THE OTHER SIDE OF
Quiet

ALSO BY TARA C. ALLRED

Sanders' Starfish
Unauthored Letters

www.taracallred.net

THE OTHER SIDE OF
Quiet

TARA C. ALLRED

Patella Publishing
P.O. Box 493
American Fork, UT 84003
First eBook Edition: 2015
First Paperback Edition: 2015

ISBN: 978-0-9864215-0-1

Patella Publishing

Cover design by Anne Darling and JT Niekamp
Layout design by NovelNinjutsu.com

to

Kelley

AUTHOR NOTE

Dear Reader,

Two weeks into my fourth grade year, I transferred to a special elementary school. Since I joined the class late, I didn't receive specific instructions regarding Mrs. Jackson's journals. But I already was actively writing in a journal, so I was pretty confident I knew what to do with this assignment.

In fact, I made great use of my class journal!

I wrote about how I didn't like my new school, or my new teachers, or any of my new experiences. I even went so far as to declare my confident plan of being transferred out of this school.

Then, soon into these valuable writing days, Mrs. Jackson announced it was time for her monthly collection of these journals.

As a shy, obedient child, I was horrified! I was absolutely mortified that my unfiltered account of my private life would have such a reader.

Now I chuckle to think about Mrs. Jackson as she read my first entries.

Yet she handled it beautifully.

She expressed concern for my sorrows, offered help through my troubles, and encouraged me in my growth as a writer. To this day, I am profoundly grateful that I chose to stay at this school. The years that followed were some of the most formative and influential years of my education.

I owe a great deal to Mrs. Jackson and all the exceptional educators at Harbor Math/Science Magnet! I'm also deeply grateful for every teacher who has dedicated his or her life to help make the world a better place through education, specifically those educators from

Dodson Junior High, San Pedro High, and Rim of the World High Schools. Thank you!

It has been a joy to revisit my past as I have worked on this novel. Much of my ground research for *The Other Side of Quiet* came from writings gathered during my teenage years. I'm grateful for all the amazing friends I had during such a critical, difficult, and important time of life.

As I moved further into the research of this novel, many talented individuals provided perspectives that further enhanced and diversified these characters' stories.

However, one dilemma I encountered was how to provide authentic teenage writing in regards to spelling, grammar and language errors. Yes, in the real world these writings would most likely have atrocious errors as well as some crudities. Not to mention the pointless boring entries too. So I had a choice of which way I would offend. Some readers will be looking for the raw teen writing which would include poor spelling, grammar, profanity and pointless ramblings. Other readers will be seeking a more polished story without any of these distracting items. I erred on the side of storytelling. Although there may still be some of these writing vices, I tried my best to be strategic and intentional when inserting such errors.

More than anything, I aimed to build a world where I could share these characters' lives with you.

I hope I have done that.

—*Tara C. Allred*

JOURNAL VOICES

Imagine Goldilocks, who learned to explore and survive among bears, suddenly being transported to Ken and Barbie's dream house. Well, that's me and it's wild.

—Todi's Journal

I want to do something important, something really important. Once I've done what it is, everyone around me will know that it's important.

—Blake's Journal

How Mrs. Childs describes this journal, I think it's more like a diary. I won't start each entry as *Dear Diary*, that is completely lame. But I'll write from my heart. That's what Mrs. Childs told us to do, and that's what I want to do.

—Abigail's Journal

I heard a loud sound, like glass shattering on the floor.
Something's broken.

—Dillon's Journal

I love my mom.
I would tell her this if I could.

—Anya's Journal

I have to share this with someone. But it'd be like a pirate's curse if the wrong people knew. And it's hard to know who you can trust, especially when you're new and just making friends, or at least trying to make friends.

—Tracey's Journal

This year, I'm going to look super pretty! Not like last year, where I felt ugly every day! This year, my hair is going to be perfect ALL the time! This year, something really good BETTER happen with me and boys! (And I SO hope it's with Hamilton!)

—Priscilla's Journal

When I made the football team, I thought that was good enough for Dad. He'd worked me hard. He didn't want me to get there because I was his son, but because of my own skills.

I've never worked so hard for anything before.

—*Hamilton's Journal*

Mrs. Childs says she won't read this. All I have to do is fill the pages. That's what she says she'll look for. If there's stuff on the paper, then I get credit. So that's what you get, Mrs. Childs.

—*Kyle's Journal*

The cops didn't have to take our journals. They didn't have to read about our personal lives to find out what happened to Stella. What happened to Stella has nothing to do with our class.

—*Darby's Special Journal*

PART I
The Class

CHAPTER
One

I HELD MY CLASS'S ATTENTION, BUT THE POLICE OFFICER, standing next to Principal Truss near the doorway, held mine. My voice remained steady as I lectured my small band of ninth graders on the power of tone, but as soon as I made eye contact, Principal Truss stepped in.

"Mrs. Childs." He motioned with his forefinger. "May we speak to you for a moment?"

I caught the stern face of the officer which caused me to nod my consent. I stepped toward the door only to turn back to see all ten of my creative writing students focused on these men.

"Just a moment of your time," Principal Truss said again.

My students' eyes shifted. When they looked at me, I shrugged.

Abigail twisted around to give Dillon a quick glance, while Anya, the principal's daughter, stared at her father's face.

Through his dark-rimmed glasses, Principal Truss stared back. Then quickly he turned away, ran his hands though his flaxen hair, and stepped back into the hallway.

3

Before I followed, I said to my class, "Use this time to examine the tone in your narrative draft." Then I left my room and stood face to face with a morose Principal Truss and an austere officer of the law.

"Thank you." Principal Truss spoke with caution. "This will be brief."

I nodded while an *okay* slipped from my lips like a whisper.

"Mrs. Childs," his voice quivered in a way I'd never heard before, "this is Officer Bond."

I nodded at the dark-haired distinguished man, who barely gave me a smile.

Principal Truss pointed to a neighboring class, vacant during our Junior High's last period of the day. "He needs to speak to you."

The officer stepped toward the empty room, then paused at the door to wait for me.

But I glanced back toward my class.

"I have Ms. Atherton coming," Principal Truss said. "And until she arrives, I'll stay with them."

I drew in a breath, brushed my dark hair from my face, and followed Officer Bond into the room.

After he shut the door behind us, he approached a nearby desk and placed his hand on a box labeled Helam City Police. Then he looked at me. "Do you know a Stella Fabrizio?"

"No." My heart began to race. "Should I?"

"Her body was found this morning, five miles outside of town, in a pasture."

"Oh dear." My hand reached for my chest. "Did she go to our school?"

"The high school," Officer Bond said. "She was a senior."

From the box, he pulled out a photo in a sealed bag. The girl had dark hair, large brown eyes, olive skin, and was wearing a low-cut cream tank top.

"Her parents divorced two years ago," he said, "which is when she and her mom moved here."

"From where?"

"Just up north, near Salt Lake."

I stared at the picture. "That's why I didn't have her as a student," I said more to myself than to him.

"I know," he said quietly. "Right now, no one knows how she's connected to your class."

I gave him a puzzled look and handed him back the photo. "My class?"

He studied my face for a moment. Then he said, "Do you recognize this?" From the box, he produced another sealed bag. This one contained a black vinyl drawstring pack with the green National Coalition for Families logo on the front. He flipped it so I could see the back logo: *Let the Children Speak: Identities and Families* with the current year *2004*.

I nodded.

"It was found around her neck."

The gasp slipped out before I could cover my mouth. Suddenly, I felt sick.

Our school, my class, these students were the only Utah recipients who had received these bags. This was tied in with our class's special project, our final essays which would be a part of a temporary exhibit in Washington D. C. Almost a year before, I'd endured the grueling application process to then be awarded a special invite from this nonprofit organization, a group designated to help children and strengthen families. Yet now, I stared at the logo and the cheap welcoming bag which had been used to end another teenager's life.

Officer Bond reached into the box again. "What about this?" He produced another sealed bag with a ripped sheet of paper inside. He handed it to me.

It only took a second for me to recognize my own words.

These journals are a place for expression, a place to write freely, and to feel safe. I ask you to write respectfully and to write your best, since this is still a class assignment. But your words will not be shared with others. Even I will not examine what you write. Rather, once a month I'll ask you to flip through your journal pages to show me you are writing. This is how you will receive credit for the assignment.

On this sheet of paper, I even recognized the black pen mark where I'd manually ~~went~~ gone through each copy and changed my small typo from *on* to *in*.

Now its presence haunted me. "I purchased journals for my class, and then I slipped a letter with a journal into each bag."

"So we can assume these two items came from the same person?"

"I guess." Then suddenly I understood. "Wait!" I took a step back. "No! My students didn't do this. Not this." I quickly handed him back the letter. "They weren't involved with this."

He turned the letter over and handed it back to me. In large flowing cursive it read, *The truth is found here.* An arrow followed and below it was a quick sketch of a heart.

I followed the arrow's order and flipped the letter around, back to my typed phrases where the information about my class's journals stared back at me.

"It can't be," I said. The idea was inconceivable!

From behind me, I heard footsteps. I turned to face Principal Truss. In place of the traditional twinkle, I saw the fear in his eyes.

"We want to collect your class journals," he said.

I looked at both these men. "I still don't understand."

"I've spoken with the Board." Principal Truss stepped toward me. "They've spoken with our attorney. Of the present options, this has the least liability."

"What?" I gave him a confused look.

"We need you to collect their journals."

"But they're confidential." I handed the letter back to Officer Bond. "I told my students that. I told them this was a safe place to express themselves."

"I understand." Officer Bond spoke with no emotion. "But right now our goal is to find information."

"I'm sorry," I restated. "I can't accommodate this request."

With one hand, Principal Truss pressed his fingers into his temples. "Well, we can't interrogate each member of your class. If we do parents will be here with pitchforks, screaming at the school, at the police, at all of us on how we handle what's next."

"What's next?" I felt bewildered. This was ridiculous.

"How did Stella end up with your class items?" Officer Bond asked.

I glanced at both of them. "I don't know!"

Principal Truss tried to speak in a soothing voice. "I've explored the other options. At this point, this makes the most sense."

"No! We ask each member of the class where their paper got placed, where their bag is." My voice only grew louder. "You don't just take their private journals."

Principal Truss rubbed his forehead, then glanced at Officer Bond's box. "Anya no longer has those things."

"What?" I resented his response. "You did this because your daughter no longer has her bag, or the handout?"

He glanced back at me. "I did this for every child in that classroom who didn't feel a need to keep a cheap bag and a sheet of information. I did this to not penalize *all* of them due to the concern we may have with *one*."

"This is absurd! They are not your journals to take."

"Aren't they?" He gave me a sorrowful smile. "I can do a routine locker check anytime I want at this school. And we do. So when you stamped 'Property of Helam Junior High' on every one of those journals, you made them school property."

"I did it," my voice trembled while my eyes fought to keep back the tears, "so I could require them to use these journals for the designated assignment, and not for their own personal use."

"I'm sorry, Savannah," Principal Truss said softly, "but if this is murder, at the hands of one of our students—taking these journals will be the least of our worries."

I stared at the ground, thinking. Then slowly, I glanced back at him. "You're sure there isn't another way?"

"I wish there was. But it's not as simple as you want." He turned to face Officer Bond, who had remained silent near his box. "It's not as simple as *all* of us want."

"Okay," I whispered. With the back of my hand, I swiped at the first tear before it could roll down. Then I headed toward my classroom.

8

CHAPTER
Two

L IKE A DEATH MARCH, I WALKED BACK TO THE FRONT OF
my class while Principal Truss and Officer Bond lingered in
the doorway.

At first I said nothing. I didn't need to, all ten students
watched me.

I exchanged a quick farewell with Ms. Atherton, then, while
knowing I was about to be a traitor, I turned to my students and
sought to sound strong. "Class, if your journals are not out, please
pull them out."

For the moment, my instructions were standard. Still, no one
moved.

"Quickly, students." I clapped my hands together, knowing the
respect I'd rightfully earned would soon be gone. "Pull out your
journals. I don't care if you're caught up. You have four minutes left
of class to jot something down for the day."

Like how it feels to have your personal journals taken from you, but I
refrained from speaking such thoughts.

Although my students appeared confused, they obediently followed instructions, until all journals were open and resting on desks. Then while the seconds ticked away, I observed the contrast. From days past, pens had danced across the pages. Now their writing movements were crippled and slow.

Hamilton set his pen on his desk, folded his muscular arms and watched me. Abigail softly touched her pen to paper, but then hesitated while her flawless complexion scowled at the pages. Tracey drew up the sleeves of his white blazer, looked down at his dark arms, then uncapped his green pen, only to gnaw on the pen cap.

Priscilla tugged at her long blonde curls and stared at a blank page. Blake pressed his pen against the paper, but kept pausing to look at me. Whereas, Dillon drew his baseball cap down while he flipped back and forth among previous entries.

Todi watched the officer in the doorway, until he looked directly at her. Then she flipped her head down so that her auburn ponytail fell behind her and kept her eyes glued to some former words she'd written in her journal.

Then there was Kyle. He'd already shut his journal, lifted his hood, and slipped earbuds into his ears.

I glanced at the clock. One final minute remained. "Okay," I said.

Darby shot me a quick glance. Then her pen hastily scribbled out her writing.

"Please close your journals." My tone remained even. "And place them on my desk." I headed to the back of the room only to hear the sound of silence.

When I turned back, all students stared at me. "Quickly, class." I snapped my fingers as if my authority could lessen the sting. "I need your journals now."

This time a cacophony began.

"What?"

"Mrs. Childs?"

"No."

"You said . . ."

"How come?"

Dillon shifted as if prepared to slide his journal into his pack, while tiny Anya stood with her journal in hand.

Sadly, I smiled at her. Of course the principal's daughter, with no secrets to hide, would be first.

Her writings would be filled with sweetness. No conflicts there. Yet, although I appreciated her respect toward my betrayal, her eagerness left me wondering if she'd truly expressed herself.

Then I caught the quick glance she shot her father. Perhaps she was the wise one, wiser than us all. Perhaps her words had remained guarded and her inner world kept safe.

Once she placed it on my desk, my fingers grazed across it. "Thank you, Anya."

Yet she did not return to her seat. Instead she tugged on one of her golden braids. "I thought you said you'd never collect these?"

A huge pit formed in my stomach. My head hurt and my eyes watered slightly at such a simple, well-deserved question.

I swiped at the moisture and spoke loudly against the eruption which had commenced among the rest. "Class, I told you since the beginning, and on repeated instances, that these are your personal journals. But now circumstances have changed that."

Tracey's lean body sat up in his chair. "You can't do that."

"No!" Darby said. Her hazel eyes shot me a scalding look. "You can't tell us one thing and then change your mind."

Abigail's face scrunched up as if in pain. "We trusted you."

The pit inside me was expanding, the heartache increasing, and my tears still fought for expression. As expected, I was losing control of this situation. So I did the only thing I could; I turned to Principal Truss. "Can you explain?"

The bell erupted, signifying the end of class, the end of school, the great sound of freedom. Yet no one moved.

In fact, to make matters worse, as the ringing subsided, Principal Truss stepped into the room, followed by Officer Bond, who shut the classroom door behind him.

Suddenly the walls felt close. The students stared at these two men whose presence suggested there was no exit until the completion of this required task.

Slowly, Principal Truss walked the short distance to the center of my room. He observed these teenagers and then said, "Right now, I cannot share a lot of details. I can only say that Mrs. Childs needs to collect them."

"How come now?" Dillon asked clearly.

"It's not right!" Darby added. "That's not what she told us!"

Principal Truss shifted his weight from side to side. He released a strong sigh and I saw a twitch in his eye. He rubbed his neck, and cleared his throat. "Well, my role is to protect my students, and today I was approached with a difficult choice. In order to protect all of you, Mrs. Childs and I have chosen a path that is best for the majority of this class. Yes, I recognize this is difficult. But at this point, your responsibility is to turn your journal over to Mrs. Childs."

"But why?" Priscilla looked at him with wide eyes.

He stared back at her, and the agitation increased across his face, suggesting he was at a breaking point with questions. "This is required of each one of you. You will be unable to leave this class until you hand over your journal. At this point, that is my final word on this action."

He motioned at my desk, resumed his position next to Officer Bond, and let his eyes gaze over the classroom. Meanwhile, he avoided eye contact with everyone, especially his daughter.

And while her journal was the first on my desk, Anya did not leave the classroom. Instead she kept playing with her backpack's zippers, as if waiting to see if the other nine students would follow or successfully revolt.

Perhaps she wanted to reclaim hers, if she had the chance.

Seconds passed and no one moved. Finally, Blake looked at each adult and then stood. He tugged on his pressed button-up shirt and then walked the distance to my desk.

All of us watched him. With somber obedience, he set it down and quietly said, "Here you go, Mrs. Childs." Then he turned back to the class, unsure of what to do next.

But his effort spurred Priscilla to break the silence. She jumped up and said, "Darby and I have dance practice. We have to go." In haste, she moved to my desk and dropped the journal down with a thud. Then she turned back to stare at Darby, who remained frozen in her seat. "Come on Darby, we gotta go!"

Darby looked down at her journal, acting oblivious to Priscilla and the entire class that watched her. It seemed each remaining class member was still waiting, hoping another would raise the cry that would stop this injustice.

Instead Priscilla grew more impatient. "Come on, Darby!"

Slowly, Darby slid out from her chair and stood. She tugged at her tight skirt, rolled her shoulders back, and lifted her head high. Then she strode up to my desk, dropped her journal on the stack, and spoke with a chilling coldness. "There you go, Mrs. Childs, there's our secrets."

It was Darby who broke out of the classroom first; it was she who strode past all the rest and pushed open the door to let the sounds of carefree students roaming the hall enter the room.

Once Darby exited, Priscilla, Blake and Anya followed.

And once the door shut behind them, the statement had been made.

The other six had no choice.

It was Todi who rose next, followed by Hamilton, then Kyle.

Abigail kept shooting Dillon glances. But once he stood, Abigail reached for her pack and accompanied him down the aisle. Finally, it was Tracey who remained.

When he dropped his journal on my desk, he looked me square in the eyes and said, "Not cool, Mrs. Childs. Not cool."

CHAPTER
Three

THAT EVENING THE HOUSE WAS QUIET. OF COURSE IT was quiet. For the last seven months, this was my lonely norm.

And for those seven months I had told myself I was okay with the silence. I was strong, I was supportive, I was independent. I didn't need Peter here.

Yet tonight I did.

Because tonight's silence hurt more than ever before.

To cope, I prepared my standard meal of stir-fry. This had become my routine for almost every night over the last seven months. My only variation came in the chopped vegetables I chose. Tonight it was bok choy, peppers, mushrooms, carrots, bean sprouts and baby corn.

Then, as had become custom, I saw no need to sit alone at the table, so I sat at the bar. I said a silent blessing on the food and reflected on how Peter wouldn't eat this meal, even if he were here.

My hunter husband—meat was the meal.

15

So, after nine years of marriage, I was now on a meat sabbatical using this time to avoid the carnivorous life.

But as the months had passed, I found myself craving its return. Vegetables were no longer enough.

After dinner, I hunted for something to free my mind from the unsettling events of the day. Instead, I gravitated toward my own private journals.

Soon I pulled out volume after volume, as if starving for an answer until my king-sized bed was covered with its own history of my life.

Then I stared at it all.

These were my personal insights and were never meant to be loosely shared. In these I'd written from the heart, which is precisely what I'd told my students to do. Today's classroom event was a violation. A horror of what had been required of us all.

With this injustice looming hot in my mind, I grabbed my previous year's journal and a half container of ice cream. Then I headed to the soft sofa and slipped back into my past.

SEPT 2, 2002

I want a child.

Yet my husband is blindly content with his world, spending all our discretionary funds on his hunting hobby, filling our lives with trips and plans and accessories. Each time he brings another toy home I want to yell, I want to curse him, I want to hit him. Can't he see I'm dying inside? Can't he see that this is his hobby, not mine, not ours? His alone, but I willingly let him drag me along, because there is nothing in life that brings me joy except him.

Yet he is lost in another world, lost in his joyful state of hunting, so busy investing in his own love that he doesn't see time is passing.

He doesn't see our parenting days are slipping away.

SEPT 3, 2002

Deep down I know he wants this.

He feels the void.

The hunting is to dry up his sadness too.

But why hunting? Why take away life, when we hunger for the gift of life?

While we are being deprived of this power to create, why kill another life?

SEPT 24, 2002

We don't speak about it. We can't speak about it. There are no words, or plans, or actions which solve this longing, this loss, this endless grieving.

I declare to myself enough. Get over this. Move on.

Yet I can't.

FEB 19, 2003

Already it's been a difficult year for us, a painful companion to the previous few.

I'm caught in a stalemate. I want a child, I deeply desire a child, yet my body rebels, and announces loudly that I'm ill-fit to be a mother. I inquire of my body if this means I'm ill-fit to carry a child or also that I'm ill-fit to run after a child.

It gives no answer. I must discover this for myself.

So I re-examine all we've tried over the years.

Each procedure we've tried has failed.

Then IVF gave us brief news of a pregnancy, only to miscarry.

When an adoptive mother selected us we thought it was our miracle. But during the final weeks of carrying her child, she avoided our calls.

More attempts, more failures, and we're emotionally, physically, and financially spent. And yet I still hurt.

I want Peter to fix this hurt.

But he doesn't know how to fill this void which consumes me.

Instead I wonder if he's caught in the midst of an early mid-life crisis—because, like me, his life didn't shape into what he thought it would be.

MAR 2, 2003

I feel the emptiness taking shape, letting me know I no longer am the person I know I should be.

It's time to move on.

Time to find something which will adequately challenge me, something which forces me not to give up.

Something which will keep me living inside.

CHAPTER
Four

A FTER CONSUMING MORE THAN A QUARTER GALLON OF ice cream and two dozen journal entries, I retreated to my bed, only to feel lost in confusion. Like tangled knots, I thought about this girl named Stella, my creative writing students, and Peter.

Last Spring I'd applied for this special project with the National Coalition for Families. During the process of being selected and then selecting my own talented small group, I found purpose again in living. By the end of the school year, I had the start to a strong curriculum and an exciting class list.

But when summer hit, I faced a new form of sadness.

And for the entire summer, I only wrote in my journal once.

AUGUST 12, 2003

Whenever something unfortunate occurs I always return to the sore place in my heart labeled *unknown infertility*. My emotions return to it again and again, like it's a favorite spot on a beloved blanket, the spot worn thin from continuous caressing.

I've reached a point that I don't know *me* without this longing. Because this hurt now defines me, gives me an identity of who I am—or more correctly, who I am not.

Yet I'd always assumed we would keep trying.

But what do you do when your partner is done trying?

Then what?

Yet I, like Peter, dislike this weight.

Trying is a different term for fertile couples versus infertile couples. Fertile couples *try* by stopping any preventive measures they'd invested in. *Trying* for infertile couples is investing every spare expense and every spare thought into every scientific, alternative, and snake doctor technique that exists. *Trying* is trying everything on the spectrum, from solid research to any wives' tales shared. *Trying* is discarding romance to focus on the grand goal of creating a child, to make love for the biological criteria of conceiving, only to have month after month declaring that your partnership is a failure within the creative realm.

Trying

Trying.

Trying!

Trying!!!

After seven years of trying in any way we could define the term, Peter was done with the spending, done with the failures, done with the heartache, done with the empty nights filled with my tears. He was done trying to know what to say when there were no words that could heal.

And truthfully, I feared I was done trying too!

Then I lost all hope.

I plummeted.

And the plague has spread until Peter doesn't know how to support me.

In June, he reenlisted in the National Guard.

Without telling me.

We got through that.

Until in July, he volunteered to go on a ten-month service to Afghanistan.

After 9/11, he said he enlisted because he had to do something. He had to find his way to serve, to leave his mark on the world, to do something of worth.

And I'm not ready to hear this!

So, I will kiss him good-bye in the comfort of our home—not at the base—not at the airport.

I have failed in my efforts to be a mother. And now, I've failed as a wife.

CHAPTER
Five

S O PETER RAN FROM IT, AND I BECAME SUFFOCATED BY IT. And tonight the wound started to bleed again.

I truly needed to find sleep and do what was necessary to emotionally survive.

Instead, from my nightstand, I pulled out my current volume. Then I wrote, letting the pen help me sort through my emotions of guilt and despair.

FEBRUARY 27, 2004

Like a raging river below me, I watch the dangers of depression flow. In fear of myself, I've erected a protective barrier, a guardrail which will not let me pass over into the deadening water. Yet I still watch it, mesmerized by its power, its acceleration, its ability to control.

Lately my toe dangles over the edge, finding a gap in the guardrail where the current can flow over my flesh. I want to submerge my whole body, just slip away into the river, and let it wash over all my cares. It promises it will carry my pain, but I know it lies.

So I begrudgingly pull my entire foot out, noting how unintentionally I'd let my ankle get wet. I step away from the guardrail. Yet I wonder how soon I'll return to this place.

I'm an infertile woman, lost, trying to figure my purpose, wishing to know where I belong, searching for peace in my life, yet being haunted by this void.

But then I took action. After finding the darkness unbearable, I pulled myself out. I formed my talented creative writing class.

This project prevented me from submerging myself into the river. This class saved me.

And in return I have disappointed them.

Today the river scares me. My body slips into it, while my voice of reason vehemently screams and then prays I don't drown here.

CHAPTER
Six

I BELIEVE I FELL ASLEEP AROUND 2 A.M. WHEN MY EYELIDS finally drooped, I had finished off the container of ice cream and had another stack of journals by my side.

At 9:42 a.m., I awoke to the chirpy sound of my ring tone. The call was from Principal Truss.

"They've all been read," he said.

I glanced at my personal stack. "I figured."

"Now they want someone from the school to come to the station."

"To collect them?" I asked hopefully.

"No." He paused, which concerned me. "Officer Bond is looking for more details about the students. More than what's already been provided."

My frustration from yesterday returned. "They're good kids!"

"I know," he spoke like a father.

"Thanks," I said weakly.

"But Savannah," his tone was solemn. "He has specific questions, and thinks someone from the school should read these journals."

"No!" I said firmly.

"He thinks it'd be wise to have someone from the school involved in this."

"Why?"

"He only said as a precaution."

Anger rose in my throat. "This isn't right!"

"I know. But they need to find out who did this."

"So—" My voice cracked against the emerging emotion. "Who's going to read them?"

"It needs to be you."

I glanced again at my own journals spread across Peter's side of the bed. "I can't do that to my students."

"Well, it's going to be you, me, or the school counselor. Who do you think would be best?"

I sighed into the phone. If Principal Truss or Mr. Tate read those journals they'd feel obligated to authoritatively act based on what was shared.

I reached for one of my volumes; this was a captured short segment of my life. Compared to Principal Truss or Mr. Tate, I understood the assignment. I knew what had been asked of these students. Through that knowledge, I could be the buffer between truth and action.

"Fine," I said. "I'll do it."

"Thank you!" He sounded relieved. But then an awkward silence followed.

Finally he said, "We should connect afterwards. In fact, could you come here, to my house, after you leave the station?"

"Sure," I said gravely.

"Savannah, it's already out of our control. This isn't what any of us wanted, but for now, help this investigation. Read the journals. Answer the questions. And let's pray we're able to quickly establish that our school had no connection to Stella's tragedy."

Two hours later, I sat in a bare room, on a hard chair, with a long table in front of me. The stack of my familiar class journals towered over three glossy photos of Stella Fabrizio.

In addition to the photo I'd seen on Friday, there was a photo of her staged in a cheerleading pose. Her legs were muscular, her physique strong and shapely, her smile inviting. The final photo was her with two girlfriends. Their arms were around each other, their smiles energetic, and their eyes caught in laughter.

In all three photos, Stella's face stared back at me. She was turning into a real person, a person who had a favorite food, likes and dislikes, goals and aspirations, hopes and dreams. And now all that was gone.

A heavy sigh slipped from my lips.

Perhaps it was the room, the photos, the "private" journals, the pathetic night of wallowing in my own self-pity, or the lack of sleep, but suddenly I felt empty. I felt scared. For the first time since the event, I looked at the photos of Stella, and felt a need to truly start questioning my students.

So, I took a deep breath and selected Todi Spencer's from off the top.

PART II
The Journals

TODI'S JOURNAL

MY MEMOIR

BY
TODI SPENCER

NOTE TO READER:

This is my memoir of living in Utah. I like that word, *memoir*. It makes me sound like a professional. I don't know if I could be a professional anything, but writing a *memoir* makes me feel like maybe I could be. So this is my author's note to you, the reader. I wrote this after I wrote some of the chapters of my memoir. I haven't finished my memoir yet, 'cause it'll take me the whole year to finish this, 'cause I'm still living in Utah. But it seemed like you might need a note to understand why I wrote this.

The reason I'm writing this is due to my English teacher, Mrs. Childs. She was my English teacher first, then she encouraged me to join her special class. In her special class, she gave us these journals.

Before I got invited to join the class, 'cause you have to apply and all and it's kind of a big deal, I told Mrs. Childs about my *dysfunctional* family. That's a word I really hate! I especially hate it when others, like my social worker, use it to describe me. Usually teachers or foster families say it like this when they describe me: "She comes from a . . . (pause, pause, then they lower their voice) . . . a *dysfunctional* family." Not my social worker, she says it superfast, like it's an obvious fact, and the faster she says it, the sooner she can move on to other big tasks. She says it this way: "Since Jodi comes from adysfunctionalfamily." And then she keeps right on talking. It's a label slapped on me, like it defines who I am. And it's how people pass me along from one group to the next.

I hate the label. But it's an easy way for people to think they know me.

Even though it's not just who I am.

That's why I'm writing this memoir—to help that.

So let's start from the beginning of the school year, before I was in Mrs. Childs's CW class.

CHAPTER 1

Imagine Goldilocks, who learned to explore and survive among bears, suddenly being transported to Ken and Barbie's dream house.

Well, that's me and it's wild.

For the fifteen years of my life I've been searching for just right and suddenly I'm living now with Carroll and Paisley Johnson.

When I first heard I'd be living with a man named Carroll I thought it was one of the funniest things I'd ever heard. I'd never met a man named Carroll before so I pictured him having a squeaky voice, horn-rimmed glasses, and a bowtie. Instead Carroll is tall, but not super tall, and thin, but not pencil-thin. White hair, but not ghost white, mostly gray, and he has an oval face with kind eyes. He just left the software industry doing something I don't understand, and he and his wife are saving up to serve a mission for the Mormons. Carroll likes to correct me and say, "We are going to be missionaries for the Church of Jesus Christ of Latter-day Saints." But I like to tease Carroll and so I call them Mormons whenever I can.

Before I moved here, I didn't even know what a Mormon was. My mom, Clarissa, never really had a religion. I guess she believes in God, 'cause I remember at least one night where she stayed in the bathroom all night crying, "Oh, God . . . Oh, God."

For me, the verdict is still out whether God answered her prayer, 'cause the next morning I took my first ride into foster care. Since then, I've been in and out of twelve different homes. Meanwhile, Clarissa's been in and out of jails, halfway houses, and crazy hospitals. I have a sister named Cassie (really it's Cassandra, but she goes by Cassie). I think it's a brainless name 'cause it's a lot like my mom

35

Clarissa's name. But whenever I tell her what I think, my mom says that it's my sister's dad who named her.

Even though it's a brainless name, Cassie has a dad and she gets to go live with him whenever things get bad.

I don't have a dad.

But for this round I have Carroll. And his wife Paisley, too.

Paisley is an odd name. It belongs next to a chalkboard, where someone can run their fingernails down the board as they say the name – *Paisley*. It gives me the chills, maybe 'cause paisley belongs on wallpaper, or a dated shirt, or a businessman's tie—or a Mormon's tie. What does Carroll think when he puts on a paisley tie and takes his wife Paisley to church? Does she ever get lost in the wallpaper?

At first, I didn't want to like Paisley. But it was hard not to 'cause she bakes fresh bread every day. Before now, I'd never had home-baked bread. When I lived with Clarissa, it was always cheap loaves and only when she could afford it, which was hit and miss at times.

Now how can you not like a woman who fills her Barbie dollhouse with the smell of fresh bread all the time?

Carroll and Paisley chose to be the place where kids come stay for about a year. For as many years as I've been alive, they've housed twenty-five children. I guess they really like kids.

But this last year, they'd stopped doing the foster care stuff because they were preparing for their church mission. So they were busy with other stuff, when they got the call about me.

Over a year ago, my mom went to jail for supporting her boyfriend Jake, who built a meth lab in our apartment. Plus, she'd been forging stolen checks. Not smart of her, but thinking's never been her top quality.

I never liked Jake. Once my mom asked him to marry her, but he looked over at me and said, "No, because then she'd be my ugly redheaded stepchild." He thought he was funny. Clarissa didn't. She hit him real hard, not because I'd be his stepchild or because I have red hair, even though Clarissa and I like to call it auburn, but because he said I was ugly. I think that made Clarissa especially mad, 'cause we look alike. We both have lots of curls, except she keeps hers frizzy and wild, whereas I just want mine out of the way. Right after I wash it, I pull it back in a ponytail and that's how it stays.

But on the day I headed back to foster care, I met a guy named John Sanders. I wanted him to help me, but he couldn't. He had his own set of problems.

But every once in a while somebody shocks you, and that's what happened here. I'd forgot all about Mr. Sanders, 'cause enough time had passed, and I'd been living in a foster home where the dad said his goal was to smooth out my rough edges. I didn't like him—the foster dad, that is—but I guess I'm *better* than before, whatever that means. I do like Mr. Sanders, 'cause even though I'd forgot about him, he hadn't forgot about me. And even though I already was in that foster home, I just still didn't like it there. So when Mr. Sanders tracked me down, he said he'd found someone who could help me, and they worked something out, and that's how I ended up at Carroll and Paisley's.

Actually Carroll prefers to call it a *miracle* (that's a word Carroll uses a lot), because Carroll and Paisley had lived in California all their married life, and Carroll had known Mr. Sanders at some juncture in their careers (I like the word *juncture*, starts out like the common word *junk*, but then it transforms into a brainy word). So Mr. Sanders knew Carroll took in foster kids. But what he didn't know was that Carroll and Paisley had sold their home and moved to a town called Helam,

Utah 'cause Carroll grew up here. He says that back in the early '60s, most the town was rural, but it's not like that anymore. Still, Carroll chose to come back to this place 'cause he says it *feels* like his home here (*feel* is another word he uses a lot).

So that's where Carroll's miracle came in. Like I already wrote, Carroll and Paisley were no longer taking foster kids. Plus their license was for California, but now they lived in Utah. But somehow they drove to California, picked me up, and we drove to Utah. I'm not sure how it all worked out, but it did.

For this next year, I'm living in Utah. I won't get to see my mom, but that's okay with me. I don't really need to see her at the jail. And she writes me letters. Basically she warns me that the Mormons will try to convert me. I don't like the word *convert* so I'm not too worried, but Carroll asked me to go to church with him and Paisley, so I said sometime I would. I figure I can be a good houseguest while I'm here. I do try and be good when I'm living with other people. Sometimes it's easy, sometimes it's hard.

But back to Paisley—she has what she calls a grandma shape. She calls it that because she says she has a lap for her grandkids to sit on and strong arms to carry them—and hug them tight. They have seven kids and a *whole* lot of grandkids. And like I wrote, she really likes kids. And I do like her laugh. So even though she has a funny name that belongs on drapery or around a man's neck, she's still a nice lady.

Oh, and the vinyl. I probably should mention the vinyl. I didn't even know what vinyl was until I got to Paisley's house. Probably as much as she loves kids, she loves vinyl lettering. She has it everywhere. You come to Carroll and Paisley's front door and next to the doorbell it says *Welcome Friends* and on the door in vinyl it says *Johnsons,* and in a not too discreet but not too obvious spot, in vinyl, it says *No Soliciting.*

Then once you walk in, there is an arch in the entryway, and in vinyl it says, *Our Story Begins Here.* Other vinyl says: *Don't Count Life by the Breaths You Take, But by the Moments that Take Your Breath Away, Count Your Many Blessings*, and *Seize the Day.* Plus, she has what I like to call her vinyl wall. On the top of the wall, it says *All Because Two People Fell in Love.* There are framed photos of all their children and grandchildren with all their names in vinyl, which is kind of dumb, 'cause it's not like she is going to forget their names or anything. But I don't tell Paisley that.

Then, tucked away in another part of the house, there is a wall with each foster kid's school picture. Their vinyl names are stuck right onto the frame, so she'll always remember us kids' names, which is probably why I especially don't like the large vinyl lettering, near the dining room table, which says *Families are Forever.*

Carroll explained to me that families are real important to Mormons. But I pretty much hate that sign. It feels like it's speaking to an exclusive club—like I can't talk about forever if I don't even have the first step that might be required for it. Maybe I'm reading it wrong. Maybe forever is a dark place without families. I just don't like it. And what I really don't like is sitting underneath it each time we eat, and we always eat under it.

That's 'cause Paisley is adamant we *all* eat together. Clarissa never made dinner, let alone required us to sit in the same room when she ate, or I ate, or my sister ate.

But this year I eat with Carroll, and Paisley, and I sit under a forever family sign to remind me that all this is temporary.

Still, I'd rather eat fresh-baked bread in a house that looks like Ken and Barbie's than cold porridge in the woods any day, because like Carroll says, "It just *feels* right."

CHAPTER II

After I moved to Carroll and Paisley's home they got me enrolled at Helam Junior High School. It's an okay place, nothing special. Except for my English class. I like to write, which is good 'cause someday I want to be a writer. So by the first day it was easy to already love that class.

But lunch comes right after English and when the bell rang, I just had a real hard time leaving. I kind of hung around until all the other kids left the room. Then I just stared at the door for a while. Until Mrs. Childs said, "Todi, can I help you with something?"

Now I just remembered that in this memoir, I haven't helped you understand my name. It's Jodi. But in Kindergarten I wrote my "J's" like "T's," and then one time, my teacher accidentally called me Todi. All the kids laughed. From then on, they never could remember my real name. By first grade, I asked the teacher to call me Todi. And it just kind of took over from there. So every time I move (and I move a lot), I always say my name is Todi. Even my mom and sis call me Todi. But my social worker, she always has to call me Jodi. She introduces me to everyone as Jodi, like using my proper name will make me proper or give me a proper life.

But my name is Todi!

And that's what Mrs. Childs calls me. So of course I like her. And I only had to tell her once. Since then she's always remembered it. Plus she likes how I write. And she says she can help me to write even better. So someday, maybe I could even become a real writer.

"What do you need, Todi?" she said in that sweet voice, that really meant, *"I know you are new here, you are a foster kid, and are totally lost, so what can I help you with?"*

When I told her I didn't want to eat lunch with the other kids, she listened. I expected her to try to trick me out the door, like by lying to me and saying I'd have friends in no time, which I wouldn't. Most of the time I eventually find some goof-off boys that'll let me hang out with them. Sometimes girls will let me hang out with them too, but not very often. But I've never had *friends* in no time. It takes work to make a real friend. Sometimes hard work! And I get real tired of trying because then I move, and I lose that friend that I worked hard to make. So that day, I didn't feel like *trying* to make friends.

Mrs. Childs didn't force me out her door. Instead, she said she sometimes ate her lunch in her room. And she told me that if I wanted to stay I could.

So I did. Every day for a week, I pulled out a lunch packed by Paisley with her special homemade bread and ate at my desk.

But by the next week, Mrs. Childs seemed worried about me still being there. I could hear it in her voice. She came over to the desk next to mine, set down her salad and said, "How are things, Todi? Are they getting any easier for you?"

I shared a little about me—not too much—but a little. She listened.

Then the next day, I shared a little more. And she listened again.

Clarissa says I talk too much, so I figured Mrs. Childs must be pretty cool 'cause she was okay to ask me questions, and let me sit in her class, and talk to her. So on the third day, I figured I wouldn't just talk about me, but I'd ask her some questions too. So at the start of lunch, I twisted a desk around to face hers and said, "Mrs. Childs,

41

there's a lot of people in Helam who have big families! Is that a Utah thing or a Mormon thing?"

She grinned at me and then said, "Yes. There are some large families around here."

But she didn't answer my question, so I figured I'd approach it another way. "Are you Mormon?"

"Yes," she said.

So I asked, "Do you have lots of kids?"

I thought it was an easy question, but Mrs. Childs looked at the papers on her desk and her big salad and took a long time to answer. Finally she said, "No."

"Do you got any?"

She kept looking at her salad, like she didn't know the answer, or she didn't want to talk to me about it. Maybe 'cause it was about her life outside of school and I'm just a student and all.

So I decided to stop asking her questions and I just started eating my lunch.

But when I looked at her again, this time she looked at me and I saw she had little tears hanging out in the corners of her eyes. She gave me a real small smile that didn't look happy.

Now I've seen Clarissa cry lots! When she wants, she's the grand master at the whole basket case thing. But I like Mrs. Childs, so I didn't like that I'd made her cry. So, I decided my question was a bad one.

"I didn't mean to make you sad," I said.

She used her hands to wipe her eyes so that the little tears were gone. But then she said, "I don't have any children."

I thought of Paisley with all her kids, so I rolled my shoulders back, and spoke real soft and polite, "I'm sorry you don't have any kids."

Then she burst into a real painful laugh. The kind that means *I don't really think it's funny but I have to laugh anyway.* "Cruel, huh?" she said to me. "God plays one cruel joke. Every day, I'm stuck with this married name, Childs, that reminds me I don't have any."

I wanted to correct her, and tell her that her name could also mean that she was once a child (which was true). But her face scrunched up into a painful contortion and then she started sniffling, like she was trying to hide her tears. So I figured me correcting her, might make it worse. So I didn't say anything.

But it was real awkward. I didn't have any tissues in my backpack and I noticed that the box on her desk was empty. I wondered if that's 'cause she cries a lot, being Mrs. Childs with no children.

So I kept glancing around the room while she tried not to cry. In the movies, they usually give the crier a tissue, 'cause that's the best way for the non-crier to make the situation better. Or at least it shows that the non-crier cares. I've given Clarissa a tissue a couple of times before, but usually we can't afford them. So I give her a whole roll of toilet paper instead. (Unless we're running low, then I don't want her to waste it, 'cause when she needs 'em, it usually means she's going to cry a lot.)

But with Mrs. Childs, I didn't think leaving the classroom to go get a roll of toilet paper would solve things. Plus, they lock the toilet paper in place so no one steals them (which I wouldn't be stealing, but still I couldn't borrow it either). So I kept looking around the room, especially 'cause right then I couldn't look at Mrs. Childs. She had gone back to eating her salad, but she kept wiping her eyes, and she kept sniffling. She even whispered real quiet, "Sorry, Todi."

But I barely heard that, 'cause all I kept hearing was the sniffling. I'm not a crier. But I've cried a few times around people, and it's a real pain to make sure those tears that want to roll out through your nose—don't. It's just gross! For sure, Mrs. Childs didn't want that to happen in front of me. And I did *not* want to see it!

I don't think Mrs. Childs could be my favorite teacher if I saw snot-tears coming out of her nose.

So I thought of a solution. If I ran, real fast, there was Mrs. Bernstein's science class down the hall. In her room, she had a sink with a paper towel dispenser.

"I'll be right back." I said it without looking at her. Then I raced out into the hall, ran all the way to Mrs. Bernstein's room. She was writing on her board, and I said, "I need some paper towels from you." She turned around and said, "Sure, Jodi." And I pulled out two perfect sheets. Then I dashed back and handed them to Mrs. Childs.

At first she had a real confused look on her face. But then she laughed, and it was a real laugh this time. And she smiled at me.

From there, we became friends.

CHAPTER III

Pretty soon after that, I learned about Mrs. Childs's special CW class.

It was after English class. Once the bell rang, and all the other kids left, I looked over at Mrs. Childs. Since the day I made her cry, I hadn't tried to eat lunch anywhere near her desk.

Instead I reached into my backpack and pulled out my lunch box. But before I could even unzip it, Mrs. Childs took a seat in the row next to me. She clapped her hands together, and leaned her head toward me. "I have some exciting news, Todi." She was grinning real big, almost to the point that she reminded me of the cat from Alice in Wonderland.

So I wasn't sure what to do. I didn't open my lunch box lid yet ('cause I figured if Mrs. Childs was this excited, I shouldn't be rude and start digging through my lunch—even though I was real hungry and I saw that Paisley had slipped in a strawberry roll-up after I told her it was one of my favorite snacks).

So instead of eating (like I wanted to), I turned in my seat and looked at Mrs. Childs.

"Bria Roberts is moving," she said, which I thought seemed like a funny thing for a teacher to be excited about. I didn't really know Bria. I mean, I sat next to both her and her best friend Priscilla in Homeroom, but they've never talked to me. And I had Math with Bria, but I've never talked to her there either. But Bria and Priscilla talk about boys in Homeroom *all the time*. And before Math class, I've seen Bria in the hall looking at her reflection through a window while

45

she fixes her hair, or puts on lip gloss, or sticks out her chest. Then she goes into class to sit by some boys and giggles the whole time!

So to tell the truth, even if Bria and Priscilla wanted to be my friends, I don't know if I'd want to be their friend. 'Cause I'm not like them. And 'cause boys aren't celebrities—they're just boys!

But even though Bria's not my friend, it seemed not right that Mrs. Childs would act so happy that Bria was moving. Unless Bria talks about boys all the time in Mrs. Childs's class like she does in Homeroom.

So I said, "Do you not like Bria?"

Mrs. Childs laughed. Then she said, "Of course I like Bria!" But she still had a huge grin on her face. And her eyes were real big. It was like she had a giant surprise that she couldn't wait to tell me, but yet she could wait to tell me, 'cause she still hadn't said why she was so excited (only that Bria was moving).

Then Mrs. Childs slid a paper off her lap and placed it on my desk. It was a form with a bright green circle at the top. I leaned forward and saw the words *National Coalition for Families* in the center of the circle.

"Bria was in my Creative Writing class," Mrs. Childs said, "but now she's moving, which means there's an extra spot. Todi, I think you'd be perfect for the class."

In my 15 years of life, I don't think anyone's told me that I'd be perfect for something. So you can believe me when I say that right after Mrs. Childs said that, I sat straight up, and kept my eyes glued on Mrs. Childs. I tried real hard not to look too close at the paper on my desk, 'cause I really just wanted to listen so I could learn about this class that Mrs. Childs thought I might be perfect at.

"I've already talked to Principal Truss," she said. "You'll still need to apply and submit the required writing assignments. And I spoke with our school counselor, Mr. Tate, about how this might impact your schedule. He said that if you're interested, this Creative Writing class would replace your Drama elective, and then you'd need to move Biology to third period so that your sixth period is free for this class."

She clenched her hands together and watched me. She looked real eager for what I was about to say. Let me try a metaphor here. Mrs. Childs looked like a teapot. She looked like the kind with the little flap over the spout that vibrates right before it flips 'cause of the steam. She seemed like she was boiling inside, and that flap was going to pop up at any moment.

I don't know if that's a very good metaphor. But I wrote it 'cause each morning I watch Paisley's teapot as she sets it on the stove to let the water boil for hot chocolate. The first morning that she offered me some, with marshmallows too, I thought maybe Paisley was really an angel from heaven.

So I was thinking about Paisley and how excited I get each morning, and Mrs. Childs's face reminded me of that teapot flap.

I told Mrs. Childs that I once had a foster mom tell me I'd already had enough drama in my life, so I was okay not to be in Drama anymore. And I didn't mind changing my Biology class if that meant I could be in her sixth period class.

That's when the teapot flap flipped up! Mrs. Childs clapped her hands together, smiled super big, and then handed me the form and told me *all* about her special class.

CHAPTER IV

Right away, I liked Mrs. Childs's CW class. I especially liked it, 'cause it was the first place I started making friends.

It started when she gave us a class assignment where we had to answer a 110-item questionnaire, which is a lot of questions! But she said it'd help us for when we create characters in our fiction writing and for when we write stuff about ourselves in our nonfiction writing. But I think she just gave it to us 'cause she thought it'd be fun, 'cause it was one of my most favorite class periods yet.

My partner was Tracey and I learned lots about him.

First, he really, really likes the movie *Pirates of the Caribbean*. He's watched it seven times this summer, and for Christmas, he already knows he's getting a life-size cut-out of Captain Jack Sparrow for his room. And his goal is to build his wardrobe so he can dress just like Johnny Depp. He likes Drama. He likes to act. And he likes to make people laugh. But he says that people at this school don't think he's funny.

Second, he likes to do all sorts of things with his hair. I don't know what nationality he is, but he's got dark skin and thick hair, but not like an Afro. But he loves his hair. He likes to do all sorts of things to it. He's dyed it auburn, purple, and lime green, 'cause lime green is his favorite color, but he says since his hair is naturally so dark, the lime green didn't work real well. But right now he's got it bleached blond. He used to perm his hair and then shave the sides. Last year, he had a ponytail but he didn't like it that much. This year, he spikes it out real straight.

The last thing I learned was that he had lots of friends before he moved here, and he's only living here for one year due to his mom, Cori, being a professor. But he's real ready to move back to Berkeley, which is in the Bay Area, near San Francisco. I told him I also lived in California, and I was here in Helam for just this year too. He asked me if I'd made many friends here, and then us first being friendless is what turned us into friends.

I ate lunch with Tracey the next day.

CHAPTER V

Over the next while, Tracey and I hung out together during lunch time. I like Tracey as a friend. And I keep learning lots about him, like the first time he came to Utah was for the Olympic Winter Games in 2002. Then his moms liked it so much, his mom Cori did a one-year job swap with a professor at the University of Utah. Tracey said they swapped everything! And Tracey says he hates living in someone else's house.

I didn't tell him how many different ones I'd lived in.

He also says he hates Helam, 'cause he doesn't fit in.

I said, "How come?"

"Cause I'm dark."

Where I lived in California everyone was a different color, so it just didn't matter.

"Diversity's good!" I said. I like the word *diversity*, so I was glad I could say it to him. But I don't think he liked that word.

He gave me a real dirty look. So even though I like Tracey a lot, 'cause he likes to sing, and he likes to act like all sorts of characters, and he can be real funny, he's also got a chip on his shoulder, so I didn't like what he said next.

"You know that's why we're in Mrs. Childs's special elective class."

"'Cause we write well," I said.

"No!" He said it like it was a fact. "Because she wanted *diversity* in her class." And he said it like *diversity* was a bad word.

I'm not a crier, so I wasn't going to cry, but my eyes did burn a little, and I did bite my lip, because what Tracey was saying made it sound like Mrs. Childs thought I'd be perfect for her CW class for a different reason than what I thought she thought.

Tracey said, "When we were getting ready to move here, my mom Cori called the school and talked to them about what classes I could take. And when she heard about Mrs. Childs's elective class, and the national project we get to do at the end, she made sure I applied and got in."

He kept talking like it had nothing to do with our writing skills. Instead, it had to do with us being different. And he never said *dysfunctional* but I figured that was what he meant, so even though I hate that word, I was starting to get mad, so I said, "Do you have a dysfunctional family too?"

Well, even though he'd hurt my feelings, I think I hurt his feelings even more 'cause his eyes got real big, and his face turned red. Tracey's taller than most boys, but he's super, super thin. I could probably wear his jeans, I just would need to roll up the cuffs. Or maybe I wouldn't fit in his jeans, 'cause he is really that skinny. So since he's so skinny, he doesn't scare me. It's not like he's going to hurt anybody, but seeing how red his face was, I sure felt like that word hurt him. And I sure did understand, 'cause I hate that word too. So I guess I shouldn't have said it.

"My family is not dysfunctional," he told me. "My family is non-traditional. I have two moms. And we have a super *great* family!"

"Lots of people have two moms." I thought of my sister Cassie, she never called her other mom "Mom" but she did call her "step-mom", which has mom in it. And I have my foster moms, which are types of moms too. So I didn't think Tracey needed to be so upset.

But he said, "My moms are lesbians, okay!"

He kind of was yelling this at me. But I didn't think it was such a big deal, 'cause instead of having to take turns at both of his moms' houses, they all lived together, which was nicer than what Cassie and I had to do. But I wasn't going to say that, especially 'cause Tracey seemed all upset at me, even though I hadn't said anything. And he just kept talking about it, and while he did . . . well, I hate to write this, and maybe I should erase it from my memoir . . . Tracey, if you ever read my memoir, please don't be upset that I wrote this . . . but while Tracey kept talking about what he was upset about, he did cry just a little bit. It was the type where the eyes well up with tears first, and then slowly, one by one, they start to spill over. I hope it's okay that I wrote that, Tracey.

He said, "It's not just my skin that makes me different here."

I wanted to tell him what Clarissa had told me when I was real young. That just like I thought the best part of the apple was past the peel, she said people are like that too. The best part of people is always past their skin. It's one of the few things Clarissa told me that I really liked. But I didn't tell Tracey that, cause his eyes were still wet and real big.

Instead he said, "I don't fit here because I'm not a Mormon like the rest of the school."

I wanted to tell Tracey what Carroll had told me. That back when Carroll was a kid, almost the entire town was Mormon, and it was the Mormon pioneers that had settled Helam, and that Salt Lake City was to the Mormons like Rome is to the Catholics, but nowadays Helam is only 50% Mormons, which would mean that only 50% of our school is Mormon, and 50% doesn't really mean the whole rest of the school. It means half. But Tracey wasn't done talking, so I didn't say anything.

Then he said, "I also don't fit here because my moms are lesbians, which means I have double the moms and no dad."

52

At this point, I had some options. I could tell Tracey that I didn't have a dad either, so he wasn't that odd to me. But the other thing I could tell him was what we'd learned in Biology this week about sexual reproduction. To be completely accurate, I could say we both did still have dads, because of the whole egg and sperm thing, but I was pretty sure Tracey didn't really want to hear any of that.

So I got a different idea. I reached into my backpack and pulled out a little pack of tissues I'd made from a box of tissues at Carroll and Paisley's house. I made this little packet in case Mrs. Childs ever needed them again, but turns out right then, I decided Tracey maybe needed them too.

CHAPTER VI

Eventually Anya from our CW class came and ate lunch with Tracey and me. Then sometimes Blake would come too.

Blake is a funny kid. He's kind of like a teddy bear. He isn't really fat, just someone you could really wrap your arms around and squeeze tight. Whereas Tracey is so thin that if you wrapped your arms around him, your wrists might touch. With Blake, I don't think your fingers would come close to touching. Of course, I don't know. I haven't hugged Tracey or Blake, but they're my friends, and I do like hanging out with them.

Blake is super, super smart. Tracey is smart too, but in other ways. Blake is smart like a nerd. He wants to be an engineer someday and build bridges or ships. I guess he likes the ocean or something. He also reads books—a lot of books. I like books too, but Blake reads them at lunch, and while he walks down the halls, and every night before he goes to bed. And they aren't school books, or fun books, but grown-up books about business guys. I ask him if he understands it. He says not all of it, but that's why he's reading them—to try to understand it.

I like Anya a lot.

I don't know how to describe her, other than to say she's just nice, and super sweet! And she's real short. When Tracey stands next to Anya he is over a foot taller than her. And she has honey-blonde hair that she always wears in braids. She looks young, but cute young.

She says she doesn't have a lot of friends, but she seems to know everyone at school. I don't know if that's 'cause she grew up here, or if she just has more friends than she thinks she does. To be honest, I don't really have much in common with Anya, but I'm still glad to have her as a friend.

One day, it was just us at our side of the lunch table. Blake doesn't always eat with us, and especially not that day because he was helping the student body president get ready for an assembly after lunch. And Tracey said he wanted to be by himself so he could practice some lines for Drama. Lately, he doesn't even try to make us laugh—and I miss laughing with him.

So while it was just Anya and me, we got talking about the rest of our CW class. Anya says everyone at the school knows who Hamilton is because his dad is Thad Forbes.

When she saw I wasn't impressed, she said, "Thad Forbes used to play for the Steelers."

I just shrugged at her.

She said, "The NFL football team!"

I said, "I don't know much about football." I said it 'cause I really didn't care who Hamilton's dad is. But it was real clear Anya did.

She said, "He does a lot of good for Helam now, and helps with the high school's football team, and my dad says they're going to name a street after him."

"Oh," I said. I started to think maybe it was a big deal, 'cause Anya's eyes got real big while she kept talking about him.

"Dad says that the Forbes family has been in Helam for like a hundred years. And when Thad Forbes played for the NFL, everyone was super glad he put our little town on the map."

I wanted to tell her that Carroll says that Helam's not little anymore, but instead I asked her if she likes football.

"So much!" she said. "I love watching it with my dad."

The only sport I ever watched was baseball, and that's only 'cause I lived with a foster family who liked it a whole lot, so I learned some stuff. But once I left there, I haven't watched a game since. So I asked Anya, "Would you watch it by yourself?"

She said, "Maybe, but probably not. When I'm by myself, I strum my guitar, or write song lyrics, or play with my dog."

I'd been eating a strawberry roll-up and my mouth was full with the last bite when I said, "Do you like being Principal Truss's daughter?"

She gave me a funny grin, like she thought my question was dumb. "I was his daughter before he was my principal."

I guess that made sense.

"So I know Abigail and Dillon are boyfriend and girlfriend," I said.

She said, "Yeah. They are."

I'd already figured that out, 'cause they sit by each other all the time, and a couple of times I've seen them passing notes, and they hold hands. "Abigail's nice." I said. "She always says *hi* to me in the halls, and in Creative Writing and Geometry."

"Dillon's nice too," Anya added.

"I figured," I said. He usually nodded at me in the halls. So, of course, I nodded back. "What about Darby?" I asked. "She never smiles!"

Anya rolled her eyes. "Yeah!" She said. "I know! Darby and I were really good friends when we were little. Like we played together from Preschool to third grade, but then from third grade to sixth grade we just stopped hanging out, and now she won't even say *hi* to me."

"That's rude!" I said.

She shrugged. "I know."

"And I know what Priscilla likes," I said.

Anya and I looked at each other, and at the same time we both said, "Boys!" Then we laughed!

The only person left was Kyle, who I didn't know at all. That's 'cause he sits way in the back, he hardly talks, he slouches a lot, and I'm pretty sure he doesn't even want to be in the class.

So I asked Anya if she knows why he's there.

"My mom is best friends with Kyle's mom's sister and she said that it was 'cause Kyle's dad made him take the class."

"Really?" I couldn't imagine anyone in our CW class being *made* to be there.

"Kyle's *big time* into video games," Anya said, "and Kyle told his dad he plans to design them someday. So his dad made Kyle write a storyline for a game, and it was that story that got him into Mrs. Childs's class."

Must have been a real great story, 'cause we both know other kids who are sad they didn't get into this class.

"I don't think Kyle really wants to design games," Anya said. "I think he just said that so he could keep playing his video games, and he doesn't really want to be in Mrs. Childs's class, which is too bad."

"Yeah!" I said "'Cause it's like the best class ever!"

"I know!"

Then we both laughed.

It was a super, great, fun lunchtime!

CHAPTER VII

I just had the best weekend. It might be one of my favorite weekends ever!

Over a week ago, Priscilla had invited all of us girls from the CW class to her house for a sleepover on Friday. The whole year, she's hardly talked to me except when we were paired together for group discussions, so I thought it was kind of strange, but I was still excited. So was Anya.

Anya told me what *girly* stuff to pack for the sleepover, and she let me borrow a sleeping bag, and then her dad and Carroll called and talked to Priscilla's mom. He said he did that phone call because it's a good practice. He said he learned the hard way during his early father years. Then he hugged me and said he hoped I had fun. And I like it that Carroll cares.

And the sleepover was amazing! Before, when Clarissa had some bad episodes and other adults had to step in, they'd say I got to go have a sleepover, and then they'd take me to someone else's house. So I thought I'd done sleepovers before, but they were nothing like this! We stayed up until three in the morning 'cause we were talking, and laughing, and playing games, and watching movies, and eating so much junk food. I learned something about each girl, and now I feel like they're all my friends.

Then Saturday morning, after the sleepover, Anya invited me over to her house. It was bizarre to see Principal Truss at his house in a t-shirt and jeans, and it was even more bizarre to hear the corny jokes he tells Anya. I'm glad he doesn't share any of these at school with us students, 'cause they aren't funny. But I laughed at them anyway, just to be nice.

Then on Sunday, I went to church with Carroll and Paisley. I especially went 'cause Anya goes there too. My favorite part is when we sit together in a class called Young Women's, which I bet you could guess that only women are there, and most of them are young, but some of the leaders look real old! And this Sunday, I snuck in some snacks, which Anya shared with me.

I know I already said it, but I just want to say it again. This was one of the best weekends I've had in a very long time!

CHAPTER VIII

I'm real mad right now and I feel bad 'cause I came home from school today and I slammed the door to my room. Carroll came and knocked and asked if I wanted to talk, but I kind of yelled back and said, "No!"

He said, "You sound angry."

And I knew I was, but I lied and said I wasn't.

But I am, 'cause all day I haven't been able to stop thinking about my phone call last night with Clarissa. And the more I think about it, the madder I get.

Here's a metaphor! What Clarissa said is like a brain worm. I can't get it out. It's stuck in my head and it just keeps moving around, inch by inch, until I can't think about anything else but what she said!

The brain worm's been bothering me all day, and especially in my CW class, which now I think is a stupid class 'cause I don't like it now when Mrs. Childs talks about our last project. And she did today and I couldn't stop thinking about what Clarissa had said.

At first, Clarissa said she should have never listened to Jake, 'cause he's who got her into this mess.

Then I said I never liked Jake.

And she said, "Then why didn't you tell me?"

I said I did, but she swore I didn't and then she said, "Todi! If you would have told me, you could have stopped this." But that wasn't enough, 'cause then she said, "Todi! I wouldn't be in jail right now if you'd just spoken up." And then after she said, "If you'd have done something, you wouldn't be in foster care.

"We would still be together." That's what the brain worm keeps saying, "Todi, it's 'cause of you."

I don't want to listen to the brain worm. It's not my fault.

But it still causes a lot of pain!

Dillon's Journal

September 18, 2003

I like this class and Mrs. Childs and her assignment with these journals. Writing doesn't bother me. When I was in grade school, a couple of teachers told me I was good at it. I am not sure this is something I want to do all the time as in a profession, but I don't mind it. Not like some kids. So far I don't know what I want to do for a job. I'm thinking about being a dentist, but it's a lot of schooling.

My dad is a businessman. He works for a computer software company that documents and tracks information for other businesses. He works in the sales department and he has worked there since I was five years old. He's very good at what he does. He travels some for work, but usually he brings us back a gift when he gets back, so that part's cool.

I am the oldest of five kids. Then there is my sister Rachael who just turned thirteen. Then it's my sister Lexi who is nine, my brother Lawrence who is seven, and the baby, Rusty.

For the most part I don't mind being the oldest, although once I turned twelve my parents started leaving me to watch Rachael, Lexi, and Lawrence. Since Rusty's been born, Mom usually takes him with her. But sometimes I watch him for a little bit. I don't mind every once in a while watching all of them, but sometimes it's a lot of work.

October 22, 2003

Two nights ago, my mom was yelling at my dad. It was so loud it woke me up. She was pissed. I can't remember ever hearing her so pissed before.

Last night was my dad's turn. He yelled—not as loud as mom, and not as pissed as mom. But he yelled tonight.

They're fighting more and more.

I hate it when they fight. It makes everything feel unsteady. And I have a hard time sleeping because I'm wondering which kid did something wrong. Sometimes I wonder if it was me who did something that made them mad.

My mom has told me several times how I make her happy. She talks about boys in other families and all the trouble they cause. I've never been a troublemaker. I plan to go to college, get a degree, and work hard. I wish I knew what I wanted to be, but for now college is the next step after high school. Especially this year, now that I'm in ninth grade, I have to work hard so that I'll have choices and so that I can get a scholarship when I graduate.

Being in this class was a good first step. My mom was proud of me. My dad was proud of me too, but he also was proud when I got picked for the freshman basketball team. I have practice starting in a week, and games starting in December. Dad says he will be at every game. Both my mom and dad say I'm on the right track, which makes them happy.

November 7, 2003

Last night, I heard my dad leave in the middle of the night. They had been yelling again. This time both of them. When Dad slammed the door the whole house shook. Then Rusty started crying. I didn't know if I should go get him or pretend I was still asleep. When the door slammed, it scared me.

Then I heard a loud sound, like glass shattering on the floor.

Something's broken.

Since Rusty kept crying, I got out of bed. Our rooms are right next to each other, so I crept quietly into his room, picked him up, and held him. Then I walked down the hall until I could see downstairs. Mom was hunched over on the couch crying. She looked old. But she must have heard me or Rusty because she looked up. We both looked at each other for a while. Then her shoulders sagged, and she looked real thin. I kept holding Rusty, and it was like she couldn't move. It was like she wasn't my mom, like what was broken was her.

She just whispered, "Thanks Dillon."

Then she stared at Rusty for a long time. Longer than when she'd stared at me. Finally, she said, "Can Dillon put you back to bed? Mommy needs to be alone right now."

I've always expected my parents to fix things when they break. But looking at my mom, it just seemed like this was bigger than what they could fix. But then I thought that maybe I could fix it. So I said, "I can take care of him."

Those words made Mom jump for her car keys. "Thanks Dillon," she said it like three times—over and over again. "I need to go for a drive right now. But everything will be okay." Then she turned back to look at me and started crying again. Then she said, "It'll be okay, Dillon. I love you."

The only way I could fix anything was to say, "I love you too." Then she ran out the front door.

November 10, 2003

My parents finally told us what was going on. Well, Dad did. Mom sat in the corner twisting a tissue to shreds. She didn't cry. She didn't say anything mean, and she didn't yell at Dad. She just stayed quiet. Sometimes she gave Dad looks. Sometimes she scanned her eyes over all of us. Sometimes she just stared at the tissue in her hand.

Dad hadn't been back to the house since their last big fight. At least, not while us kids had been home. Lexi had asked Mom if Dad was on a trip. "No, he's just staying somewhere else."

Lexi asked when he would be home. Mom said, "I don't know. He needs to come and talk to you."

"Me?" Lexi had sounded all excited, like she was someone important if Dad just needed to talk to her. Or maybe she thought he had some special surprise just for her. But Mom was sharp back when she said, "All of you. He needs to come talk to all of you." Then she stormed off. Lexi looked at me like she was confused. She didn't get why what she'd said had made Mom mad. But I did. Mom's still mad at Dad. Mom is super pissed.

So when Dad came to talk to us, I already knew it was bad news. I'd been hoping that something would change. Maybe they really could fix what broke. But as soon as Dad walked in the door and acted way too friendly to all of us, I knew he hadn't come to fix things. He'd only been gone for three days, but he acted strange. He asked Mom if he could get a soda from the fridge. That was odd. Just like it was odd when he asked her where they should all sit. Both times she shrugged at him. The only thing she said while he was there was, "This is your thing, Danny. You figure it out."

When he sat us all down in the living room, Mom sat in the back, behind all of us. At first, it felt like she was watching us like a hawk would. She was so angry. But then my dad started talking, and he started sharing all these great memories we'd had as a family—our vacation to Yosemite, the Christmas we all got bikes, the trip to Disneyland, our first jumps on our trampoline, and building our tree house. He talked about some of the funny times and Lexi and Lawrence laughed. Rachael smiled.

Mom was silent.

I felt like I needed to follow her. Dad was *lying* to us. He sat in front of all of us, smiling and *lying*. I could see it in his smiles and hear it in his voice. And when he finally got to his point, I knew for sure he was lying.

He said, "All those great memories will continue, and we'll make even more great memories, but in a different way, because Mom and I have decided I need to move out."

I snuck a look at Mom. Her face pulled back as if one of us had just slapped her. But she didn't argue. She just listened to Dad as he talked about him moving out. He said it would be the best for everyone. He said he needed to do this. Rachael started to cry. Lexi kept asking questions, "What does that mean? Dad wouldn't be living with us? But why?" Lawrence just wanted to be done with the talk so he could go out and play. And Rusty was upstairs asleep.

I couldn't say anything. I glanced at Mom and then stared at Dad. Once, Dad looked at me, eye to eye, long enough that I think I saw the truth—I think he was sad. But I don't know for sure, because then he was back talking about taking us all to the zoo in a couple of Saturdays, and I saw Lawrence jump for joy, and Lexi stop with the questions, and Rachael, who was still upset, wipe her eyes as if she could play along with all of this. But all I could do was look back at Mom and see her clench her tissue.

I know the truth. Mom doesn't want Dad to leave. She doesn't want this to happen to all of us. This isn't her fault. This is Dad's.

Dad's leaving us, and none of us can stop him.

December 10, 2003

Thanksgiving was different. Christmas will be different too.

January 7, 2004

Best thing about being back from winter break is that Christmas is over—worst Christmas ever.

January 12, 2004

I don't like to write in this journal anymore. I don't like to write. Mrs. Childs started asking us some questions that had to do with our final project about our family. But I've got nothing I want to write.

I hate my dad. I hate being around him. All he does is lie. We could still be a family if he wouldn't lie.

February 23, 2004

I will be a better dad than my dad.

Priscilla's Journal

Sept. 18, 2003

I like my journal. Mrs. Childs gave us these for our Creative Writing class. They are sturdy like a lot of our school books, but mine also feels smooth, and I like the color of mine. A kid named Blake called them moleskin, which sounds totally disgusting! So I won't call them that. There are three different colors: black, brown, and blue. I am SO happy that mine is blue. It's really pretty and reminds me of the ocean!

Mrs. Childs told us to make an extra effort to include thoughts, feelings, emotions, and memories about our families, since she says it'll help us get ready for our final writing project, but she also said that she isn't going to read these, so I'm going to write whatever I want in here.

Like how this is about to be the Best Year Ever!

I'm so excited for 9th grade. First, Bria, my best friend since 4th grade, and I, made it into Dance Club together. We already started rehearsals and it is SO much fun! It's supposed to help prepare us to get into Drill Team at the High School next year. Plus, my older brother, Josh, left for college, which means I don't have to share a room with my little sister Caitlin anymore. That is seriously one of the greatest things that happened this new school year! The other great things are that Bria and I have four classes together: Homeroom, English, Social Studies, and this Creative Writing class. It was Bria's idea that we apply for this class. We had to send in sample essays last April. I don't like to write, but Bria thought it would be fun. So she talked me into it. Then we both got in so I was excited. And so far I like it. Mrs. Childs gave us a cheap black backpack with an ugly logo. I'd never actually use mine (not to mention mine already has a hole in the corner), but what was inside was cool. There were our journals, some other papers, a keychain, an eraser, a pen, and a mirror. Of course, the mirror is my favorite.

But the VERY best part of this year is that Hamilton Forbes is in this Creative Writing class too. I was SO shocked when I found out. I would have never ever guessed he would apply to be in this class. EVER! He is super, super good-looking. He has sandy-blond hair that he keeps short, and he spikes up the front part perfectly. He has nice blue eyes and the best body! So many girls like him, and he's been my number-one crush since 7th grade. I usually have about two classes with him each year, but he sits with all of his friends, and only once in a while does he look at me. Well, I hope he is looking at me. But I don't know for sure.

But this year, everything will be different. There are only ten students in this class because Mrs. Childs wants time to do stuff with our writing, and with this class so small, Hamilton will have to notice me, and even sit by me sometimes. Plus, we have group discussions where we all have to talk, so this means for sure we'll need to talk to each other. I'm so, So, SO excited about this!

Bria is such a good friend, she really thinks this is the year that Hamilton will ask me out. She thinks it's a sign that both of us ended up in this class, especially since I first didn't want to try to get into the class. I so hope so! This year, I'm going to look super pretty! Not like last year, where I felt ugly every day! This year, my hair is going to be perfect ALL the time. This year, something really good BETTER happen with me and boys! (And I SO hope it's with Hamilton!)

Sept. 25, 2003

This is going to be the worst year ever!!!

Last night, I found out Bria's family is moving in eight days. I'm so mad I just want to cry!

She doesn't want to move. I doubt anyone in their family wants to move, but they've been renting their house for six years, and now the landlord wants to sell the house. There are seven kids in Bria's family, and they don't have enough money to buy the house right now. I want them to stay here, but Bria says that it is hard for them to find a house that's big enough for all of them that their dad can afford. He works a lot at the copper mine and now her parents say they're going to move closer to his work. I HATE this! I asked her if she could still go to our school, but she said no.

They are moving and I don't know what I'm going to do without Bria. It's just not fair! I won't have any really good friends—definitely nobody like Bria!

I haven't been able to smile all day. And now that I'm writing in this journal, I keep thinking about all the writing I have to do in this class! It's a REAL good thing Hamilton is in here otherwise I would be SO mad that I ended up in this class!!!

Sept. 26, 2003

Right now I don't like Hamilton cause every day he always sits by Darby, and they talk a lot to each other, and they always walk down the halls together, and I DO NOT LIKE DARBY!

And I don't like 9th grade.

Oct. 2, 2003

Today was the first school day without Bria. It's been such a HORRIBLE DAY!!! I don't have any friends in Homeroom. I just sit there while everyone else around me talks.

I don't like English or this Creative Writing class anymore (even if Hamilton is in it), and Social Studies is the only class that is okay because the teacher, Mr. Willis, is funny.

I don't even like Dance Club anymore. It was fun when Bria was there. It's not fun now. And Darby is in it too, which makes no sense to me. Why would she be here? I thought for sure she would rather be a cheerleader next year than on the Drill Team. Lena is one of the best cheerleaders at the High School and is the most popular girl ever. Everyone knows who she is because she's totally perfect. She has perfect hair always, if she wears it curly no strand is out of place, if she wears it straight, there are no flyaways. Everyone wanted to be just like her when she was at the Jr. High. That year half of us 7th graders tried to do our hair like hers or dress just like her. And she has boys around her all the time. So does Darby.

Today, Darby said "hi" to me, but it wasn't a "Hi, want to be my friend?" hi. It was a "Hi, aren't you in some of my classes?" hi. The rest of practice she didn't talk to any of the other girls, cause she's so stuck-up. But she did keep standing by me through practice.

It took me a long time, but I finally got up the nerve and said, "Are you going out with Hamilton?"

Darby shook her head and then stared at me for a long time. I was so mad at myself that I asked her that. Now she'll think I like him, and then she'll tell Hamilton, and I hate it when a guy knows that I like him.

But I was happy with her answer. She said they had been boyfriend and girlfriend in 7th grade but now they're just friends.

That news made me VERY happy, even if she did look down at the spot of mud smeared across the toe of my shoes. Darby or her sister, Lena, would never have muddy shoes. I'd seen the mud, but I didn't wipe it off. And now Darby saw. She looked at it long enough that I hope she doesn't say anything about it to Hamilton. I hope she doesn't think I like Hamilton.

Oct. 17, 2003

Something really great just happened. It made today a very, very good day!

I got to Creative Writing a few minutes before the bell. Some of the other kids were talking, but I was stuck fishing in my bag to find a pen. Then I looked up and Darby is standing at my desk. And Hamilton is there too. Darby says, "Hi, Priscilla." And then Hamilton smiles at me.

It was the BEST DAY of my life. Hamilton smiled at me!!!

Of course, I was a fool and said, "Hi Darby." But didn't say anything to Hamilton. I wish I could have said "hi" to him too, but suddenly I got real nervous.

Then they both took their seats two rows away from me, and they talked to each other through most of class. But still Darby said "hi," and Hamilton smiled at me!

Plus, today was picture day and I'm pretty sure my hair was PERFECT for it. Best hair day EVER! That's never happened before, it usually goes all flat right before my photo time. But not today. And Bria says she has a cousin who can photoshop out my zit. Awesome, AWESOME day!!!

Oct. 29, 2003

Today was the worst day ever!!! I had planned to talk to Hamilton today, so I already planned to wear my favorite black leggings with my tangerine silk skirt, only to find out my skirt was not there. I was SO mad! Turns out it was in my closet, but not where I had last hung it up.

When my brother Josh left for college and Caitlin moved into his room, I finally got the whole closet to myself. I organized it so my tangerine skirt was right between my black knit skirt and my flower print skirt. But today I found it between my leather jacket and my black and white striped shirt on my lower rack. I know Caitlin has been going through my stuff again because this time there was a smear of red lipstick on my skirt, and I KNOW I would have never worn red lipstick with a tangerine skirt. I was mad. Not just that Caitlin had got into my stuff again, but that she lied about it when I asked.

She lied about it until she started to cry. I didn't mean to make her cry, but she shouldn't be in my stuff.

She cried until Mom came and then I got in trouble, which was SO not fair.

After Mom left, I told Caitlin I would make her wish she'd never touched my stuff. That only set her off into a full-blown six-year-old meltdown. She yelled, "I DIDN'T touch your stuff!" and that put me face-to-face with my dad.

Except now when I wear heels I tower over my dad. Not by much, but enough that he has to look up at me when he tries to give me a talking to. When I hit my growth spurt, I rose slightly above my family's short genes, and that's when I stopped being scared of my dad.

Still, I don't like making him mad.

"I'm sure it was an accident," he said.

(Mrs. Childs gave us an assignment to try and use dialogue at least once in our journals. Here's my attempt.)

"She shouldn't be in my stuff," I said. "If she wasn't in my stuff, then there would never be an accident, huh?"

"Priscilla, be patient with her. She's only six."

"A six-year-old who likes to wear my skirts like they're her dresses!"

"Priscilla." He said my name all soft, like he wanted me to calm down.

But I didn't want to calm down. I said, "And she shouldn't be touching my clothes, or my makeup, or my jewelry, or my perfume, or my mirror, or ANYTHING!"

"She just wants to be like you."

"Dad, even if she was thirteen, I still don't want her touching my stuff!"

He looked at me with his sad eyes. And that's why I don't like making my dad mad at me, because he doesn't know how to get mad at me, only to give me sad eyes. The eyes of 'I'm *disappointed* in you.' Like I should spend my whole life trying to make him happy so I can avoid the 'I'm *disappointed* in you' look. I hate that look!!!

So I try to avoid it as much as I can. But today I couldn't! I'd wanted to wear that exact outfit since I'd already planned that this was the day I was going to talk to Hamilton.

But instead, I was late to school because I got into a fight with everyone in my family (except Josh, but he doesn't count). I had to redo my entire wardrobe plans, and I didn't have the full hour I needed on my hair. So it fell out by 4th period! I hate my outfit, I hate my hair, and I hate me. Today has turned into the worst day of my whole life!

Before, I'd been planning to sit near Hamilton while Mrs. Childs set us up in our groups. But after feeling so ugly, now I'm just trying to avoid him. I know it seems silly, but if he doesn't really look at me today, then maybe I'll still have a chance some other time.

And he didn't end up in my group. Instead I was with Kyle, Blake, and Anya.

But next week we'll be in new groups . . . so I can still hope for next week. As long as Caitlin stays out of my stuff!!

Nov. 6, 2003

Not only did Hamilton end up in my group, he asked to borrow a pen from me. I was SO excited and nervous! When I pulled out the pen from my pack it dropped onto the floor, then we both went for the pen, and when we both touched the pen, our fingers touched too! I'm SO HAPPY!!!

He knows who I am, and we talked, and then he gave me back my pen at the end of class and said, "Thank you."

If he were to like me, it'd change everything! This could be my BEST YEAR EVER! A boy would like me—not just any boy, but Hamilton!!!

And if Hamilton liked me, I'd never feel ugly again. That would let me know for sure that I was pretty. And if he liked me, he might ask me to be his girlfriend.

That would mean I'd kiss Hamilton. I would LOVE to kiss Hamilton!!! I so want him to be my first kiss!

Although I know he's kissed lots of girls before. But I don't care. If he were to kiss me, I would be the happiest person ever! This is what I want so badly!!! And then I'd be SO HAPPY!

Nov. 16, 2003

Darby says hi to me in class still, and stands by me in Dance Club still, but I don't like her still!

She talks to Hamilton a lot. I still think she likes him, but she just didn't want to tell me!

She's really pretty. And I bet if she liked Hamilton, he would like her back.

She's so lucky—God just gave her beautiful hair. And beautiful skin. And a beautiful figure.

And the ability to talk to boys.

Lots of boys.

All the boys!

She does everything right. She has tons of boys at her table at lunch. She always has a boy walking her to class. She's had boyfriends since 5th grade.

I just wish I was a little bit more like Darby—enough so that Hamilton would notice me, and want to be with me, and want me to be his girlfriend, and want to kiss me . . .

That's all I want.

If Hamilton would like me, then life would be perfect!

Dec. 2, 2003

So far, since he borrowed my pen, Hamilton hasn't talked to me again. Once he waited at the door at the end of class, and I thought maybe he was waiting for me. Maybe he was going to talk to me. I wanted to believe that SO much!

I got real nervous and took a little longer to put my notebook in my bag, only to see he was really waiting for Darby! Then they walked out together. I should have known!

81

Made for one of the WORST afternoons in my life, because I ended up walking behind them.

I could hear Darby laugh, and I could hear Hamilton teasing her. I even saw him slide his hand down her back until he touched her butt. I SO wish I wouldn't have seen that!

Darby just let out a giggle and playfully nudged him away. But they kept talking and laughing. Darby must like him! And he must like Darby. He will never notice me! I'll never have a chance! I hate school!!!

I hate my life!

Some things just aren't fair.

Jan. 9, 2004

So I figured it out. It's a GOOD idea! I'm quite proud of myself for thinking of it.

In fact, I saw Bria lots over the Christmas break and I told her about my plan. She thinks it's the perfect plan!

The only way I'm going to get Hamilton to notice me is through Darby. So I have to get Darby to become my friend.

And I know how to do it!

I'm going to invite all of the girls from my Creative Writing class over for a sleepover. I decided it is a great way to get to know all the girls. Especially Darby!

Because at a slumber party, secrets naturally come out. Darby's bound to share what's going on between her and Hamilton. I just know that's how she'll answer all the questions I'm dying to know. Like if they're going out. And if so, how serious are they? And if not, maybe I can find out if there's a chance he might like me. Maybe Darby could even help me.

I LOVE my plan!!!

If I ever have a shot at Hamilton, this is it!

Jan. 13, 2004

Today I invited the other girls to my house this Friday. I promised them there would be manicures, pedicures, facials, pizza, hot fudge sundaes, chick flicks, and more.

Anya was over-the-top excited. She kept saying, "Really?!?" and then again "Really?!?" and then "That will be so much fun." I hope she doesn't think we're BFFs now! But it was super nice to have her excited!

Abigail said she would be there and it sounded like a lot of fun.

Todi said she's never been to a sleepover before—not like this. She said she's slept over at other people's houses for like a night, sometimes a week, or for months, but she'd never been invited to a party like this before. She talked for a while. She LIKES to talk! She totally seemed excited but nervous too, and I started to wonder if maybe it would be odd to have her there. She isn't real into girly stuff. I mean, maybe she could be, but I've never seen her nails painted before. So I wasn't sure if it was going to be a mistake having her there. Still, she was SO excited which was good, because on the other hand, Darby appeared real *cold* toward my invite. It was to the point I didn't think she'd even heard the invite. Or she didn't want to acknowledge it! Maybe she had a date with Hamilton that night instead! Or maybe she hoped she did.

And really I knew she'd heard my invite, cause she cocked her head slightly and then she examined each one of us with her eyes: Todi first, then Anya, then Abigail, then me. I didn't like being examined.

Fortunately, Todi broke the silence. "Darby, you have to come! We're a team now so it's part of working together!"

"Well, it's not like it's an assignment or a requirement," Anya said. Her voice was VERY chirpy. "It's just for all of us girls to get

83

together and have SO MUCH fun!" She was treating my slumber-party invitation like I'd offered her a ticket to Disneyland!

I SO felt like Darby wanted to say, "I have a real life, one with boys, and adventures, dates, and make-out sessions, I don't need to hang out with a bunch of losers like you to have fun."

I felt the words coming, and I was SO scared she was going to humiliate me and my party in front of everyone. And then I realized that if she said no, I'd still have to have this party with the other girls. Suddenly I was starting to think that maybe this was a SUPER STUPID plan!

But after a few more LONG seconds, she looked at me and smiled. It wasn't a warm smile, it wasn't even a *"Hi, I haven't noticed you before, but now that you invited me to your party, I think you must be quite cool"* smile. Rather, it was a *"Your breath smells fishy, but I have to tolerate it for the moment"* smile.

Maybe it wasn't as bad as I remember it, but for how eager Anya was, Darby was the opposite and she showed me that through her sophisticated and calm way that she talks. She said, "Let me check and get back to you."

It was Abigail who saved the day! She said, "Darby, I really hope you can make it. It's a great idea for all of us to get to know each other even better! Thanks, Priscilla!"

"Yes, thank you! Thank you so much!!!" Anya said.

"Sounds like a BLAST!" Todi grinned at me like I'd done something really good.

Then all three grinned at Darby. And I think it was their grins that did it. She stopped cocking her head. Instead, she stood tall and gave all of us one more long glance. Then she said, "Okay, I'm in."

I was TOTALLY elated!!!

Jan. 20, 2004

My slumber party started out real good, and I thought everyone was having a great time. We ate pizza, and sundaes, and did each other's nails, and we were all laughing lots, even Darby laughed a couple of times

Then when we started a movie, Darby stood up and said, "I need to go now, my sister's coming to pick me up."

Anya said. "You're not staying?"

And Darby said, "No."

So Anya said, "Cause why?"

Then Darby kind of seemed flustered. She reached for her bag and threw it over her shoulder. She said, "I promised my sister I would help her with something."

"So you're going home?" Anya kept pushing her to answer.

"I'm helping my sister!" Darby said real strong.

I don't know if Anya was upset. She didn't show it. And then the other girls all said bye to Darby from the living room where we were watching the movie. But I walked her down the hallway. That's because my mom went to great pains when I was a child to teach me the proper steps of entertaining guests. Anytime a friend came over, I had to walk my friend to the door, and say *"thank you for coming"* before they exited. Bria loved to make fun of me, and my *"entertaining"* manners.

"Darby, thank you for coming," I said.

She stopped at our entryway mirror and looked into the glass. "Sure," she said. Then she reached into her bag, pulled out some lip gloss, and applied it to her lips.

I watched her perfect lips, the perfect color, the perfect application. I was SO jealous!!! Especially as the pieces began to fall into place!

"You aren't going home, are you?" I asked her.

She paused and looked at me. Then she tilted her head to the side. It was like she was deciding what she needed to tell me, or why she even needed to tell me anything!

I was getting a bit annoyed with her, leaving my slumber party for a better reason. So I got real bold and said, "Are you going to make out with a guy?"

"Hopefully with more than one!" She winked at me and I felt my jaw drop.

Then she pulled off her burgundy V-neck t-shirt, right in front of me. I stood face to face with Darby in her bra! This wasn't the locker room! She reached into her bag and pulled out a very thin lacy top. It was black, as was her black lacy bra that covered her perfect boobs. I turned away. I was super embarrassed!!!

But Darby didn't seem to care, her arms slid right through the thin straps, and she just slipped right into her tiny top. Then she pulled the lace down and stuck out her chest, and I noticed her bra kinda showed through the lace. Honestly, she looked like a supermodel, and I think she knew it!

Once I caught my breath, I said, "Is Hamilton going to be there?"

"Probably not," she said. Then she shrugged at me and hoisted her bag onto her shoulder.

"Do you wish he was?" I studied her eyes. Her lashes were real dark and thick from her mascara.

"Why? Do you like him?"

I stepped back and from the mirror I could see my face blushing. "Please don't tell him!"

"Why not?" She grinned at me.

My heart was racing! This sleepover was about to backfire big time!!!

I whispered at her, "Do you like him?"

She chuckled at me. "Hamilton's not looking for a girl to distract him from football." Outside a car beeped its horn three times. "He's just looking for a girl to have fun with!" Darby reached for the door. "Bye, Priscilla."

I said, "Don't tell him. Please!"

But she just smirked at me. "I can help you if you want."

My heart was racing again! I said, "Really?"

The car outside beeped its horn three times again. "You bet!" she said and then headed out my door.

Feb. 17, 2004

It's almost been a whole month since my sleepover party and Darby has done nothing to help me! I'm so BUMMED!!!

I asked her once about it and she said, "I already told him that you like him."

My face turned SO red!!! I just stared at her and I got real mad at her, because I told her *NOT* to tell him! Then I said, "What? You told him?"

She said, "Just kidding!" Then she laughed at me because I believed her. And then she said, "Do you want me to tell him you like him?"

I told her "NO!!!"

Then she just shrugged and walked away.

I don't know what I'm going to do. The school year's more than half over and I thought Hamilton and I would be talking to each other by now!

I'm so DEPRESSED!!!

I really, really, really want Hamilton Forbes to LIKE me!

BLAKE'S JOURNAL

Course: Creative Writing

Teacher: Mrs. Childs

Period: 6th

Assignment: Keep a journal throughout the course. Grade is based on participation, not on specifics of the written journal entries.

Requirements:

- Complete 10 – 15 entries for the entire year, or approximately 15 pages.
- Entries should provide insight into family unit.
- Entries will help to spark ideas to be shared in class discussion.
- Entries will aid in the discovery of tone and content for final writing project to be submitted in May.

09.18.03

"The chief cause of failure and unhappiness is trading what we want the most for what we want at the moment." –C.S. Lewis

My mom told me she was a bit wild in her youth. As a result I was born. She doesn't know who my dad is, which means neither do I. Which oddly means he doesn't know who I am either. Or that I exist.

I think I'm okay with that. I just don't want to mess up.

I want to make my mom proud, and I want to do something important, something really important. Once I've done what it is, everyone around me will know that it's important.

I want to have a purpose for why I came to my mom.

I've been told that really successful businessmen don't chase after money, they chase after excellence. Not that I have to be a businessman. But an entrepreneur of some sort, and I've studied some of the greats: Carnegie, Buffett, Marriott and Covey. What I've read is that the greats have higher goals than just making money. They want to be the best at what they do, and then they know, as a side result, the money will come. They seek after products or ideas that improve the quality of life for the people in their communities or within their business environments. Anything that will lift or build rather than diminish or take down society. That's their number one objective.

I want to do that too. I don't know what I'll do or how I'll do it, but whatever it is, it's going to make a difference.

09.30.03

We've been reading *Lord of the Flies* in our ninth grade English class, so Mrs. Childs used it as an example in our Creative Writing class discussion today. We examined the use of symbolism and then the discussion shifted to talking about stereotypes.

Todi, who has no filter on her mouth, declared when she met me she viewed me as an adolescent still growing out of that awkward plumpy kid stage, but now that she's gotten to know me some, she sees me more like a loveable teddy bear. I wasn't sure if this was a compliment, but I decided to take it as one.

Early on in the book, stereotyping begins. Piggy doesn't know Ralph, yet he makes assumptions about Ralph right away, like that he can trust Ralph. So he tells him many personal things. Later, Ralph sees Jack as a natural leader and places him in charge of a group of boys.

In class we talked about how stereotyping helps us make generalizations about people, so we know how to act around people and can seek out the type of people we want to be around. But stereotyping can also be negative. It can create wrong impressions, unfair bias or opinions about people. Yet we all tend to stereotype.

Tracey talked about how there is a lot of stereotyping that happens in Helam.

Anya shared the benefits of this.

Todi shared the disadvantages.

I found it impressive that Mrs. Childs just let us talk. She didn't correct us or tell us we were wrong. She just let us talk and she listened. And we listened too, to each other.

It seemed today, more than in any other class, we as students began to break down some of the stereotypes we have of each other.

10.05.03

Another very good discussion from *Lord of the Flies* in Mrs. Childs's class. We talked about the Lost Boys and about wanting to belong, and about love and esteem. Early on, when the conch was blown, the other boys came. They came because they wanted to belong. They held a meeting because they wanted to feel united. They elected a leader because they sensed that they needed to stay together and be a group.

Mrs. Childs turned the discussion toward each of us with this phrase: Human beings need to belong to a group.

We identified that the first group we belong to is our families. Then we said usually the leaders of a family are our parents. Our families are the first to shape us. But over time, and especially now that we are teenagers, we begin to look at other groups. We start to take an interest in other places where we can belong, and in these new groups, certain leaders also emerge.

Next Mrs. Childs led us into a discussion about large groups and the needs within those large groups to have smaller groups within. Todi brought up our Creative Writing class, and how it is a special group. Mrs. Childs smiled. I think she liked that praise. And I agreed with Todi about us being a group within a group.

We all sat at our desks, forming a crooked circle, and I thought about us as a group and about the importance of needing a group within a group. At the beginning of the year, I didn't know most of these other students. Sure, I knew some of their names, but they weren't my friends. Yet today, not only do I look at all of them a bit differently now, some of them I also feel a sense of belonging with. I can tell that some of them are smart, and like me, they want to succeed in life. We have our goals and we feel a need to become something important.

And just like in *Lord of the Flies*, we can destroy each other, like in our high school years, or we can help each other.

Since Todi is the one who identified us as a group, and Mrs. Childs is the one who motivated us to work hard and try to succeed together as a group, I spoke up and said stuff about us helping each other and not letting one another fail. How we need to support each other in the years ahead, especially this year and next as we transition into high school. Then I said we can also help each other as we prepare ourselves for the best college experience we want, and then even further into our careers and in life.

Mrs. Childs nodded and she said she believes in all of us and thinks this is a very special class.

After our class discussion, I was motivated. I really want to do something now to help this group. I don't know what yet, but I want to be a leader in my own right, within my own role. Not like Jack. In *Lord of the Flies*, Jack shows how dangerous it can be if you don't have the right values as a leader. I would never want to hunt after power like Jack did. I want to add to our group. I want to help all of us succeed.

11.18.03

My mom has a new boyfriend who she says makes her very happy. When I was younger and she brought home a new guy who would start to stay with us, she would always tell me I had a new dad. She would be real excited and say, "I found a new dad for you" and soon I associated *dad* with *a man who comes to live with us for a bit and then hurts my mom in some way.*

Over time she stopped calling them "a new dad," which made me glad, and she also stopped trying to fill that void in our lives. I think the term *dad* should come with some level of commitment. It should be a term for dedication—dedication to the woman, to the family, to their lives. A dad stays, he doesn't leave. He helps, he doesn't hurt. He loves us. And when we call him *Dad* we all understand what that means.

01.04.04

"The last shall be first." –Matthew 20:16 (King James Version of the Bible)

I just found the most incredible story from History. It was the *Lord of the Flies* but in reverse.

The Sudan Lost Boys created a group that saved their lives.

They lost their families in a war and only had each other.

They formed their own new family in a strange land.

From what I can tell, there is no hierarchy. They all have to consult one another.

I plan to study more about the Sudan boys. They have formed a society that is worth understanding.

01.19.04

Tomorrow I have a Biology test. But instead of studying tonight, I went and got my mega set of Legos that I've had since I was a kid, and I dumped them out right in front of my mom. She laughed, which was good, because she had red eyes, and I knew she had been crying earlier.

Her boyfriend isn't her boyfriend anymore, but he's still a manager at the hotel where she works. She says it was all a bad idea. Then she picks up a Lego and starts building with me, and we build an enormous bridge, just like we did when I was a kid.

And she tells me her story, one that I've heard many times when she is sad. She tells me how as a girl, she dreamed of being one of the best architects in the United States. In high school she excelled at science and math. By the time she was a freshman in college she was at the right school, with the right classes, and she had the right ambition to reach her dream. But she hasn't always made the best choices, and her first set of real bad choices happened early in college, which led her to make many bad choices, and by her sophomore year she had dropped out and moved hundreds of miles away from her family so she could live with a friend. Together they picked up work with a catering staff at a hotel.

The friend moved on, but Mom stayed. She's been at the hotel ever since, and she reminds me that *my dad* was a man who paid all his bills with cash and was just passing through town.

She's met many boyfriends through her work, but she also works really hard, and through the years she's moved into management. She says she has no regrets, but I know she wishes she had finished college.

That's why she's raised me differently. She's taught me to be smart and she's going to help me to succeed.

She wanted to build houses, and I want to build bridges, so tonight we built the most awesome Lego town.

01.24.04

"There never has been, and cannot be, a good life without self-control."
–Leo Tolstoy

After Mom's recent relationship disappointment, I promised her I'd do everything I could to avoid any type of image that would cause me to appear to others as if I'm a bad person. I aim to respect others. I want to be mindful of their circumstances, their troubles, and their heartaches.

Any time after my mom has had her heart hurt, she first tells me her story of bad choices, then a few days later she gives me her lecture. Because she is repeatedly drawn to players, she's talked to me extensively about this. She wants me to like girls, to someday have a girlfriend, and to have fun, but she wants me to be honest with girls, to be up front with them, and never lead them on.

I told her I don't think that it's my personality to lie to another person. She agreed.

However, I don't feel I could ask her the question I really want to know, which is "What is acceptable conduct?"

There is a girl I'm interested in getting to know better. But I may get to know her better only to discover I don't want to continue to get to know her better. Yet if she seems she wants to continue to get to know me, but then I'm done getting to know her, then am I a player?

Certainly I wouldn't plan to lose interest. But if I did, how would I tactfully communicate this?

"I was curious about you, but you have adequately satisfied my curiosity, so there is no need for me to explore this relationship further." Could I say that?

I'd like to approach girls as if I was conducting an experiment. I'd use the scientific method to create a hypothesis, plan my procedures, conduct my observations, record my data, and draw my conclusion before I declare my results. However, somewhere in the process I'd have to take into account the feelings of the subject under investigation and this could complicate things considerably.

So is there a safe way to make this discovery about another without jeopardizing their feelings?

Also, I'm curious about how to conduct this research while always maintaining a sense of quality and integrity of self.

As I continue my own research of great men in history, I recognize their knowledge and their wisdom. I see how their great acts have aided the human race, yet I am perplexed by those who gave up their families in order to invest in their own worldly fame.

Does it have to be one or the other?

I can't look to my mother for an example of relationship success. I find science has yet to discover any natural laws which may define the process in which to achieve a happy nuclear family.

I dream of success, I see myself accomplishing something great, yet I can't see myself with a healthy family someday. I don't think I have those social skills, so I'm still not sure how this is to be done.

02.08.04

"You gain strength, courage and confidence by every experience in which you really stop to look fear in the face. You must do the things you think you cannot do." –Eleanor Roosevelt

And fear is preventing me from moving forward.

I don't believe in failure. I only can pursue success, but asking out a girl could equal failure.

And I don't know if this is worth it.

I'd rather be safe than hear a "no."

But I keep thinking about her. A lot.

To the point that she is distracting me from my goals.

Maybe I need to tell her to at least stop. Stop talking to me. Stop looking at me. Stop sitting near me. Stop giving me clues or suggestions that she might also find some positive charge between us.

Please stop. For the sake of my sanity and goals, please leave me alone.

Of course, my mom is sensing a change in me. If she gets note of this, I'm done for. She will encourage and pressure me into acting, and then I will have to say something to this interesting girl.

I'd rather not complicate life. I'd rather stay on my clear course.

My mom says men can be dangerous.

I think a pretty woman can be just as dangerous!

02.13.04

"No one is useless in this world who lightens the burdens of another."
—Charles Dickens

I want to write something super profound today; instead I'm stuck, because my mind keeps thinking about her.

This is not good. She's a real distraction, a real nuisance in my life.

Because she's also addicting.

I find a lot of joy in being near her every school day.

But I also feel like I'm losing control of my thoughts. Which means I must say—I don't know what to do next.

Abigail's Journal

Tuesday, Sept 18, 2003

I've never written in a journal before. I've wanted to, but I never have. I don't really understand the difference between a journal and a diary. I think a journal is where you write down facts like "I ate tuna for lunch today", although I hate tuna. But the point is a journal is a place where you record what you did for that day. I think a diary is more personal, a place where you really share who you are and what is important to you.

How Mrs. Childs describes this journal, I think it is more like a diary. I won't start each entry as *Dear Diary*, that is completely lame. But I'll write from my heart. That's what Mrs. Childs told us to do, and that's what I want to do. I'm excited to have a place to share me, all of me—the good and the bad, the happy and the sad. And to know no one else will read it, because this is for me. This is mine. It is safe.

Monday, Sept 22, 2003

So at least once a month we are supposed to write. Mrs. Childs says even just two paragraphs is a good goal, but hopefully we write more. I'd like to write once a week, but I don't really know what to write about. I guess something about myself. I'm fourteen and in ninth grade. I will turn fifteen on January 15th. I am the middle child in my family. My older sister Paige is sixteen and perfect. She is beautiful, smart, Mom's favorite, and so nice you have to love her. My little sister Maraline is ten and she is just cute.

My mom is great, but sad lots. My dad died when I was nine. I miss him a lot. But I don't remember him very well. I think that frustrates my mom. She says it's hard to raise us without him. She works, and she takes care of the house, and she takes care of us, but she also sleeps a lot, at least whenever she can, and she just always seems sad. I'm sure she misses my dad a lot.

Monday, Oct 6, 2003

I didn't write last week, but Mrs. Childs says that's fine. She says I don't have to write once a week, but if that's my goal, and I miss a week, then I can just write more the next time, which sounds good to me. This time I want to write about my boyfriend, Dillon. He is really cute and smart and fun, and I love him. We met in seventh grade. It was our first year at Helam Junior High. We were both in choir and we immediately became friends.

Tuesday, Oct 14, 2003

Today Dillon surprised me. At lunch, he walked me out onto the P.E. field, gave me a piece of my favorite gum, and then he kissed me. He kissed me once, then twice, and then three times, and then we laughed. Then we held hands all the way back to class.

Monday, Oct 20, 2003

I want to tell Dillon I love him, but I don't know if I sound too serious. I don't ever want to lose him. I really do love him.

Monday, Nov 3, 2003

Dillon is sad and I don't know what to do. He doesn't want to talk much. At first I thought it was me. I worried he was losing interest in me. But he finally told me it was his family. His parents have been fighting a lot and he doesn't know why. His dad sometimes doesn't come home. His mom is sad. He has two sisters and two brothers, he is the oldest. He says sometimes it is hard, especially right now. None of the kids know what is up, but Dillon knows something's up.

Wednesday, Nov 12, 2003

Dillon found out what's going on. His dad called everyone in their family together for a special meeting. His mom never said one thing during the whole meeting. But his dad talked a lot.

Dillon said he had a yucky feeling in his stomach the whole time and he thinks his dad is telling him lies.

Monday, Dec 1, 2003

Yep. Dillon's dad lied. He lied big time. Not only did their dad not come to Thanksgiving dinner, his mom said he didn't even want to come. Instead, his dad forced them to go visit him in his new place. His new place with his girlfriend, Antoinette.

But they already had met Antoinette. Dillon was mad his dad had forgot. They had met Antoinette when Dillon and his family had visited their dad at work two years ago. She is ten years younger than Dillon's mom and she likes to say that a lot. And she doesn't wear a lot of clothes, and Dillon's dad kept touching her. He would put his arm around her waist, or touch her cheek, or kiss her forehead. Dillon felt sick the whole time.

Then a few days later, he heard his mom on the phone. She said Antoinette is a home wrecker. That she had done this before, but that Dillon's dad doesn't acknowledge that. Dillon's mom is very sad. And Dillon is angry that his dad lied to him. He is angry that his mom made him go. He swore to me he would never visit his dad again. Ever.

I don't know what to say to Dillon. I wish I did. I am sad for him too.

Thursday, Dec 11, 2003

Dillon doesn't talk to me about it anymore. He wants to pretend it never happened and that it doesn't exist. He wants to pretend his dad is dead. But it is different. I know that, and I wanted to tell Dillon that, but I can tell it would only make him mad.

But at our holiday choir performance, my mom and Dillon's mom met for the first time. While all the kids were off getting cookies and drinks, and Dillon was helping his little brother, I was next to my mom, waiting to ask her a question. But sometimes she does this to me, it's like she doesn't see me there.

So I stood there waiting, listening to them talk, and both our moms talked about our dads. My mom was saying how she had lost her husband a few years ago. Dillon's mom said that she had lost her husband too, but not to death. Then Dillon's mom said my mom was lucky because at least my dad still loved her.

I glanced at my mom, who still didn't see me there, and I thought my mom looked hurt or angry. But later that night she seemed quiet, but in a good way. She smiled more than normal.

She came in to say good-night to me, which she had stopped doing a few years ago, and I had missed it, but I had never wanted to tell her that. She was always tired, and the least I could do was put myself to bed. I didn't need her to tuck me in or say good-night. I didn't need those things, I just still wanted them.

But tonight she stood in the doorway and watched me crawl into bed. Then she looked at me, and I looked at her. Then she said,

"Abby, your dad loved you very much. He loved all of us a great deal. We're very lucky . . . and he would have stayed with us if he could have."

I nodded because she was talking to me with a lot of respect. Like from one grown-up to another, and I was scared if I said anything back, she'd remember I wasn't a grown-up and would stop talking to me.

But since I didn't say anything, she kept talking. "Sometimes I still feel his love. I hope you do too."

I nodded again. Not because I felt my dad's love. I really don't remember lots about him. But I didn't want to say that to my mom because it would make her sad or angry. And she would stop looking at me. Right then, she was *really* looking at me, and that made me so happy. All I could do was smile and nod. Because I just wanted her to keep looking at me.

But then she said "Good-night" and turned off the light. I pulled up the covers and was sad that she was leaving. But then as she shut the door, she said, "I love you Abigail, I really do."

And even though I say it to her a lot, it still felt good to say, "I love you too."

Monday, Dec 29, 2003

That last entry was a long entry. So I didn't think I needed to write for a while, plus it got busy with the holidays, but some things happened, and I really want to write in here. Mrs. Childs said this was private and just for us to record our own personal things, so I want to share what happened over the last couple of weeks.

As the holidays started to get close, Dillon got sadder and sadder. I've never seen him so sad before. I didn't know what to do. The only thing that seemed to help him was when we would go be by ourselves. His family has a tree house that no one uses anymore, except for us right now. Even though it's cold, we've brought blankets up there, and we've made a bed on the floor, and then Dillon kisses me. He doesn't just kiss me like he first did. Now he gets really into us kissing. I like it a lot, but sometimes I get a little scared too.

But he is so happy with me there, when it's just us. And we do some things that we probably shouldn't do. But he calls it experimenting, and I want him to be happy, and it seems like when we're together, alone in his tree house, it helps him.

Monday, January 5, 2004

I pictured the first time different than this. But Dillon just seemed really hungry for sex, like it was the only way he could forget about Christmas.

I didn't want to tell him how much I thought maybe we shouldn't. But I didn't want him to stop either. I'm not sure what to think right now. I'm feeling happy and sad and confused. I wish there was someone I could talk to.

Monday, January 12, 2004

I wish I could tell Paige about all of this. I wish she would understand. But she wouldn't understand.

My mom asked us not to date boys until we are sixteen. Paige is seventeen but would rather be studying for her AP classes than looking at boys. She says boys will mess up her plans. She wants to be a lawyer. I wish I knew what I wanted to be.

Instead I tell my mom and Paige that Dillon is just a good friend. And they believe me. Why would I lie? I don't lie to them.

THE OTHER SIDE OF

But I can't tell them about this. Even though I love Dillon, and he loves me, it would break my mom's heart if she knew I was doing this. I once asked Dillon if his mom would be upset if she found out. He said he didn't care.

I don't ask him about his dad anymore.

Thursday, January 15, 2004

Dillon really loves me. I know he loves me. He says it now. Just like I say it now. Things are really good between us. I see him every day. And we are having fun together, lots of fun together.

Sometimes I don't like the secrets. I don't like hiding from everyone. But I love him. I love to make him happy. And I love being with him.

Monday, January 26, 2004

I don't know what to do. I'm so scared. I took a pregnancy test. Three times.

How could this happen?

It can't be true.

I don't feel pregnant.

But I don't know what it's supposed to feel like.

I'm hungry all the time, but maybe that's just because I'm so scared.

This can't be true.

I need to tell Dillon, but I can't yet. He can tell something is wrong, that something is different with me, but I just tell him I've been feeling sick, which I have. Right now I don't want to see him. I love him, but I don't know what he will say. I don't know what his mom will say, or worse, my mom. I especially don't know what Paige will say.

My mom will cry. She will cry lots. But she already cries lots. She already is sad. I don't want to make her sadder, but maybe it won't be so bad if she already is so sad. I don't know. I really don't know what to do.

I feel so alone.

What will Dillon say? What do I want him to say?

I just turned fifteen, and I'm pregnant.

Thursday, January 29, 2004

I have cried a lot. But only at night, when I am all alone. I've never been one to keep secrets from anyone, but I still don't feel like I can tell anyone.

I am ashamed.

I don't understand. At school, people talk about sex all the time. There are always rumors going around. Some talk about it like they are bragging.

But once you become like me, people talk different about you.

I don't want people to talk about me at school. I don't even know if I can keep going to school. Maybe I won't be showing for a while. Maybe I don't have to tell anyone for a while. Maybe I can wait until the summer.

And then what?

Once I start to show, then what?

And once the baby comes, then what?

And once Dillon knows, then what?

Friday, February 6, 2004

I told Dillon. It didn't go as good as I'd hoped.

Maybe I thought he would tell me again that he loved me. Maybe he would tell me everything was going to be okay. Maybe he was going to hug me and stroke my hair, like he used to do before we started having sex. But he doesn't hold me anymore, and he definitely didn't hold me when I told him. In fact, he didn't want to touch me. He stared at me for a long time and kept saying, "You are sure?" I told him, "Yes." And he asked again "You are sure?" "Yes, Dillon, I'm sure." Then his voice rose even more. "Abes, are you totally sure?" Then before I could answer, he cussed. He cussed a lot. Over and over again. And he didn't touch me once. And once I started to cry, he left.

He was supposed to take me in his arms and hold me and tell me it was going to be okay. I need someone to tell me it is going to be okay. If he won't tell me that, who will?

Thursday, February 12, 2004

For the past week, I hadn't talked to Dillon.

I tried to talk to him at school, but he didn't want to talk to me.

Finally, today at lunch he told me to follow him out onto the P.E. field. It was cold enough that snow was starting to come down just a little bit, but not too bad.

Dillon had us walk all the way out onto the field, where no one was around us. Then he said, "Who knows?"

I told him no one.

"Don't tell anyone," he said. And he made me promise. He didn't hold my hand, or hug me. He barely looked at me. I wanted to cry, but I didn't want him to see me cry. He doesn't need me to cry.

Then he said, "I need my space right now, Abes." I didn't know what that meant. I wanted to ask, but I was scared. So I listened to him say it again and then he walked away.

He left me all alone on the field. I watched him walk away while the snow kept falling down.

I have a baby inside of me, and I don't know what Dillon thinks. I don't know what it means and I don't know who to talk to. Right now, Dillon told me to talk to no one about it. So I won't. I will just give him some space and wait a little longer.

Thursday, February 19, 2004

It's been another week, and Dillon keeps avoiding me. He doesn't sit by me at lunch, he doesn't wait for me on the bus, he doesn't look at me in our classes, he avoids me as much as he can.

My heart hurts. It feels like it's breaking.

My friends at school all ask what's going on between us. They ask if we've broken up. I told them I don't know. Paige asked if I was okay. I just told her I was tired, but once I snapped at her, and then I apologized and told her that Dillon is mad at me. Even though I lie to Mom and her and tell them he isn't my boyfriend, and that we are just friends, Paige still hugged me. And I cried. I cried a lot, and she just hugged me for a long time. I really needed her hug. She is perfect, and I wish I was a little bit more like her. Instead I'm pregnant, and the only person who knows won't talk to me. I really don't know what I'm going to do.

Tuesday, February 24, 2004

Dillon surprised me today. First he came to school wearing my favorite shirt on him. And he smiled at me, and he passed me a note in Ms. Fielding's class. He wanted me to meet him at our favorite spot near the field during lunch. When I got there, he was waiting for me. He had a smile on his face and he said he had missed me, and he was sorry, but he had needed time to think about things.

I said I understood. I didn't want to say anything else, cause Dillon was smiling, and he was smiling at me. He reached for my hand and pecked my cheek, and he asked me how I was feeling, and he was being super sweet, and I knew again that it was okay. He loves me, and I love him, and it will all be okay. Everything will be okay.

Then he told me to come to his house after school, that he had a late Valentine's Day surprise for me.

When I got to his house he escorted me up to the tree house and the place was all decorated. There were flowers for me and a card, and my favorite Skittles candy in a dish. And he kissed me again. Really long and really hard. I thought he was going to undress me, but instead he got down on his knee and asked me to marry him. Dillon asked me to marry him.

I'm getting married.

I'm so happy. Everything is going to be wonderful. It will all be perfect now.

But Dillon told me not to tell anyone yet, especially not our moms. They both are so sad, and Dillon is right. Even though we are doing the right thing, it will still make them sad. He wants to wait. He says he is thinking of running away, and if he does, he of course wants me to come with him. He asked me if I would.

I told him yes. I love him, and I am carrying our baby, and now we are getting married and we can raise the baby together. Of course I'll run away with him.

Otherwise we stay and have to tell our parents.

Hamilton's Journal

9/18

When I made the football team, I thought that was good enough for Dad. He'd worked me hard. He didn't want me to get there because I was his son, but because of my own skills.

I've never worked so hard for anything before.

There were lots of days I didn't know why I was doing all this extra work. There were days when I hated Dad. And there for sure were days I thought my body was going to quit.

But I also knew I wouldn't quit.

Dad taught me that. I am not a quitter.

I am a fighter.

I am a champion.

I succeed in what I do.

I'm on the freshman high school team.

I am a Helam High School Fighting Scot.

And I am a Forbes.

9/26

Last night was our fourth game. We played the Wildcats. For most the game, I played like an All-Star running back. For the 38 minutes I was on the field, I played well—real well. I was proud of my runs and I could hear my dad from the side yelling good things at me.

When there were just two minutes left in the game, and we were up by three points, the plan was to let the clock run out. The play was for me to run the ball. And I did real well. Until I fumbled. The Wildcats got the ball and scored an easy 30-yard touchdown. My entire 38 minutes of good plays were nothing to match the last two minutes of the game – my two minutes of shame.

Dad left the game before I got out of the locker room. Mom was waiting for me outside. She hugged me and told me I'd had a great game. But we both knew what would be remembered. My mistake had cost the game.

When I got home, Dad said nothing.

For the evening, it felt like he'd disowned me.

I was mad at him too. I'd spent the last year building up, beefing up, working hard, to be part of this team. Then one upset, even with my other successes, and he won't talk to me.

Tonight I don't love the game. I'd rather quit the game, and be another man's son.

10/02

Tonight's game was a different story. Dad was proud of me. I played harder than I've ever played.

I'm happy. We won by six points, due to me! I gave us most of the yardage and I scored two of the touchdowns.

When we left the field, I knew Dad was proud. He kept saying "Good job, son." He left the NFL when I was two. The day he left, he knew my future. Tonight he slapped me on the back and reminded me that our competition will be fierce, but games like tonight will get us closer to our goal.

10/08

Through calorie counting and regular weight lifting, my dad helped me reach my target weight. I now weigh 180 pounds of muscle.

My next goal is to shorten my time on the 40-yard dash. At the start of the summer, it was at 4.9. The goal is for me to run it at 4.5

by my senior year of high school. This year I need to be running it at 4.7 by the end of the season. Tonight I ran it in 4.71 seconds.

I'm close, and I'm counting down the days until I reach that goal.

And I'm counting down the days until my first high school football season is over.

10/15

I know I don't belong in this class. I'm a slow reader, my writing is slow, and my reading comprehension is listed as average.

But this was a class I really wanted to take. My parents told me this was not a great choice for my elective. Still, I wanted to take it because I want to learn how to write.

And this journal is good.

I don't know what I want to be. I haven't told my dad yet, but sometimes I don't think I want to be an NFL player. Sometimes, instead, I think about being a writer.

I know I don't really know what I need to do to be a writer, but I do like to dream about it.

I picture my life real simple, where I sit in a quiet office with books, lots of books, and I write in a room all by myself. I type away at my keyboard and write about a boy who takes on quests, and who has to fight a big dragon, and who has to tackle his world to grow into a man who wins the respect of his village.

I like to listen to Mrs. Childs when she talks about really good literature. She calls it the *sirens* that pull her in.

And it makes me want to write a book like that someday.

10/16

Mrs. Childs returned our first big writing assignments today. It was a first draft of our fiction stories. Only one person smiled. It was a girl named Anya. The rest of us groaned or sighed real loud. When the bell rang, nobody looked real happy as we left, but then Mrs. Childs specifically called me back.

I got a C on my assignment. I was bummed and didn't want to talk to her.

But she wanted to talk to me.

She told me a long story about a golfer and how he had good days and bad days when he played the game, but no matter what, he always still enjoyed it. The story was okay, but I could tell she wanted me to learn a lesson from it, and I didn't really understand what she was getting at. Then she said that even though I got this low grade, she did not control my worth as a writer.

I still didn't get what she was saying. Then she asked how long I'd worked on the assignment.

I told her I had football practice, and when I got to my homework, even though I wanted to work on my story first, it's an elective, so I didn't start until 10 pm. It was rushed.

And she knew.

She said she knew I could do even better with my story in my rewrite.

Then she said that's what a good writer does. They study, read, read more, and write, and write more, and rewrite and rewrite more, and edit and edit more. And they learn to love the whole thing, because all of it is part of the *writing craft.*

Then she asked me what my goals were, and what I wanted to be.

I have a set answer to that question. Since preschool, I've always told every adult the same answer.

And when I say, "I want to be a football player like my dad," they always smile.

So I knew what I would say, but all the sudden, when Mrs. Childs looked at me, I said a different answer.

"I'd like to write," I said.

She nodded at me, like she'd expected that answer. Then she told me I was given a C because she saw not only talent from all my previous assignments but motivation. She saw commitment and determination. Just like I run through all the football drills and work hard every single day of practice, if I were to run through similar drills, I could be a very good writer—the kind of fiction writer she thinks I want to be.

She said again that I had talent. But then she said I still have to learn lots, and work at the skill of writing. Then she said, "I'm proud of you, Hamilton. There are creative seeds inside of you, and they're ready to sprout. Don't let them turn dormant. Water them. Nurture them. Feed them. You have a lot of other obligations, but if you want, you can be a good writer too. Don't get discouraged, Hamilton. Keep writing."

At that point, I knew she really thought I could.

And now I keep thinking, maybe I really could be a writer someday.

10/22

I heard all about it at our last football practice. The news is spreading fast among all the players.

One of the sophomore cheerleaders says a coach touched her inappropriately.

There are at least three problems with this story.

Problem 1: If you touch this girl's shoulder it's considered inappropriate by her standards. She has a long history of exaggeration, misunderstandings, and tattling on anything she thinks is questionable. So all the football players don't believe her.

Problem 2: This girl causes issues with others, especially other teachers at the high school. She gets upset when people speak to her in certain ways, or place her in an uncomfortable situation, or as mentioned in Problem 1, touch her. Logan, on the JV team, told me three weeks ago this girl caused their Science teacher, Miss Wagner, to cry because this girl told the principal that Miss Wagner was bullying her. So either this girl wants a lot of attention or her "standards" don't even exist in the same universe as the rest of us.

Problem 3: This is the biggest problem - the coach she accused of touching her inappropriately is my dad.

10/23

Dad is fuming. Mom is livid. I'm sure they want to keep this gossip quiet, but they sure weren't quiet last night. My bedroom is in the basement, and at certain times when they talk directly over the vent, I can hear them clearly, especially when they speak loud, which they were doing last night.

Mom said a lot of unkind things about this girl. I sort of know the girl, her name's Layne. I don't like her. And neither does Mom. She kept repeating the phrase, *Layne is a Liar*, until it became a chant in my head.

Dad repeated it several times too. *Layne is a Liar.*

I feel sorry for Dad.

Tomorrow he has to go visit with the head coach, the high school principal, and then possibly the Board.

He told Mom it was last week, which was an away game. They ran into each other in a hallway. There was no one else there – no witnesses. She was distraught. Her boyfriend had sent her a text to end their "minor" relationship, and she freaked out. Dad didn't know what to do. He asked her if she was all right.

Then he recalls her leaning into him for a hug. He said it was awkward. But he did let her cry for a few minutes.

Nothing inappropriate—it was only for a moment, but Mom says that "moment" will change his whole career.

He tried to laugh, but it wasn't real convincing. He said, "You really think everyone's going to believe her word over Thad Forbes?"

Mom swore several times. Then they stepped away from the vents and I couldn't hear them anymore.

From there I stayed up for over an hour wondering what Dad will do.

10/27

Right before Dad was set to meet with the Board, Layne changed her story. She said Dad seemed too touchy for her comfort level, but she could accept that some people are more touch-oriented than she is. Her family is not the hugging type. And she didn't ask for a hug.

But according to her, Dad pulled her into the hug, and held her tight, and for a long time. She was uncomfortable but that was it, whereas before, she said his hands had wandered, and he'd touched her breasts. But now she says she made a mistake and misunderstood. It was her error.

Dad says she walked right over to him and leaned into him. He suspects he was set up.

From what other players have said, Layne doesn't talk to anyone anymore.

When Dad found out I knew about all this, he talked to me. It was kind of awkward, but he told me that this is the price of fame. Sometimes people attack you, because they want their own fame or they think they can get money out of you through payoffs or lawsuits. He said the more people that know you, the more troubles they bring with them. And being his son, I need to start being careful now. That sometimes there are bad people out there whose only intention will be to stir up harm in my life.

Dad says it was fortunate that all this didn't get out of control. Other than the football teams, the cheerleaders, and some of the HS administration, it didn't get out to the media like some false accusations do. He says once the media gets a story like that it can sometimes get a whole lot more complicated.

But I think somebody must have told somebody something, because two days later the *Helam Herald* had an article on Dad. It was a real nice account. It talked about his glory days, and how he now volunteers as a coach and helps the players at Helam High School. It even talked about his private business that he started four years ago and how he works with college recruiters and high school coaches, from all over, to help them identify future talent.

Everyone, except maybe Layne the Liar, knows Dad is a good man.

11/11

When Dad talks about his glory days, his face lights up. I like listening to him talk about his team, his fans, and his fame. It stirs an excitement in me too. Not to be a copy of my father, but to be my own famous person.

Maybe living in my dad's shadow has caused this. Maybe if I lived with an average man, with an average place in town, I'd want an average plan too. Instead I feel like I need to be something.

I want to write.

I want to tell a story and I want others to read it.

I want to see my name on a cover.

I want to have a voice.

And I want to be heard.

I don't want to be in my father's shadow forever. Instead, I want to be my own something great.

12/01

My fiction story isn't perfect. It still needs a lot of work. But I've made lots of improvements on it after I got it back from Mrs. Childs.

Plus I'm writing the next chapter, which I'm not ready to show anyone.

In fact, no one really knows I'm expanding the story and turning it into a book.

But I'm going to keep working on it, I'm going to write it, and rewrite it, and edit it, and do all the things Mrs. Childs has been saying I need to do. Then when it's super good, I'll share it.

For now it's my own secret world of Thomas and his adventures. I've been writing about his training camp, and how he is working on becoming a warrior, and how his ultimate quest will be to defend his village from the dragon, Divulgamen.

01/13/04

I got an A on my last assignment. Now that football's over, I've been able to give more time to my assignments, and Mrs. Childs says she can tell a huge difference in my writing.

But I still haven't figured out if I can be both a writer and a professional football player. I'd like to be both.

02/02

Last Sunday was the Super Bowl. It was the Panthers and the Patriots. Dad was quieter than in the past. Usually leading up to this game, Dad starts reliving his own glory days and sometimes he re-watches footage from his games. He never got to play in a Super Bowl and I've started to wonder if he gets a little sad leading up to the game.

This year, during the first half, he seemed sadder than in years before. Then at half-time, he got real mad when Justin Timberlake pulled on Janet Jackson's outfit and showed off her boob. Dad's voice roared at me. "Shut your eyes, Hamilton!" Then he started to yell. "Idiot people! Kids are watching!"

My sister Kira gave me a funny smile, almost like I'd been caught doing something I wasn't supposed to be doing. And she's always been like that. She loves watching me get in trouble, especially because she thinks Dad favors me with football. Then she whispered, "Hey Hammy, Dad thinks you've never seen a girl's boobies before."

"You think this is funny?" Dad started yelling at Kira. "It's things like this that make it so hard to keep you kids safe."

Then for the first time in all my life, Dad shut off the TV during the Super Bowl and stormed out.

After half-time was over, he returned. The rest of the game he cheered, but he was still quieter than in other years. Sometimes I yelled at the game before he did, which had never happened before. So either he was real angry at Janet Jackson and Justin Timberlake, or he was angry at me or Kira. But he sure was angry at something.

02/23

Tonight I took my writing notebook with the story about Thomas and the dragon and climbed up our backyard wall. It's a rock wall that's eight feet tall and I had to use a tree to hoist myself up. But it was amazing. A storm is supposed to come tomorrow, so tonight was the warmth before the cold. I looked out over the neighborhood. Then I looked out toward the snow-covered mountains, and then up into the sky right before it started to get dark.

And then I wrote!

I wrote for as long as I could see. Then I climbed down the wall and hid in my room for the rest of the night to write.

It worked out since Dad's out of town. He left this morning, and I don't think he'd like it if he knew what I did tonight. Especially because I didn't stay the whole time at weight training, even though Dad arranged for Malcolm, who's on the senior team, to train with me. I did train with him some. We went to the high school and I stayed for forty minutes, but then Malcolm got a call from his girlfriend, and I told him I had to go. And since Mom and Kira went out shopping, I was alone to write.

It's almost midnight now and Thomas has just finished up his training camp and now he's off on his first solo quest.

Tonight, I learned that writing is one of my favorite things to do!

TRACEY'S JOURNAL

18 SEPT 03

I'm in this class for my mom, Cori. She wanted me here. She made sure I got here.

It's not a bad class, but not my favorite either.

I like Drama. I like to act, I like to make people laugh.

But I also like how Mrs. Childs says we can write anything we want in these journals. If that's true, and these are really ours to write who we really are, and ours to share our own personal thoughts, and we can really know these items are safe, then I do have something to write.

I have to share this with someone. But it'd be like a pirate's curse if the wrong people knew. And it's hard to know who you can trust, especially when you're new and just making friends, or at least trying to make friends.

Before we moved from Berkeley, I'd have shared this with my best friend Sophia, since she was the one who told me about it anyway. But she has a boyfriend now, and she's way too into him, and this isn't just something you share in an email. Some things you only share with a person when you are with them face-to-face. So since I don't get to see Sophia until next summer, this journal will have to do.

Sophia's my best friend and has been almost all my life. She calls me a freak of nature. And it's okay, because she's one too. She calls us both freaks. But never around our parents. They wouldn't think it was funny like Sophia does. I never understood why it was funny to her, but I laugh when she says it because she laughs when she says it.

But up until this last year, I don't think I really understood exactly what it meant. Sure, I was made fun of, but it got better through the years, and my moms always made sure we were around people who understood us. And I had Sophia, and my other friends, who just all understood that this is how it is.

All my life, my moms have told me that when two women love each other and want to have a child, that one of the appropriate ways to bring life into the world is how I came to them. In their way they have told me how natural it is. And they love me so much—which of course I know that, because they tell me that all the time. And I tell them that I love them back too. Because I do.

And all my life they've shared the stories with me of all they've done to bring me into the world and to protect me from a world that's still trying to understand tolerance and love.

But I'm not a child anymore. Before when I went to them for answers, they gave me their answers. Sophia's two years older than me, and she likes to tell me the other side of things. She told me to wait until I took Biology, wait until I heard about what it takes for an organism to reproduce and survive. She wants to be a doctor, and she loves genetics—genetic coding she calls it—and she also calls it a mystery of information that her and I are missing out on.

This year, I'm taking Biology and learning all about how an organism recreates to produce life. But truthfully all I hear is that somehow I don't have a dad.

What I do have is what I learned from Sophia. I have some sperm bank donor's DNA. Some man made his deposit, got his pay, and I now exist from his coding.

He doesn't know I exist, doesn't care I exist, and even if I ever were to find him, he doesn't owe me anything. He has no connection to me, to my moms, to my identity. Yet I'm a part of him. My personal cell structure carries his identity.

So I find myself thinking about him—a lot. The man who has no connection to me, yet I'm biologically intertwined with him.

134

What does he look like? What does he like? Does he have his own children (besides all us other kids who are just his donations so other people can be our parents and raise us)? If he has his own children, does he play ball with them? Or teach them how to drive? Or build tree houses, rocket ships, or a future with them?

Not that my moms never played ball with me. They did. And we built a model car together once, but it wasn't really their thing, so I told them it wasn't my thing too. Maybe it wouldn't have been my dad's thing either. I did like building the car. I wanted to build more, but my moms want me to be happy while they're happy. And it just wasn't their thing.

But we did build rockets together and laughed as the rockets shot up in the night sky. And we watched the stars together. I know 25 constellations thanks to Cori. And I know how to make crème brûlée thanks to Paula. And I'm good at school thanks to both of them. And that makes them both proud, which makes me happy. We are close, and I'm lucky. I know I'm lucky, because they love me a lot. And they're certain I'll never forget that or question it, because they tell me it almost every day.

And it's not like if I had a dad I'd be any better than I am now. I'd certainly never be able to pick which mom I'd keep and which I'd give away to have a dad. It just doesn't work that way, and that's what they always have told me. This is just how it is, and it isn't any other way. I exist because two women love each other.

But in Biology, it's talked about differently. Organisms need to reproduce. It's part of their function.

Which leaves me with a lot of questions—and a bunch of answers I don't understand.

Now that I'm studying all this and trying to understand what I'm hearing in Biology, Sophia's right. I am a concoction of experienced

135

scientists, a Petri dish, Cori's egg, a nameless donor's sperm, and Paula's uterus. Nature didn't bring me here, but a lot of money and some grand advancements did, which would make my birth unnatural, which then makes Sophia right. She and I are freaks of nature.

15 OCT 03

Cori tells me I can like girls or I can like boys. They want to talk to me about my development. I learned about it in Health class, but they think I should hear it from them too, because I have choices, and they want me to be sure I understand my choices. And they want me to feel loved no matter what.

What they don't understand is I've grown up all my life seeing those choices. Ever since I can remember, we've been a part of the LGBT culture. My friends were the children of their friends, and we all played together. We all lived within this community.

I don't understand those who have gay-phobia. I don't understand how people aren't just people. But that doesn't mean I haven't heard the slurs, the negative statements, the whisperings— not just about my moms, but about me. But I didn't know how different I was until my moms decided to come to Helam.

I don't fit here.

And just like my moms want me to know I have choices, I'm seeing a different choice. It's a different lifestyle here, which makes me real curious about what a "traditional" family must be like. If I wanted a traditional family, I maybe wouldn't have to go to a doctor and ask for help to become a father. Instead I could get that right from nature.

But I don't think I want to be a father.

I know both moms, especially Paula, want to be a grandmother someday. But I don't like the idea of being a father. I'm not really sure what a father is.

Paula says a father is like a mother.

Cori says I've seen fathers all the time. I've played with them when we hung around Glen and Rocky. And I followed Glen around a lot. He often treated me like I was his own kid. And Cori hates it when I bring up anything about wanting a father. She says many kids wish they had two mothers, and most straight couples never go through the effort and dedication that same-sex couples go through to bring a baby into this world. All that my moms did to get me here is a lot of proof that I'm loved, even more than other kids out there.

So Cori tells me not to focus on a father's absence, but instead to focus on what I've gained by having two moms who love me so much.

And I can't argue with them.

I like seeing them happy. And we are a family. They love me, and I love them, and that should be enough.

18 NOV 03

A girl named Todi asked me why I call my moms by their first names. She calls her mom by her first name but it's because she doesn't respect her. I told her I do respect my moms.

So she asked me why I do it then. This is the long story of what I told her.

At first I did call them *Mom*.

Actually, when I was little, Paula was Mom or Mum, and Cori was Mommy or Mummy. But when I was seven, I told Cori she should dress up like a mummy for Halloween since she was my

137

Mummy. I laughed so hard, milk came out of my nose. She asked me to stop calling her Mummy after that.

When I was eight, I started to not like calling her Mommy either. It sounded like I was still in Kindergarten or first grade. Since I was now in third grade, I really didn't like calling her Mommy around other kids. So one day I stopped. Instead I called her Cori and she smiled at me and said, "Tracey, some names are just a bit cutesy for my liking too. If you like this better, you can call me Cori."

But then when I was nine, I felt odd calling my one mom *Mom* and my other mom Cori. It just didn't feel right, like I was playing favorites. They both were my Mom. So I tried calling them both Mom for a little while.

At first, it worked great when I was in trouble and needed help real fast, because whoever was closest came. So I did like that part. But when we were sitting at home together, or driving in the car, and I said "Mom," then they would say "Which one?" For a little while, we laughed, but after a while it wasn't funny anymore. It just got confusing.

One day, I said to my mom Paula, "I call Cori, Cori. Can I call you Paula too?"

She gave me one of her big smiles and then she wrapped me in a real strong hug. When she pulled away she looked me in the eyes and said, "When you were little, your mom and I decided that we'd let you choose once you were old enough. Maybe today is that day. Tracey, you can call me whatever is best for you."

She thought it was pretty neat that I was old enough, but I didn't feel like I was asking because I was older, I was just confused. Still, I was glad Paula was smiling at me, especially because I didn't want to offend her or Cori.

"Promise it's okay, because I don't want to hurt anyone's feelings," I said.

"It's fine," she said.

Just to make sure, I said, "I promise to think the word *Mom* whenever I say your name."

Then Paula took me by the hand and led me over to the couch and had me sit by her. She said, "Tracey, *Mom* is a very, very special word. And straight couples have had thousands of years to come up with the right names to use when they become parents, but we haven't had all that time to come up with another word that's just as important and special as the word *Mom*. Until then, we want you to decide what you'd like to call us. Okay?"

I said okay, and since then, I still sometimes call them *Mom*, but mostly I call them Cori and Paula.

06 JAN 04

I haven't been feeling like myself lately. Paula thinks I'm depressed. She thinks I need to see a therapist. Cori thinks I'm fine, that this is just part of adolescence and that I'm a typical fifteen-year-old boy.

I watched Johnny Depp movies all weekend. I'd planned to just watch *The Curse of the Black Pearl* and *Edward Scissorhands*, but then I watched *What's Eating Gilbert Grape*. I actually watched it twice, while Cori and Paula went to dinner and then the symphony with some professors from the university. Paula would be worried if she knew I watched that movie, especially twice. Cori would just be upset that I spent the whole weekend watching movies, over and over again.

Cori would say it's not really a *life* watching movies all weekend. But I don't feel like doing anything else. And I don't really know what I should be doing, because I don't have a whole lot of friends, I don't like my Drama class anymore, which means I now completely hate school. Cori heard me say that over the phone to my best friend Sophia, and Cori got upset with me. But it didn't really matter, because Sophia didn't have time to talk, because her boyfriend Joey was there, and they were going up to San Francisco for a weekend with Joey's parents. Sophia doesn't even miss me.

I started to study Biology, but it was all about Punnett squares, and dominant traits, and it made me angry. Angry enough I wanted to throw the book against the wall, or find a rope and hang myself.

Some days I don't really care who I am, or what my genes really say about me. But sometimes I do want to figure out my identity.

What I don't want, while I live in Helam, is for people to keep asking me about my dad, or if I'm a member of their church, or what race I am.

It's hard being different here.

Sometimes I'd rather just slip away.

I wasn't really meant to exist, so it'd be easier if I just didn't.

22 FEB 04

Paula asked me if my recent mood swings have anything to do with her and Cori being lesbians. Of course not! But what I do hate is that both Paula, and especially Cori, try so hard to make sure everyone knows we are such a happy, loving family. Because we are *non-traditional*, to them it's even more important that we always look so happy.

Today is Sunday, and I've just stayed in bed most the day. I only can get away with it because they went snowshoeing up in the mountains today. I was supposed to go too, but I told them I was sick. Paula took my temperature. She said I looked kind of flushed. Cori left me money to order pizza, which meant she felt bad leaving me here alone. But I wanted to be left alone.

So, I stay in bed and think about having all the money I need to leave here, to go back home and pick up Sophia, and then go anywhere we want. Maybe we could travel to South America, or Africa, or to New York where we could both be in Broadway plays. Or even just to L.A. Sophia has friends in L.A., and we could be stand-ins for a movie, until we both get discovered, and then maybe I could star in a movie with Johnny Depp.

But none of that's really going to happen.

Instead I just feel weird. So I try not to think about me, or my school work, or Punnett squares, or genetic traits, or the writing project about what my family means to me, and how my parents have helped shape my identity. I hate that class. I want out, but I can't tell Cori why. Even if I lied and told her it was because I had to write too much, she would tell me that she believed in me, and this would help prepare me for future tasks in high school, and especially college. Then she would smile at me and wait until I smiled back. She's taught me respect and self-esteem, and I know I'm a good person because of how she's raised me.

But today, I got to be separate from every person on the planet. I got to pull the covers over my head and think about never coming out. About not breathing, or thinking, or existing anymore, just slipping away.

That's the way I feel, smothered by my own life.

Tracey's journal was the last in the pile.

Kyle, Anya, and Darby's journals were missing.

PART III
The Confessions

CHAPTER
One

I SET TRACEY'S JOURNAL DOWN NEXT TO STELLA'S PHOTO. Over the many years, I'd caged in my heart, protecting it from all emotion. But these students, this special project, this class of expressive creativity—my attachment, my hope, my love for them—somehow the cage door had swung open and suddenly I felt vulnerable again.

I found Abigail's and Dillon's. I let them touch as I placed them next to Tracey's. Next I placed Todi's, Blake's, Hamilton's, and Priscilla's on the other side of the photos, until all their stories circled around Stella Fabrizio's smile.

I was still staring at her smile when a knock broke my silence.

Officer Bond walked in and offered me bottled water and a bag of potato chips. I accepted them like a peace offering. "You done?" he asked.

"Where are the rest of them?"

He pulled out a chair and sat near me, our knees were only inches apart. Then his eyes studied my display. "Darby's is with her

145

mother. Principal Truss picked up his daughter's. And Kyle's— well, I've some questions for you about Kyle's."

"Why does Principal Truss have Anya's?"

Officer Bond studied me while anger swirled around my tender heart.

"These were collected to protect the students," I said, "especially his daughter, but if he pulled a double standard—"

"We read the journals, all of them, including Anya's." His tone remained calm and soothing.

"But he has her journal now?"

"I called him to discuss our next steps. He asked to pick up Anya's. He asked for you to read the rest. He called you after he left the station."

A sigh slipped from my lips. "This was meant to be a simple, *private* writing assignment."

He nodded.

"So why does Darby's mom have hers?"

He looked over at the wall and gave it a crooked half-smile. Then he chuckled out a sound of pain. "Story is Darby came home from school enraged. She demanded her father do something. But he didn't. That evening when her mom got home from work, I got a call, around quarter to eight. She wanted answers, sort of demanded to know if we had a right to take her daughter's property. I explained we did, and we chose that option rather than bringing her in for questioning. She said she'd prefer to have Darby questioned than have her journal circulating around the station. So I asked her to bring Darby in, as well as her older daughter Lena. Had an insightful visit with all three of them. And it may have given us a good lead."

I glanced over at the photo. "Are you saying Darby's a part of this?"

"Right now we have no suspects, only people of interest," he said firmly. "Though Darby gave us a little more history about Stella, more than what Stella's parents shared."

I squared my shoulders back, looked directly at him, and said, "So did you read Darby's?"

"We read enough." Our eyes connected for a moment. I could tell he knew things and that bothered me.

I glanced back at the table, scanned the journals, and thought about the seven students' lives still vivid in my mind. When I looked back at him a question was on my lips, and he answered before I asked.

"A lot of anger. She hates her father, claims he's a deadbeat. He drinks but her mother denies it. Meanwhile her mother works two jobs and is gone most the time, but keeps the girls in designer clothes. She wants them to have everything, and *experience* everything, so either she's been turning a blind eye or been clueless toward the extreme partying and drug use."

"She's not clueless now." I waved my hand toward the journals.

"Nope."

For a few seconds, we both were silent. "So her mom has her journal?" I asked.

"Yes. And she claims her daughters will have a severe lesson on what the word *consequences* means."

"Oh dear!" These journals had snowballed into an out-of-control assignment.

Again he glanced at the journal display and cleared his throat. "I also handed off Darby's sister's name to our narcotics team." He glanced back at me. "Seems like she might have some other information for them."

147

"Oh dear!" I said again and my heart sank. What the project was not meant to be was a self-attacking tool. It was never intended to spin around and harm the students, especially due to their own words. I glanced at a far wall then released a heavy sigh. "So tell me about Kyle's?"

"I'll have you look at it first."

Officer Bond disappeared from the room and within seconds reappeared with the familiar journal. Kyle's name, and his artist doodles, were graffitied across the cover.

"Here." He handed it to me, then sat down to watch me read.

Kyle's Journal

9-17-03

Mrs. Childs says she won't read this. All I have to do is fill the pages. That's what she says she'll look for. If there's stuff on the paper, then I get credit. So that's what you get, Mrs. Childs.

A bunch of pages filled with important research and facts.

My completed assignment for you.

10-5-03

A war that changed the world.

Victory was not achieved by one man but by the death of many.

10-10-03

Mrs. Childs says I need to write more than my last entry.

How's this:

Abc def g stupid class ijk lmn

Op qrs t I hate this class uvwxyz

Aaa bbb ddd idiot sts assignment tbilk

Ulabk how asdl is tlakjb this for doing ajblkag my alkjaf assignment?

10-30-03

Chaos Bleeds

Defiance

Evil Dead

Angel of Darkness

Invisible War

Devil May Cry

01-06-04

Oh hey, great! Remind me to thank the captain for this.

Shut up!

I can't believe I agreed to do this.

You didn't, remember? You volunteered.

Death to the fascists!

Hurry up!

Whose artillery is that?

Ours. Not that it matters. They don't know we're here.

Would they stop if they did know?

Hard to say.

Ever steal a car?

Only when I need one.

01-31-04

Are you blind and dumb or just stupid?

02-09-04

I hate this class.

Oh man! This is nuts, I can't believe I'm doin' this.

Believe it, unless you sprout wings and wanna fly. It's only six miles – just shut up and do your job.

02-16-04

Hit List

    1. 0890

    2. 5430

    3. 9130

    4. 123,590

CHAPTER
Two

I SHUT THE JOURNAL AND DREW IN A LONG BREATH. I didn't exhale until my eyes met Officer Bond's.

"Explain it to me?" he asked.

"I don't know." I shrugged. "He hates the class, that's no big secret.

"Why's he there?"

"His father pushed him into the class."

Officer Bond looked up at the ceiling and then rubbed his chin. "We've called, no one answers. We've driven by the home, no one answers. What do you know about him? Should we be concerned?"

I shook my head. "He hates school. His dad's trying to motivate him to get some ambition with his life. At parent-teacher conference, Mr. McConkie said he coaxed Kyle into my class. Kyle had written a fantasy story that was pretty good, and so with the help of his father he submitted it as his application. But since then, he doesn't turn in a lot of the assignments. Right now, he won't pass unless he starts applying himself soon."

Officer Bond nodded. "Principal Truss said Kyle previously had been a skater."

"He still has the long bangs. And the baggy pants. I suspect Principal Truss told you Kyle hasn't always hung with the best crowd."

"He did. He also said his father intervened and now Kyle keeps more to himself."

"That's pretty accurate," I said. "More and more, I just see him alone at school. And his dad is frustrated because Kyle just sits at home and plays video games, and he can't get Kyle motivated to do much."

Officer Bond glanced at Stella's photo. Then he tapped Kyle's journal on the desk. "Should we be concerned?" he repeated. "Is there any correlation here? Or is this just some *form* of creative writing?"

I shrugged. "Before yesterday, I considered you a fool for approaching my class." I shot him a quick glance, followed by an apologetic grin. "But, now I know more about my class then they, or I, ever wanted me to know. I don't know Kyle well enough to make a judgment call on this. Clearly, he didn't do the journal assignment. But prior to today, he didn't seem like a threat. But none of them do."

"Okay." He stood and looked at all the journals again. A long sigh followed before he tossed Kyle's in with the mix.

"We now have a few leads," he finally said. Then he turned to face me. He offered another half-smile and extended a hand. "Thanks for your assistance."

CHAPTER
Three

I LEFT THE POLICE STATION AND WOUND MY WAY through the old part of Helam. Main Street was a conglomeration of old and new. Buildings with pioneer ancestry, dating as far back as the early 1900s, offset the new professional suites, strip malls, and business plazas. Many old buildings had For Sale signs in the windows since the mom-and-pop businesses had been replaced by the national box stores on the west side of town. Caught between shadows of the past and the wealth of a hopeful tomorrow, Main Street was morphing, and all of Helam's identity was being redefined too.

Two blocks down from the main artery was Principal Truss's Victorian home. I parked on the street and paused to look at the two-story structure. Its wrap-around porch, circular columns, fish-scale siding, and hipped roof made it a landmark of Helam's past.

And its history gave me my answer.

Time heals wounds. Time heals anger. Time heals the sting of lies. Time would fix all that was broken.

155

Time was my only friend.

I rang the doorbell and soon faced Anya, dressed in a baggy t-shirt and black leggings. Her blonde hair was tied in a loose braid and she offered me a small smile.

"How are you?" I asked.

She shrugged. "My parents and I already talked about my journal."

"Oh." I hadn't come here thinking to check on Anya. Suddenly, I wasn't sure what to say.

Instead she filled the quiet space. "I wasn't ready for them to read it. But we talked this morning, and we read it, and it's okay now." She used her smile like a mask to cover her true face.

"I'm sorry," I said quietly.

Our eyes connected and the innocent, happy aura I'd always associated with Anya was gone.

"It's okay." She shrugged again. "Dad explained. It wasn't your fault. He's sad for you. It's just now a bigger deal than he expected."

"For me too." My voice cracked and I coughed to cover up my emotion.

"Come in." She motioned me into a home filled with antiques and a deep history. I glanced at a stunning fireplace's hearth in a neighboring room.

"How old is your home?"

"1910. Dad," she called out, "Mrs. Childs is here."

Other than vintage photos, Anya's pictures were the only child's smile that filled the walls.

Through the hallway, two doors down, Principal Truss appeared. His hair was ruffled, and like Todi's comment in her journal, it was a bit *bizarre* to see our principal in jeans and a disheveled t-shirt. Yet the most apparent change was the visible gloom in his eyes.

156

"Come in." He pointed me toward his study. "Thank you, Anya," he spoke even-toned and softly to her. Then once he shut the door, his tired eyes looked at me. "How are you?"

I glanced around the room. Book spines lining the walls announced theories of learning, adolescent development and administration, as well as classic literature. Photos of Principal Truss through the years with an array of students and teachers, plaques of degrees and honors intermingled with scribbled notes and thank you cards framed the room.

When I finally turned to face him, I answered his question like Anya had answered mine. I shrugged.

His eyes searched mine. "So you read the rest of them?"

I found looking at him difficult, and selecting the right words to say even more difficult, especially since I was unsure what he knew. "All except Darby's and Anya's," I said and then pressed my lips together.

"Here, sit." He motioned to a winged-back chair in the corner then twisted his office chair to face me. "I know I owe you an explanation," he said quickly.

I nodded while I tried to avoid his eyes, which were only four feet from my face. "An explanation seems fair."

He clasped his hands in his lap and cleared his throat. "Officer Bond phoned me late last night. He told me all the events that played out with Darby and her family." His tone was tight. "I'm sure he's shared this with you."

Again, I nodded.

"It was late. And after a very difficult day in my career, I admit I overreacted. All I understood was that a mother had gone into the police station naive and when she came out she knew of a completely different world that her daughters were now a part of. So I asked

157

Officer Bond if Anya's had been read. He said yes. So I asked if he had any concerns. He said for what they were searching for, Anya's journal had nothing of interest. His answer didn't surprise me. But what did surprise me is what I said next: 'As a parent, could I also retrieve my daughter's journal?' He told me that'd be fine, so early in the morning I did."

Once again I pressed my lips together tightly.

"After breakfast, Anya, my wife Claire and I all sat around the table and discussed it. I told her others had read it, and I asked if there was anything in there she didn't want us to know. I'd meant anything illegal, shameful, immoral, etc. I admit my vision as a concerned parent obscured my own voice of reason. But as a public figure in the community, I wanted to know if there was anything that I needed to be aware of about my daughter, especially now, with other adults who knew those things. Of course, I didn't truly believe there was an issue, but if there was, I wanted to hear it myself, from my own daughter's mouth."

Since I'd first stepped into the room, his eyes had not stopped studying me. And I'd tried to look everywhere but at him. When he paused, I looked at my hands clasped together in my lap and examined the small cuts and rough patches due to my seasonally dry skin.

"Savannah." He waited, until I made the mistake of looking up. Rather than seeing Principal Truss's face, I saw a father pleading with me.

"I made a mistake," he said. "Anya mistook my question. She thought I was telling her we *needed* to read it. So she said we could. But I'm a fool. She didn't want us to, not really, but of course I didn't understand that. For me, we've always been an honest and open family. We've shared everything at the right time, and in the right way, especially in regard to Anya. And we've always felt like she's been honest with us. When I took her journal, I expected no secrets, no unnecessary drama, nothing to hide."

Suddenly I wanted to yell at him. I wanted him to understand that I was not responsible for what he found. And neither was Anya. She only had been doing her assignment!

But I refrained.

Instead, I rubbed my dry hands and focused on how lotion would soothe the ache. Then I put on my teacher voice and calmly said, "It wasn't yours to read."

"I know," he said softly.

"I gave them permission to let their pens flow and not be concerned about an audience."

"I made a mistake," he said. "I was caught in the moment of thinking about Darby's mother, about Darby, and her sister Lena. I hurt for them, Savannah. This morning, I hurt for their whole household. But not ours. I really believed we wouldn't hurt from Anya's words. Our family was fine," he said in sarcasm. "So Anya offered and we read. And now Claire is upstairs in bed because a scab which she thought had healed has now been pulled off and the wound re-exposed. And it's my daughter's words which inflicted Claire's pain."

I dropped my guard and finally looked at him. Moisture filled the corners of his eyes, which sparked a similar reaction in mine.

"Claire hurts," he said. "And Anya hurts for unintentionally hurting her mother. And I hurt for putting all of this into motion." He leaned back in his chair, looked up at the ceiling and rubbed his head, which tousled his hair a bit more.

My words stumbled out as a whisper. "Are you blaming me for this?"

"No, no." He glanced back at me. Then with the back of his hand he swiped at his eyes. "I feel like I'm on a pendulum with these journals." He shifted his gaze to the wall across from us. I glanced over too and saw a hanging graduation photo, five students with enormous grins and diplomas encircled around Principal Truss. "The steps we took on Friday were meant to prevent further harm," he said.

"The journals were never meant to inflict harm," I said.

He looked at me again. "This is all out of control. Between last night and early this morning, I thought parents had a right to know about these journals. If police officers were reading these, if crimes are being committed, if there are reasons for concern, then I need to understand what my responsibility is here. Should parents be aware of all of this? Are we obligated to give parents the option to know about their child's life, especially when poor decisions are being made? Decisions that are hurting these children? For every Darby in your class, if I was a parent of that child, and these things were taking place, I'd want to know. As a concerned parent, isn't it our right to know?"

I hated questions phrased in that way. Questions that spoke to me as if I was a parent and could weigh in on a subject I knew nothing about. I had no idea what a parent of a teenager should expect. Besides, each parent drew their own moral line of what was normal growing-up behavior versus that which was deemed a violation. "I can't answer that," I said softly.

"Well, as the principal of the school, I let the parents of one of your students know—I let myself and my wife into the private world of our daughter—and now I wish I could go back and restore the trust I've broken. I tested this in one situation and that approach did

THE OTHER SIDE OF

not work. So now I don't know what to do. I don't know what's right for the other children in your class, but right now Darby and Anya are hurting, right now parents are hurting, right now those journals have caused a divide with these two families."

I shook my head. "That was never the intent of this assignment."

"I know, and I still expect none of our students to be connected to this tragedy. If they are, Officer Bond will follow the correct protocol in addressing it. Meanwhile you know the rest of their stories. You know if certain things need to be shared with parents. If not, then you were right. You understand this was a time of free expression, which means we can all move on. I respect and trust you, Savannah."

"Do you?" I challenged him.

His eyes pierced into mine. "Yes. Make the best choices for these students and their families and I will support you."

CHAPTER

Four

WITH THE WEIGHT OF INFORMATION PLACED IN MY care, my brain felt fragile. As soon as I collapsed into the driver's seat of my car, I stared at Principal Truss's home and knew I needed ice cream—lots of ice cream!

I fired up the engine and detoured over to the west side of town, where I shifted into my weekly shopping routine. I purchased my standard stir-fry vegetables, a large piece of ginger root, a giant bag of rice, and in preparation for a rocky week, my emergency supply of ice cream.

With my groceries bagged and paid for, I maneuvered my cart through the parking lot until a neighboring scene caused me to pause.

A few cars over, a child, around four years of age, sped through rows of parked cars. Until a woman fervently grabbed him. Assuming it was his mother, I held my breath and waited for her strong reprimand.

But no scolding came.

I'd reached my car but I held still, while tilting my head to observe.

A girl, a few years older than the boy, now joined them. The woman knelt to be at the boy's eye level. "You ran out into the road. Why would that not be a good idea?"

She paused.

I opened my trunk, and started to unload a bag, but then I couldn't hear their voices. So I turned my head again.

"Watch me," the woman said, "tell me what I'm doing wrong." She tilted her head to the far right, and her arms and legs moved up and down in an exaggerated form, much like a cartoon figure who was stuck running in place.

"What's wrong?" she repeated, raising her arms and legs up and down with her head jerked completely to the far right.

The young girl piped up, as if eager to teach the younger boy, "You're not looking both ways."

I smiled at the engaging teacher. She'd used an effective teaching strategy to share her message. Our eyes connected briefly and she grinned back.

After my long day, I valued this scene. It gave me a much-needed smile. I resumed loading my groceries with my smile still in place, only to hear the final piece of this teacher's message. "You can't run through here without looking. You're too precious."

My hands froze, my head turned, my heart ached. I saw the boy, still with uncontainable energy, move swiftly through the final stretch of road and join the rest of their group. Another woman quickly hugged him.

I shot one last look at the scene and questioned which of these women was the boy's mother. But it didn't matter. His teacher clearly understood an important truth about this boy.

You're too precious. The words rang in my ears.

You're too precious. And I thought of Todi. Her dreams, her wishes, and her void. I wanted to sit down with her, look her straight in the eyes, just like this woman had, and say, *Todi, you're too precious to not have a stable family in your life.*

And *you're too precious, Dillon, to give up your dreams, to destroy your own life because your father hurt you.*

You're too precious, Abigail, to face these intense and critical decisions alone.

You're too precious, Tracey, to underestimate your true worth.

You're too precious, Kyle, to give up on life.

You're too precious, Anya. You're too precious, Blake. And Hamilton. And Priscilla. And Darby.

If only I could! I'd take each one of them, grab them by the shoulders and tell them this. And I'd gently shake them with just enough force for them to see that they can't give up on themselves, on who they are or who they are yet to be.

Instead I thought of this parking lot scene, this teacher of example and precept. And more words came, not so much from me, as toward me. *Savannah, you're too precious too.*

CHAPTER

Five

I GOT THROUGH THE EVENING. BUT THE NEXT DAY WAS ITS
own battle.

I attended church, as I do every Sunday, and just like every
Sunday since Peter's absence, I sat alone and watched legions of
young families, full of new life and new hope, remind me of this way
of life I was excluded from.

Amid the congregation, I saw a few of my English students—
not my Creative Writing students; they were not part of my
congregation—but other students whose presences and nods were
enough to remind me of the Monday I soon must face.

I also heard the whisperings, gossip and truth mixed together to
spread information about Stella's death.

That evening, I watched a small segment of the news but found
no further revelations, or leads, in her investigation. I turned off the
TV, sat on the couch, and listened. The refrigerator hummed and the
clock counted off seconds which led me closer to the new day.

Finally I sought solace the only way I knew how. I grabbed a half gallon of ice cream and turned to my journal to write about last Friday. Thankfully, words poured out and brought comfort to my troubled heart.

When the alarm rang Monday morning, I couldn't move. Life was calling, yet my heart felt dead.

Sunday journal writing had buoyed me up, but sleep had brought back my turbulent fears.

And while continuous beeping announced a new day, I thought of Darby's journal which had exposed her. And Anya's words which had slapped her mother with grief. And dear Abigail and Dillon with the unknowns they faced. And I thought of Kyle's terrifying words.

Then I thought of Priscilla. Blake. Todi. Hamilton.

And Tracey.

The beeps continued to nag me to action, even though I'd rather remain safe and catatonic in my bed.

However after four minutes, the chirping alarm received its desired response. I shut it off and proceeded to shower, hoping droplets of warmth would soothe my sore heart.

For the first six hours of school, I managed.

But right before sixth period, my forced smile began to fade.

To offset the chill from the other students, Blake said hello to me and Todi gave me a small but somewhat disappointed grin.

Then the tardy bell rang and I faced the moment I'd dreaded. In the hours leading up to this moment, I'd considered a standard opener, a teaser into my prepared lecture, a few remarks to set the stage for all that we'd learn that day.

Instead, three minutes after the bell rang I stood at the front of the class and still had nothing to say. Then one by one, due to the silence, my students began to look up at me.

We all knew today was like no other day. So I decided to break the silence with the truth.

"I'm sorry."

A huff from Dillon. "They were our journals."

"It's okay." Todi was the first to hold eye contact. "Sometimes adults lie."

"Yeah." Dillon slouched in his seat, his voice barely a whisper. "That's what they do."

Tracey released a sarcastic laugh. "So did you read all of them?"

I scanned the faces of my students. Other than Kyle, who was absent, all of them watched me. "They were handed over to the police."

"What does that mean?" Priscilla looked confused.

I drew in a breath, but before I could speak, Anya interrupted, "They needed to know who committed a crime."

"We haven't committed a crime." Abigail spoke so hastily her voice cracked.

"How do you know?" Hamilton sounded tense. "Maybe one of us did?"

"I hope not," I said strongly. "Not this crime, at least."

I saw Darby shift in her seat and look down at her desk.

"What crime?" Priscilla pressed her words together.

Darby's eyes darted up. "The cops took our journals because of Stella."

"What?" Abigail shot a look at Darby.

"Yeah." Darby nodded her head.

"The girl who died?" Priscilla practically yelled.

"Yes, Stella Fabrizio." Darby's voice cracked briefly, but then she covered it with more anger. "The cops asked me all about her."

All students now stared at Darby and she looked at her desk.

"Why?" Tracey asked.

Todi looked around the group. "Who's Stella?"

"It's been on the news," Blake offered. "They found her dead out in a field, and they're not sure what happened to her."

"She went to the high school," Abigail said. "My sister Paige knew her."

"She's a cheerleader," Hamilton practically whispered.

"Is that how you knew her?" Anya asked Darby.

As if she didn't want to talk, Darby turned her head away. Yet she answered in a low voice. "My sister and she got in a fight over a guy."

Todi's face scrunched up in concern. "So is your sister busted?"

"No!" Darby huffed out the word. "Not because of that."

"So," Dillon's tone was harsh, "why did the police take our journals?"

Anya twisted her body around to look at everyone. "When they found her, they also found a bag from our class."

"What bag?" Tracey asked.

All the students now looked at Anya and her face reddened.

I finally broke in. "Where did you hear that, Anya?"

She shrugged her shoulders. "All weekend my dad's been asking me to find that bag, even though I told him I don't have it anymore. And he keeps saying sorry about the journal stuff, and the police have called him twice. I just know—I heard my dad say something over the phone. It's one of our bags from the family project." She looked at the class again.

"They think one of us did it?" Tracey stared at me.

"Are you sure?" Priscilla asked Anya.

But the rest of the class no longer looked at Anya. Instead, a silence fell over the room while eyes darted around to look at each other until all eyes settled on Kyle's empty chair.

168

"Where's Kyle?" Hamilton asked.

The remaining students twisted to look at me and then back at his vacant spot.

"It's always the quiet one," Todi said.

"Kyle's not a suspect." I aimed to restore a sense of dignity and respect within my classroom, so I quoted Officer Bond. "There are no suspects yet."

"But why did you take our journals?" Dillon asked again, while Abigail shot him a quick glance.

"This has been difficult for everyone." My voice remained firm. "But it's how they chose to conduct the investigation."

"That doesn't make sense," Dillon said.

"So whose bag was there?" Todi looked at the class.

"It could be anyone's," Anya said.

"Not if you still have yours," Blake offered. "I still have mine." He looked around the room for a simple confirmation from others.

But fear ran across Priscilla's face. "I didn't like mine. I threw it away."

"I don't know where mine is." Abigail also appeared a bit panicked.

"My room's a bit messy right now," Tracey said, "but I'm sure it's at the bottom of my stuff somewhere."

"So we all find our bags and bring 'em in." Blake looked at me. "Right, Mrs. Childs?"

"I threw mine away." Priscilla looked like she was near tears.

"I never got one," Todi said.

Priscilla shot me a quick look. "Bria threw hers away too. I promise!"

"It's fine," I said firmly. "If you have your bag bring it in, and if you have information that you think can help the investigation, let me

169

or Principal Truss know. Otherwise I don't think any of you have anything to worry about," I aimed to sound convincing, but I caught Anya's eyes before she glanced down at her desk. Then she bit her lip.

Meanwhile Dillon glared at me. "So did you read them?"

Darby shot me a spiteful look. "They've been read."

"You did?" Tracey asked.

My heart beat quickened. All students stared at me with wide eyes. "Yes," I said quietly, and frowns followed.

For a brief moment, I considered shifting the dialogue straight into a writing lecture. Instead I said, "I didn't choose to do this, but I did violate your trust. And I'm sorry."

"So who did it?" Tracey asked me.

I didn't want my students to play this harmful game of Clue, but before I could speak, Priscilla interrupted, "Did Kyle?"

"No," I quickly said. "No," I said again. "Nobody here has done anything that anyone knows of."

"Why's Kyle not here?" Tracey asked.

"He's just not," I tried to say with more composure.

"It's not Kyle," Darby said roughly.

Todi whipped around to look at her. "Then who?"

"I already told the police," Darby said.

Hamilton's voice was low. "You did?"

Priscilla's eyes grew huge. "You told them what?"

Everyone focused on Darby. "I can't say," she said.

With that statement everyone turned back to face me, like I was going to force Darby to share something clearly quite confidential. I shook my head, ready to be done with this conversation, ready for all my innocent students to return to their descriptive writing.

"It's time to work on your next assignment," I said.

"That's hard to do," Dillon dropped his pen on the desk, "after what you did to us."

His statement voiced my fears. Even after the *why*, my students were still disappointed in me. Because for the past seven months I'd given them a treasure box, where I'd promised them freedom to unload all their thoughts, expressions, and emotions. And now I'd broken in and robbed them.

Instead of reprimanding Dillon, I nodded. They didn't feel like they could write today, and I didn't feel like I could teach. In horrible defeat, I said, "Under the circumstances, let's step back from our writing for a day. You can all work on homework from another class."

Then I retreated to my desk and let the earth rotate on its axis.

When the bell finally rang, I looked at my students, who quietly filed out and never looked at me.

Although Todi did bellow, "See you tomorrow, Mrs. Childs."

"Have a good evening," rested on my tongue, but the word *good* seemed heartless, so instead I softly said, "Bye."

After the doors closed behind my students, a heavy sigh expelled from my lips. That was a difficult period! One of the most intense in my career. I glanced at the fourth period English papers on my desk and shuffled them into a file. Then I stood and reached for my bag.

"Mrs. Childs?"

I whipped around to see Abigail on the far side of the room.

"Yes," I said cautiously.

She moved diagonally across the room until she stood six feet away from me. Her voice remained low. "Please don't tell my mom."

"What?" I asked as I thought about Abigail's plight.

"You know." Her words were direct. Her face said *I don't have time for games.* "Don't tell her yet."

171

I wasn't in the mood for games either. "It wouldn't be my place to tell her," my voice came out strong, "but she needs to know soon."

Abigail's gaze dropped to the ground. "I can't tell her, not yet."

"But," my tone softened, "you'll need to soon."

She watched her shoe trace a pattern across the floor. "Dillon and I are still figuring out our plans. Only he knows . . ." She glanced up, and briefly looked me in the eyes. "And now you."

Her words felt acidic. Yes. I did know.

To lessen the gap between us, I stepped out from behind my desk. "Abigail." I took another step and our eyes met. "I'm sorry."

She shrugged. "It'll be okay."

"It will." I matched her solemn tone, until her face tensed up slightly and I couldn't hold back. "Are you scared?"

"Yes." She nodded.

"I've never really been pregnant." The words startled me—not the statement, but how smoothly I spoke from my heartache. "But if you ever need someone to talk to, I'm here."

"Thank you." She nodded again. A tiny smile crept across her face, and I wanted to believe that for that moment, she'd forgiven me, and perhaps even felt relieved someone else knew. But then the moment snapped. She flung her backpack onto her shoulder, flipped around, and batted at her eyes. "Good-bye, Mrs. Childs."

I stepped back.

The magic was gone. Instead I fell back into my role as the cautionary teacher, and an infertile woman who'd danced too close to a situation she did not understand. As Abigail reached for the door, I said loudly, "You need to tell your mother soon."

"I know," she said without looking back.

CHAPTER
Six

THAT EVENING WHILE MAKING STIR-FRY, I PHONED Officer Bond.

"Kyle wasn't at school today," I said.

Officer Bond's tone was deep and stable. "I know."

I held my breath and waited but when he didn't say more, I added, "The other students are now asking questions. They want to know what's going on with him and the investigation."

"I just got off the phone with his father."

Silence followed.

"And?" I prodded.

"They've been out of town. They took their camper to a campground near Zion and were out of service, which is why we couldn't reach them. He's bringing Kyle in for questioning now."

"Oh," I said cautiously.

"Once I shared a few lines from Kyle's journal, Mr. McConkie seemed extremely concerned."

I stared at my hot wok, watching the snow peas darken from the heat. "I guess we all are."

"His father seems very willing to work with us, especially since Kyle initiated the camping trip."

My fingers tightened around the phone. "I really hope you find the answers you need." Then I quickly added, "Will you let me know?"

He responded back with, "I'll let you know what I can let you know."

From there, all through the meal, my thoughts circled around Kyle.

He had given me a fabulous fantasy story, centered on a remarkable quest, with a warrior who could "story hop" and build bridges between worlds in order to rescue his own world. It was clever, engaging, and actually well-written. And it was the only piece of quality writing I'd yet seen from Kyle.

Otherwise, he was my mute student who carried around a load of angst, the loner who never said *hi* to anyone in class, the distant boy who had scribbled threats throughout his journal. He hated my class, but I didn't hate him.

The truth was I didn't know Kyle.

Although he sat in my classroom, unless I could painfully coax the words out of him, he didn't speak. He didn't turn in his assignments. His grade fluctuated between a C- and a D. His status in my ninth grade English class was even worse.

I thought of the interrogation and wondered if Kyle would speak more to Officer Bond than he'd ever spoken to me.

Chaos Bleeds, Angel of Darkness, death of many, Invisible War, I can't believe I'm doing this.

His journal words replayed in my mind, until my over-active imagination saw Kyle in Stella's room. One moment she was alive. The next minute she was dead.

I stared at the food on my plate and my stomach revolted.

Quickly, I threw plastic wrap over my meal and stuck it in the fridge. Then I sought a distraction from my dangerous thoughts. I flipped on my computer and hoped to find an email from Peter. But nothing was there.

I opened a new email to tell Peter about the journals, about life, about me. But no words came.

Instead I stared at a blinking cursor and waited for something.

CHAPTER

Seven

I FELL ASLEEP ON THE SOFA AWAITING OFFICER BOND'S phone call. When I awoke it was morning. I had a kinked neck and a sour mood. Tuesday had begun no better than Monday.

At school, I walked the halls, searching for Kyle. I scanned the crowds of students for his five foot frame, his dark blond hair, and his taut face, but nothing. By fourth period English, my fears were confirmed. Kyle's seat was empty.

During sixth period it remained empty. I rubbed my neck and tried to soothe my unsettled mood. I had assumed Officer Bond would notify me. But he had not!

And I was not the only one who noticed Kyle's absence. Across the aisle Tracey tapped Todi's arm. "Where is he?" He nodded toward Kyle's empty seat.

Todi shot me a look, but I shrugged determined to not turn his absence into a class discussion. Still, Hamilton caught my expression and leaned forward to whisper in Darby's ear.

Darby shot a look at Kyle's seat and then shook her head. "It's not him," she said strongly.

Quickly, I dove into my creative writing lecture. Back when I'd built my syllabus, I'd envisioned today to be a stirring lecture. Under other circumstances, I believe I could have led a collaborative discussion with excerpts from literary giants on style, syntax, and rhythm. Instead my questions boomeranged out, swirled around the classroom, and returned without a grasp. On a few occasions Blake or Todi commented, but otherwise, even Anya remained silent and disengaged.

Like the majority of students, Hamilton slouched in his seat, although once he looked up, and his eyes revealed an interest, like his heart had been drawn back into this magical art form. Yet too quickly, after our eyes connected, his head twisted away as if no longer listening.

The only time a real conversation returned was near the end of class, when I had once again resigned my class time to other course homework. Then Anya turned and spoke to Darby, a couple of rows behind her.

"Are you going to Stella's funeral?" she asked.

"Of course not," Darby said coldly.

"I am," Hamilton volunteered.

Anya gave him a soft grin. "My dad thinks we'll go to the viewing."

"When is it?" Abigail asked.

In order to face her, Anya twisted diagonally in her seat. "Tomorrow night is the viewing."

"I bet my sister will go then." Abigail looked at Dillon. "I'll probably go too."

Right then the bell rang. Darby scowled at the group then gathered up her notebook. But instead of walking out the door like the other students, she approached me.

On top of my second period's neat stack of assessments, she dropped a spiral notebook.

"Here," she said coarsely. "Thought you'd like to read this too." Then she strode out, hitting the door's crash bar with a thrust.

She was long gone before the door swung back and latched itself into place.

I sank behind my desk and listened. Other than Darby's display, no other students, not even Todi, had acknowledged me.

The former days of happy chatter were now gone. Smiles and good-byes had been traded for anger and silence. I glanced down at Darby's notebook. It was not her original journal but rather a new spiral notebook, with a swirling design across the corner and her name boldly drawn in black block letters.

Darby's Journal

Monday, March 1, 2004

Last Friday, Mrs. Childs took our journals from us. She said she wouldn't, but she did.

She said we could write whatever we wanted in them. She told us to share our soul in these pages, like we could share secrets, and feelings, and expressions. She promised us our privacy and respect.

Now she pulled that from us. And I've had to pay for that.

The cops didn't have to take our journals. They didn't have to read about our personal lives to find out what happened to Stella. What happened to Stella has nothing to do with our class.

But instead, ever since my journal has had an audience I've been punished. Because like Mrs. Childs said, writing for an audience is quite different than writing for yourself. So if I'd known I was having an audience for my writing this is what I'd have said:

Being a teenager is hard.

Being popular and pretty and liked takes work. You have to watch what you say, do, feel, and think. You have to be someone for everybody else. You can't just be you. You don't even know who *you* is.

I know I'm pretty. And that pretty is temporary. It's a clock that will tick itself away.

I know I'm smart. But I got to do something now, or I'll be left behind in the race to get into a good college.

I know I can have friends, lots of friends, but none of them are real friends. None of them are people who I can really bare my soul to.

But I did in my journal, Mrs. Childs.

So now what are you going to do about that?

181

CHAPTER
Eight

O N MY WAY HOME, I DROVE OVER TO THE POLICE station. I asked for Officer Bond and found myself waiting in a plastic bucket chair in the skinny lobby for over twenty-five minutes. Twice I thought about leaving; once I even stood up. But I always found myself slumping back into the curved chair.

Finally Officer Bond appeared in the doorway; his gray blue eyes scanned my face as if he didn't recognize me. Boldly I stood, and heat filled my cheeks.

Then he said, "Sorry to keep you waiting, Mrs. Childs."

"Savannah," I huffed out my name.

"Come on back." He motioned me through a door and we stepped into a long hallway, where he led me to his office. Right away I scanned the room for signs of who he was, noting no photos of a wife or kids, but three photos of him with a St. Bernard. "Yours?" I pointed at a dog photo.

"Yeah. His name's Rex."

"He's huge."

"He is." Officer Bond motioned at a seat and I sat. Then we both stared at each other awkwardly.

"What can I help you with?" he finally asked.

I clutched my hands together.

When I'd entered the station, I'd felt entitled to answers. I'd held to that belief as I'd painfully waited for almost a half-hour for this man. Now I sat across from him, and suddenly I had no idea what information was deemed confidential and out of my grasp.

"I . . ." My boldness felt long spent.

Still, I looked at the door, braved myself forward, and spat out the words, "I just need to know about Kyle." I glanced back at him. "Is there anything you can tell me?"

His palm hit his forehead. "Oh," he said as if in pain. "I got a call last night about another homicide case. A messy case that's taken priority over everything. I've been entrenched in it for the last twenty hours."

I heaved out a relieved sigh. "So you didn't meet with Kyle?"

"I did." His eyes pierced into mine. "And I think the interrogation had an impact."

"What happened?"

"He fumbled around a lot, asked to use the bathroom, asked his dad to leave the room. But I asked his dad to stay."

My hands clasped together tightly, and my throat tightened.

I dreaded to hear the words, yet I still waited for the confirmation.

But when the words didn't come, I closed my eyes and asked, "Did you arrest him?"

My eyes shot open to the low rumble of laughter. For the first time since I'd met Officer Bond, he had a grin across his face. Not a full grin that reached his eyes, but a grin nonetheless.

"It was video games," he said.

"What?"

"Those phrases in his journal were from video games. Call of Duty, Killzone, Grand Theft Auto – all games he'd smuggled past his father."

"What about the hit list?"

"High scores, his goals of what he's aiming for." Officer Bond spoke in sarcasm. "And here his father thought he had no drive or ambition."

"So . . . no correlation with Stella?"

He shrugged. "Not that I could find."

"Video games," I repeated.

"Yep."

I bit my lip and scanned the room one last time. There were filing cabinets, bookshelves, framed diplomas and recognitions, but no personality cues other than the man's dog. "So where was he today?"

"You mean at school?"

"Yeah. You said his family got back from a trip yesterday. But what about today?"

"Well, he didn't look too good when he left last night. My bet is, by being here, his nerves got a little shook up."

"How was his father?"

Officer Bond shook his head. "Not pleased with how Kyle approached your assignment. Or his son's video game selection. Or the lies. He pulled me aside and asked if there were charges we could throw at his son. I believe he was kidding. But he did ask if there were laws against underage children purchasing mature video games."

This meant another student was condemned by his own words, courtesy of my journal assignment. Darby's fury echoed in my mind. *What are you going to do about it?*

184

"So what does this mean for Stella's case?" I asked.

He pushed his chair away from the desk and folded his arms. For a brief moment he looked at the wall behind me. When he spoke again, his words were soft. "Stella's case is still open. We're still actively investigating."

"Darby mentioned she talked to you about a possible suspect."

"Yes. She's given us a good lead."

I held my breath until I couldn't refrain, then I blurted out, "So are you still questioning my students?"

"At the end of the week, Coach Forbes will be back. Then we'll bring Hamilton in."

My shoulders tensed. "I doubt Hamilton had anything to do with it."

"Probably not directly." He offered me a very small smile.

"Then why?" My defensive tone was back.

"Darby shared some information about an activity between the football players and cheerleaders at the high school, and if she's right, then the question is how did this particular *person of interest* end up with your class's bag. And I suspect after we talk with Hamilton and his father, we'll have our answer."

"Anything you can share with me?"

"Not yet."

CHAPTER
Nine

O N WEDNESDAY, TIME SEEMED TO CREEP FORWARD during my creative writing lecture. Eventually, I needed to instruct them to pull out a sheet of paper and write.

But I struggled with this request.

Still, we needed to move past the wounds of the journal assignment. Yet with ten minutes left, I offered my students, once again, time to work on homework from other classes.

From there, my wish was to retreat back to my desk and let the final minutes of class slip by. But my job was not over yet.

Since reading their journals, all the students' entries had rung in my ears, but Tracey's echo had been the loudest. I knew I had to say something, but my heart and mind were at war over what I needed to share. Still, I approached his desk. "Tracey."

He looked up and said nothing, but I saw the fear trapped in his eyes.

"After the bell rings, please stay after. I'd like to speak with you briefly."

He shifted his eyes down, stared at his three-ring binder, and let his fingers glide along the edges. Then he slouched down before nodding his acceptance.

When the bell rang, all students quickly departed. Except Tracey. His bag remained open, his binder and textbook stayed unfolded on his desk, and his eyes stared ahead at the whiteboard.

I stood near my desk, and watched until the hallway noise faded and quietness settled around the room. Once he reached for his pack and slowly loaded it, I braved myself forward, meeting him right as he stood over his desk.

He towered above me. I looked up, opened my mouth, and still felt unsure as the words tumbled out, "I don't want to overstep here, Tracey, but it seems like I have to talk to you about some things."

His gaze dropped to the ground.

"Our school has a specific policy on how I handle a student's suicide comments."

His foot tapped on a discarded balled-up gum wrapper. "Well, you *weren't* supposed to read my journal."

"Fair enough," I said, and wished the conversation could end here.

Fortunately, Tracey helped me out. "For what it's worth, I don't have suicide thoughts anymore. It was just that entry." He pressed down on the gum wrapper, smashing it flat, and then scratched at his neck. "And they weren't really suicide thoughts, you know, they were just thoughts. They were just words used for expression. Like the assignment was, right?"

"Yes." I let his words sink in. Then, when his light brown eyes met mine, I added, "But under the circumstances, I've something very important to tell you."

"What's that?"

"I've researched and studied a lot about what a child is, because I can't have a child," I said boldly. "And so, through that research, I've learned how complex and amazing science is." His eyes stayed on me. "It's remarkable that it starts with two critical pieces, and from there life begins to form. And yes, in some instances, it's almost like scientists have the ability to play *God*."

"They do," he said matter-of-factly.

"I also very much understand your moms' longings to be parents."

"Which is why they have me." He slung his arm through his loose backpack strap.

The window to talk was shrinking, so I chose my words quickly. "I know there's a lot of talk about what makes up a family, and I can't tell you what's right or wrong with how families are formed, or what makes up a family in your own home. But I hope you know you're no less than anyone else."

"No matter how you came to exist," he spoke as if mocking the phrase.

"No matter how you came to exist," I repeated back confidently.

Suddenly the backpack slid off his back and thudded against the ground. Then Tracey stepped onto his chair and sat on the desktop. He faced me squarely, his eyes studying me, and I paused, unsure of what to say next.

As a distracting thought, I wondered if I was being responsible allowing Tracey to sit on the desktop like that. Yet in contemplating this conversation around his existence, I reckoned the chair's strength was a lesser concern for both of us.

"Mrs. Childs," he spoke with a tone much older than a ninth grader. "I've done my research too. Do you know who the first test-tube baby was?"

I slid into a neighboring chair. "No."

"It was Louise Brown."

"Okay?" I gave him a quizzical look. "Is that name supposed to mean something?"

"She wasn't supposed to be the first test-tube baby." He folded his arms and looked down at me. "It was supposed to be another family, the Del-Zios. I did a report on it last year. My friend Sophia found the story. My teacher thought the story was interesting, and my mom Paula did too."

"So what's the story?" I asked.

"Well," Tracey cleared his throat as if ready to recite a prepared speech. "It was 1973 and Mrs. Del-Zio really wanted a baby. She'd decided she'd do anything, so she took all the drugs, and did everything her doctor told her to do, and then this doctor got ready to build the first human test-tube baby. So he removed her *stuff*, and gathered Mr. Del-Zio's *stuff*, and once their stuff combined he put the fertilized egg in the test-tube so it could grow for four days. Then after that, he was going to put this *baby* into Mrs. Del-Zio. Only problem is the doctor's boss found out, and he got super angry. He didn't know the doctor was experimenting like this. And he thought it was wrong. He didn't think a doctor should be building a baby in a test-tube. So he removed the test-tube from the incubator, and he stopped the experiment. That was it! Everything that Mrs. Del-Zio and her husband had done, and it was over, just like that. Then in 1978, someone else created another test-tube baby. And that became Louise Brown."

My jaw dropped. "Tracey. That's a lot of information you know."

"It's all true."

I shook my head. "Why do you know all this?"

189

"If you were a test-tube baby, wouldn't you want to know?"

This discussion was not going at all how I'd planned. "I don't know. I've never thought about it."

"Do you know who your father is?"

I nodded, knowing I hadn't spoken to him in over a month, and in looking at Tracey, I suddenly missed my father.

"My friend Sophia talked to me a lot about it." Tracey tapped his feet on the chair. "Because I do have a father, biologically speaking, and Sophia likes to talk to me like she's a scientist. She calls it the *old debate*. She says, 'Does nature or nurture shape us into who we are?' She says it's because it's a question that bothered her lots in middle school, but over time it got easier. I hope so. Because I want this pain, about wanting to know who my father is, to go away."

"Do you have a father figure in your life?"

The feet tapping paused. "My parents feel like Sophia's dads were there for me." He lifted up one of his heels slightly, only to let it freeze in place. "And before we moved, they were. They've always been nice. And kind. And just good to me." He rotated his heel around and watched it. "But they were Sophia's parents, you know. And you sort of depend on a parent, kind of like an anchor. I feel that with my parents, but not with Sophia's parents. Because they aren't my parents."

"What are you saying, Tracey?"

He set his foot back on the chair. "I'm not saying anything." Then the feet tapping began again. "My mom Cori says I should be proud to be part of the first generation of new families. In California, my moms can get married now, so for Spring Break we're heading back home. Then a document from the government will bind us together as a family, and I'll be part of history, you know?"

"And what do you think about that?"

190

He stopped the tapping, stopped looking at his feet, and looked at me. "Sophia always said, 'I fully support equality and rights, but it's not my fight.' She says it's her parents' fight, you know? And I think," he shrugged his shoulders, "I agree with her. Someday I'll have something to fight for. But right now, I just feel a lot of pressure from my parents."

"What kind of pressure?"

"Just to be part of this first wave of new families, and to turn out okay. That I have to be perfect for them and their cause. And I don't feel perfect. I feel confused. And sometimes I just want to know about my dad—because I'm still a part of him too."

"Have you ever told your parents this?" I asked softly.

"They wouldn't understand." His voice cracked. "It'd hurt them too much, you know."

"Have you tried?"

"No." He balled his hands into fists. "I can't." He choked away some of the tension in his voice. "They'd feel like I was attacking what they've given me." His voice cracked again. "And all that they've done for me—but I want to know who he is."

"You may never know who he is." But this was the wrong thing to say, since I saw tears well up in his honey-colored eyes.

"Mrs. Childs, do you believe in God?"

"Tracey," I kept my tone reserved, "even though this school doesn't have a specific policy on it, I tend to not talk about—"

"But do you?" He cut me off.

"Yes. I do."

"Then why don't I have a dad?"

"I don't know." I shrugged. "Why don't I have any children?" For a moment, we both stared at each other. Then Tracey brushed a tear away, while I tried to prevent my own tears from falling. "I ask

God that a lot," I confessed. "And I don't have an answer. From my perspective, you're right. Somehow when the father card was dealt out you were skipped in the truest sense. You got two mom cards and no dad cards. Some may say you got a lucky hand; others will tell you that you were given an unfortunate hand. I don't know, Tracey. I'm here to tell you neither."

"Cori doesn't believe in God. Paula says she does. I don't know what I believe."

I spoke softly. "Someday you'll know what you believe."

"Do you think if I believed I'd understand why my family is different than the rest of the families here?"

"I don't know." I offered him a kind smile. "I believe in God, but I don't know why every family is different."

The eyes that looked back at me weren't satisfied. Instead, he hungered for something more.

"Tracey, I don't understand lots about life, but there is one thing I do understand."

"What's that?"

"Well," I was crossing a gray moral line, yet Tracey's eager face caused my words to tumble out. "Before the radical and amazing act of science helped to create you, you still had a soul. And that's what God knows and understands about you."

"Really?" A tear rolled down his check. He used the back of his palm to swipe at it. "You really believe that?"

"I do."

He studied my face as if trying to read something deeper.

I studied him back and said, "So I guess, if I had to make sense of things, I'd say that even though you don't have a father here, you still do have a Father who knows you."

"Who?" He whispered out the word. "God?"

"If you choose to believe in deity, then yes. He's who created you. But that's for you to decide." I stood up. "Okay Tracey, as your teacher I can't talk to you about this anymore. In fact, I'm not sure I should have shared any of that."

But he smiled back at me.

"Well," I said, "after reading your journal, I needed you to know how very important you are. You are no less than any other human being. So Tracey, if we need to, let's get those statements in your journal addressed. Okay?"

"No." With the back of his wrist, Tracey wiped the tear residue from his face. He slipped off the chair, hefted his backpack onto his shoulder, and gave me a direct look. "I'm okay. Thanks!"

I tried to smile at him as he walked out of the classroom. Perhaps I was wrong to have crossed this line. But it was true! Tracey was much more than what he thought he was.

And I couldn't bear for him to believe otherwise.

CHAPTER
Ten

THAT EVENING, I ATTENDED STELLA'S VIEWING. At first, I didn't know why I was there. Perhaps I was like the other long-time residents of Helam who stood in line. We were there hoping to pay our respects due to this terrible tragedy that had shaken our beloved town and wedged Stella's life into our hearts forever.

From where I stood in line, I could see members of Stella's family. A woman I presumed to be her mother stood closest to the casket. A daughter older than Stella stood next to her, another young man, with grandparents near, and then another man I presumed to be her father. A similar look of shock covered each of their faces.

For those of us in line, a video played nearby and I watched segments bring this deceased girl back to life.

Then I felt a squeeze on my arm and turned to see Principal Truss, his wife, and Anya at his side. I tried to smile at them.

"How are you?" he asked.

I let the sober smile answer. "You?" I asked.

He nodded back. Then he introduced me to his wife, and together we exchanged awkward talk, until a woman from the line stepped forward and tapped Principal Truss on the shoulder.

It was Hamilton Forbes's mom. I turned back and nodded at Hamilton and Kira, his sister, who both stood a half dozen people behind me.

"Thad wishes he could be here," Mrs. Forbes said. "We're all just still completely in shock." The line moved. I stepped forward, while she slipped back into her place in line. The Trusses remained with her to further converse. However, Anya remained near me.

But her focus was directed at a young man sitting alone in a far corner on a folding chair. He was bulk and muscle yet his plump cheeks still held a bit of youth. He faced us with a lost look in his eyes.

"Do you know him?" I asked Anya.

She nodded. "I know about him."

He'd never been one of my students. "Who is he?"

"Skyler Benson."

The name didn't mean anything, but I kept watching him too. His torso remained still, but his feet shuffled under his chair as if he were running. Then his hands balled into fists and he pounded at his eyes.

"Is he okay?" I whispered.

"He was her ex-boyfriend," Anya whispered back. Then she tugged on my sleeve and I leaned down to hear, "I think he's who Darby thinks did it."

I drew up my head and watched him. The kid was scared.

I looked back at Anya. "How old?"

"He's a senior. He's eighteen."

I tried to look away, but the more I tried the more my eyes shifted back to watch him. "How do you know this?"

"I just listen," she said. "And I know when to ask things."

Right then Mrs. Truss reached for Anya's arm and we exchanged good-byes. Then I watched Skyler a little longer, until it was my turn to approach the family line.

My introduction was brief. I said little, as did they. And then I stood at the casket and stared at Stella's lifeless body. She was dressed in pale blue with a neckline and makeup that hid the truth. And at that moment I truly understood why I had come. Desperately, I wanted to believe the innocence of my students. But one of their bags had done this.

When I stepped away from the casket, I brushed my wet eyes. Then I shot a glance in Skyler's direction, but he was gone.

Instead, on the opposite side of the room, Officer Bond stood in street clothing, observing.

When our eyes met, I gave him a soft smile. He returned the smile and nodded.

He was there to bring Stella justice.

Later that evening, with life and death and family and love heavy on my mind, I checked my email in hopes of a message from Peter. Over the months, due to different schedules and time zones, email had proved to be our best form of communication.

Then that communication had morphed into a loose schedule of once a week correspondence where I'd recap my teaching week, items about the house, updates from his parents if I'd actually reached out to them, which seemed less and less as time moved on, news about neighbors, our friends, our congregation—anything I could think of. Sometimes the emails felt forced, which made me keenly aware of the distance between us. But I tried. Once a week, I tried to consolidate my life into one email and send it off as if a weekly email would make everything right in our marriage.

196

Similarly, once a week, I found his mutual attempt at our marriage waiting there in my inbox.

And tonight I needed contact from him. Anything would do.

But nothing was there.

With my heart still lost in the sorrow of the evening, I pulled up his last email from the previous week.

Hi Love,

Miss you. Seven months now, and I find myself more anxious to be home.

Still in the village. Thought our unit was relocating to the city. But so far nothing.

Don't know how I feel about it. Sometimes I want to be in the city with more of the action. Otherwise it can get easy to feel like we aren't doing anything here, at least that's what some of the guys have said.

But then I take a moment to interact with the villagers. The ones who are glad we're here, and it makes me glad too.

You'd love the school we're helping to build. Every time I step into it, I think of you. Makes me hear your words: that "real change comes from educating the children." Once, before the sheetrock came, I carved your name into the frame.

And the thanks! Fathers and mothers come to us with tears in their eyes thanking us for this opportunity for their daughters. It's nice!

With all its problems here, there's also much good happening too.

A lot of talk about the upcoming elections. We hope this is what the country needs. That after so many years of war, and the Taliban, and all the unrest, they can at last move toward peace.

Hope you are well.
Remember—we both sleep under the same bright moon.

Peter

That night, out of habit, I knelt and prayed for Peter.

Then I prayed with more fervency.

Perhaps it was due to the recent email void, or the lifeless body of Stella, or my earlier talk with Tracey, but some ache in my heart kept me praying.

Until the tears welled up in my eyes, and I felt, at last, a soft spot in my heart.

It was deep inside, but still it was there; tenderness still lived inside me—my heart still cared!

This discovery sent more tears spilling down.

I began praying for others, for Tracey, then Abigail, then Darby, next Kyle. And Todi. Anya. Dillon and Blake. I prayed for Hamilton, followed by Priscilla. Each creative writing student by name. Then, in a general prayer, I prayed for all the rest of my dear students.

Followed by prayers for Stella's family, for Officer Bond, and for his efforts with this case, and then for all people who grieve.

At last I crawled into bed, and for the first time in a long time, I rejoiced that I felt alive and that hope still existed within my heart.

But deep in the night, a dream came, one that drew me away from my peaceful state.

It started fine. I was a child again. Six years old on my grandfather's farm, the field wide open, the sun beating down on my face. Then a bunny darted through the dry grass and I chased it through the field. With each of its little hops, I ran faster, chasing it straight toward a large oak tree, until the bunny jetted behind the tree and disappeared from view.

Still intent on my catch, I dashed around the oak, only to run smack into a human body decaying on the ground. The face was blue and puffy. It didn't look like her, but I knew it was Stella.

198

I yelled. And I ran. I was a grown woman now, stretching my legs wide, sprinting across the field, calling for help.

Until his sinister eyes froze me.

His hands held a gun, his fingers firm on the trigger. The barrel aimed at me. It was Kyle McConkie and he was going to shoot me.

"No!" My yell rippled through the open field.

"Don't worry," Kyle said calmly. "It's only a game."

He stepped closer and my body trembled. "Please, no."

Then Peter appeared, his firm body in uniform. I wanted to run to him, to feel his strong arms around me, but Kyle saw my face. From there he knew my wishes. And the gun turned swiftly on Peter.

Kyle fired. Hitting Peter. Again. Again. Again. And again.

I crumpled to the ground. Sobbing. Waiting now for Kyle to kill me too.

Instead a shrilling alarm filled the land. Kyle glanced around, our eyes connected, and then he ran.

When I looked up, I caught a faint glimpse of Peter's lifeless body. My heart moaned while the shrilling beeps continued.

Slowly my perception sharpened, my eyes opened, and I saw my tranquil bedroom.

I reached for my alarm and shut it off.

I'd found my heart's soft spot, which also meant I could bleed, and I cursed this weakness.

A heart with love, and hope, is liable to hurt.

Still bleary-eyed, I arose from my bed, flipped on my computer, and went straight to my inbox.

With fingers trembling, I hit the keys. The dream had showed me a new life, one far more painful than being childless.

My email was short and direct. *I miss you. Please come back safe.*

CHAPTER
Eleven

THURSDAY'S CREATIVE WRITING CLASS WAS QUIET.
Kyle was a no-show again and I felt relief. Then immediate guilt for that relief, like I had caused his absence.

Nine students and I silently survived the fifty minutes of class.

That evening I had no email from Peter.

Again I dropped to my knees, this time praying even deeper than the night before. Rather than peace, a great wave of despair rushed over me, sending me back into the strong, turbulent, destructive current. My own cold heart was my silent killer.

And then I knew!

This was *not* the person I wanted to be.

I wanted to *love*. I wanted to feel! But I needed help to face the vulnerability that accompanies love.

Perhaps God had been waiting for this. Because after I asked for help, God sent me a day of miracles.

The first miracle occurred at the end of sixth period.

Blake lingered until everyone left, then he said, "Can I talk to you?"

"Of course." I motioned to two classroom chairs, but before we could sit, my classroom door opened and in walked Kyle—my second miracle.

"Kyle." The tone of my voice sounded as if we were dear friends. "How are you?" After a week's absence, and despite the dream, I truly was happy to see the return of my lost student.

"I owe you this." He set a pristine spiral-bound notebook on a desk near me.

"What is it?"

"My real journal. I wrote it this week, while I've been sick." He looked past me, clearly avoiding my eyes. "I'm sorry I didn't do the assignment like I should have."

I couldn't stop staring at him.

"You can read it." He looked down at his feet. "When I wrote it, I knew you would."

I glanced at the journal. The cover was simple, a dark purple seventy-page spiral-bound notebook.

"I doubt there's anything anyone really wants to read in there," he said. "But I just want you to know I did the assignment, and I did it right."

I was speechless. I nodded until I was able to say, "Thank you, Kyle."

He grunted an acceptance, and shifted his head so our eyes caught briefly. Then he left.

With both hands, I picked up the journal while the slightest smile danced on my face. Lightly I touched Blake's shoulder, then headed to my desk and set down the new notebook. When I returned, I sat, faced Blake, and said, "Okay."

He smiled at me. "Mrs. Childs, I need your help."

Seeing Blake's smile strengthened my own. "Then let's hope I can help."

He cleared his throat as if preparing to launch into an important speech, and then sat up straight. "Mrs. Childs," he said my name again. "Do you ever feel like you're meant to do something really great? I mean. . ." His thick fingers tapped on the desk, a gesture reminding me of a business executive contemplating summary points or debating a critical decision. "Something that could change the world?" His voice grew in intensity. "Like even improve the world?"

I nodded, smiled again, and reflected on the irony. Growing up, my dream had been simple. I'd change the world through motherhood. I lived in a society that valued this goal, even claimed it was a female's God-given right to be a mother, a woman's noble gift to share her talents and skills in raising other strong, capable, virtuous human beings. And all my life I'd held firmly to that belief.

But since life hadn't followed that plan, and Blake's question wasn't really for me, I simply said, "How do you want to change the world?"

"I don't know!" His voice was excited, his eyes wide. He leaned forward, and I saw again a business executive in a boardroom, frantic over the bottom line. "I just want to know if everyone feels this way."

"We all have a purpose," I said calmly, hoping to soften the anxiety I saw before me. His face still held some baby fat, but it also had early marks of stubble, sideburns, and wrinkles of concern. "What do you think your purpose is, Blake?"

"I don't know yet. But I need to decide soon."

"Why?" My tone remained even.

"Because if I don't know soon, then I could be on the wrong path, and I don't want to be. Because that's when I'll make a mistake."

A cynical side of me wanted to laugh at Blake, to tell him it didn't matter what he chose, because life never worked as planned. His worries were silly because there was too much of life he couldn't control. But this embryo of a man didn't need my doubts. From his perspective, his issues were huge.

And he was looking for someone with a compass, so he could secure his path and not get lost. But I did not have that compass.

Still, I wished to say something of use. "You're fifteen, Blake. And you have a lot of goals, a lot of ambition, a lot of focus. Those are all tools you'll need for whatever you decide to pursue."

"I want to become an engineer and build bridges. But I don't know how that changes the world."

"It helps people get places. And it makes you a responsible person, someone who contributes to society."

He pounded his fist on the desk. "So what should my goals be right now?"

"Well," I stifled a laugh. If he wasn't careful he was going to get an ulcer before he was eighteen. "You can talk to Mr. Tate, that's why he's here. He'll help you with your career goals."

Blake gave me a puzzled look. "I don't mean those goals."

I mirrored his look. "Then what do you mean?"

"I want to improve things. I want to make a difference. I want to empower others so they can succeed in their own goals. But I don't know how to do that. And I don't see how building bridges does that."

"Then become a teacher," I said.

He pulled back and gave me a repulsed look.

"I didn't mean to offend you," I laughed. "But you did describe a teacher."

"No. I want to be an engineer."

"Then that's a wonderful career goal."

"But what if that's the wrong career? I don't want to ruin my life. But at the same time, I don't want to spend so much time trying to decide for sure what I want to be that I miss out on my career."

"Blake." Suddenly my tone was low and serious. "You're young!" I clutched my hands together and leaned forward. "It's great that you're trying to figure out your goals, but you don't need to stress about it. You have a lifetime to figure things out."

"But Mrs. Childs," his face tensed up as if my words had stung him, "I don't want to fail."

I leaned back, drew in a breath, then slowly released it. I didn't want to reference his journal, yet I gave in and said, "Is this because of your mom?"

He gave me a lopsided shrug and his face still appeared in pain. "I don't know."

"Blake, I know you want to succeed for her. And that's a beautiful expression of love. But she already loves you, and no matter what you choose, that doesn't change her love for you. She'll always love you."

"I know," he said, unconvinced.

"You keep developing you. Build courage, take risks, step outside your comfort zone, and then be okay that sometimes you don't know exactly where you're headed. But keep working at your goals and you'll succeed."

"Thanks." He sat for a moment. Then he reached for his bag. When he stood up, his forehead was still creased with concern.

I stood also. "I can tell this is deeply troubling you."

He hefted his bag onto his shoulder. "I don't know," he said nonchalantly.

"Well, I wish I could give you some priceless advice."

He stared at me, as if waiting for that advice.

"But I can't," I said. Still his face waited, so I said, "All I can do is give you what I've found to be true in my own life. See, sometimes things don't work out how we want them to. Sometimes no matter what our best efforts, life deals us a different hand than what we expected. Perhaps your mom had a different life than she envisioned for herself, or for you, but she's done an extraordinary job in helping you have ambition and goals. Her greatest goal is to help you succeed, even while she's struggling to find her own place for herself. So the best advice I can give you, from my own experiences . . ." his eyes watched me intently, ". . . is that you're going to fail."

He stepped back. His eyes narrowed and he shook his head.

"I know that's the worst thing you could have a teacher tell you. You're all about A's and achievements and awards. You work hard for your accolades, and you deserve all of them. Most likely you'll be your high school's valedictorian, and you'll get to go to the college of your choice, or you'll get a full ride scholarship to a great school."

"I need to." Fear overtook his voice. "My mom's already told me she can't pay for my education."

"And Blake," I said softly, "I'm confident you'll have those wishes; those desires will work out for you. However, somewhere along the way I hope you challenge yourself at something and you fail."

He shook his head. "I can't fail."

"You need to fail at something." Our eyes locked. I nodded at him until his shoulders slowly started to relax. "You have to get over this fear, and you have to find peace in failure. Because part of success is failing. Because once you fail, the next step is to get back up and keep following your dreams. If you don't fail, you won't ever really be able to push yourself to your greatest success."

He rubbed his lightly-stubbled chin, and with his creased forehead, he again portrayed a future business executive examining the data before him.

"Right now fear of failure is what's motivating you," I said. "But once you've tasted failure, then you can let go of that motivator. You can find a different one, a true motivator, which will be your real quest for success."

His hand still rubbed his chin, and he looked unconvinced. "Like what?"

"Like what you've already mentioned. What's deep in your heart, that passion to help improve the world. To help others."

He bit his lip as if deep in thought, analyzing and inspecting every word I gave him. So I spoke with more force.

"Once you've failed, you can let go of worrying about you, and then you can truly focus on loving others, loving the human race, and helping the world be better. Failure can be a gift."

He stopped biting his lip but then shook his head. "I don't think so."

"Well, I know it sounds like a riddle, that failure can give you a deeper sense of fulfillment in everything you do. But it can. It can give you a glimpse into how fragile and imperfect we all really are. If used correctly, failure really can be a tool."

He looked at a far corner of the room. Then his words were calm and slow. "I might, maybe, understand."

"You don't need all the praise from the world to tell you you're great. And you don't need countless recognitions to validate that you're doing good things in your life. You don't *need* all that, but I have no doubt that praises will still come. Just remember those are byproducts, not the destination."

He looked at me and nodded his head slowly.

"Blake, you're only one person, just a very, very small piece of this grand world, but an important piece, and as you do your part, in whatever role you pick, you're going to make the world a better place. Now, have I given you enough of a lecture?" I grinned at him.

His forehead still wrinkled in thought, and he rubbed his chin again, but his eyes looked at me with determination. "Okay, I think I can do that."

"I know you can. And I know you'll be very successful at it too."

He wrapped his hand into a fist as if he were a fighter. "Okay." Then he grinned, dropped both hands to his side, and the muscles in his face relaxed. "I know what I need to do."

"Good." I smiled.

"Even if I fail," his shoulders dropped, and he smiled more to himself than at me. "I think I'm ready—I'm going to do it. I'm going to ask her out. Thanks, Mrs. Childs." With an eager grin on his face, he quickly turned and strode out of my room.

CHAPTER
Twelve

A GRIN ACCOMPANIED ME AS I APPROACHED MY DESK. I'd misunderstood Blake's great internal struggle. But I'd been right about his overall goals. No matter the career he chose, the mindset he held would steer him toward a quality life.

Then I glanced down to see Kyle's notebook.

For a moment, I debated what to do, until I slowly peeled back the cover, glanced at the first page, and saw this:

Dear Mrs. Childs,

I've tried to write you a journal like you said the assignment was but I can't do it. I've tried. But my dad says I owe you this, the real assignment, not the other I submitted. So I hope a letter will do. It's easier for me to write to somebody, I guess. Otherwise it feels like I'm writing to someone inside my head. And that's weird.

I don't really know what you want me to tell you. But my dad says I'm grounded and that I can't play video games until I make up my assignments. I don't care that I'm grounded. That's happened tons of times before. But not playing video games really sucks. Especially cause I've been sick ever since we got back from Zion's.

I thought maybe it was food poisoning. It happened that night after we got home from our trip. But it also happened right as we were heading over to the police station. My dad tells my mom he thinks I got the crap scared out of me. (You said one of your rules were we couldn't cuss in any of our assignments. Dad said the same thing to me. I hope I can say crap cause that's the truth, so I have to use that word. The other word I can't use.) Monday I felt like crap, and I ended up on the toilet most the night.

Nobody was sending me to school after that. And it just worked out better for me to stay home the rest of the week too. But Thursday morning, Dad called the school and got all my assignments. Plus he said I had to do this one, so I've been busy.

My mom's been trying to tutor me. She sucks at tutoring.

I get pissed with her, and she gets annoyed with me. I usually say something that upsets her, so then she leaves me alone. Which is what I want. If I have to do my homework, I'd rather do it myself. Killer better than having my mom or dad be in my face about it—like they like to be.

My mom is real bad at Math. She says she barely graduated from high school and it was the Math that almost stopped her. Then she didn't go on to college. Neither did my dad. They say they had to get married. That's because my mom was pregnant with me. They didn't want me. It was an accident. So I threw off their plans. They got married and took care of me after that.

So Dad talks about what he missed out on. Mom too. They say they made lots of mistakes when they were first parents with me, and then they laugh about it.

They waited five years to have my brother, then came my other brother, then now a sister. Mom and Dad say they know what they're doing now with them. And they tell me they're sorry they didn't always know what to do with me.

All I know is they talk about how dirt poor we were. And how they didn't even have a car that worked for a full year. They had to take the bus to my dad's work, to the grocery store, and to the doctor's office cause I kept having ear infections. They said I'd cry on the bus and everyone would look at them real pissed. But they'd smile and act like they didn't care. But my mom says that sometimes she did care and sometimes she would cry cause she didn't know how to get me to stop crying. They did have one family that was their friend who took them to church. That family has a daughter my age. Her name is Krysti. They're still friends with my family. And my mom and her mom want us to get married someday. I really don't like it when they say that, especially in front of Krysti.

Also my mom said they had a laundromat in the apartment complex. Which was good, cause I was always spitting up, or throwing up, or pooping tons of crap. So she had a crap load of laundry to do. She says I kept her busy. And she says it was hard being a mom and she was only nineteen. But she did it.

So now my dad wants me not to mess up like they did. He wants me to serve a mission for our church, but I don't want to.

He always says if he'd been getting ready for his mission, like he was supposed to, that he wouldn't have messed up. That if I focus on a mission then things will be better for me too.

But I don't want to go.
This year I've just started telling my dad that I'm not going. He doesn't like it when I say that. He says, "We'll wait and see when you get older." But he also hasn't said it as much anymore, instead now he says, "What's your goal, Kyle? You got to have a goal."

He says it ALL THE TIME!!!

I finally told him, my goal is to get him to stop saying "What's your goal, Kyle."

Then he said if I got a goal, he'd stop saying it.

So if I want my dad to leave me alone—then I have to give him a reason to leave me alone.

So I did think about it. He and my mom hate it when I sleep in my school clothes. My mom hates it when I wear the same socks two or three days in a row. And also when I don't shower.

I don't really care. But if I tell my dad I'll shower at night, brush my teeth, and change my clothes, maybe he'll get off my back a little.

And once I finish this assignment, he says I've earned one hour toward video games. Video games that he's approved.

So Mrs. Childs, I hope this will do for my assignment. That's a little bit about me, my family, and whatever else I was supposed to write about.

Signed,
Kyle

CHAPTER
Thirteen

I SET THE JOURNAL DOWN ON MY DESK.
At least he did the assignment.
And in our Creative Writing class, he hadn't missed much this week, but for English he still had quite a bit more catching up to do.

But for now, I'd celebrate his small steps in the right direction.

However, later that evening, as I curled up on my couch, I thought more about Kyle. It was only 7 p.m. and I seriously considered dozing there, most likely for the entire night.

Since Peter had been gone, there had been four or five nights that I'd fallen asleep on the couch, slept in my work clothes, and ignored my own nightly grooming ritual.

"What's your goal?" I asked out loud, trying to sound like my own father. "You've got to have a goal, Savannah." I laughed at myself while fighting the dregs of fatigue from my emotional week. Eventually, I summoned enough energy and shuffled into the kitchen to find the dinner's dirty dishes awaiting me.

Once those were clean, I thoughtfully looked at the dining room table. *What's your goal, Savannah?* The obvious, my motherhood goal, was out of reach. But there was another goal, one that I'd tucked away due to my own fears. Now echoes of Blake's words hung over me. *I want to make a difference, but I don't want to fail.*

"Me too, Blake." I said out loud, while retrieving my laptop.

It'd been almost a year since I'd opened the file, and I hadn't touched it once since Peter left. All this free time, yet no motivation. Now I pulled up my manuscript, my story of a teacher on a quest to make a difference through teaching others. My aspiration was to write a powerful story, but I knew enough of literature to know my weaknesses—and in this case, the story lacked a plot. It lacked movement. It desperately needed something big to drive the events forward, which is why it'd been abandoned for this last year—plus my own fear of failure and my little thundercloud of self-doubt.

But with the reality of a murder heavy on my mind, I gave the document a quirky grin, then I began skimming, wondering if any of my characters might possess a hidden dark side, one that could bring new life into my decaying pages.

Finally, I reached the end of my 138-page work-in-progress and stared at the screen, still unsure if any of my characters could be driven down such a horrific and violent path.

Then an announcement filled the bottom corner of my screen. Peter was online. My heart skipped a beat, verifying yet again that emotions still ran through it.

Hi! My fingers quickly typed out the word. I hit Submit, held my breath, and eagerly waited for Peter's reply.

I just came on to email you, he wrote.

I smiled. *I've been waiting for your email.*

Yeah. We moved to the city. But the move didn't go as planned.

Typical Peter, so few words. Then of course, with much lost in the realms of military confidentiality, most of my questions spun around the safe topics of his meals and the weather. Truthfully, I never knew what I should ask. *You okay?* I finally typed.

A landmine went off.

Peter! R u OK?

I'm fine. A bit shook up, but I'm fine. Should be asleep, but needed to let you know where I am. And that I'm okay.

I didn't know I'd been holding my breath until I exhaled it. *Others ok?*

Someone lost their hand. That's all.

My heart pumped madly, and I swallowed a large lump in my throat. *Do you know the guy?*

Yeah.

I waited, hoping for him to type more, but nothing came.

You okay? I typed again.

I will be, came his reply.

I waited, staring at the cursor as it blinked at me. It appeared then it disappeared, appeared, then disappeared.

Glad things weren't worse, I typed.

Again I watched the cursor and its consistent blinking. Just like other moments from the past, it seemed this instant messaging would be short, awkward, and quickly coming to an end.

I'm sure you're exhausted, I typed. *Glad you're okay. Get some sleep.* Then I positioned my hand on the top of my laptop while waiting for his status to switch to offline.

I was no longer in the mood to work creatively on my novel. Instead I glanced at the couch and thought about retreating there, another simple curl into the cushions, where I could drift off and forget about our limited chatter. Every time we instant messaged, Peter's lack of words made me feel betrayed all over again.

I revisited my anger that he'd volunteered for this duty. He could have easily not been in harm's way. Instead he chose to be there rather than in our home, and even now, after a deep scare, he had nothing more to say.

The fury boiled in me.

One last time I glanced at the blinking cursor. "Curse you, Peter," I said while my finger reached for the power button. But right then he started typing. Deep from within, a sigh expelled out of me. I waited for what seemed like elongated minutes while Peter kept typing.

Then his reply came. *I don't know if I can sleep. Since this happened, I've been thinking about you a lot.* Then he typed some more. *Sorry about that delay, Sergeant just came by and gave a report on the guy who got injured. They're here now gathering up some of his stuff.*

Do you need to go? I typed back, my fury cooling to a weak simmer. *No. They just left now.*

I bit my lip and shared the truth. *I've been worried about you.*
Thanks. There was a moment I was real worried too.

That little piece of my heart that kept telling me I could still feel—I couldn't hold back what it screamed to let Peter know. *I miss you. A lot.*

I miss you too. Then he typed, *Deeply.* There was a long pause, with neither of us typing. And this time it was okay.

Then Peter wrote. *I don't want to die out here. Especially without you knowing how much I really want you to be happy. I really do, Love.*

I smiled at his words. Then I began typing furiously. *First, don't die out there PERIOD. Second, then why did you leave me?*

No, that's not it.

I bit my lip, and then pounded out the words. *Is it because you didn't know how to deal with me?*

No. Then he began typing again. *I don't think so. I left because I wanted to make something of my life. And right then—for you—your wounds were deep. I couldn't do anything or at least I didn't know what I could do. I couldn't control any of our outcomes. So I went where I was needed.*

Did you? Even through the miles between us, he heard the sarcasm.

I'm not perfect, Savannah. But I did try. And yes, I'm glad I'm here. It's hard, but it's good. For what it's worth I've thought a lot about you, how much I miss you, and how much I want you to be happy. If I can help that, then I want to. But I'm not sure I know how to help you, especially if I can't give you what you really want.

I watched the cursor blink at me, over and over again. *Happiness.* I thought of the last container of ice cream, patiently waiting for me in the freezer, there to help me get through the rest of the evening, after Peter and I said good-bye.

You there? Peter asked.

I drew in a long deep breath. This was a dangerous moment for me. After all this work of conditioning myself, finding a way to manage my emotions through a hard, cold heart, one that seemed incapable of emotion, especially when it came to Peter, now that very heart roared inside, and I hiccupped out a cry.

I laid my fingers on the keys and I typed. *I don't know what will help me. But I want you to be happy too.*

I want both of us to be happy, Peter replied.

Then come home. And please, Peter—let's figure out something for us. I don't know what that something is—but something. We have to do something, and we have to do it together. Not alone.

You know I've tried, Savannah. Everything you've asked of me, I've tried.
Then let's keep trying. Whatever that means.

He sent me a smiling face. Then added, *Yeah. Whatever that means.*
Please!

Ok.

Just come home, safe, with all your fingers and toes, and your charming
nose—all of you—okay. And then together, we'll figure us out. I typed the
words: *Even if us always just means two* but then I deleted those words
before I hit Send.

I never meant to be away forever, he typed back.
Then come home and let's figure us out.

Ok.

Promise?

Yes, Love. It's a deal.

That was the third miracle of the day. A miracle that sent me to
bed, not needing ice cream, or to roll up into a ball on the sofa, but
rather to respectfully glide through my nightly routine, thinking about
Peter, of his promise to come home, and for us to work together
toward something, a something where I could once again place my
hope.

After teeth were brushed, face washed, hair combed, and
pajamas in place, I looked in the mirror and smiled, truly smiled, not
so much at these hopes, which did give me cause to smile, but
especially for my vibrant heart, which was busy announcing to me
that it was still very much alive.

CHAPTER
Fourteen

I WOKE UP SATURDAY MORNING WITH A SMALL CASE OF
lovesickness.

My main symptom involved thinking about Peter—often. Warm
memories soothed me. I wandered through the house in a daze, only
focusing on reflections of us young and deep in love.

But this daze also led me to our guest room, where my thoughts
of our earlier life intermingled now with the struggling hopes of our
future family. This had been deemed our nursery. Yet it had served
more as a storage room than anything else, and each time I stepped
into it I felt the void.

For years, I'd daydream over how I'd prepare this space for our
baby. Now again the disappointments crept into my heart, and I was
flooded with the memories of our efforts and the shattered hopes.

The river of despair beckoned me to approach, but before I
could make that dangerous step, a phone call interrupted me.

It was Principal Truss and his voice brought me back to the
disheartening events of the past week. "Officer Bond says you can
pick up the rest of the journals whenever you want."

"Does that mean he has his answer?" I asked.

A long pause filled the distance. "I think so."

Less than an hour later, I sat at the station.

This time, I sat in the lobby for under five minutes before Officer Bond surfaced. But this time he wasn't alone.

He didn't even glance at me as he held the heavy door open, and I watched Skyler Benson walk out. The two did not exchange words. But Officer Bond kept watching Skyler as he walked through the lobby and out the main door. Not until the main entrance door shut and Skyler was long gone did Officer Bond acknowledge me. "Come on back."

He led me past his office, down the narrow hallway, and into a new smaller room, where I spotted the stack of journals. I headed over to the corner table but I hesitated to pick them up since Officer Bond had stopped and was looking through a large window that looked down into a vacant room.

I glanced at him. "You okay?"

"Yeah." He turned from the window. "Thanks." He stepped toward the journals. "These helped."

"Really?"

He didn't respond. Instead he lifted the eight notebooks and handed them to me. "Here you go."

"So?" Their weight rested in my hands. "Anything you can share?"

His eyes darted back to the large window. "It was Darby's specifically."

I nodded. "I heard she thinks that kid, Skyler, did it."

"Well," Officer Bond pressed his lips together before he responded. "We don't consider him a kid. He'd be tried as an adult if that were the case."

219

I stared at the stack of notebooks between us. Had this man, who was not rich with words, just given me my answer? "Is this looking like a possibility?" I asked.

He shot me a stern glance. Perhaps I'd pushed too far. But then he moved to the window, stood in a military at-ease position, and studied the empty room below. "Darby shared a ritual," he said. "At the start of the school year, a select group, usually cheerleaders, football players, and a few others, focus on some newbies, usually sophomores, and a few ninth graders who are *lucky* enough to be invited."

I held my breath, anxious for what he was about to reveal.

"It's called *Merry Moments*," he continued. "Basically a combo of Spin the Bottle, Seven Minutes of Heaven, and Truth or Dare. The older kids are in a circle, and the newbie spins the bottle. Whoever it lands on takes the newbie into a room for seven minutes, with the older one determining what happens to the newbie."

I folded my arms against my chest. "Any restrictions?"

Officer Bond shook his head. "Not that was shared. Kissing games have been around for centuries. But it's the hazing that's concerning. It's this removal of choice. It's when these newbies aren't brave enough to stop a situation—especially when it should be stopped."

I glanced back at the journals, still heavy in my hands. I drew in a quiet breath and set them down, hoping he'd keep talking. "How bad do things get?"

"Often it's sexual." He watched me and I frowned. I held no prior knowledge of the town's partying teens, so I was relieved when he said, "It's not always though. There are times it's just simple truth or dare. But then other times, it's not. Sometimes it's swearing the newbie to act on the senior's behalf. To do some deed that's meant to be done in secrecy."

My stomach felt queasy. "So a slave for a set time."

"Or for a set task."

For a silent moment, we both watched each other. Then he broke out of his stance and stepped closer toward me.

When I spoke, I heard my voice tremble. "Skyler didn't ask one of them to hurt Stella, did he?"

"No." He shook his head and my shoulders collapsed in relief. "But Darby did end up with Skyler."

CHAPTER
Fifteen

I TRIED TO GATHER MORE FROM OFFICER BOND. BUT WITH all my prodding, I only got short snippets of answers. However, I did learn four alarming things.

First, when Darby went with Skyler, he'd been drunk, high, angry, and depressed over his terminated relationship with Stella.

Second, Darby's sworn task was to learn who Stella's new interest was since Skyler felt keenly aware she liked someone else. Instead, all Darby learned was that Stella was completely over Skyler with no other interests revealed. But other guys were trying.

Third, Skyler began making threats toward Stella and anyone she dated.

Finally, Skyler attacked another football player who asked Stella out. He also hit Stella. Once Coach Forbes heard about it, he kicked Skyler off the team.

Now in the last four hours, Officer Bond had met with Hamilton, Coach Forbes, and then Skyler. Yet with all these unfavorable accounts, there was not enough to arrest Skyler.

As for the connection with my class, Officer Bond had said, "Best I can come up with is Skyler raided Hamilton's locker during football practice. Or he got it from Darby. Or from her sister Lena."

"Why Lena?" I asked.

"Skyler's now dating her."

I was shocked.

But Officer Bond said nothing further about these things.

By Monday's Creative Writing class, I needed to change my focus. I stepped into my classroom, wanting my former innocence to return. I wanted to be around children who I naively believed that as an adult I could protect.

Instead I made eye contact with Abigail. She looked at Dillon, who then scowled at me. I turned to see Darby using her pen to ink a flower onto her arm. I took a step back and scanned the rest of the class. All these students were struggling in their own states of existence, almost as if at war.

I cleared my throat. Then I started into words that I hoped would transform into some profound lecture. Instead I kept getting lost in my own thoughts about these students, as well as Stella.

So I switched gears and spoke about our final project, hoping to drum up former excitement about our participation in the O Street's temporary exhibit. I touched on how we had eight weeks to outline, craft, revise, write and rewrite a creative essay that focused on the theme of family and identity. Then I delved into the schedule and the detailed tasks to ensure each student had a top-notch final project.

Todi circled something on her paper. Tracey smiled at me twice. Blake focused on me the entire time. Anya, whose smile had been missing all last week, finally offered me a genuine smile. But my greatest highlight came from Hamilton's pen, which moved quickly, grabbing notes from everything I said.

In contrast, the rest of the class offered no affirmative eye contact, no engaged smiles, and certainly no hopeful feedback. Instead, Darby used her eyes to hurl daggers of hate. Priscilla examined hair strands and pulled at split ends. Occasionally she'd look at others, with her eyes often pausing on Hamilton, but never at me. Abigail looked at me, but with blankness, showing her mind was elsewhere. Dillon scowled at his desk. And Kyle doodled on a paper.

To pull all the class in, I boldly announced, "Let's do a practice reading, one that will help us prepare for our special reading in May where you'll be sharing your final essay with your family and friends. Here is your short assignment: one paragraph, 300 words or less, describing a family member through the use of a metaphor. I'll give you the rest of class time to work on this and tomorrow we'll share our paragraphs. And Dillon, I'd like you to go first." At the mention of his name, Dillon's eyes shot up. I smiled at him, and he frowned back.

That evening, to break away from my cycling thoughts of the week, I picked up my laptop and for the first time in a very long time, I wrote aggressively. Then I wrote some more.

I wrote until it was the early hours of a new day. This act of creating left me eager, with an energy that outlasted my tired mind and guided me through the day.

On Tuesday, I called Dillon up for his reading of this simple enough assignment, or so I thought.

But Dillon proved me wrong.

When he reached the front of the class, he read, "My father built a house, he moved us all in, and he told us he'd protect us. He promised my sister Lexi he'd protect her from monsters that she swore lived in her closet. And he'd protect Lawrence from the loud thunderstorms, and Rachael from the big spiders that sometimes show up on our porch. And he'd protect Baby Rusty from too many of Lawrence's *love hugs*. I don't remember what he said he'd protect me from, but I know he said he would. He said he'd protect all of us. But he failed to say he'd protect us all from Antoinette, who is like the wrecking ball that hurtled herself at the home my dad built. Dad was supposed to protect our home, but he did not."

When Dillon sat down, I didn't know how to respond. It was clearly not the reading I'd expected, or what any of the other students expected either. Abigail's face was white, yet she swiftly reached out her hand, holding his once he returned to his seat.

Blake was the first to break the silence with a clap, followed by Anya. Then all of us clapped.

Still, it took me a moment to find my voice. Finally, I said, "Thank you, Dillon. That was a strong metaphor." Then I casually added, "And it's always hard to be the first."

He nodded at me, acting as if it was no big deal, but I saw his knee jittering under his desk while the angry tone still covered our room.

I instructed Priscilla to go next.

"I didn't really know what to write." She gave me an apologetic look.

I tried to reassure her. "It's only practice. Just to help you get comfortable reading in front of a group."

She shrugged. "Well, here you go. My short essay is about my sister. She is like a parrot, but she doesn't just repeat what I say, she wants to act like me, look like me, take anything she can to be like me. It's really annoying! But she also is like the favorite family pet. Mom says someday she'll be my best friend. I doubt it. Especially because my parents love her the best, so why does she need anything else from me? Except maybe a cracker!"

She laughed at herself then shot Hamilton a look. When he grinned back, she grinned at the whole class.

Blake was next.

"My mom is like the ocean. Her heart is soft, calm and soothing like rolling waves at low tide. Her courage is strong and powerful like the crashing waves at high tide. She is my defender, my force, my energy that drives me to—" His face flushed. "I don't have the last line," he said.

"It's okay." I led the class into a strong applause. "It's a good metaphor, Blake."

Suddenly the shrill sound of a fire alarm filled the room. I'd been forewarned, but I'd forgotten about the scheduled drill. Now I stood in my trained position, watching my students start to chat, until I told them to quietly file out. Together we moved through the routine while this exercise absorbed the rest of our time.

Once the all-clear was given, only five minutes of class time remained. I excused my students early and they quickly gathered up their bags. Soon all were gone, except Todi.

"Hey," I smiled at her.

"Mrs. Childs, while we were out on the field, I asked Abigail about what Dillon shared."

I was silent, unsure of what to say.

"I get why he's so angry with his dad."

I held my breath for a moment, until I finally said, "I was a little surprised by what he chose to share."

"Well, I've kind of been thinking, and maybe I'm luckier than Dillon."

"With what? Your writing?"

"No. With life. My mom's always had her boyfriends, but I've never had a dad. So if I had two parents who had lived together and then they didn't, I think it'd be worse than if you'd never had that at all."

"Perhaps," I said slowly.

"Do you think Dillon thought his family was forever?"

"I don't know, Todi."

"Well, Dillon's piece made me sad. And I think you should tell him not to read it."

A short chuckle slipped out. "I'm not sure I can do that."

"Sure you can."

"Okay. Why would I do that?"

"Because if he reads that at the reading, it'll make lots of people sad. And the museum exhibit doesn't want that. They want lilacs and daffodils."

I grinned at her phrase. "Lilacs and daffodils, huh?

"Yeah."

"I don't think that's true, Todi."

"Sure they do. People don't want to hear about sad things. They only want to hear happy things. I've been thinking about my memoir. Mrs. Childs, no one will want to read it, because at the end of the year I go back to living in California with Clarissa. Once she gets her checklist from the judge done, I move back home. I used to like hearing that I got to go *home*. But now I hate it. My *home* isn't like Anya's. Or Tracey's home that he talks about in Berkeley, or Blake's home where he's always been able to stay with his mom. My *home* isn't a place, and sometimes it's not even a person."

I looked at her eyes. They were dry. Mine were not.

"Todi," I choked on her name. "I need you to tell me the truth."

Her voice was grave. "Sure."

"The exhibit wants to hear about your experiences. They want you to have a voice, and they want to listen to what you are willing to share with others. But what's more important is what do you feel comfortable sharing with them?"

She pulled back and folded her arms against her chest. For a moment, she looked at the ground and was silent. Then, in time, she looked back at me. "You want me to give it to you straight, Mrs. Childs?"

"Yes."

"The honest to goodness truth?"

"Please."

"Okay." She let out a long, heavy sigh, as if what she was about to say was going to be painful. "Is it okay if I use a metaphor?"

I blinked my few tears away and smiled. "I'd love it if you did."

"Well, when Dillon was reading his piece, right at the end, I looked at you, and you were like a boa constrictor that'd just swallowed a real active mouse."

I drew my head back.

"No, no, Mrs. Childs. Don't get upset. Maybe it's not a good one. I'm still working on this whole metaphor thing. But let me explain before you throw it out."

"Please." I tried to picture how I looked like a boa constrictor.

"See, just like I'm hungry for a *real* family, you're hungry for something too. You might even be starving for it! I think you opened your mouth real big with this project and I think you thought you'd found your dinner—so you wouldn't be starving anymore. But the mouse you ate, it's just too darn active. It's not cooperating like you

228

thought it'd be. So I don't think you're getting your dinner like you thought you were, and if you are getting your dinner, I don't think you're enjoying it, 'cause you have to keep fighting it and all."

"Todi," I stared at her for a very long time. "Why do you think I'm not enjoying this project?"

"Ever since you read our journals you've been different."

I dropped my gaze to the ground.

"You're also different when you talk about our writing now," she said. "And today when I looked at you, I don't think you liked watching Dillon hurt. And he's hurting."

I glanced back at her. "I think all of you are hurting."

"Well," she shrugged her shoulders. "I know the boa constrictor needs to eat. And the mouse is part of the food chain. I guess it's part of the mouse's duty in a way. But I just don't think this project is what you thought it was supposed to be."

I could feel myself turning defensive. "Todi, I want to do this project."

"But you don't want to hurt." Our eyes connected again. "Neither do I," she said.

Slowly, I nodded. "I don't think most people want to hurt."

CHAPTER
Sixteen

TODI'S WORDS STUCK TO ME LIKE COBWEBS. I TRIED TO free myself, tried to not even think about the National Coalition for Families and their invasive project, but the more I tried not to think, the more I did.

On Wednesday, after listening to more metaphor writing from my students, I still replayed Todi's words. With one minute left on the clock, I finally called Dillon over.

"Could you stay after for a bit?" I asked.

He scowled at me but nodded. Then he returned to his desk and whispered something to Abigail right as the end-of-class bell erupted.

Seconds later, the scowl stood in front of me again.

"Thanks for reading yesterday," I said.

He nodded then focused on the bookshelf behind me.

"I know you've been through a lot this year. So I just wanted to check, find out if you're okay with our last project's topic."

He shrugged. "I'm fine."

"Once it's complete, you'll read it to your family at the library reception, so I just want you to feel comfortable with whatever you decide to share."

He shrugged again. "I will."

Then I stepped into dangerous territory. "How are you and Abigail?"

He shot me a look. "I know you know. She told me what was in her journal."

"So do your parents know?"

He stared at me like I'd spoken to him in a foreign language.

"I'll take that as a no," I said.

He looked at the ground. "No. They know."

"Okay," I said. But when he didn't look up, I stepped further into a trespassing zone. "So what's your plan?"

He folded his arms and shook his head like I'd asked him a dumb question. "I don't know." I waited, until he said, "I just don't want to be like my dad."

"I know," I said softly.

There was sorrow in his eyes. "My dad won't regret what he's done, but he tells me that I can't be selfish. He says I have to be *accountable* for how things are. But when I try to ask him about what he's done, he just says I'm too young. That someday, when I have the whole picture, and more experience, and more wisdom, I'll understand. What he's really saying is that he can talk to me about what I do, but I can't talk to him about what he does."

My mind raced for words. I'd initiated this chat, yet I now felt like I stood on ice that was too thin for my liking. It was not my role to bad-mouth a parent. Rather, I wanted to support parents, and trust they were doing the best they could. Yet I also hurt for Dillon.

231

"Okay." My voice was strong. "Then what are *you* going to do? How will you be different? How will you avoid some of your dad's mistakes?"

"I just need to not mess up. And I won't because I love Abigail."

I tried to grin, but I wasn't sure that *love* was enough for what lay ahead.

Still I nodded, trying to accept his perspective. "You're making huge decisions. Tough decisions. And whatever you finally decide, your dad is right. You'll need to be ready to own those decisions."

"Yeah," he said sarcastically, "just like my dad owns his."

I watched pain flash across his eyes, so I pulled the conversation back to his writing. "What you wrote was good, Dillon."

He stared at me.

"You shared a very effective metaphor," I watched the anger in his eyes soften. "You are a talented and smart young man. So here is your next challenge as a writer: know your audience. What you shared for us in class had a powerful effect on your audience. That shows good writing. And for your upcoming final, you'll also have your family as part of your audience. So keep exploring what you want to share with this larger group."

I smiled at him until his deep scowl softened too.

"I'll figure it out," he said.

"Well," I stepped toward the doorway, as if excusing him, "under the circumstances, finding that right balance may be tricky, but I'm here to help you with any part of it, okay?"

"Okay, Mrs. Childs." And he walked out of my room.

CHAPTER

Seventeen

BY THE END OF THE FOLLOWING WEEK, I WAS AT LAST
ready to dive into the final project. I gave a short lecture,
then ran through a review of literary tools we'd discussed
over the past six months. Then I gave the students class time
to begin their project outline.

As I strode back to my desk, I felt pleased. It'd been almost
three weeks since the disruption, but at last we were resuming the
class's structure.

Even Dillon and Todi looked a bit more at ease as they pulled
out their papers.

However, in less than three minutes, the room's acoustics were
just right for me to hear Darby's loud whisper. "Is it true?"

I turned to see her leaning across her desk to speak to Abigail on
her left.

"Is what true?" Abigail asked.

"I heard you're pregnant."

Abigail's face dropped. "Who told you that?"

"Lena was in a bathroom stall at the high school when your sister and her BFF walked in and were talking. Your sister said you're pregnant."

Abigail's eyes were wide, her mouth wider.

"What'd you say?" Todi twisted in her seat to look at Abigail who sat behind her. "Who's pregnant?"

I stood just in time to see Dillon's rigid body, sitting directly behind Abigail, lean forward.

"Abigail is," Darby said matter-of-factly. Then her voice turned questioning, "At least that's what her sister's saying."

Priscilla, who sat behind Darby, leaned forward. "You are?" Her large eyes stared at Abigail.

I stepped toward the front corner of the class, expecting my presence to end the chatter.

Instead the girls didn't even see me. Abigail quietly said, "I just told my family less than a week ago."

"You are?" Priscilla asked, as if making sure she'd heard correctly.

Abigail shook her head. "I didn't expect news to travel so fast."

Anya, who sat on Abigail's left, turned back to look at Dillon. "Are you the dad?"

"We're getting married," Dillon said dryly, his shoulders tight, his lips stiff.

I cleared my throat.

"You are?" Priscilla asked again. This time her wide eyes stared at Dillon.

Other than Blake, who sat in the front row, directly in front of Anya, no one else noticed me.

Abigail turned to face Anya, a nervous smile covering her face. "Yes, on June 2. The Saturday right after school gets out."

With thoughtful eyes, Anya studied Abigail. "Really?"

This time the smile reached Abigail's eyes. "Yes. You're invited to come. I'll make sure you get an invitation."

Suddenly Blake stirred too. He twisted his body around and in a tense whisper said, "You're not even sixteen." He looked diagonally, past Abigail, to ask Dillon, "How are you even going to get a job?"

"I'll be sixteen in December," Dillon said. "I'll get one then."

I moved to the front of the class and folded my arms. Naively, I thought my presence would stop the chatter. Instead the whispers grew louder, almost reaching a full discussion level. And even Kyle, who always sat in the farthest corner and often appeared disengaged, stared at Dillon and Abigail.

"So you're dropping out of school?" Tracey chimed in.

Abigail twisted in her seat to look at him. Then she turned in a full circle to see all eyes watching her. Even mine.

Only Hamilton acted as if he wasn't listening.

"We're transferring," she said calmly. "We weren't planning on announcing this to the school yet." Her tone slipped into a flustered sound. "But we're going to finish up ninth grade, and then after graduation, we're getting married. Next fall we'll start at Horizon."

"What's that?" Tracey asked.

"*Horizon*," Darby said it like it was a dirty word, "is the alternative high school."

"What happens to the baby while you're at school?" Anya asked.

"Our moms said they'll help us, once they work out their work schedules, and the school has a daycare . . . I think."

Blake turned around and looked at me. He shook his head then rolled his eyes at me.

I started to speak, but my voice was cut off by Priscilla's "Are you excited?"

235

Abigail softly grinned. "A little." She turned around to make eye contact with Dillon. "I'm excited to get married." She touched his hand then turned back to face Priscilla. "And . . . for the baby too."

While the majority watched Abigail, I watched Dillon's strained face.

"You don't have to keep the baby," Anya said evenly.

Everybody shifted to look at Anya. Except Hamilton, who kept his pen in hand and his eyes on his paper.

Anya's voice dropped in volume. "I mean, you could give her to another family who wants a baby."

"We want the baby!" Abigail snapped.

The terse tone threw Anya back. "I didn't mean it like that." Anya's voice broke up a bit. "Just someone older, who has a place for the baby."

"We have places," Dillon said coldly.

From across the room, Tracey said, "So you're going to keep living with one of your families?"

"We don't know yet," Dillon said quickly. "We're figuring things out."

With both hands, Abigail touched her stomach. Her voice was weak. "The baby's wanted."

From the corner, Kyle slid up from his slouch. "You sure?"

The entire class whipped around to notice him in the back corner. Even Hamilton tilted his head to look. Then Kyle sunk back, slouching down farther than normal in his chair.

"Were you scared?" Priscilla leaned across her desk, almost touching Abigail. "I mean when you first found out?"

Abigail's hands remained on her flat stomach while she smiled softly. "I thought maybe it was the flu at first. But it wasn't."

"No. It's much worse!" Darby said. "A sickness that'll stay with you for the rest of your life."

I clapped my hands together strongly. Everyone looked at me. Abigail appeared the most surprised, as if I'd thrown her back to another world. "Let's get working on those outlines," I said. "We only have fifteen minutes left of class."

Heads went down, pens went into hands, but as I returned to my desk, I still heard zero writing. Before I sat, I stretched my eyes toward Hamilton's paper to find even his sheet was blank.

I sighed as I slipped into my seat. Then I retrieved my red pen and successfully graded three quizzes from my third period before the whisperings resumed.

Again the acoustics of the room channeled students' voices over to my desk corner. "You love each other, right?" I looked up, knowing the voice well before I saw Priscilla's tilted head staring at Abigail.

Abigail shot Dillon a glance and then smiled. "Of course."

The large grin that fanned across Priscilla's face made even me wish that love truly could make everything right.

"Congratulations," Priscilla said. "I want to come to your wedding, if I'm invited."

"Of course you are," Abigail beamed. "I'll bring you an invitation once they're ready."

I dropped my head back to grading, and offered a silent quick prayer for Abigail and Dillon, only to be interrupted by a harsh whisper. "Do you really want this?" I glanced up. It was Darby speaking to Dillon.

I stood. Dillon kept his eyes down, as if looking at his writing. His pen hovered over the paper as if waiting for words to spill out. When he replied, his tone was masked. "It's the right thing to do."

"It sounds messy."

I stepped toward the front of the class. This time, Dillon glanced over at me and nodded. Next he looked directly at Darby. "We'll be okay."

His pen hit the paper and he began scribbling down words.

I returned to my desk and for the final minutes of class the room remained silent other than pens jotting down text. But there was not enough of this sound for the writing to be universal.

Once I glanced up to specifically see Abigail's pen abandoned on her desk. She just stared at it. My heart, which had grown stronger and louder as of late, wished to pull her into a hug. Instead I tried to focus even more intently on my grading.

When the bell rang, I stood to make eye contact with my departing students.

Tracey was the first to exit. But no one else followed. Even Kyle was slow to shuffle items into his bag.

When Abigail stood, Dillon followed. But then Darby reached out and grabbed Abigail's arm. "You know there are other choices, easier ones."

Abigail stepped away from Darby's touch. "I don't like those options."

"Well, you don't have to go through with this." Darby cocked her head back like she was offended. "You do have choices."

Dillon placed his hand on Abigail's shoulder and nudged her down the aisle. When he was directly across from Darby, he paused. "Mind your own business, Darby."

"I am." She put her hands on her hips and leaned toward Dillon. "My business is I care about your *fiancée*." Her last word came out hot and hostile.

He leaned forward until his face was inches away from hers "Shut it!"

Darby leaned in even closer. "Make me."

For the first time in my career, I feared a boy/girl fight was about to erupt in my classroom. With fearful eyes, the remaining students all stood watching Dillon, Darby, and Abigail.

Finally Abigail tugged on Dillon's arm. "Come on. She means well."

With her arms crossed, Todi took a step toward Darby. "You need to leave them alone."

Hate spread across Darby's face. Blake's eyes darted from Todi to Darby. Quickly, he said, "Todi, she's trying to help them! She just says it'll be a lot of work, because it will."

Tears had formed in Abigail's eyes and she swiped them with her palm. The other hand interlaced with Dillon's. "Let's go."

When they walked out Darby, Blake, Todi, Anya, and even Kyle watched them leave. Meanwhile Hamilton still stared at his blank paper.

CHAPTER
Eighteen

S OON AFTER ABIGAIL AND DILLON LEFT, KYLE USED THE opposite door to slide out. Darby followed. Blake and Todi shot me a look before exiting the main door together. Then Hamilton slowly loaded up his bag and headed out the same door as Kyle and Darby.

Only Anya remained.

She met me at my desk while I sorted through the ungraded third period quizzes. When I glanced up at her, her eyes were soft. "I didn't mean to upset them," she said.

"Who? Abigail and Dillon?" I played dumb, even though lingering tension still hung over my classroom.

"Yes, I think I did. At least Abigail."

Something held me back. As much as I didn't want to admit it, I felt a stab of envy. Envy that a fifteen-year-old would be experiencing something I'd never yet known. How was life fair? "I don't know if *you* specifically did," I said. "It's a very tender time for them. I'm sure right now many things are difficult for them."

She drew her long golden braid from behind, and let her hands glide up and down it. Meanwhile her eyes watched me. "I don't want to hurt her. I just want her to think about things."

I set my red pen down. "It sounds like this is really bothering you." I hoped my own *bothered* feelings stayed masked in my reserved tone.

She kept stroking her braid. "You know I'm adopted, right?"

"No," I said, surprised. Yet my mind reflected back to nine years ago, when I'd first come to the school. Had I known this? "From Russia?" I asked.

Another teacher had briefly described the principal, or one of the assistant principals, having a child that was born in Russia. When I first heard this, Anya would've been five, almost a decade before she'd become one of my own students. Now I shrugged. "I guess I didn't remember that."

"When you came to my house a few weeks ago, I thought you knew why my mom was upset."

I leaned back in my chair. "No. I didn't."

She looked at my face, as if studying it for more details.

"I still don't," I added.

"I don't know my birth mother, but I love her." Her hand gripped her braid. "That's what my mom read in my journal. How I wish I could meet my birth mother and tell her that . . . that I love her." She dropped the braid and folded her arms. "What my mom didn't understand was why I love my birth mom."

I studied Anya like I never had before. The soft coloring of her skin, the high cheekbones, the strong nose and lips. She was one of the shortest girls in the ninth grade, yet despite her height, I could see the marks of a girl on the brink of beautiful womanhood. Perhaps her features weren't exactly like Principal Truss or his wife, but she didn't look vastly different either.

"I'm sure it was the hardest decision she ever had to make," Anya said. "Sometimes I think a lot about her and that decision."

Knowing now that Anya was adopted, my imagination began envisioning a girl, close to Anya's age, but a little older, a little taller, with a swollen belly and scared eyes, placing an infant Anya in the care of the government—a choice that would lead Anya into a completely different world.

Such thoughts rubbed at the rawness in my heart. Quickly, I tried to sweep away my creation of Anya's birth mom. There were many reasons why children in Russia were placed in orphanages. Instead I managed to say, "It's beautiful you can say that. That you love her."

"Because she did the very most important thing that could've been done for me."

"Hopefully your *mom* can understand that," I said softly, emphasizing the woman who now carried that important title.

She bit her lip and then nodded. It took her a moment, but then she said, "I can't imagine my life any other way. Yet it all came down to her choice. Had she made a different choice, who knows where I'd be? Most likely not here."

I nodded, because her words had touched the tenderest spot in my heart, a place where I truly hurt. I glanced down at the papers on my desk then I reached for my bag. I wanted to look at Anya, I needed to look at her, but if I did, I knew I'd break. Instead, I shoved the papers into a folder and tucked them into my bag. "I don't think you offended Abigail. No more than the rest of the class."

"I did if Abigail's making the wrong choice."

She hoisted her backpack onto her shoulder and headed toward the exit, but before she reached the door, I gave in.

"Anya." She turned, and I said, "You're right. In your case, your biological mother made the right choice."

Her smile, which I'd always seen as simple, innocent, and naive, now flashed across her face and warmed the lingering cold section of my heart.

"Yes," Anya said, "she did."

CHAPTER
Nineteen

THE FOLLOWING DAY I WAS DISAPPOINTED TO SEE Abigail and Dillon's chairs empty, but I wasn't surprised either. What did surprise me was the class eruption.

First, I led my creative writing students into a great discussion on symbolism. I spoke of beginnings. I used the sun's constant setting and rising anew as a symbol of a fresh start. I spoke of a caterpillar entering a cocoon and emerging as a butterfly to be symbolic of a beautiful new beginning. Then I spoke of the initial stages of life: an egg, a seed, a baby. With each new life, there is a new beginning and new hope.

Priscilla raised her hand and said, "So is Abigail and Dillon's baby symbolic of the new life they're starting together?"

The tangential reference threw me off my literary flow. Before I responded, Darby jumped in, "Maybe she shouldn't even have the baby!" All eyes turned to look at her. "Well, nobody even wants to talk about that."

"I think that'd be an awful tragedy," Anya swiftly said.

"Girls," I spoke in haste, determined to stop a continuation of yesterday's mutiny. "This is a personal decision between Abigail and Dillon."

Yet words continued to fly. "I think neither of them have any idea what they're signing up for," Blake spoke with authority.

"There's no way I'd want to be a dad right now," Kyle offered.

Darby gave him a look of disdain. "Or a husband, at that."

Kyle shrank down into his chair. "Yeah," he whispered.

I had to stop this discussion. Yesterday was bad enough, but today without Abigail and Dillon's presence it felt voyeuristic.

In the context of literature we could defend and debate fictional lives, but not this—not the real lives of fellow classmates. I cleared my throat, determined to put an end to this wrong, when the sudden words of Todi shook my core.

"Mrs. Childs could take their baby. She could adopt it."

Anya whipped around to look at me. "Yes, you could."

"No!" The statement came from Kyle, his voice surprisingly strong. "It's their child."

"Well," Tracey looked at me, "would you want their baby?"

The entire class watched me.

"Do you even want a *baby*?" Darby added.

"Stop!" Hamilton said. "I don't think this is any of our business. It's their life."

His voice of reason had rescued me. I kept my tone guarded, quick and even. "Yes. Hamilton's right."

Todi had a large grin on her face. "But it'd solve everything."

"Sounds like a big mess to me," Blake inserted.

"Well, they already created that *mess* by getting pregnant," Darby said.

"This is not a topic we have any right to discuss." My angry tone surprised me. "Dillon and Abigail made a mistake, but all of us make mistakes."

"Except Anya," Darby said sarcastically.

"Enough Darby," I commanded. "We *all* make mistakes. This is one that sadly has long-term challenges."

"You don't know the baby was a mistake," Kyle said strongly.

"Of course it was," Blake added.

"I'm not talking about the actual baby." My voice was rising. "I'm talking about Dillon and Abigail's lives right now! They're still too young to be making some of these decisions they have to make!"

"Maybe they'll do better at it then some adults do," Hamilton offered.

Priscilla looked at Hamilton and then nodded. "Maybe they will."

"I think they're stupid," Darby said.

"Well," I put my hands on my hips and glared at her, "please keep that opinion to yourself."

"I think they need to think about what they're doing," Blake said firmly.

I spun around to face Blake. "They are." My words spit out. "They're going through the steps that they need to go through right now; they're doing what is best for them and their own circumstances. They're facing things that none of us understand. What we *can* do is let them know we aren't here to judge them, because none of you really know what you'd do if you were in their situation."

"There are things they could have done to prevent their situation," Tracey said dryly.

"Well, they can only live in hindsight for so long," I responded. "They're now in a situation which requires great sacrifices, difficult decisions, and tough consequences. No matter what step they take it's going to require facing some heartaches, working through challenges, and then going forward confidently with whatever choices they make." Now that words were coming, I couldn't seem to stop myself. "What they don't need is to know we, as a class, have talked about this two days in a row. So please pull out your outlines. In fact this seems timely. Let's have you start writing about *your* family and how it's shaped *your* identity. What makes it strong, and good, and right for you?"

The transition had come in desperation, but I walked back to my desk feeling satisfied. It was time for them to take these last months and begin shaping their ideas. Time to use their learned tools. Time to get past the journal episode, and the secrets it had exposed, and write!

CHAPTER
Twenty

THE CLASS PERIOD FLEW BY IN SILENCE. AFTER THE BELL rang, students quietly filed out, except for Todi, who approached me.

"Mrs. Childs?"

I set down all the first drafts I'd collected from the class. "Yes, Todi."

"I'm sorry if I upset you by saying you should take the baby."

"I'm okay."

"It's just that you know how I feel, and I couldn't be a mom right now."

I saw the freckles scattered across her nose and the energy bouncing within her. It was true. At this moment in her life, I couldn't imagine Todi as a mother.

"I've lived on my own for a short while," she said, "and it was tough."

"Todi." I gave her a sympathetic look. "I'm sure that was quite tough!"

"Tough enough that it brought me back into foster care. I couldn't be on my own and have a baby too."

"I understand," I said softly. "But she won't be alone."

"Dillon's not going to stay with her. Maybe he will for a little while, but not always."

"Todi," I whispered, "we don't know that."

"Clarissa wasn't ready for me when I came. And back then she had more smarts than she has now. Most definitely, she had more smarts than Abigail has right now."

Her earnest eyes and her tender words tugged at my heart. "It's not our place to decide her path," I said.

"But it's a mistake."

"But we can't decide that for her."

"But you can fix this for her."

"Todi. I can't."

"You want a baby. But you can't have one."

No. I can't have one. The words echoed in my ears.

"Abigail shouldn't be having a baby," Todi continued, "but she is. So help her out."

I shook my head and looked at the door. This conversation had crossed a line, making me quite uncomfortable. "I can't imagine what Abigail's facing right now."

"Well, she thinks Dillon is going to find her a white horse and the two of them are going to ride off into the sunset. She's ridiculous silly. And I like her. I like her a lot. And I don't want to see her end up like my mom. Or the baby to end up like me."

"Todi! You are a beautiful young woman!"

"I'm not, Mrs. Childs. And you could prevent this baby from becoming me."

"Why do you say that?"

"'Cause my mom's told me."

"That's wrong!"

"It's what she's said," she whispered.

"Todi, does your mom always speak the truth? If she does, then she's told you you've had a hard life at your young age. But you have a strong soul! And yes, other people's choices have made things tough, but you have your whole life ahead of you!"

She shrugged off my words as if she hadn't heard them. "Then it all comes down to the baby, doesn't it? What's going to be the best life for it?"

I laughed, which softened my intense emotion. "You sound like Anya."

"And how can you argue with Anya?" Todi gave me a soft grin. Then she hoisted her pack over her shoulder and headed toward the door. Briefly, she turned to say, "I can see you as a mom, Mrs. Childs. And if I was a baby, I'd want you to be my mom."

That evening I stood in my guest room, scanning the layout as I had so many times. I knew where the crib would be, the changing table, the wall décor. In my mind, everything was there, and it was perfect, minus that one critical piece.

Then I felt it. That deep fear inside me that despite all my wishing this room would never actually transform.

And I thought of Peter.

I'd always blamed him for holding us back, because it'd always been my suffocating biological need which had forced us to face the hurdles time and time again. Each time, I was the one who got Peter ready for what was next, only to see our wishes and efforts dashed time and time again. Yes, it felt like we'd tried everything, which made each *new* defeat even more exasperating.

But now what?

What was that next something which was right for our marriage?

CHAPTER
Twenty-One

S UNDAY EVENING, AFTER FALLING ASLEEP ON THE SOFA, I slipped into a nightmare. I stood facing Abigail and immediately I knew we were fighting over an infant.

"You thief!"

"Imbecile!"

"Liar!"

"Fraud!"

Then the name-calling escalated into verbal threats.

"I'll kill you."

"Not if I kill you first!"

She stepped toward me, infant still in her arms. I touched the baby's hand, only to growl at Abigail like a mad woman.

Until King Solomon stepped in. He drew the infant out of Abigail's arms, produced a large cleaver, and without asking either of us about love, he drew the blade up.

We both screamed. Horrific screams coming deep from within my heart. Screams which awoke me and made it impossible to fall back asleep.

My face felt wet with tears, yet I felt dirty, ugly, and ashamed, like I was responsible for my own nightmare. I considered showering, as if water could wash the dream's residue from my mind. Instead, I crumpled into my bed and hugged my knees. I stared at the other side, the vacant side, and missed Peter deeply.

I regretted the words my students had shared about Abigail and her baby. It was her child. And Priscilla was right, life could be good for Abigail. She got to play house earlier than the rest of the girls. Yes, she'd have to grow up faster than the rest of them, but she'd be okay. She'd survive. If this was what she chose, she'd survive.

And if she chose another path for her baby, it'd be her choice, hers and Dillon's choice alone. Not ignorant opinions, a class vote, or group persuasion.

My body shuddered into the bed. No longer could I think about her or her baby.

Yet my traitor mind still wandered off and I slipped into envy's scorching heat, a danger which could smother me.

To face such intense envy, I allowed myself to cry and while the tears plummeted, I assigned them to heartaches. First, I cried for me, I cried for Peter, I cried for us. I cried for a life we should have had, but we did not. Then I cried for every expecting parent who didn't want their child, at least not at first. I cried for every child who went to a place they weren't wanted, or to a home that didn't surround them with love. Next I cried for all ungrateful arms which held a child, arms that didn't know the literal ache of those wishing to hold a child. I cried for all the human race, for every child that came into the world and none of them, not a single one, was mine to love. Finally amid such tears, I laughed. I laughed long and deep and intensely, laughed myself into hysteria at how unfair life could be.

The next morning, I went straight for the tea bags, entreating them to soothe my puffy eyes. Then I showered, dressed, and ate a sensible breakfast of hard-boiled eggs, toast, and half a grapefruit. I brushed my hair, applied some lip gloss, and gathered up my belongings. One last glance at the mirror and I was done grieving. It was time to move on. It was time to face the life I'd been given.

---CHAPTER---

Twenty-Two

THE FOLLOWING WEEK I SPOTTED THE NOTE GOING back and forth. Priscilla started it and Darby responded, then back to Priscilla and again over to Darby.

Meanwhile the rest of the students were working on rewriting their first drafts so I didn't feel generous toward these girls squandering away this important time. I kept my eye on the note and approached them from behind. Darby had just jotted down her last correspondence and folded it up, slipping it low, extending it toward Priscilla's outstretched hand. "I'll take that," I said.

Priscilla's eyes doubled in size and her mouth froze open while I held my stern look. Darby huffed out a grunt and handed me the note. Then she picked up her pen, as if the consequences meant little to her, and started to write.

Once I reached my desk, Priscilla still watched me. I stared back, so quickly she grabbed her pen and looked at her assignment.

Then I unfolded the note and read.

Darby – Could you still help me get Hamilton to notice me?
I'd really like it if you could!

What did you have in mind?

Well, what did you have in mind? Did you forget?

No Priscilla—I haven't forgot. I've been grounded.

Oh! What happened?

**This damn class. And that stupid journal assignment. My
mom read it and I got in some trouble. Both me and my
sister. It's been over a month! But on Friday I'm no longer
grounded.**

Just in time for Spring Break—COOL! But that stinks about
being grounded.

**Yeah! It sucked. I hate this class and Mrs. Childs. It's her
fault!**

I don't think she meant it to happen.

**I don't care. I still hate her—but soon I can do what I want
again.**

Good.

Yeah!

So do you think you can help me?

With Ham—Sure.

Cool!

There's a Spring Break party on Friday. My sister's still grounded, but my mom's working and my dad doesn't care so I'm sure she'll take us. Want to go?

For sure! Will Hamilton be there?

I'll invite him too.

That would be TOTALLY COOL!

There will be a game, and I'll make sure you get to play. I'll ask my sister, maybe she'll get you paired up with Hamilton. Then you and him will have time alone to do whatever you want.

Like ... him kissing me?

It's possible.

That would be TOTALLY RAD!!!!!!!!!!!

Yeah. No matter what – you'll have fun! Want to stay the night at my house?

I set the note down and then looked at these girls. Priscilla was writing. Darby was not. She glanced over at me and our eyes met. A sad smile crossed my face. Quickly she looked away.

I had eight minutes to figure out my next move. The note, like the journals, placed me in a position that weighed me down with accountability, like I had some type of ownership or responsibility over these students' behaviors.

There was an option to brush off my concerns and allow these children to experience life without my interference. But then I thought of Stella.

My next option was to speak to them. But one's warning would be different than the other's. So right before the bell, I positioned myself near Darby, her eyes well aware I was there. I used a strong tone. "Darby, I'd like you to stay after."

She huffed out her consent.

Then the bell rang, leaving her to watch the rest of the class file out.

As Priscilla shuffled toward the exit, she kept turning back to look at Darby. Meanwhile Darby stuck her chest out a little more than normal and cocked her head as if preparing for combat. At last at the door, Priscilla mouthed the word *sorry* then darted from the room.

With no one else left, I waited for Darby to look at me, but she did not. Finally I said, "Who are you angry with?"

She whipped her head around and stared at me with her hot eyes. "What?"

"Are you angry at me, your dad, your mom, or your sister?" I folded my hands across my chest, stood diagonal from her desk, and looked down at her. She stared back.

"What are you talking about?" She hissed out the words.

"The note says you hate me. I'm sorry you feel that way."

She dropped her gaze down to study her black leather boots that were kicked out in front of her. She rotated her right heel and stared at it, while silence wedged more tension between us.

Still I waited stubbornly, not feeling a need to say anything yet.

At last she stopped rotating her heels. She set her feet firmly on the ground and looked up, her eyes shifting to the note still in my hand. Then she looked at me. "So are you going to tell my mom what I wrote?"

"I'm going to give the note to Principal Truss and let him decide what he feels should be shared with your parents."

Her shoulders dropped and her mouth turned into a severe pout. "Everything I write in this class gets me in trouble."

I tapped the note. "This was not an assignment."

"I hate your class!"

"I know. You said that in your note."

"Well, *it* wasn't for you."

"Why are you in this class?" The question came out sharper than I'd intended. "I want you in this class, Darby. I just don't think you want to be here."

"I don't!" She stood up. We now were at eye level.

"Yet here you are. So what are we going to do?"

"I want to become a doctor." She tilted her head back. "And so for all the schooling I have to do, I heard I need to learn how to write. I thought your class would teach me that. But right away, it was totally obvious it wouldn't! Instead it's just been. . ." She pressed her lips together and shook her head. Then she glanced down at her boots. She looked at them for a while, then leaned back on her left heel, letting the toe point toward the ceiling. "This class has been a waste."

"Okay. Tell me how?"

"All you talk about is the *craft*. Or *families*. Or how writing is supposed to magically make our lives better, which it's not. When I write for this class, it makes life worse!"

THE OTHER SIDE OF
Quiet

I took my time responding. "I'm sorry you feel that way, Darby."

"Yeah." She folded her arms. "Me too!"

"Lots of things I'd planned didn't work out like I'd hoped. Certainly I didn't mean for your own writing to cause issues for you. I know I wouldn't like my private journals read by others either." That sentence caused Darby to drop her heel to the ground and her arms fell to her side.

So I kept speaking. "Lots of things in life aren't always what we think they'll be. Dreams aren't always realized. Some hopes aren't achieved. But it's vital we have those ambitions to work toward. I love hearing that you plan to be a doctor. That's extremely admirable, Darby. But how are your choices helping you work toward that goal?"

"I just told you." Her voice was slightly softer than before. "I took this class to learn how to write."

"Okay." I steered the conversation away from my class. "What about your other choices?"

"What?" Her angry tone was back. "I'm getting good grades in most of my classes."

I held out the note again. "What about these parties?"

She focused on my eyes as if playing a staring game. Her deep brown eyes looked intent on winning. But it was too late. I'd already seen a softer side to this girl.

"Something has to change," I said. "Otherwise you're on a path where you could lose control, a path that may be incredibly difficult to regain perspective of who you are. If things don't change, Darby, it's likely your journey of fun will shift into a muddy road. Do you really want to be a doctor?"

"Yes." Her voice was firm, but she'd abandoned the staring game. Instead, she now glanced at the classroom walls.

259

"Well then, you may want to start looking for the first opportunity to make a U-turn. As soon as you can, find the path that's going to offer you better options in becoming the person you want to be."

She stared at the floor, then twisted her head to another corner of the room, clearly intent on avoiding my eyes.

More of my lecture rested on my lips, but instead I let the silence speak. Eventually she glanced at me, and her eyes had softened.

"If you want to change," I continued, "if you really want to have a good life, get away from the bad environment. Stop hanging around people who aren't good influences, friends who aren't helping you become a better person."

"They're not *my* friends!" she said harshly. "They're my sister's."

"Really?" I asked softly.

"And my sister Lena is more invested in my happiness than my mother and father combined. She's the one who's there for me. She's who's taking care of me. It's been that way all my life."

"Is she still dating Skyler?"

I caught the shock in her eyes, then quickly she filled them with anger. "Maybe."

"Does that worry you?"

"She's wanted to be with Skyler for a long time."

"But," I was treading down a dangerous path, "do you have some concerns about Skyler?"

"No," she said quickly. "There were things I didn't know, but Lena set me straight. And she told me not to talk about it again. And definitely not with you! Besides, she told me I was wrong."

Her statement left me unsure of what to think, let alone what to say.

But Darby quickly filled the silence. "Don't judge my sister, Mrs. Childs! My dad sleeps in most the day, and my mom gets up early for work, and it's always been my sister who's been there helping me to get ready for school. She helps me know what to do, and how to do things, and how to handle every situation. And she's the only one who does! So I don't buy what you said! I don't care if you think she's a bad influence. I know I can count on her. I can trust her. She'd give me anything! So I'm sticking with her. She's got a plan! And she's the one who will keep me safe!"

I glanced down at the note while I sorted through my words. Early in my career, I'd promised myself I'd never tell a student their parent was bad. My role as a teacher was never to diminish the work a parent had done. Now I questioned whether I needed to extend that promise out to siblings, to other role models: good or bad.

Then I studied the beautiful girl in front of me. For the first time, rather than the confident, cocky girl that many at school saw, I clearly caught a glimpse of a young, insecure girl who idolized and walked in the shadows of her big sister.

And I felt an urgency to forewarn Darby against the danger I saw.

So I spoke boldly, "Then ask Lena, in her plan, to include the gift of your freedom. Ask her to let you find your own identity." She shot me a look of hate, so I softened my tone. "You need her, but she may need you too. You might be the person who benefits your sister's life right now."

Darby leaned back on the tips of her heels and looked at the ceiling. She pressed her lips together, and then slowly lowered her feet to the ground. When she finally spoke she didn't look at me. "It's not like that, Mrs. Childs. Lena knows what she's doing. She's got a

261

plan."

"A *plan?*" I asked cautiously. "What does that mean?"

She hoisted her bag onto her shoulder and avoided my eyes, letting me know I'd said too much. She tossed her head back and stuck her chest out once again. But as she headed toward the door, I saw her wipe her nose with the back of her hand and I heard the short sniffle. "She knows what she's doing," Darby repeated. Then, a bit softer, she said, "See you tomorrow, Mrs. Childs."

CHAPTER
Twenty-Three

PRINCIPAL TRUSS'S OFFICE DOOR WAS OPEN, AND WHEN he spotted me, he beckoned me in.

"How are you?" His words were solemn and kind.

"Still hanging in there," I said, as if everything referenced my students' journals.

He gave me a soft, compassionate smile.

Then I extended the note. "I picked this up today, and I'm not sure how to handle things." I waited for him to unfold it. "It's between Priscilla Putnam and Darby Johnson." While he scanned the note, I said, "I'm wondering if it's the *Merry Moments* game. Have you heard about it?"

He set the note down on the far corner of his desk. "I'm friends with Priscilla's mom. I'll mention this to her."

I nodded. He made it sound so simple. "Thanks." I turned toward the door, then paused over thoughts about Darby.

But before I could decide what to share, he called me back. "Don't leave yet." He motioned at a chair.

I sat while he shut his office door.

Then he slipped back into his chair and said, "I have an update for you."

Immediately, I thought of Officer Bond, of Skyler, and of a possible confession. "Is it about Stella's case?"

With a somber face, he shook his head. "No." He folded his arms and looked at his desk. "I got a message to call Abigail's mom today. Last week I'd contacted her to see if she had any questions, anything I could help with. But she wasn't ready to discuss those details yet, so I figured that's why she was calling now." He shook his head and rubbed his chin, while his eyes still studied his desk. "I'm sure you noticed Abigail wasn't in class?"

"Neither was Dillon."

"You won't see her for a little while." He glanced up at me.

"Oh dear!" Based off the look on his face, I shared my fear. "Have they run off together?"

"No," he said. But his voice seemed distant. "Last night she had severe cramps, then bleeding. When they arrived at the doctor's, it was confirmed there was no longer a heartbeat, then she was given medicine to complete the process."

"She miscarried?"

He nodded.

And silence filled the room.

Finally he said, "My wife couldn't get pregnant. Then once we thought we'd fixed the issue, she never could keep a pregnancy. I know it's difficult for a woman who wants a child, but surely it's different for Abigail, with an unplanned pregnancy."

"You would think," I said.

"She has to feel relieved."

I pressed my lips together and nodded.

"It gives them another chance to put their lives back on course," he said.

Surely Abigail and Dillon had to see this as good news. But I couldn't help wondering if, for a season, some *what ifs* lingered around their lives. Or even, just pangs of guilt around the relief they must feel.

"You okay?" He looked directly at me.

A bit too anxiously, I nodded again.

He drew in a loud breath and his shoulders dropped with the exhale. "My wife's recently been re-living her miscarriages. She's again dwelling on her own condition. More than she has in a long time. You think you're over things, and then they resurface."

I looked at his desk, suddenly feeling unsure whether I wanted to hear about the Truss's private life.

"As the husband," he continued, "watching the woman you love torture herself through all this makes you feel quite helpless."

I looked at him and he nodded. He'd seen the hints of tears in my eyes, which meant I'd answered his earlier question. Like his wife, I wasn't sure if I'd ever be completely okay with my inability. It was a loss, like a death, a shattered dream based on expectations of being able to carry a child. My choice rested in how I faced this, but it would always be a deep loss.

"With Abigail," I said, aiming to change the subject, "what do you think she needs?"

He spoke calmly. "She'll most likely be out the rest of the week."

"Okay." I stood and approached the door.

"Her mother says your class knows about the pregnancy."

I spun around. "Yes. My creative writing students know."

Principal Truss gave me a short nod. "She wants you to tell them about the miscarriage. She wants all this cleared up before Abigail returns."

I felt my shoulders collapse. Suddenly the news felt heavier than it should.

"You okay?" he asked again.

"Yeah." I nodded then turned back toward the door.

"Savannah." His voice caused me to turn back. "Thanks for all you do." He offered a kind smile. "The students are fortunate to have you."

CHAPTER
Twenty-Four

THE OLD BLANKET OF SORROW WAS BACK. I stroked the memories of my own miscarriage while I recalled the detailed path of in-vitro. Peter and I had endured shots and medicine, we'd invested all our savings, and more importantly all our hope, into this procedure, only to have the grand return be disappointment. Such immense joy, followed by such sadness.

But this was entirely different!

Clearly, I had no idea what a fifteen-year-old must feel after an unexpected pregnancy ends in miscarriage.

Still, it was now my responsibility to share the news with my sixth period. "Class." My voice was more timid than I'd have liked. And I sensed the surfacing of my deep, unwanted emotion. "I was asked to share some information about Abigail and Dillon and why they were absent yesterday and today." The class glanced around at their empty chairs. "The night before last, she miscarried."

Then all eyes shot up at me, even Hamilton's, who rarely had in days.

"What?" Todi demanded.

Anya was next. "Really?"

"How sad," Priscilla said.

Tracey whipped around to eye Priscilla, his tall body leaning toward her. "No. That's good."

"Is it?" Anya looked at me.

"Of course it is," Darby said. Then quickly she added, "I mean, if it was me," her tone turning considerably softer, "I'd be glad."

"Well, it's hard to know exactly how they must feel right now." I matched Darby's soft tone. "I'm sure there are a lot of positives here, with this change, but at the same time there might be some sadness too."

"Are Abigail and Dillon still getting married?" Priscilla asked.

"I don't know," I said. "But I wouldn't think so."

"Oh." She looked down at her desk.

I scanned my students' faces. Half now looked down at their desks. They, like me, knew there was nothing more to say. The news had been shared, and no matter the feelings, it was time to move on. However, other students looked at me with wide eyes. Especially Kyle—despite the bangs that covered half his face, he stared at me as if I'd just told him his grandmother had passed away.

Meanwhile Blake, in his starched button-up shirt, spoke in a studious tone, like an expert telling all of us that this was the best outcome. But Anya and Todi glanced at each other as if they did not agree with Blake. Then they glanced at me with a clear sadness.

But I looked past them to meet Darby's eyes. Her extreme anger from yesterday was gone. "Will they be okay?" she asked quietly.

268

Such a simple question, but coming from her, that's when I felt the emotion trapped in my throat. I nodded my head, strong and affirmative. They would. They were young, they were tough, and once again they were free. I nodded again then whipped around to the dry erase board and wrote *Identity*.

For the next twenty minutes I lectured, letting my words take over, letting my focus on the upcoming big project control the class time. A two-to-three page paper was due the following Wednesday after Spring Break. I wanted them to write about themselves and their interactions with their family over this next week, and to share how their family dynamics helped in shaping their identity.

Then I boldly said, "If you like, you can treat this assignment like a journal entry—but I *will* be reading this entry."

Each student looked at me. I held back any additional words about the journals. Instead, I moved on to further review literary elements we'd discussed throughout the year.

After class was over, I felt a sigh of relief pass through me. I'd kept at bay the unconquerable emotion that still haunted me.

As all the students filed out, I smiled at them. Except for Todi, because she remained in her seat.

When our eyes met and I saw her downtrodden face, I thought about the beginning of the year, when I'd broken down in front of her. I couldn't do that again. I drew in a strong breath and spoke boldly. "How are you, Todi?"

"Anya and I thought you were going to take the baby."

The memory of my King Solomon dream resurfaced and my bruised heart pumped through a few beats. "No, Todi. In the end, the right thing has happened."

"You sure?" she asked.

"Yes!"

"Okay." She shrugged, stood, and slipped one of her arms through a backpack strap. After taking two steps, she said, "Then I'll be happy for them." She took a few more steps, then paused and looked down at her Converses.

"How are things in your life, Todi?"

"Fine." Suddenly she kicked at an imaginary something, then her leg kept swinging back and forth, swaying like a pendulum.

"You sure?"

"Yeah." She dropped her foot to the ground then let the other leg swing like a pendulum.

"You practicing for something?" I asked.

"No." She stopped the swinging and planted both feet on the ground. Then she shoved her hands in her jean pockets and her torso began to sway. "Just found out Clarissa's ready for me to come live with her again."

"Oh." My heart pumped through a new pain.

Todi looked up at me and shrugged. "I'm supposed to be happy, I think."

"When are you going back?" My voice sounded tense.

"She wants me to come home." Todi stared at her feet and kept swaying. "Soon."

"No!" The word flew out before I could catch it. Todi looked up. "You can't."

She stopped moving and watched me. Finally she said, "I know. I want to finish school here. Actually, I want to live here." She spun her arm around the room. "Not right here at the school, but in Helam."

My body ached with sadness. "Can you?"

270

"Carroll and Paisley leave in July." For a moment, she stood still. "But I don't want to go back."

My heart started racing in search of hope. "If you had a place to stay, would you not have to go back?"

"I'm not sure." She started to sway again. "I'd like to think I could stay. But Clarissa needs me."

"We all need you, Todi."

She gave me a small smile, then looked down at her feet and rocked back and forth.

Her quietness spoke volumes.

"You really don't want to go, do you?" I said.

She bit her lip, shook her head, and kept rocking. I thought maybe she was going to cry. I leaned across my desk for a box of tissues, only to see the box was empty. When I glanced back at her, she laughed at me.

"It's okay." Her smile was back. "I don't need those."

I tried to smile too, but I couldn't make mine last. "I'm sorry about your mom, about her timing, about all the circumstances." This was hard.

"Carroll's trying to convince the caseworker I need to stay here until the end of the school year."

"Well, he's right!"

She stopped moving.

I gave her a strong smile while I fought off my own tears.

"Mrs. Childs," she paused and pressed her lips together before she said, "I need to tell you something else." Her face was more somber than I'd ever seen.

"Yes, Todi." I braced myself, ready for an even greater tragedy that she was about to confess.

Her face scrunched in pain and the words tumbled out. "Blake asked me out yesterday and I don't know what to do."

My face smashed into a huge smile. "Blake did, did he?"

"Yes!" Now she really looked like she was going to cry.

"What did you tell him?"

"I said I had to think about it."

"Oh."

"But then when I told Carroll and Paisley they said that anyone who is staying under their roof abides by the rules, and one of their rules is that us kids can't date until we're sixteen."

"Were you sad?" I asked, wondering if Blake had the slightest chance with her.

"I don't know. I'm sort of mad."

"At Carroll and Paisley?"

"At Blake."

"Blake?"

"'Cause before we were just friends, and now he went and messed that up." She shook her head in disgust. "Now if I stay, I got to decide whether I like him or not. Why did he have to do that?"

"But if you can't date yet, then do you have to decide?"

"Well, Carroll suggested I have a party at our house next week, during Spring Break. He said I could invite Blake, and Anya, and Tracey, and anyone else I want to, and I've already talked to Anya. Her birthday's that week, and so I told her we'd have a cake for her, and ice cream, and she could invite some other friends that she wants to come, and she has a boy she likes that I said she could invite."

"Anya likes a boy?"

Todi shook her head swiftly. "Don't tell her dad. Please don't tell her dad, and don't tell her I told you."

"Do I know him?"

"He's in eighth grade but started Kindergarten late, so he's almost our age."

"Well, Todi, that sounds like a lot of fun."

"But then Blake might think I like him."

"Oh, so you don't want to have the party then?"

"I don't want to like Blake."

"Can you just tell him that you like him as a friend?"

"But I might like him too. Like the other like. And now I'm just confused, and it's all Blake's fault. Why did he have to mess stuff up like that?"

I grinned. "I bet it's been hard for him not to like you."

"He wrote me this poem, Mrs. Childs, and it's . . . well, it's . . ." She shuffled through her open bag and handed me a crumpled-up paper. "Here, you read it."

I smoothed out the paper to find a poem with her name spelled out vertically and starting out each stanza.

Terrific, tenacious, tomboy beauty
O how I hope I don't sound too fruity
Delightful, dynamic and fun, definitely a special one
I hope you say yes, 'cause you compare to none

I grinned and handed her back the paper. "Definitely sounds like you have an admirer."

"Tomboy beauty?" she huffed out the words. "What does that mean?"

Dressed in her simple jeans and basic t-shirt, her unpainted nails, and her hair pulled back in a ponytail, with the auburn curls falling loosely down, she wasn't a Priscilla—and Blake liked that. Still, I chose my words carefully, "He likes you for you. You don't have to try to be anything else for him."

"Why would I try to be someone else?"

"Todi—you don't have to like Blake. No one's making you."

She scratched her head and leaned back again on her Converses. "But what if I do?"

"Why don't you have your party, and get to know him better, see what it's like to be around him besides just at school."

A huge grin spread across her face. "You think that's okay?"

"Of course it is. When you're old enough to date, that's what dating is—getting to know people better."

"I don't have to be his girlfriend then."

"Of course not. You don't have to do anything you don't want to do."

"Well, it's just that he's a real nerdy teddy bear, but he's a nice kid. That's what I told Carroll."

I laughed. "Yes, he's a nice kid. And so are you."

After Todi left, I spent thirty minutes grading a batch of assignments. Then I packed up and headed toward the door. Before flipping off the light switch, I did a mental check and scanned the classroom just as the opposite door flew open and Kyle came rushing in.

"Can I turn this in, Mrs. Childs?" He spoke to me as if I stood near my desk.

"Kyle?" My shifted location made him jump. "What is it?"

"Three of my English assignments." He hustled over to me, papers extended.

"The one due today?"

"No." He shifted to gaze at the ground. "I haven't started that one yet. These were the ones from January."

I accepted them. "Thank you."

"You said I've less than half the semester left, and if I catch up, you'll pass me, right?"

I was glad to hear my warning from two weeks ago had not fallen on deaf ears. "This is a good start, Kyle."

"Yeah." When he flipped his head, and his bangs fell away from his partially-covered face, I caught the admiration in his eyes as he stared at the papers in my hands.

I looked at the large calendar hanging in a corner near my desk. "Do you think you'll be able to catch up on your other missed assignments?"

"I'm pretty sure I can."

"Good."

I expected him to turn around and head out the door he came in, but he didn't move. I stepped away from the door that I currently blocked, giving him a closer exit. But he stayed. I peeked at the clock above his head; school had been out for over fifty minutes.

"Did you go home and then come back to turn these in?"

"Yeah. I had 'em ready this morning, but I left 'em at home in the printer. My mom just dropped me off while she gets my brother from Little League practice. She says she'll be back in twenty minutes."

His feet made no movement, as if indicating he planned to stand right there for each of those twenty minutes.

If there was one student I didn't feel a need to lecture, it was Kyle. Not that he couldn't use a lecture, but I'd already told him the danger he faced due to his grades, and now he had responded to the warning. There was no need for a follow-up one. Besides, his parents seemed quite capable of providing this in regard to his goals.

But if not a lecture, I also couldn't stand here and praise him for his work. He was still two months behind on missed assignments.

I knew nothing of video games.

Finally I said, "I'm glad you're in the creative writing class. I know it's a lot of work, and writing isn't one of your favorite things, but I think it's a great opportunity for you."

He shrugged. "Me too."

I tried to build on this topic. "So you want to write stories for video games?"

"It'll probably be better if I learn to do the programming instead of just writing."

It was a proactive statement—and it had come from Kyle. "That's great!" I said a bit too enthusiastically.

I searched for another question, frustrated that my knowledge of video games was so limited, when he instead voluntarily spoke. "What happened to Abigail?" He studied me as if searching for something.

"You mean the miscarriage?"

"Yeah. What happened to the baby?"

"It died," I said softly.

He drew his bangs to one side. Both eyes watched me intently. "Did she kill it?"

"Oh no! No. She didn't kill it."

His hands dropped to his side. "Then how did it die?"

"Sometimes that's what happens. For a baby to develop from something so microscopic, and to keep growing inside a female, that's huge. It's one of the greatest miracles of life. Sometimes some things go wrong, and to protect the baby, or the mother, it stops developing, and it just can't survive."

"I don't understand why it would die."

I didn't understand what Kyle needed to hear. "It just does sometimes."

"Did Abigail want it to die?"

"I don't think so."

"But you don't know that."

"Abigail didn't hurt the baby on purpose."

"Well, it doesn't seem right. The baby shouldn't have died."

My own feelings around Abigail's baby were still a bit confused. I certainly didn't know how to make sense of it for Kyle.

"Some people," he said, "kill their babies before they're born."

I nodded. "They terminate a pregnancy early."

"I don't like that."

For the first time, quiet Kyle was now sharing his opinion. "Why is that?" I asked.

"Because before my mom had me, her aunt told her she'd help her get rid of me."

"Oh."

"My mom doesn't know I know. Neither does my dad. But my aunt told me."

I gave him a sympathetic smile. "I see."

"You ever almost died?"

"Once," I said.

"Me too. Twice if you count my aunt."

I reflected on my tire blowing out on the freeway, me spinning into traffic, people rescuing my shaking body, telling me they witnessed the whole thing and thought for sure I was heading straight into my death. I'd been twenty-two at the time. "It's scary, huh?" I said.

He nodded, his face incredibly solemn. "Makes you think about things a little."

"Did yours just happen?" I asked. "Your other one?"

"Last weekend. But don't tell my dad, okay?"

I nodded. "Want to talk about it?"

"No. I just wanted to find out if Abigail hurt her baby."

"She didn't."

"Okay. I'm glad to hear that, Mrs. Childs." Then he nodded at me before turning and walking out.

CHAPTER
Twenty-Five

S PRING BREAK CAME AND I FORCED MYSELF TO LEAVE MY house. I packed a bag and road tripped along the Wasatch Front. I visited my two brothers, separately, spent a day with my father and his wife, and then visited my mom's grave.

Next, I made a point to visit my in-laws, which they much appreciated.

Turns out I did too.

We talked about Peter, his youth, his deployment and his return.

His return. Twice I spoke with Peter over the phone, always short, but full of plans. A clear date was not determined, but the estimated time frame for his return was eight weeks. Each time I heard his voice my heart did somersaults in my chest.

Eight weeks!

Proudly, Peter's parents and I began our joyous countdown.

After a week's break, I came back to school anxious for time to fly by. School would end around the same time Peter would be home, which meant Spring Fever attacked me with vengeance. I struggled being back in the classroom. Until I saw Abigail walking alone. Her eyes watched the ground. Her feet scuffed along the floor. She was the first student to arrive for fourth period English.

"How are you?" I asked her as we stood in the doorway.

"Dillon and I broke up."

"Oh." I studied her flawless face. "Are you okay with that?"

"Not at the moment, but my mom keeps telling me I will be." Her face tensed up, as if trying to fight back the tears. "She says time will help heal some of the wounds."

"It does, Abigail."

From the other door, a crowd of noisy students entered the room. I touched her shoulder and repeated the words. "It does." Then I turned to face the other students.

Two days later, at the start of our creative writing period, I asked the class to pass forward their Spring Break assignments. When Blake handed me his, there was a science report on top. I handed the report back to him, but he gave me a comical grin. "No. It's for you. It's connected to my assignment." I glanced at it briefly then grinned back at him. I added it to the stack and continued gathering up the rest of the assignments.

Later, when I flipped through the collection, I was surprised to find Priscilla's was the longest, and Kyle's was the correct length and on time!

Hamilton's was missing, even though he'd been in class. Todi's was missing, but she'd not been in class.

I selected Abigail's to read first.

Abigail Night
April 12, 2004

Spring Break 2004

Sometimes life doesn't give you what you feel like you deserve.

I'm too young for a family. I'm not too young to be a daughter, or a sister, a niece, or a granddaughter, but too young to be a mother. And a wife.

I thought it was going to be okay. I thought that even though we were young, we'd figure things out.

I didn't know love could be complicated. That love could hurt. And that what I didn't want, and then did want, and then didn't get, could leave me with so much sadness.

If there was one positive thing about being pregnant, and then being engaged, and then miscarrying, and then breaking up, and having the entire school know my story, it's that my mom knows it too.

And for the first time in my life, because of all this pain, my mom finally sat me down and talked to me, really talked to me, like two adults. She talked to me like an adult that she respected and cared about.

I expected her to yell, to cry, and to be real angry with me. I deserved all of it. I got all of it too.

And then she told me that these were important choices and then asked me more questions about what I was going to do.

She sat down with a blank checkbook, a cookbook, cleaning supplies, a collection of bills, and a pregnancy book. She handed all of them to me and asked me what I needed help with. Her tone was not angry, or sarcastic, or demeaning. She was sincere.

We talked about some of the things. She gave me instructions, but not like she was criticizing me, like she really, really wanted to help me. Because I knew she would help me, it just seemed like everything would be okay. And that she still loved me.

I especially knew she would help me after the baby was gone. I was in pain and confused. Dillon and I had a plan—a good plan, I thought. So I cried when I told him what had happened. And he didn't cry. He said it was really good news. Really, really good news.

So I shoved him away from me. And then we fought.

And then we broke up.

And then I felt even more confused.

I would have cried all night, but my mom came and held me like a child. She let me rest my head on her lap and she stroked my hair, and touched my cheek, and dried my tears. She didn't say much. I didn't say much either, but I felt closer to her than maybe ever.

She did say we would get through this together. And I knew we would.

She is my mom, and she knows pain. She will help me through this. And I love her.

Kyle McConkie
April 13, 2004

My Family's Spring Break Trip

I went camping with my family for Spring Break. My dad likes to go as much as we can. He says it's so we're out in the middle of nowhere. We don't have electricity, not even cell phone reception. He says he does it so I get a break from video games. But really I think he just likes to camp. I don't mind it either.

My mom likes to cook. She cooks some real good stuff.

I play cards with my brothers and sister. Sometimes my mom and dad play too. My favorite game is called *Buttman*. But when my parents play with us they make us call it *Janitor*. I also play *War*. But that's usually so my little sister Macie feels included and happy. It's our special game with just her and me. I play *Speed* with my brother Daniel and *21* with my brother Reed. Also the whole family sometimes plays *Nertz* or *Hearts*. But we team up for *Hearts* if Daniel or Macie want to play cause they don't get the game.

I also like time around the campfire. Reed tells good jokes. Daniel tries to copy, but his are real dumb. Sometimes I laugh at his jokes. But most the time it's fake because they're so stupid.

I really like it when Dad tells ghost stories around the fire. Mom usually tells him not to. She says she doesn't want to be up all night with Macie. Or Daniel. Because they get scared. So most of his stories end up just being goofy.

This time for Spring Break we went to Flaming Gorge. It was fun. We looked for petrified wood and did some fishing.

But I especially liked the time we spent around the campfire. Instead of jokes or ghost stories, Dad just talked about when he was a kid, and what he liked to do, and what he got in trouble for. All of us listened. Reed asked Dad some questions. So did Macie.

And then Mom shared some stories.

And before I knew it they were talking about when they first got married. They told a story about how when I was two they moved a whole state away from family. But the station wagon that had all their belongings broke down on the side of the highway. They said all they had was $40 and a prayer. So they let the car rest until it had strength. Then they'd start it up again and travel for as far as it could go. Then let it rest, over and over again, until they finally got to their new home. Mom and Dad kept laughing while they told that story. I'd never heard it before. Then Dad reached for Mom's hand and they kept telling each other stories of things that they remembered. For a while it was like they forgot us kids were even there.

I went for a walk later. Dad found me and asked if he could walk with me. Then he asked me questions about my video games. But they weren't like his usual questions that when I answer I get in trouble for. These were about what my favorite game is, and why I like it, and if there's a game that him and I could play together like on a team when we got home. That was a wicked surprise!

I told him yes. But then I thought he'd tricked me. I thought he was asking me questions about video games so he could find something to chew me out about. But then he said, "Kyle. Remember family's your biggest advocate. Not your enemy." He said it like he was torn down or something. Then he said, "That's something it seems I always have to re-learn."

How he said it, it's now like stuck in my head.

Blake's Experiment

Experiment:
Ask a particular female of interest out on a date.

Hypothesis:
My hypothesis was that if I shared my intentions of dating this individual, she would reciprocate similar intentions.

Procedure:
My procedure involved asking her out, which led to her explaining that a party at her location would be the better fit.

In addition to asking her out, I supplied her with a poem that shared my sentiments for her. This was to ensure that my feelings for her were clear.

Advanced Preparation:
Prior preparations included eager help from my mother and Cleon (see my Spring Break Writing Assignment). I obtained a new shirt, a haircut, and coaching from both parties on how to approach the female, Todi, at the party.

Data Table:
A sampling of my appearance was provided by my mother before I attended the party.

Description	of stated times
you look good	10
you look real good	6
you look hot	4
you look sexy	0.5

*Mother said "you look..." Cleon inserted "sexy, Man"

285

Results:
My findings were obtained through my participation in Todi's party. During most of the evening, she spent less time talking to me than in our normal circles at school. Although I don't have the exact data on this, I estimate a variation of 10:1 words shared in school vs. party setting.

Two times I headed to sit by her on the couch when she called over her friend, Anya, to sit near her instead.

My prior understanding was that this specific party had been created to stimulate an environment where Todi and I could get to know each other better. However in this controlled environment, I observed that she made very little effort to interact with me.

Conclusions:
From my findings, I conclude that the female of interest, Todi, is not interested in me. These findings eliminate earlier concerns that I might possibly hurt her feelings someday. Instead I discovered she has the ability to hurt my heart. I also discovered a positive outcome from this experiment. Based on recommendations by Mrs. Childs, I have attempted something and have failed at that attempt. Therefore I have been successful in my attempt to fail.

Blake Wells
April 11, 2004

A Spring Break to Remember

How does my family shape my identity and how did I see manifestations of this during my Spring Break? Historically, Spring Break may go back to ancient Greece and Rome, when people liked to plan a celebration around spring. They called it the "rite of spring". Adults found it a time to relax and enjoy the warm weather. My mom agrees that it's about enjoying the beautiful weather, and it's a time to fall in love. That didn't work out for me, but it did for my mom.

This last week she brought home her new boyfriend. She likes him a lot. He likes her a lot too, so much he wants to marry her.

They haven't dated more than a month, but they've known each other for two months before, and he's already asked her to marry him and she said yes. It's going to change a lot of things for my mom, for me, for all of us. But she seems really happy.

I wasn't that excited to meet Cleon at first. I thought this was one more guy who would end up making her sad. But then I met him.

Mom had already told me he's African. Not African-American, but from Africa, with a visa to be in America. He's working on getting his citizenship and keeps practicing really hard to get ready for the test. Mom's pretty sure he knows more things about our government than she's ever known. She thinks he may even know more than me too.

He's from Botswana and has been in America for seven years. He came here to go to school and then he found work that's let him stay. Mom says he is smart. And nice, and good to her, and she can't wait to take him home to meet her parents because he's black and they will *flip out over this*. And she's looking forward *to shocking them again over her life choices*.

My shocker was when he told me about Africa and then I asked him about Sudan, he said he'd never been there but he was friends with some refugees that live in Utah. I asked if they are Lost Boys and he says some of them are.

Cleon let me share all the research I'd done on the Lost Boys. I told him about how they worked together as a group, and how they wouldn't have survived had they not had each other, and how they made sacrifices so they could all make it to Kenya where there is a UN refugee camp. My favorite part is how since they didn't have a family anymore they all became each other's family. Cleon said he was impressed. He asked if I wanted to meet the ones he knew. I was extremely excited!

That Friday we went to a park in West Valley City for a party for all sorts of people from Africa. There were drums, song, dance, and food – really good food, with all different types from what they would eat in different parts of Africa.

Mom was very happy; she told me three times that she was very in love with Cleon. Then he let me meet his *brothers*, as he likes to call them, from Sudan. It felt like I was meeting some celebrities, but cooler celebrities than the ones you'd meet in Hollywood, like people who really did something amazing. When I first sat down with them, I was nervous, but Cleon helped me. Pretty soon, I was able to ask them questions and they were super nice. Sometimes I had a hard time understanding everything they said. Even though they spoke English well, they had an accent that was really thick. Still, they told me stories about leaving their country, traveling to Kenya, and then the announcement when they got to come to America. Not all of them got to come and they said it was hard to leave their other brothers behind. They also found out coming to America was hard, but they've been here for over two years and it's gotten easier for them.

It was unbelievable. I'm pretty sure I'll never be the same after talking with them. After hearing about the things they saw, and what they did after their families were killed, and then what it took to make sure their *brothers* survived, how they wouldn't leave each other, how they stayed together, how they made each other their family. It was amazing.

When it was time to go, Cleon promised I could talk with them again. I was glad because they were just starting to talk to me about how they missed their country and wanted to go back someday, after the fighting is over.

When we left, I looked at my mom, and she was looking at Cleon. Then she looked at me and winked, and I winked back. I like Cleon. And Mom is extra glad that I do.

She told me she hopes he can be the father I never had. I don't know what Cleon thinks, but I'd like him to be my father too.

And even though my experiment with Todi failed, I still found out how helpful and smart Cleon is. On Saturday, when I was getting ready for her party, I was really nervous. But Cleon gave me some advice: he told me to be myself, because the *worst* thing that could happen is if this girl did end up liking me just because I was trying to be somebody else. How he said it, it just made sense. Somehow he just helped me feel like it would all be okay. Still, I told Cleon I hoped Todi liked me and he said she'd be a fool not to.

Also he helped balance Mom so she didn't go overboard in pressuring me about Todi. She did buy me a new shirt and gave me a haircut, and hugged me really hard when she dropped me off in front of Todi's house. It was so long, and most definitely embarrassing. Good thing Todi didn't see it.

At least I hope she didn't.

Tracey Wade-Brown
April 12, 2004

My Family

We went to California so my moms could get married over Spring Break. The drive there was long but I got to watch, on my portable DVD player, *Edward Scissorhands, Benny and Joon, Cry-Baby,* and *Pirates of the Caribbean* (twice) without either mom complaining.

That's because they were busy. They were talking about their wedding, about seeing old friends, and if they should leave me with Sophia's family so they could take a short honeymoon if they wanted to.

Mostly, I just listened to my movies.

Once we got there, it was so good to see Sophia. I almost cried, because I'd missed her a lot.

I guess I should write about the wedding, because Paula says their wedding is part of history. That's cool. And she says we paved a way for a better America, where my children will have more rights and more opportunities. I didn't want to tell her I don't like to think about my children, and I don't know if I want children. Instead I tell her how happy I am. Because they're both happy, so of course I'm happy.

And I'm happy because for the wedding they let me get my hair cut and colored, any color I wanted, so I wanted lime green, because it's my favorite color, but the stylist told me we'd have to bleach my hair first and Cori said not this time. So I got it a purple burgundy color and it looks extraordinary. I got a new pair of Doc Martin boots and a rayon crème shirt that looks like something Captain Jack

Sparrow would wear. Cori said I could wear that shirt to the wedding. And then Paula asked me to give her away even though my grandpa, her dad, would be there.

I told her I didn't think that would be traditional and Paula and Cori laughed. They said they didn't want traditional, they wanted memorable.

As part of the wedding, both moms gave me gifts. I asked them if I was supposed to get them gifts, because I hadn't. I think maybe I was supposed to, but they both told me no. They told me I was their gift.

And now because they were legally married, we were stronger as a family.

They were super happy. And I knew they were super happy.

But then I made a super big mistake.

So even though Spring Break started good, it kind of ended bad.

We were on our way home from California, and they were trying to get me to talk, but I didn't feel like talking. Instead, I was thinking about what Sophia had showed me while I stayed at her house. It's a website that helps you find out about your donor parent. Sophia thinks I should try to find my dad, so she signed me up. But then she told me not to tell Paula and Cori. I'd been planning not to, but on the drive home I was thinking about it a lot, and I don't like to keep secrets, so I just blurted it out.

I said, "I'm going to find my dad."

Before they'd been talking lots, but when I said that, nobody said anything. Instead the car sped up.

Finally Paula said, "Honey, slow down." Cori almost had the speedometer at 100.

When the car slowed down, Paula said, "Tracey, sweetheart, what do you hope to accomplish by doing this?"

My heart was racing, but I tried to remember what Sophia had said, so I said, "I want to see what he looks like. And how he acts and see if I act like him. And I want to find out if he has a brother or a sister, or any of his own kids. And I want him to see me. And I want to tell him I want to be an actor someday."

Cori sounded mad. "He's not really your father."

"Then who is?" I asked.

Paula pointed at the speedometer again. "Honey!"

Cori said, "What if he doesn't want to be found?"

I guess that's why Sophia told me not to tell them. I said, "I don't know."

Cori said, "You know he didn't do this to be your father. He did this so we could have you."

"Fine." I was getting mad now. So I said, "Then I want to meet my siblings. I want to find out what we have in common. If we look alike. Or if we act the same with some things."

Paula tried to calm me down. I could hear it in her voice. "Tracey, sweetheart, we've already talked about this, how you didn't need a sibling. But if you've changed your mind, and it's important to you, let's talk about it. Maybe we could adopt. Or maybe I could carry the baby this time."

Cori still sounded mad when she said, "Well, this is something we can talk about later. But not now! Let's just enjoy what we have right now."

Paula said, "Yes. Let's enjoy that we have each other. That we're *at last* legally a family now."

And we stopped talking any more about my dad.

Anya Truss

April 13, 2004

A Surprise!

During Spring Break, I had my birthday. I celebrated it with my friends at Todi's house. She threw me a really fun party. But on my actual birthday, there was a big surprise. One I don't think even my parents saw coming.

It started in the morning. My mom made my favorite breakfast of Belgian waffles with peaches and real maple syrup and whipped cream. It was on our *Special Day* red plate and then they handed me an envelope that had a huge gold ribbon wrapped around it. I thought for sure it was going to be money. That my mom was going to take me out shopping, which she loves to do. I love to do that with her too. But if it was shopping, she didn't really have a smile on her face like she should have. But she hasn't really smiled since she read my journal. I talked to Dad about it and he said there's nothing we can do about it, it just has to run its course.

Still, he must have got tired of it running its course, because he suggested they give me the envelope for my birthday.

I first learned about the envelope, and the letter inside, when I was twelve. At the time, Dad said I could have it when I turned eighteen, and then I'd need to pay to have it translated.

But he changed his mind. I think he convinced Mom, and then they decided that maybe we all needed it now. So when I opened the envelope, it felt strange staring at a letter written to me in a foreign language. Since my mom was glaring at it, I didn't know if I was supposed to be excited, since it was my gift, or not. Dad smiled, but it was a plastic smile, like a smile that belonged on one of my old dolls.

We all drove over to this guy's house that Dad had hired to translate the letter for us. It wasn't long, just one page. On the drive over, Dad talked. Mom was quiet. He told me the same story that I'd heard before. A woman in her sixties, most likely my grandmother, took me to an orphanage and gave them my father's name, but said he was recently deceased. She said she couldn't give my mother's name. But she wanted me to have this envelope from my mother and she said it must travel with me.

Soon after that Mom and Dad got the call from the adoption agency. All my life they've told me about that moment, and how they'd been waiting a long time for that call.

I still wonder if someone did read the letter, but I guess they didn't because the envelope was still sealed, and even though we thought the letter was written in Russian, we were wrong. The translator took one glance and then made two phone calls before he sent us to another man's office in Salt Lake. Turns out the letter was written in Estonian.

I don't really know what to think about the letter. I guess I can say it left me feeling a bit mixed up inside. Rather than try to make sense of it now, I'll just rewrite it. Maybe if I'd waited until I was eighteen, it would make sense. Still, I hope it helped my mom. Over these last few days she seems to have started smiling again, so I guess it's been good. I guess.

Here's what it said.

Dear Laps,

I am married to Andrus. Andrus is not your father.

Your father is Jaak. He is hard working, strong, and has a beautiful voice. I first heard him sing for independence at the Tallinn Song Festival Grounds for what Jaak calls the Singing Revolution. But Andrus is a wealthy man from Russia who supports the Soviets. He would never forgive me that I met Jaak.

Andrus is powerful among his friends in the Soviet regime, and he is very liked by women. He likes to find out how much he is liked, which I do not like.

I guess I was lonely. But when I saw Jaak passionate about the revolution, his voice loud and strong, and then when I saw him with his three girls, all under the age of six, something happened to me.

I have two boys. The oldest, Hillar, is preparing to take over Andrus's business someday. He is 14. Kristjan is 12. And then we have an angel daughter, Eliisabet, who is 8.

For many years, I thought no more babies for us. I thought my body knew I was too old, or maybe just my heart was.

Your father Jaak says between his three girls and his wife, there is a lot of chatter in their home. Lots of girl cries, and lots of laughing, lots of happiness. But all that would change if Jaak's wife found out about you and me.

Your Grandmother, Kaja, my mama found out about you, and figured Andrus would kill you, or me, or both. Better to avoid the truth, so we did.

I went traveling with my mama for three long months. I don't know if Andrus even has missed me. I hope so. I have missed our children, your siblings.

We would like to meet you someday, but if you find us, PLEASE say you are the illegitimate child of my cousin, Paavo. He was quite wild and is now deceased. Everyone will believe that to be true. That is whose name Mama gave to them as your father when she helped you find your new home. For me, Jaak, and Andrus, it's better for all of us if you don't share who you really are.

I pray you have a good life. May the love of God shine down on you.

Love,
Ema

Priscilla Putnam
April 13, 2004

Worst Spring Break Ever

I was grounded ALL of Spring Break. It was HORRIBLE!

I thought it was going to be the best week ever. I thought I finally was going to get what I've wanted for so long, from a perfect person, like Hamilton. Instead—I got grounded!

First, I asked my mom if I could go to Darby's house to sleep over. She said no. That made me mad. She didn't even know Darby, so how could she say no?

But she did.

When I told Darby, she said she was pretty good about working around those things. But I think I shouldn't have believed her.

I snuck out. I know I shouldn't have, but I did. I wanted to see Hamilton so badly outside of school, because then we could talk, and then I could know if maybe he likes me. So at the time, I didn't care that I had to sneak out to see him.

Only problem is, Hamilton didn't go!

In fact, the only person I did know at the party was Darby. It was a bunch of people from the high school, and they all seemed so cool, like they knew so much. I was super shy. I just stuck to Darby and she promised she would help me.

When Lena and Darby picked me up down the street from my house, Darby loaned me one of her shirts to wear. It had no sleeves, was my favorite color, and was SUPER sexy. When I got home that night, I was still wearing it, and my mom was there waiting for me. She wasn't too happy with me about a lot of things—Darby's shirt being one of them.

But Darby told me I looked REAL good, and although I felt real young at the party, she told me the shirt didn't make me look young. It didn't fit me perfectly cause my boobs are smaller than Darby's, so it kept slipping down. Darby told me not to worry about it, that I still looked real hot. But sometimes it was a pain to keep trying to pull it up.

Then I found out Hamilton wasn't there, and I was VERY, VERY SAD! Darby told me not to worry, that there were lots of other cute guys I could like, even just for the party. I said okay and then we started to talk about some of the hot guys we saw.

But some guys weren't hot. There was one guy who wasn't super cute, and he had real bushy eyebrows, and slicked-back hair that was kind of dark and greasy. I know it was greasy because I touched it later.

When it was time to play the game that Darby had told me about, I wasn't real excited, but that's when lots of the older kids started to notice me and cheer me on and say I needed to play. Darby smiled at me. She told me it would be fun and I believed her.

A bunch of the older kids were in a circle and then one of them told me it was my turn to spin the bottle, so I did. And it landed on the kid with the greasy hair. Right away he stood up and had a big huge grin on his face. Everybody in the circle cheered. He stared at me, and at Darby's shirt, for a real long time. People started cheering again. Then he stretched out his hand and said, "Let's go." I looked at Darby and she smiled at me. I tried to whisper to her, "I don't want to." But someone pushed me toward him. I shot Darby a look, hoping she'd help, but all she did was wink at me. Then he held my hand, kind of hard, and steered me up the stairs toward a room.

It was a boy's room. When we walked in the lights were on. There was a Nerf basketball hoop over the closet door, and a blue and beige bedspread, and posters of basketball players all over the room. As soon as we stepped in he said, "Hi, I'm Dale. And you're real pretty."

I just stood in the doorway. There was a pit in my stomach ever since he had first smiled at me, and it wasn't going away. I felt real nervous and shy. I didn't say anything and he was still holding my hand. I liked that he said I was pretty, but I didn't know what to say.

"What's your name?" he asked.

I still didn't say anything. He pulled me a step farther into the room then shut the door behind us.

He asked me again about my name. This time I said, "Priscilla."

He said, "Priscilla. That's a pretty name, pretty like you. How old are you, Priscilla?"

I swallowed a big lump in my throat. Then I said, "Fifteen."

He nodded his head at me for a long time. "I thought so." Then he said, "Ever done this before?"

I wasn't real sure what he meant, but I nodded my head *yes*. I didn't want him to know that I was scared right then. And I thought of Darby and didn't want to make her mad. But I don't know why I said *yes*.

He said, "Good," and that's when he stopped holding my hand. He stepped closer to me and turned off the lights. Other than a basketball-shaped nightlight, the room was real dark. All I could really still see was his face, because it glowed in a weird way.

Then his face got close to mine, real close, so close I could smell his breath, and it didn't smell very good.

"Let's have some fun, Priscilla," he said. Then he put his lips on mine.

When Bria had her first kiss last summer, I was a little bit jealous, so at first when Dale kissed me, I thought about telling Bria

300

that now I'd been kissed too. But then he kept kissing me, more and more. He pushed me back, so my back was against the door, and then he kissed me harder. He leaned his whole body against me, and then his tongue slipped into my mouth.

It felt funny and weird, and I wasn't sure I wanted him to keep doing it. But really I wasn't sure about a lot right then.

All this last year, I'd wanted Hamilton to be my first kiss so I was a little sad right then. Maybe if it'd been with Hamilton, it would have been different—like more romantic.

Instead, there were shadows on Dale's face and he looked scary! I had my hands pressed against the door, and he reached down and grabbed one of them. Then he placed my hand around his neck, same with the other one, so we were hugging, and that's when I felt his hair and knew it was greasy. And I smelled his breath again, and it made me feel like I wanted to throw up. I wanted to tell him that I wasn't feeling well, but his tongue was still in my mouth.

My first kiss was supposed to be romantic but this was yucky and gross. He was kissing me so hard that his spit was getting all around my mouth.

I really wanted him to stop. When I moved one of my hands to wipe the spit away, I wasn't hugging him anymore. So he drew back a little, and then I got to wipe my mouth.

I can't write what happened next in this assignment. But it wasn't good. It was TOTALLY GROSS! That's when I knew FOR SURE I wanted to get out of there! So I tried to think of something to say so I could leave. But I also didn't want Darby to be mad. She wanted me to play this game, BUT I HATED THIS STUPID GAME!

Then he whispered in my ear, real low and slow, "Priscilla, I'm going to take your top off now."

"No!" And I said it real fast.

"Why?" He said it real slow.

"It's my friend's!" I was still talking fast and real nervous. "I'm just borrowing it. I can't let anything happen to it."

A GIANT grin spread across his face. It was so big! I shook my head. "No!" I said. "I want to go home!"

And I did!

That's why it was such a horrible Spring Break.

I disobeyed my mom, I wore Darby's top, I went to a party that got me in trouble, I got my first kiss—which I TOTALLY hated—and I didn't see Hamilton AT ALL!

Yep!

Worst Spring Break ever!!!

Dillon Hayes
April 13, 2004

My mom told me I need to forgive Dad.

When I told her that Abigail and I broke up, she told me that.

I also told her I hate him. She says she understands. But I still have to forgive him.

Then she said it was for me—that's why I needed to forgive him. Otherwise I'd spend the rest of my life blaming him for the mistakes I make.

I thought Mom and I were on the same team. I thought we both had a common goal of hating Dad. But she doesn't want me on her team.

Instead she talks to Abigail's mom all the time. At first it was about Abigail and me, about our decisions, and our plans, and then once it changed between Abigail and me, I thought it'd change between them too. But it didn't.

They still talk a lot. Mom asked me and my sister Rachael to watch Lexi and Lawrence and baby Rusty so that Mom and Abigail's mom could go out. First it was ice cream, then it was to a movie, then another time to dinner. Now Mom says once the divorce is final, she and Abigail's mom are going dancing with people their age. She told me the next time they go out, she'd hire a babysitter if I wanted, but I told her it's okay. It's not like I have plans or anything.

The last time they went out for dinner she hugged me for a long time. Then she gave me her talk. She said, "Dillon, it's going to be hard for all of us. None of this is easy. But we have to heal." I really didn't want to listen to her. I tried to pull out of the hug, but then she grabbed my arm. She said, "We have to make a choice to forgive and move on. We have to not let your father's choices control us. We

303

control our choices. So Dillon, you need to start taking control of your life starting now. Do you understand me?"

I didn't want to agree. But I knew I had to. My dad had lectured me a lot when he first heard about Abigail and me, especially when he heard we were getting married. He told me what to do, and what not to do and I didn't want his help. Nothing he said mattered to me, but when my mom heard about Abigail and me, and our plans, she just stared at me for a long time, to the point that it hurt. Then she said, "Let's get through this."

And she still says that to me. "We're going to get through this, Dillon."

I told her okay.

I love her, and I want to make her proud of me. I've always wanted her to be proud of me, so I need to fix some things.

The best thing about Spring Break, is that one evening, my mom pulled out all the ingredients for banana splits and let us all make them as big, and as unhealthy as we wanted to. My brother Lawrence and I made them huge, and then Lawrence's fell all over the floor. He looked at my mom with huge eyes and then said real fast, "It's okay, Mom! I'll lick it off the floor." And instead of Mom getting mad, she laughed. And then Lawrence laughed. Pretty soon all of us were laughing. And Mom and Lawrence kept laughing while they cleaned it up.

It was the first time we'd all laughed together since Dad left. Later that night, when I was helping her put Rusty to bed, we were still laughing. That's when she said, "Dillon, it's your dad's loss. He's missing out on all the rest of these memories."

Still, Mom made me spend some time with Dad during the week. What's worse is she told Dad that she thought it needed to just be

304

him and I. That was a lie! The last thing I needed was to be alone with just him. But at least he didn't bring Antoinette. That would have been worse.

We went to a movie. We didn't talk at all on the way there.

After it was over he asked me how I was doing.

I said fine.

He asked how Abigail was.

I told him we broke up.

He said good. Then he said he liked Abigail, but that me breaking up with her sounded like a very responsible thing to do. He thought I was making good choices.

Just because he said that, I don't know if I am.

I miss Abigail. But I'm trying to fix my mistakes.

Darby Johnson
April 11, 2004

My Spring Break

My Spring Break with my family was boring. My mom got a promotion at her one job and was gone pretty much the whole week. My dad celebrated her promotion by buying a new video game. And Lena and I did nothing all week, except we hung out with her friends at the start of Spring Break.

Which is why we didn't hang out the rest of the week.

Since what I write in this class gets me in trouble, I guess I'll just share the truth. I've already been in trouble. What's the big deal if what I write now causes more?

It was just a game. I didn't think Priscilla was ready to play it. But Lena and Skyler said she was.

When Skyler pushed Priscilla to get a turn, and Priscilla looked at me, I started to think maybe it was too much for her.

Then I kept thinking about her, and who she was with, and if she was ready, and it bothered me.

A lot.

Enough that I stood up.

I planned to just quietly go find her. But then Skyler saw me. "No," he said.

At first I tried to ignore him. I just started walking toward the stairs.

But then he said, real loud, "No, Darby!"

The game stopped and everyone looked at me.

Lena looked at me from across the circle. She said, "What are you doing?"

306

I just wanted to sit back down. I kept hoping they would start the game again and stop looking at me.

Instead I said, "I just want to check on Priscilla."

A bunch of guys started laughing.

Lena's friend Roxie put her arm around me and tried to pull me back to the circle. Lena's other friend, Cami, tried to hand me a drink, but I just ignored everyone.

Instead I kept watching Lena and she kept watching me. Roxie got me to sit down, and then I waited until everyone was playing the game again. Then I stood up. Roxie said, "Don't, Darby!"

But I did.

I darted up the stairs and past the people standing in the way. But when I got to the top, there were a lot of rooms with shut doors.

Then Skyler and Roxie came up to talk to me and Skyler pushed me. "Lena wants you back downstairs now!"

A light turned on in one of the rooms near us and I heard Priscilla's voice. So I knocked.

It was Dale's voice. "What?"

"Nothing!" Skyler yelled back.

I tried to sound strong, but I wasn't feeling strong. "You okay, Priscilla?"

Then Dale threw open the door. "What do you want?"

I peeked into the room. Priscilla had her arms over her chest and she didn't look happy. "Time's up," I said.

Dale glanced at a clock, "No, it's not!"

Roxy said, "No, it's not."

Dale gave me a dirty look. He tried to shut the door again, but I stuck my foot in the way. "You okay, Priscilla?" I asked my question again, because her eyes were huge. Right then, Skyler yanked me back and threw both his arms around me so I couldn't move.

Priscilla said, "Move!" to Dale. She didn't even look at Dale, and she didn't say anything to any of us. She just walked out and tugged at her top until it was as high as it could go.

Skyler said, "You can't do that!"

Dale said, "Come back."

Roxy said, "It's not time."

But Priscilla just kept walking down the stairs.

Skyler released me from his tight hold and I followed Priscilla. But as soon as I got downstairs, Lena was waiting for me. That's probably when I should have tried to fix things. But instead, I walked up to Lena and said, "Take us home!"

She said no.

Skyler came downstairs and shoved me. "You're going to regret this!"

Priscilla disappeared into the kitchen. I heard her ask for a phone.

"Go home with Priscilla," Lena said.

When Priscilla came back, and we walked out together, there were *boos* and "See you, Little Darby," and "Babies can't hang with the big kids," and a bunch of other words that Mrs. Childs does not want me to write in this assignment.

Then Priscilla and I sat outside on the curb, and I asked if she was okay. She didn't answer me.

Then her dad came because she had called him. He asked where I lived and then no one said anything the entire ride to my house.

Lena didn't say anything to me when she came home, just like she didn't say anything to me all week. And of course none of Lena's friends are going to talk to me. I called Priscilla once but she only took the call to tell me she got in trouble and wasn't allowed to use a phone the rest of the week. I said I was sorry and she said okay, and that she wasn't mad at me, and then she hung up.

So how does my family help shape my identity, and how did I see that this week? Well, I sat by myself most of the week. Once I tried to play the new video game with my dad. It was a co-op game. At first we were doing well, until I made us lose. Dad got real angry at me and called me a few names. I yelled back. He told me I had no skills or coordination. I told him he was right.

Later I told my mom she should divorce Dad. She told me she doesn't believe in that.

So the rest of the week, I read my Math book—that's how bored I was! At least I'm now ahead in Math—at least I like Math.

CHAPTER
Twenty-Six

THE CANDOR OF MY STUDENTS WAS SURPRISING. NEVER in my teaching career had I witnessed such insight into my students' personal lives before. I considered the writing topic to be the cause of this response, but instead I knew that this was due to the journals.

Still, I fluctuated between feeling honored and concerned. And before first period the next day, I was still reflecting on my role over this, when Todi raced into my room. "Here it is." She dropped her assignment onto my desk. "I'm sorry it's late."

I picked the paper up. "Thank you, Todi."

"I'm real sorry," she said again.

"For what?"

"Almost all my other assignments have been on time."

"You weren't here yesterday," I said, but her face was tight with worry. "Todi, what's wrong?"

She gave me a weak shrug.

I glanced at the clock. We had ten minutes before the first period bell rang. "Come, sit," I motioned toward neighboring seats and we sat. "Tell me what's going on?"

"I was absent yesterday."

"I know."

"You can read about it in my assignment."

From the look on her face, I feared the worst. "Is it about your mom?"

She folded her arms and nodded.

"Are you able to stay here?" I held my breath, while fearing her response.

She looked at the floor and nodded again.

"Todi! That's great!"

She glanced up at me and offered me a pathetic grin.

"Yeah," she said with no expression. "I get to stay."

"Todi!" My overjoyed tone magnified her quiet voice. "This is wonderful!"

She gave me no smile.

"You want to stay, don't you?"

She bit her lip.

"Why aren't you happy about this?"

"I am." She remained reserved. "And I know what I'm doing for the final project."

"That's excellent, Todi!" But my smile did not match hers.

"I'm going to define what the word *family* means. Not my specific family, but in general what the word means. It's a good word, so I'm going to research places like Wikipedia and blogs and stuff and be like a reporter so I can write my essay and explain to everyone why it's such a good word."

"Wow!" I said softly. "I like that! I think it's a wonderful idea."

"Good," she said solemnly.

Some of my first period students poked their heads through the open door. Todi stood up. "Thanks, Mrs. Childs." She gave me a weak smile then walked out the door.

Todi Spencer
April 13, 2004

Spring Break in Utah

I've been having a real hard time writing in my memoir. I pretty much stopped.

I don't want to finish it.

During the beginning of Spring Break, I tried to work on my final project about families. It was a catastrophe. I wonder if the word *catastrophe* comes from cats getting into trouble! At least that's how my cat, Hazard, was. If Clarissa still had Hazard, then maybe I'd be glad to come home. But Hazard ran away when I was eleven, and Clarissa didn't even go looking for him. Hazard never came back.

But I keep thinking about him, actually I think about him a lot right now. Maybe 'cause I'm different than our cat. Clarissa keeps looking for me.

I mean, she knows where I am. But she thinks I'm in the wrong place. She thinks it was a big mistake that I got sent out of California. She thinks they shouldn't have done that. She plans to get them in trouble for that, and she thinks she can get me home faster 'cause of it.

Last Saturday, in the morning, I was getting ready for my party when Clarissa called.

She told me I'd be coming home soon, like next week, which made me sick. There's still six weeks left of school. Carroll said he would get it all straightened out.

But Clarissa also told me that my sister isn't coming back this time. Her dad is keeping her. Clarissa cried when she told me that.

313

Which made me extra sad for her. I don't like it when she gets like this. And it's even worse when I *can* do something about it—so that she'll be happy. Like in this case coming back to live with her.

I already knew this is Clarissa's last chance. One more crime, another breakdown, another bout with drugs, anything else, and she'll never have custody of me again.

I tried to cheer her up. I said, "Mom ('cause I know she likes it when I call her that), I'm almost sixteen. That means I'll only get to live with you for two more years, so stay clean this time, and don't mess up and we can stay together."

That just made her more sad, so I wish I hadn't said that. I said it 'cause I thought it would help, but it didn't.

During my party, I couldn't stop thinking about my mom, and leaving my friends, and how she wanted me home now.

I missed some school this week 'cause Carroll worked with my social worker and they set up a video conference with me where I said I wanted to stay the rest of the school year here.

Carroll told me I'd made a very good decision by sharing what I wanted and he was sure I'd get to stay. But now that I'm staying, I don't think my mom will stay sober.

I'm pretty sure without me, she'll mess up. And then, I'll just end up in another foster home in California 'cause I hurt my mom.

CHAPTER
Twenty-Seven

ODI'S ASSIGNMENT HAUNTED ME. ALL OF THE students' writing haunted me, but especially Todi's. I spent the weekend fighting my concerns. In the end, I contacted Carroll Johnson and shared my concerns. Then I wrote a letter to Peter three times.

I typed it up as an email, and then deleted the whole thing. I pulled out a pad of paper and wrote a lengthy letter to him, only to fold it up and slip it into a file which I tucked away. Finally I wrote another email, only to courageously save it as a draft.

Then I stepped away.

Some things are hard to discuss when a person is so far away.

The following Monday, a stillness hung in the air, almost as if my creative writing students were waiting for something.

In addition to Todi's lost smile, I attributed the universal hush to what we had all witnessed at the start of class. Abigail had arrived early and placed her bag over the desk behind her, the spot where Dillon had sat through the months of class. It was a cute ritual, one she'd done all year. But right before the bell rang, without a glance her way, Dillon took a seat on the opposite side of the room, two seats in front of Kyle's beloved spot.

While Abigail slowly pulled her bag from Dillon's former seat, the rest of us tried to look away.

Then through the class period, all students spoke in quiet tones, almost as if we were holding our breaths. I imagined others, like me, replaying Abigail and Dillon's private life, mourning what they'd lost, celebrating what they'd saved, and hurting over the gap which now grew between them.

But perhaps the class's stillness was also preparing me for something else.

Twenty minutes before the bell, I caught sight of the storm that covered Hamilton's face. It'd been brewing for weeks, but today it seemed strong, and stagnant, like a dismal cloud crammed with unreleased rain.

Then, when the bell rang, my students quietly filed out, except Hamilton. He didn't reach for his backpack, or shuffle papers, or even shift from his slumped position.

I approached him cautiously, masking my concern in a casual tone. "I'm used to you running out the door," I said.

He didn't say anything.

I filled the void with more chatter. "Back when you had practice, you really booked it out of here. It's a nice change to see you not in a rush."

Only a muscle near his mouth stirred, and just barely at that. "I have nowhere to be."

316

"Well, that's good because I wanted to check in, see how you're doing."

"I'm fine," he said tersely.

"That's good." I kept my tone casual. "I'm still waiting for you to turn in your last assignment."

His muscular shoulders slid up the back of the chair and his torso turned until his eyes met mine. Anger covered his face. "I won't be completing that assignment."

I ignored the fury. "I can still give you partial credit if you get it in."

He shrugged as if my words meant nothing to him.

I took a seat near him. "Hamilton, out of everyone in the class, you've made the greatest improvements. You have such talent! You're really a good writer, so don't give up. Okay?"

"I'm not going to do it." His voice remained flat.

"Okay," I said softly.

"Or the final class project."

My tone remained even. "Why?"

"I'm not writing anything about my family right now."

I nodded. These were teens working through the difficult development stages of becoming an adult. I'd expected some students to have some struggles around this family topic. I just didn't expect it from Hamilton.

"Is it your father?"

His stoic composure broke. "I can't do this."

I kept my voice soft, wishing not to tread where I shouldn't. "It's okay." Since this project was not ever intended to spur heartache, I cheerfully said, "I have a different assignment for you, both for the Spring Break assignment and for the final project. I'll give you a week to make up your last assignment, and I won't mark it

317

late if you get it to me by next Monday, and I'll also provide you with a new topic for the final."

Hamilton grunted, and his body slumped again into his chair.

"It's okay," I said calmly. "I understand. There are aspects of your family that you don't want to share."

Originally the journals were there to be that buffer, a safe place to share heartaches, and to gain perspective, whereas the final project was to be their selection of well-chosen words reflecting the positive side of their family.

But as the journal assignment disintegrated, and after Dillon's self-exposure, I'd become leery of some aspects of this project. "You don't have to write anything about your specific family, just don't stop writing. Okay, Hamilton?"

"My dad asked me to be something I'm not," he stated.

"I know," I said softly. "Adults make mistakes. Sometimes lots of them."

Hamilton suddenly whirled around and almost lunged from his seat. "My dad is on a trip right now. Last time he was on a business trip, he set it up that I'd train with Malcolm, since he's the best player on the Varsity team. And I did, for two nights. But one night, when no one else was home, I told Malcolm I couldn't come. Because I'd been working lots on my fiction story, and that night I wanted to stay home and work on it some more. It's the same story that you read a part of last fall, but that part wasn't really good."

"It was still good!" I said. "A great work-in-progress."

He attempted to smile, but the internal storm still dominated his face. "That night, I was writing more, and it was getting better, until I heard my truck, the one my dad had bought for me."

He stared at me like that statement alone should mean something. When I gave him the smallest of shrugs, he said, "He's

318

taken me out driving in it, out in the country, so I can be comfortable driving my truck before I'm 16. But for the past couple months it's been at the shop, getting some custom work done. When Dad has extra cash, he puts it toward the truck. When it's all done it's going to be . . ." his voice trailed off.

I nodded, as if that explanation clarified whatever I was supposed to understand. "You and your dad had an argument over the truck?"

"No!" He pounded his fist against desk. "That night, when I walked out of my room," his eyes were wild and nervous, "I saw my dad."

"And you weren't where you were supposed to be."

He gave me a small nod. "I thought I was so busted for not being at training with Malcolm. Dad was going to be ticked! I tried to come up with something real fast to explain it, but instead he just said to me real low, and real stern, 'You're not supposed to be here.'"

The muscles in Hamilton's neck had become tight. His entire body bounced with nervous energy, as if the rain inside the gray cloud was suddenly pouring down. "When I said, 'I thought you were out of town' I knew he was going to verbally slap me. Instead he made no sense! He said, 'I am—I was—I still am. But I need to be gone longer now. I just came home for a moment, to get some things, then I'm gone, longer again. But don't tell your mom. No need to tell her. I'll call her.' Then he turned around, and almost sprinting through the house, he kept stumbling, and muttering things, but quietly, like under his breath. Once I kind of followed him, but he didn't see me. Then I saw him again in the kitchen. He had two suits, but they were rolled up into balls, and they were still in their dry cleaning bags. And the plastic kept unraveling as he walked. Then he opened the fridge, took out a whole pack of cheese sticks and shoved them inside the rolled up suit ball, then he opened the pantry and pulled out a container of whey protein and headed back to his bedroom."

The nervous bouncing stopped. Hamilton clasped his hands together and looked at them resting on his desk.

"When my dad found me again, his hands were full, his suits had unraveled to his knees, and he looked real scared. He said, 'Ham, I need you to do something. And it's *extremely* important. You hear me?'" Hamilton swallowed then nodded his head as if acting out the words. "I was ready to take whatever orders he gave me, like I've always done. He was real stern, and he said, 'This is more important than anything I've ever asked of you.' Then his lips started to tremble. I'd never seen him like that. He said. 'Don't tell your mom I was here. Okay?' I nodded and he said, 'Promise?' And I nodded again and he said, 'Don't tell your sis, or anyone. And I mean anyone. I'm still gone! Understand me?' I told him yes, but then he yelled at me. 'I came back only for today! I had to take care of something, and now I'm gone again. So I wasn't here! Do you understand me?' I nodded, but that wasn't good enough. He yelled at me like I was on the field, screwing up an important play that he'd just told me to do. 'Do you understand me, Hamilton?' He clenched his teeth together and his face was shaking. I felt like I'd just made a huge mistake, but I didn't even know what it was. I said, "Yeah, Dad. I understand.'

"He walked to the front door and said, 'The truck's at the body shop, getting fixed for you. It's been there all month. I'm not here. I haven't been since Monday morning.' When he turned back to look at me, he looked pissed and he yelled, 'Understood?' His vein was protruding, the one in his neck that shows when he's fuming over a player who's fouled up a play. Then he yelled it again, 'Understood?' And I said, 'Yes, Coach,' and he left."

Hamilton leaned back in his seat. His hands were still clutched together tightly. He looked at me, and I looked at him, afraid to speak.

"When, Hamilton?" I finally asked. "When was this?"

"Wednesday, February 25."

I released a heavy sigh. That date stirred words in me that I couldn't bring myself to say, words that Hamilton couldn't say either.

I kept my tone even. "You've been keeping this from everyone for over seven weeks?"

He looked down at his hands and nodded.

"That's a long time."

He nodded again. I asked my next question cautiously. "Do you think your dad was with someone else that night?"

He kept staring at his tightly clutched hands. On his knuckles, I saw the scrapes and scabs of an active youth. "I don't know," he said.

I held onto the heavy sigh that had been growing inside. "You chose to tell me this for a reason. Why?"

The pain in his eyes answered before he did. "What am I supposed to do?"

"I don't think you'd be telling me any of this if you didn't already have an idea."

He nodded then looked down at his knuckles. His thumb rubbed at a scab. Then he spoke as if in pain. "What would you do?"

The question threw me back into the hard plastic chair. With the metal desk arm wrapped around my side, I looked ahead at the dry eraser board and waited, listening, hoping for some wisdom. But the whiteboard was empty. I'd cleaned it at lunch, and now it only offered a white void. The true answer was that I hoped to never have

321

to face such a decision. Instead I said, "If I were you, I hope, I truly hope, I'd do the right thing."

"That's why I told you," Hamilton said. I looked at him and he looked back at me. "I'm trying to get the courage to tell the right person, but it's been real hard. For the past seven weeks, I've tried, but I can't."

I nodded and turned back to face the clear whiteboard. I wasn't quite sure what I was supposed to do to help him until I heard his whisper, "That's why I told you, Mrs. Childs."

CHAPTER
Twenty-Eight

WITH THE RELEASE OF HIS CONFESSION, THE STORM cloud had eased. When he left my classroom, Hamilton's face appeared lighter.

Yet I felt the transfer of weight.

And with that weight, a sickness grew, especially as I sat across from Officer Bond and retold Hamilton's story.

When I finished, Officer Bond scanned my face. Then he stood. "I'll be right back."

I waited alone in his office and looked at the photos of him and his dog, Rex. These framed photos either emphasized the extreme closeness of owner and pet or it magnified Officer Bond's limited family condition.

When he stepped back into the room, another officer was with him.

"Lieutenant Fisher." The man extended his hand and I shook it. "I'm Carl Bond's supervising officer—and I'll be handling the case from here."

I glanced back and forth between the two men until Officer Bond gave me a solemn nod, as if this was a necessary change.

Then the lieutenant asked me to retell the story, which I did. Meanwhile his face remained expressionless.

When my account was done, he placed his hands onto the chair's armrest, and spoke quickly. "Before we haul Thad in, tell me why we should believe *this* kid?"

"It's not just a kid," I said calmly. "It's his child."

"I get that, Mrs. Childs, but I'm not a fool. This is Thad Forbes we're talking about. Before I get into some family affair, I want to know why *this* kid would come and tell you this—now, after almost two months."

His tone bothered me, and I had to pause for a moment before respectfully responding. "He was scared and he didn't know where else to go. So he came to me for help."

The lieutenant rested his elbows on the armrest and scratched his hands while his eyes scanned Officer Bond's room. When he looked back at me, his tone was reserved. "You said Thad's out of town right now."

"Hamilton said he left this morning."

Lieutenant Fisher looked at a far corner and pressed his fingers to his lips. After a long moment, he lowered his arms and said, "Sometimes a man doesn't want his wife to know where he is." When he glanced back at me, I felt uncomfortable. "I'll talk to Forbes when he's back, but right now, let's be careful not to get too involved in a personal matter."

I bit down on a corner of my lip and shot Officer Bond a glance. He nodded another assurance, trying to tell me these circumstances were okay.

But I wasn't okay.

"All right." Lieutenant Fisher stood and huffed out a long sigh. "Thank you for your information, Mrs. Childs. Carl, I'll catch up with you later."

After he left the room, I waited for Officer Bond to speak. "It's all good, Savannah." His tone was soft and reassuring.

"Is it?"

"Let Fisher handle this, for your sake, for my sake, for Hamilton's sake." His eyes appeared distant, as if he was shutting me out from all this. "If we handle any of this incorrectly, it will turn bad for all of us."

That evening, I couldn't sleep. I tossed and turned and anxiously wished Peter was near. He could make sense of all this. He could provide perspective to my conflicting feelings, could help me identify what I thought was right, and he could calm my growing fears which circled around Hamilton and his family.

-------CHAPTER-------
Twenty-Nine

THE NEXT DAY, I PULLED HAMILTON ASIDE AND TOLD him all I could.

I'd taken his story to the police and they were investigating.

After sharing my words, I don't know what I expected from him. What I got was the gray cloud of despair surfacing again across his face.

On Wednesday, I sensed Hamilton's fear, anxiety, and uncertainty, perhaps because I felt all of it too.

On Thursday, in between my first and second period classes, I had another brief exchange with him. Hamilton said his father had got in late the previous night, they'd only exchanged brief words, and all seemed fine between them. This morning, he hadn't seen his father. There was truly nothing to report, yet it was that *nothing* that gave both of us a much-needed release from the excessive unknown we'd feared.

During a break between my next set of classes, Todi appeared in my doorway. Her smile offered the greatest distraction from my constant obsessing over Hamilton's situation.

"How are you?" I asked.

"So good!" She practically danced into my classroom. "Guess what?"

"What?" I stared at her large smile. I hadn't seen it in weeks. And it was priceless to see it now.

"Clarissa called me." She clutched her hands together as if capturing all her excitement that bubbled inside. "She said thank you to me!"

"For what?"

"Well, for two weeks she says she was *freakin'* mad at me, but that's not the real word she used." Todi shot me a quick smirk. "But now, she says it's okay. She's not mad anymore."

"Oh! I'm so glad!"

"She really wants me to come home! And I know she needs me. But she says this has given her time to take care of some things, all by herself." The large grin grew even bigger. "So now everyone is okay that I'm staying the rest of the school year!"

"Oh, Todi! I can't tell you how very, very happy I am to hear this."

"And I've been working real hard on our final essay. I've thrown away like twenty-four drafts, but I've almost got it figured out."

My smile now matched hers. "That makes me very happy to hear."

"Me too!" Then she stepped closer and dropped her voice to a whisper. "And can you keep a secret?"

I nodded. "I think so."

She covered her mouth and her eyes danced with excitement. Then she dropped her hands to her side and said, "I like Blake." She giggled. Then she giggled again.

"Really?"

327

"Yeah!"

"Does he know this?"

"I don't know." She laughed. "Probably not." Then her smile softened. "He stopped eating lunch with us. He started hanging out with his other friends, and I miss him."

"How was your party with him?"

"Well . . ." She looked at her feet. "That was the day I talked to my mom, and I was mixed up inside. And I was mixed up inside about Blake too. But . . ." She looked at me, and the happiness returned. "Now that I'm staying, I want him to like me."

"Well, lucky Blake!" I said.

She paused, and then gave me a huge grin.

"Be sure to tell him you miss being around him. And you want him to eat lunch with you."

"Okay."

"He will be very happy."

"Then I will." She clapped her hands together, giggled again, and ran off.

CHAPTER
Thirty

AFTER SIXTH PERIOD, I LINGERED A BIT LONGER THAN normal. I had been oblivious to time, lost in grading English essays, when I heard my classroom door open. I glanced at the clock to see it was 5 pm. Then I shot a look at the door, expecting to see Mr. Drakes, the school custodian, in my room.

Instead, it was Coach Forbes.

"Hi," I said quickly.

"I'm here to ask you some questions." His smile was more threatening than warm.

"Sure." I stood.

"I'm trying to figure out who from this school would be messing with Hamilton's life, enough that I'd end up at the police station."

Our eyes connected but no words came out of my mouth.

"See, Hamilton talks about your class, and about you, a lot." He stepped farther into the classroom. "He talks more about you than any other teacher. Somehow your class really fires a spark in him." Three more steps toward my desk. "So when I got the call, because of something he said at school—well, that's what I'm hoping you can help me figure out."

I couldn't find any words to say. Instead I first glanced at the door which he blocked, then at the opposite door, which seemed so far away.

"Yeah," his eyes kept watching me, "had a nice welcoming phone call as soon as I arrived home."

"Oh," I said meekly.

"Seems Lieutenant Fisher had a couple things he needed me to clear up." He took the last steps, closing the final gap between us. "He asked me some questions. Nothing I couldn't answer. Nothing that wasn't the truth."

I nodded my head fast and furious, while still struggling to find my words.

"But from the sounds of things, I'm guessing that in addition to being a teacher, you're the one from this school who likes to play cops."

"No," my voice squeaked. "Not really."

He folded his arms and I noticed his bulging muscles, as well as a protruding vein in his neck, most likely the one Hamilton had referred to. "Well," he said, "I thought it might be good if I came here, in case I needed to clarify some things for you too."

"No need." I cleared my throat, hoping to dissolve the fear which was trapped inside. Even if I wanted to hide from the truth, I knew I couldn't.

With only the desk between us, Thad Forbes placed his hands on my desk and leaned forward. The little gap between us lessened even more. "Well, here's the problem. From what I've heard, sounds like you've been putting ideas into my son's head."

"No," I said too quickly. "I only listened to a concern he had."

"A misunderstood concern!"

"Yes, I'm sure." I couldn't seem to get control of my voice; it was high and rapid in tone. "A misunderstanding. He shared what he understood, and I shared what I needed to report."

"Mrs. Childs." He removed his hands from my desk and stood up straight. His eyes towered over mine. "Or may I call you Savannah?"

I nodded, while digging for the required courage to face this man.

"What exactly did you need to report?"

For the smallest moment, I questioned what I'd done.

Perhaps Lieutenant Fisher had been correct. Perhaps I'd been set up, given too much clout to a teenager who used me as his pawn in a fight against his father.

Then I thought of Hamilton. Even if he was only fifteen, I still respected his concerns. Because of this, I drew my shoulders back, stood as tall as I could, and faced the tense moment.

"I was concerned that you'd asked Hamilton to keep a secret about you being in town on the night Stella died."

His fist thudded against my desk. "This has nothing to do with Stella. How dare you! How dare you try to bring her into this, and my son into something you know nothing about!"

I swallowed a hard lump that had constricted my breathing. "I'm sorry," I said while my ears listened for another person roaming the halls. But the more silent the building, the more my courage slipped away.

"Stella was a beautiful, lively, smart, capable girl who got tied up with the wrong guy."

"Skyler?"

"I've said from the beginning that kid was responsible for her death." Again he folded his arms and let his stature fill the room. "It's tragic. Young love which turned into heartbreaks, followed by jealousy, envy, hate, and now this." He shook his head and looked at me like he expected us to share a common mistrust toward this young man.

"I don't know him," I said while my heart raced.

"Well, I promise you, Savannah," he looked me straight in the eyes, "if you're looking for the truth, like the rest of us are, then he's your man. But if you're looking for a town scandal, if you want to make yourself headline news, then keep making me your enemy!" Again the vein protruded. "But you'll ruin yourself in the process."

"I'm not looking for an enemy," I said swiftly.

"This town likes me." He cocked his head back.

"I know."

"So you better know what you're doing. I've built our high school football team to be one of the best in the State, our stadium— all donations from me. I travel all over the country training coaches, and yet I provide that training for free to all of the Helam coaches. I've given more to this town than anyone. So other than you turning my son against me, what do you hope to gain by taking such very *limited* information to the police?"

I hated that tears were forming in the corners of my eyes, tears based on fear. How dare this monster of a man stir this type of reaction in me!

A small grin played on Coach Forbes's lips, most likely at my fear, which made me feel even more vulnerable.

My throat tightened. Then I thought of Stella, breathing in her last breath, and my body shuddered.

I offered him a very forced smile and said, "I was trying to do my job." Then I grabbed my bag. "It's late, Mr. Forbes. I need to get home." I walked past, ready to abandon him in my classroom, when he grabbed my forearm.

He held me close. An acidic, cinnamon smell hit my nostrils.

"Skyler killed her. Do you understand?"

My heart raced faster. I tried to yank away but his arm tightened. "Coach Forbes, I'd like you to leave."

His grip loosened, but he still held my arm.

Anger filled his eyes.

"Let go, or I will file a complaint."

I twisted toward the door and prayed he would leave.

"You're quite the little piece of work, aren't you?" He dropped my arm and stepped in front of me so his large body stood in my path.

"Stella needed help," he said firmly. "Just like you say you were helping a student—well, I helped Stella too." His eyes watched me like a hawk. "But it wasn't enough. Her death upset me as much as anyone at the school, so don't you dare throw loose accusations around. You build trust with these students." He whirled his arm toward the empty chairs. "You teach them that you care. I know, because I've heard it in my son. I've heard the respect he has for you. So imagine, if you can, the investment, the care, the concern, the support you offer these youth, and then to lose one of them. But no, that's not enough! Instead, a well-meaning teacher, from another school, decides to throw out an unfounded accusation at you. After you've been the greatest advocate for that youth. How would that make you feel, Savannah?" He spat out my name.

I leaned my weight toward the far exit, but he glanced at that door and gave me a patronizing grin. "Answer my question first."

My fear was morphing into anger, my blood starting to boil. "I'd like you to leave, Coach Forbes."

"Not yet."

"Then what is it you want?" I shook my head. I'd either reached a summit in my quest for courage or supreme disgust had conquered my fear. "Or are you here just to terrorize me?"

He scoffed another laugh. "That's what you think this is? Me terrorizing you? I need one thing from you, Savannah." He raised his forefinger and thrust it at me. "You need to convince Hamilton of the truth."

"Of what truth?"

"Well, I'm about to tell you a little secret." He smiled at me with softer eyes, compassionate eyes, eyes of a legend that the town loved. "My son adores you. Your class has fed a need in him that I saw in myself when I first found football. He respects you, and he'll listen to you, so I'm going to give you the truth. And then you're going to let my son know that we talked and you understand why things happened as they did. Understood?"

"Really, I just want you to leave."

"I will." He offered me a smile as if we were dear friends. "But first, before I leave, I need you to help me. Do we have a deal?"

I tried to mask my extreme disgust. "I'll tell him whatever you want me to tell him."

"Then *this* is what you need to know, Savannah. I spoke with Lieutenant Fisher and gave him the truth, like I already told you. He's already checked it all out, and you can too with him, or I can give you my accountant's and my attorney's phone numbers. I don't know how much *proof* you need," he scoffed out the words, "but I have it for you. I was in town that night to take care of an urgent item with both of them."

I spoke with contempt. "And your family didn't know you were here?"

"That was my hope."

I struggled to not roll my eyes at him. "Your son says you came home and you were disoriented."

"I'd returned to my place to get some supplies because I needed to extend my trip due to bad news." He let shame cover his face. "Hamilton wasn't supposed to be there."

"So you asked him to lie to others about you being there?"

"Damn, Savannah! Damn, damn, damn! What do you want from me? I was out of town, in Idaho. I got a distressed call from my accountant. When I heard what it involved, I made an emergency trip home, knowing I needed to be back in Idaho as soon as possible. I reached out to my attorney to find out what my liabilities were if my accountant lied to get me a greater return on my federal tax forms. Do you understand me, or do I need to share more?" He glared at me and I glared back. "I really didn't want to distress my wife. And some things are better discussed with my attorney in person than through electronic archival references. Do you understand?" The protruding vein was back. "I needed to know if I was going to jail, and I wanted to know that first, before I dragged *any* of my family into this. It is unfortunate Hamilton's been dragged into this at all. So I don't know what you want to tell my son, but you sure as hell better fix the mistake you made. Do you understand me?"

My body had started to shake. I really hated this man. So I nodded my head in the affirmative and watched his iconic charming smile spread across his face. "Good. I'm in the midst of an investigation right now, and my family doesn't need to know that. So I'm glad we could reach an understanding with all of this. I expect you to adequately clarify this other unfortunate misunderstanding with my son tomorrow." Then he turned and touched the door, only to pause briefly. "I don't want to come back here. Got that?" I nodded. And he finally left.

As soon as my classroom door shut, the tears began to fall. I returned to the safety of my desk and collapsed into the chair. I drank in the air around me with thankfulness. Then with shaky hands, I retrieved my phone and dialed Officer Bond's number.

CHAPTER
Thirty-One

OVER THE PHONE, OFFICER BOND LET ME RUN through the event, let me cry out my fears, let me say anything I wanted until I brought up fears that Coach Forbes had killed Stella. "Don't go there," he warned.

"Why? Why are you protecting him?"

"I'm not," he said. "I'm protecting you."

The tears began to fall all over again. "So what are you saying?"

"Savannah, it's not my case anymore. And the only thing I can say is that you don't want to be involved in this case anymore either."

That night I didn't sleep well. The following day, I didn't feel well. And I didn't teach well either.

Before Creative Writing, Blake was talking to me, but I wasn't hearing him, until he said, "Are you okay, Mrs. Childs?"

I tried to laugh it off. "Yes. Thanks." Then suddenly I turned the subject on him. "How are *you*, Blake?"

He grinned.

So I grinned back. "As much as I enjoyed reading your experiment report, I'm not sure it counts as a successful failure."

His grin widened. "Yeah. Maybe not."

I winked and he winked back.

This left me with a smile until Hamilton sat down.

Through my class period I observed Hamilton, and near the end, when we made eye contact, I motioned for him to stay behind.

As soon as my room was empty, I took a seat next to him. "What's your dad said to you?" I asked.

"Nothing really. Not anything important."

I didn't want to travel this path. Instead I wanted this frustration, heartache, and fear to leave me. But surely my own feelings were secondary compared to Hamilton's. Plus I knew the deal I'd made. "Well, I've talked with him," I said.

His eyes grew huge. "When?"

"Yesterday evening." I would fulfill what Coach Forbes demanded of me, but nothing more. And only for Hamilton's sake. "Your father explained things to me," I said. "Just like he explained everything to the police. Apparently he was in town that night for other business reasons."

Almost as if giving himself a hug, his large forearms wrapped around his chest. His eyes studied me. "Like what?"

"He'll explain when he's ready."

"Is he in trouble?"

"I don't know." I tried to appear confident. "Not with the Helam Police. They've talked with him, and it seems they're satisfied with his answers."

"Then what?" Hamilton bit his lip and waited.

"He might owe some money."

"He has money." A calmness settled around his face.

"I know."

"So he'll be okay?" His voice was eager.

"He will be." I tried to sound casual. "He's working to get it all figured out. And he's got the right people helping him with it. So he wants to assure you that everything's okay."

"Was he mad?" Hamilton again searched my face. "At me?"

I struggled for a moment, remembering his father's large neck, the protruding vein, and his dark eyes. "Not at you," I managed to say. "He loves you, Hamilton."

He released a huge sigh of relief. He dropped his arms and his shoulders relaxed. "Thanks, Mrs. Childs." Before he headed out the door, he gave me a grin like I'd just saved his world.

Only problem was, I wasn't sure I had.

Before leaving school, I phoned Officer Bond. I had something for him, and it had nothing to do with Stella's case. He said he'd be in the lobby waiting for me.

And he was.

"How are you?" he asked.

"Just got through telling Hamilton he didn't need to worry about his dad." I shrugged, as if my lame answer summed up how I felt.

Then I reached into my bag, pulled out an envelope, and handed it to him.

He gave me a puzzled look. "What's this?"

"You'll see."

His forefinger slid open the envelope. "I hope it's not a thank you for all the disruption I've caused your class." He offered me his half-smile and then pulled out the invitation.

"You don't have to come," I quickly said, uninviting him within the same moment I invited him. "But it's a month away."

"So it's at the library." He skimmed the card.

"It's their reading," I said. "And I want you to see them for who they are. Not just for the students you read about in their journals."

He gave me another half-smile then slid the invitation back into the envelope. "If my schedule allows, I'll be there."

"Thanks." I took a step to leave, but then paused. "And I know you're no longer on the case, but I need to ask you one last thing." He cocked an eyebrow at me, which made me quickly add, "What really happened between Coach Forbes and Layne, the girl Hamilton wrote about in his journal?"

"Why do you ask?"

"Because it seems like no one really questions Thad Forbes."

Officer Bond scanned the small lobby. Other than the receptionist behind the glass pane, no one else was there. He motioned for us to sit.

"Savannah," he said my name softly. "Be careful."

"Well, what if he hurt Stella too?"

"You don't want to say that to anyone else," he said firmly. "We still have Skyler as a person of interest."

"Why?" For some reason, I couldn't accept that Skyler was responsible for this.

"Here's what you don't know." His voice dropped down low. He glanced around the lobby again. The receptionist was on the phone. "He's an evil kid. This year, during a game of *Merry Moments*, he tasked that girl, Layne Porter, to make accusations against Coach Forbes. Then when she told everyone the truth, he bullied her, unmercifully."

I watched Officer Bond and thought about Hamilton's account of Layne.

"Skyler is selfish!" he said. "The kid's always out for his own gain—and he'll brutally turn on anyone who goes against him."

"Because someone told you that?"

"Well, you brought up Layne. Skyler went into a rage when Coach Forbes kicked him off the team. That's why Skyler *tasked* Layne to do what she did. There are some specific charges against Skyler right now. He has a good lawyer, but I suspect, that through these investigations, the bigger answer will surface. And that's all I can tell you."

"You really want me to believe it's Skyler, don't you?"

Officer Bond shrugged his shoulders. "I want you to understand that Skyler is one to stir up trouble."

"Okay." I didn't mask my reservations.

"Okay," he spoke as if challenged, "here's another example. The first time I met with Skyler it was just to ask some basic questions, and when I walked him out he said, 'I need her dragonfly necklace.' I asked what he was talking about and he said, 'It's mine. I gave it to her.'"

I gave Officer Bond a puzzled look.

He chuckled out a sound of disgust. "I know! The kid told me it was his mother's, but he'd given it to Stella because she loved dragonflies. When they broke up, he'd wanted it back. But she wouldn't give it back. And to spite him, she wore it every day."

"Did you give it to him?"

"Of course not!"

"Well, if he killed her, why didn't he take the necklace then?"

"She wasn't wearing the necklace that night."

"Wouldn't he have known that if he'd killed her?"

"That's not the point. The necklace isn't important here." He rubbed his hands against his slacks as if brushing off crumbs. "The

341

point is Skyler has always been focused on himself. But this is no longer my case," Officer Bond stood up, "and there's a good reason for that. For now, I just need you to know that Skyler is not a good person."

"Well," I also stood, "for what it's worth, I think Coach Forbes is as awful a person as Skyler."

"Savannah," his tone reprimanded me. "Please. Be careful with your strong statements." He watched me closely. "It's not about what you and I think. So trust me when I say, for everyone's sake, it'd be best if the investigation confirms it's Skyler."

That evening, what saved me was an unexpected phone call from Peter.

Words poured out of me. I shared everything with him, from the journals collected, to reading them, to Officer Bond, to Stella, and to Coach Forbes. Everything I could fit in our limited window of talk. While I unloaded this weight, I wondered why I'd held it all in, why I had not shared any of this in my previous emails with him.

True to form, Peter's words, his tone, his wisdom, calmed me. And his soothing nature reminded me that all this drama I currently faced was only a facet of my life. It was a dear and important facet, but not the *only* facet of my life.

Then, with less than a minute left, Peter shared his important news. In less than a month he'd be flown to Fort Collins for debriefing and then it'd only be a matter of weeks.

Tears surfaced in my eyes. Peter, my husband, my lover, my friend, was nearly home.

In the weeks that followed, my heart soared with this news. As I prepared for Peter's return, for the wrapping up of the school year, for the Creative Writing end-of-year project, and our special reading, and all the other events ahead, I felt more life than I'd felt in a very, very long time. And the more I felt alive, the more I thought of Stella.

CHAPTER
Thirty-Two

O N A BEAUTIFUL TUESDAY IN MAY, I FELT A CALL TO BE outside. By the close of fourth period, I decided to enjoy my lunch on the grass to drink in the lovely warm day.

With my lunch container in hand, I shuffled through my desk drawer for my box of plastic forks, when Priscilla approached me.

"Hi," I said.

"Mrs. Childs." She gave me a huge, pleading smile. "Back in February, when you took my lip gloss, I know you said I'd get it back at the end of the year, but could I just borrow it real quick?"

Why I had Priscilla's lip gloss I could not recall. But if I had to guess, she probably chose to apply it during an exam.

"I promise to give it back." Her eyes pled with me. "I accidentally left mine at home. And I need to go find Hamilton. He asked me to give him something." Her begging grin increased.

I opened the desk drawer which housed my small stash of confiscated items. "Here you go." I handed it to her.

"Thank you so much!" As if she'd been on a three-day fast, she unscrewed the top and began her application, using a mirror she'd optimistically held in her hand.

I didn't want to pry, but I was extremely curious. "May I ask what you're giving Hamilton?"

"A story." She smiled at me, and her lips shimmered pink.

"Really?"

"Yeah. He said I could read his, if I gave him mine to read."

"I didn't know you were writing a story."

"I wasn't, not until Hamilton offered to swap. He told me no one else knew about his full story—except you knew a *little*." She smiled at the information that connected us.

"Did Darby help you with this?"

"With what?"

"This—exchange between you and Hamilton?"

"No." She released a string of giggles. "Better!" She set the lip gloss on my desk and then reached into her bag to pull out a spiral-bound notebook. "Here. You can read about it in my journal."

I looked at the notebook. I'd never seen it before. "Your journal?"

"Yeah." She shrugged. "Once I started writing in the journal you gave me, I loved it! Even after you collected 'em, and then you gave them back and said we didn't have to keep writing in them anymore—well, I wanted to. I finished the one you gave us. This is my second one. I've only written two entries in here, but you can read them."

"Priscilla!" I was stunned. I'd never expected this from her.

"Really." She stretched the notebook out farther. "It's okay. I want you to read it. I think it's a good story. Well, it's not the story that I'm giving to Hamilton to read. That's fiction. But the story in

345

my journal—it's true, and it's a good story." Her face maintained an enormous grin.

When I still didn't accept it, she stepped closer.

"Please," she said.

"Thanks." Still feeling a bit shocked, I accepted it. Then I added, "I'd be honored to read it."

"Well," she picked up the lip gloss and handed it back to me, "thanks for letting me borrow this." Then she spun around and said, "How do I look?"

"You look radiant."

She released a short string of giggles. "Thanks." Then she hoisted the bag onto her shoulder.

"Can I ask you a quick question?" I asked.

"Sure!"

"Does Hamilton seem okay?"

She paused, and then spoke her words thoughtfully. "I think so. Why?"

I held my words for a moment, hoping I'd choose them wisely. "You really are a pretty girl, Priscilla."

"Thanks." She grinned over the compliment.

"But more than just how you look, I think Hamilton's one who can also see your inner beauty, and there might come a time when he really needs that specific beauty."

She looked at me, and her nervous energy shifted to quiet concern. "Is Hamilton okay?"

"Yes," I said strongly. "But he has a lot of pressure with football and expectations. I think more than just a girl who's pretty on the outside, Hamilton may need a real friend. Because someday, when his world turns complicated, he needs to know there's someone who still carries a pure understanding of her world."

"Really?" She cocked her head to the side.

"Yes. I think if you look, you'll discover that beauty's inside you. And it might be what someone like Hamilton, at some point in his life, needs. So don't lose that, okay?"

"Yeah," her voice was quite serious. "You think Hamilton might need me?"

"Possibly. So above the other stuff, just make sure to be his friend too."

"For sure." She stood tall. Then she looked at me one last time. "I will. Thanks, Mrs. Childs."

After Priscilla left, I took my salad, her journal, and a blanket that I stored for such weather. Then I found a patch of grass, close enough to hear the hum of students chattering over lunch, yet far enough to slip into my own private reprieve.

After a bite of a cherry tomato, I opened Priscilla's journal.

April 12, 2004

Something pretty good happened tonight. Well, the day was bad at first.

Today, my sister got into my stuff again! It was my first day back from Spring Break, and I knew she had. She tried to hide it and she lied, but when I asked her about it, I saw one of my hairclips underneath her bed. So I got mad at her—AGAIN!

But my mom and dad have been acting weird around me lately. Like they don't yell at me like they used to. So when I yelled at Caitlin, I expected them to yell back at me for yelling at my sister. Instead my mom whispered something to my dad and then he said, "Priscilla, you have five minutes, then you and I are going for a drive."

That sounded scary!!! Like them yelling at me would have been better.

But it wasn't all that bad. I mean, at first it was.

WOW!

Dad brought up the party that I went to with Darby. They'd already yelled at me about that. And they'd grounded me for a week! So I SO thought we'd moved on by now. But he brought it up AGAIN! So I was starting to think that the STUPIDEST thing I ever did was call my dad to pick me up that night.

But then Dad said he brought it up so he could give me what he calls "an important talk about boys." And he—for sure—did talk about boys! But it was real, REAL awkward!!! He told me things I did not need to know! Like GROSS things!!!

I told him that sounded disgusting—and he did NOT need to worry about me! I mean I still want a kiss from Hamilton, but I really don't want it to be like my first kiss. With Hamilton, it's going to be nice and special.

And with that other stuff—Dad said he's glad that right now I think it sounds disgusting. But he said as I get older, I'll probably change my mind. And he said that's okay, because it's part of "maturing." But then he got super serious.

He said, "Sweetie, this year especially, you've developed into a beautiful young woman."

I like it when my parents tell me I'm beautiful. But Dad wasn't finished there.

He said, "Right now it's my job to protect you. But someday, I'm going to have to pass that job on to another man, a special young man, and I hope when that day comes, I've done my part well. I really hope, Priscilla, he's a nice man, a noble man, and he treats you well."

That TOTALLY made me smile! I LOVE thinking about my wedding!!! I think about it ALL the time! I have a book that I've been pasting pictures of flowers and cakes and dresses in since I was like thirteen. It's totally how I imagine my wedding day to be. I've never talked to my dad about it before. So when he started talking about it, I couldn't help but smile, because it's going to be AMAZING, and of course my husband will be so HOT and perfect!

Then Dad said, "Until it's time for you to leave us to build a new life with him, right now I'm the man who's been knighted to protect you. But you have to do your part too, Priscilla. Let's work together to protect you, okay, Princess?"

I said, "Okay."

But then he told me what I'd already been suspecting he was getting at. He said, "You sneaking off to an unsuitable party makes it real hard for me to do my job. Understand? In fact, if one of my biggest goals is to keep you safe, I'm still going to fail if you and I don't work together. But if we work together, we can be a team to make sure you don't run off with anyone but your special prince."

I nodded, and cause of his other talk, I could feel my cheeks turning red, but I think I understood what Dad was trying to say.

Then I think his eyes teared up, because he took off his glasses and wiped at his eyes and then he choked on his words a bit. He said, "I really want you to be happy, so help me, okay? Together, let's keep you safe. Let's protect your honor, is that a deal?" And I said it was.

Then he took me for ice cream. It was one of my favorite daddy/daughter dates. Especially cause after, he went and bought me a lock to put on my door. My parents have a key, and I have a key, but my sister does not!

And that makes me very happy!!!

May 3, 2004

Tonight was AMAZING! AMAZING!! AMAZING!!!

First, my brother, Josh is back from school. It's so great to have him back. He's here all summer to work and raise money. But the one real bad thing is I had to move back in with my sister—which is a real bummer! Especially since I was FINALLY able to keep her out of my room.

But my mom got me a special chest where I can put my things and Caitlin can't get them. Plus Caitlin got in trouble last time she took something of mine. And that was a HUGE nice change!

Plus, today Dad caught her with lipstick on her face. She'd got it from my room! So he gave her a good talk—and she cried lots! I HATE it when she cries! Everybody feels sorry for her—including me.

But then Mom had an idea. A pretty good idea.

It was Monday night, so we were all spending time together, and then Mom suggested we take Caitlin to the store and that I help her find a few things, just a few things, that would be hers, not mine. It's not that Mom wants her to start wearing jewelry or that Dad wants to start talking to her about her special Prince or anything. We just all want her to stop getting into my stuff, and maybe, if she has a few little things that are special to her, that might help.

I decided it was worth a try.

To tell the truth, I had so much fun helping her pick out a neat bracelet and a necklace, and Mom said we could also get her nail polish and some lip gloss that was so pale pink you can hardly tell Caitlin was wearing it. But she doesn't care! She's just happy to have some. And then when we put it on her she said, "Now I look pretty like you, Priscilla." And she smiled so cute I said, "You do." And then she hugged me. And I hugged her back.

That was cool and fun. Lots of fun. But the night just got better, because we went to get ice cream, all five of us, and while we were there—HAMILTON and his mom and sister walked through the door!!!

I was so glad I had put on some of Caitlin's lip gloss right before we walked in. My hair wasn't perfect but it was good enough.

At first I was feeling a little shy. I wasn't sure if he would say hi to me or not, and I didn't know if I was brave enough to say hi to him, especially with my family there, but none of that mattered cause when they came in, nobody was in line behind us yet, so my dad just walked right over and started talking to Hamilton's mom.

I guess she sells houses and she was who helped mom and dad find the house that we live in now. And I guess they all like each other, because they right away started talking and laughing. And then we just started to form one big group. Josh sort of knew Hamilton's sister from high school and then – HAMILTON CAME OVER

AND SAID HI TO ME! He even said, "Hi Priscilla"!

I was SO, SO, SO happy!

Then after we all got our ice cream, my mom and dad and his mom all decided to sit together to keep talking. But there wasn't enough room in the booth for all of us, so Hamilton said, "It's okay, we can sit over here." And when he said *we*, he meant me and him. So we did, and when we did, my dad looked at us. At first I thought maybe he'd be mad at me, but he wasn't. He smiled at me like it was okay. Kind of like he was happy for me.

Which was good, cause I was REALLY, REALLY happy!

I was still feeling real shy, like I didn't know what to talk to Hamilton about, but then he just said, "How do you like Mrs. Childs's class?"

I said, "I love it."

He said he did too.

Then he asked if I was done writing my piece for the final project and I told him not quite.

He said he was fixing his too.

Then he asked if I was a little bit nervous for the reading and I told him yes.

He said he was too.

And then we smiled at each other. It was SO COOL!!!!

Then he told me about his story that he's writing, and he asked if I wanted to read it, and he said no one else had.

I said yes, but he said only if I shared something I'd written with him.

I thought about telling him I didn't have anything to share, but I didn't want to do that. So now, I have to write something so that I can read his story.

When it was time to go, we all said bye. Dad even made a real point to shake Hamilton's hand and say bye to him.

Hamilton smiled back at my dad. My dad looked so small standing next to Hamilton, which I thought was funny, but no one else seemed to notice.

Then we left, and I'm SO excited that I got to eat ice cream and talk with Hamilton tonight I probably won't be able to sleep—which is good, because I still have to make up some story that I can give him to read. And I still don't know what to write!

All I know is that all year, I tried SO hard to talk to Hamilton, and it just seemed like everything I tried didn't work. Then my dad said "hi" to his mom and then once Hamilton and I started talking it got SO easy. It wasn't hard like before, at all.

I'm just so happy right now!

CHAPTER
Thirty-Three

L ESS THAN A WEEK LATER, I PULLED OUT MY OWN
journal.

MAY 9, 2004

Today is Mother's Day. Due to the loss of my own mother and
my loss of not being a mother, this is a day I've struggled with, a day
which historically picks at the scabs of my injured heart.

Loyal to my God, I still put on a Sunday dress and force myself
to attend a congregation. Then I endure the tributes to mothers. Why
do I torture myself?

It's the question I ask myself every year.

In the past, Peter has asked me this too.

Yet I do.

Because after all these long years, I still believe in the promises
I've made to God. And I believe in the promises He's given me in
return. Still, when there are no *delivery dates* attached to God's

promises, sometimes the bargain seems hard. Yet I've learned there's nowhere else to go. Being angry at the very entity who can save me is counter-intuitive. I need God.

And I know that now.

For on this holiday, which historically has been the hardest for me to face, God stretched forth His hand and showed me He still remembered me.

It was a doorbell ditch.

A plate of cookies, covered in tinfoil, left on my porch. Written in marker across the tinfoil were these words:

Mrs. Childs, you are an inspirational woman.
And you are a mother to many.
We love you.

On this significant day, the final pieces of my extremely bitter heart broke away, leaving me with something new: a heart rich with hope, joy, and love.

It was a kind deed from an anonymous giver. Still, if I had to make a guess who the earthly angel was, Anya's name ran through my mind. Or Todi. Or both.

I think of these girls, and the rest of my students—my children—and a wave of gratitude sweeps over me. Rather than feel cursed with the trials of infertility, I feel blessed today that I am able to serve so many.

Under my present circumstances, because of my childless state, I've been able to give more time to certain projects—and more importantly, more of my time to these children.

Years ago, a teacher told me she'd kept track of every student she'd taught. In a journal, she'd recorded every name, the dates they were in her class, and a short account of how she might have reached that child in some way through the school year. At the time, I thought her record silly, perhaps cocky, certainly a bit too detailed for me.

Yet today, I wish I had that list—my list—my record of every single life that perhaps I'd had a small, yet possibly significant, influence on, even if only for a year.

Such a list doesn't replace the role of a mother. It never will. Always my heart will yearn to be a mother. Yet some of the gifts a mother gives, I too have been able to give.

This year has saved me!

On this precious day, I feel blessed to be called a woman, I feel blessed for the inherent traits I possess, and I feel blessed to serve a child, over and over again.

CHAPTER
Thirty-Four

ON THE EVENING OF THE READING, DILLON AND HIS mom were the first to enter our room in the far corner of Helam City Library. With fifteen minutes to show time, I was in the midst of setting up the dessert table when Dillon approached me.

"Need help?"

"Sure." I handed him a bag of plastic cups. "Thanks."

He gave me a somber look.

"You nervous?" I asked.

"If my dad comes, yes!"

"Is he?"

He pulled the cups out. "My mom insisted we invite him."

I nodded, very much aware of the raw emotion still exposed in his writing. "So do you think he will come?"

He looked down at the cups and shrugged. "Probably not." Then he shot me a quick look. "I told him not to."

I masked my concern with a smile. "Well, you are listed to go first. Are you okay with that?"

He nodded. "Mom says it's okay. That I just need to share what I think." He split the cups into two stacks on the table. "But she also says I need to find ways to move on. She's asked me twice to go see a counselor. But I don't know yet."

I handed Dillon a box of plastic utensils while I fanned the napkins. "Your mom is a good lady."

He spun around to look at her across the room. "Yeah, she is."

I turned in the same direction, only to be surprised to see her chatting with Officer Bond.

"Thanks Dillon. You can put the forks here." I pointed near the napkins and rushed over to greet Officer Bond.

"I didn't think you'd come," I said. Not only was he there, he wasn't wearing his uniform. Instead he wore khakis, a checkered button-down top and for the first time since I'd known him, a casual smile, which was directed at Dillon's mom. "Hi," I said to her also.

"I haven't seen Denise since high school." He motioned toward Dillon's mom.

She looked at me and smiled. "In school, I was best friends with his sister."

"And I'd tag around with them," Officer Bond said, "when they'd let me—which wasn't often." He shot her a teasing glance.

"It's good to see you, Carl." She touched his arm. "It's been too long."

He smiled at her.

She smiled back.

Then she took a step backwards, toward Dillon, still busy lining up the forks, "Thank you, Mrs. Childs, for this event." She offered me another smile. Then she offered Officer Bond a much larger one before joining her son.

Officer Bond's smile remained stuck on his face.

"Well," I grinned, "I should have mentioned there were other good reasons to come mingle tonight." I felt the urge to playfully elbow him, but I refrained.

"When I was a kid, I had the hugest crush on her." His eyes still watched her.

"I don't think it was just when you were a kid."

And that was the comment that broke the magic. He glanced at me and his professional demeanor returned. "I'm glad I came."

"Me too," I said sincerely.

"Because I wanted to tell you, things are moving as they should with the case."

My breath caught in my throat. "Really?"

He gave me a sober look and nodded.

I placed my hand over my heart and glanced at the clock. I didn't know exactly what to make of his comment. With less than ten minutes before my class's special event, the last thing I needed was to get lost in thoughts about Stella's investigation. Instead, I turned to hear voices approaching our reception room.

Then Anya stood in front of me, dressed in white, with her golden hair pulled back in a simple fish knot. She looked like an angel.

"You look stunning, Anya," I said.

"I'm so excited!" Her face beamed.

"Me too."

Principal Truss and his wife appeared next to Anya. Next Carroll and Paisley Johnson stood in front of me and I smiled at the group.

"Hi." Todi, in her pink poofy dress and her combat boots, linked arms with Anya. She had her auburn curls pulled back in her signature ponytail, but for the first time I also saw a hint of lip gloss and eye shadow.

"You look beautiful," I said to her.

She grinned. "Thanks." Then almost nervously, she tugged on Anya's arm and they ran off.

I turned to see Blake in the doorway, accompanied by his mother and her boyfriend. The Johnsons and Trusses had already begun talking so I excused myself, and within seconds, I was listening to Blake's mom talk about her and Cleon's upcoming wedding plans.

Kyle, dressed in a full double-breasted suit, along with a haircut, entered the room. He stood next to his father. The two of them were the most dressed up of anyone in the room. I excused myself from Blake's family and greeted Kyle.

"We're really looking forward to this." Mr. McConkie shook my hand, giving me an enormous grin while the rest of his family walked into the room.

Mrs. McConkie wrapped her arm around Kyle's waist. "This is very special for all of us."

At first, Kyle appeared embarrassed, but he flung his short bangs from his face and I caught the shy, yet proud smile. I touched Kyle's shoulder. "I'm glad you're all here."

Meanwhile his younger siblings' feet slid closer to the dessert table. Mr. McConkie caught the movement and launched into a reminder of appropriate behavior, while I headed to the front.

Then Priscilla and her family entered, followed by Abigail, her mom, and her sisters, who quietly took a seat on the second to last row. At the top of the hour, I glanced at Blake, who would emcee our event. "A couple more minutes," I whispered.

Then Tracey, with his moms, walked in. He looked magnificent in his velvet cap, purple velvet blazer, dark black jeans, and black and white wing-tip shoes.

From the podium, I smiled at him as he took a seat in the back.

Now only two students were missing.

Sadly, Darby's absence did not surprise me. She'd told me if her parents couldn't come, she wouldn't come either. If that occurred, I'd asked her to read her essay to them at home. I'm pretty sure she lied to me, but she said she would.

Whereas I expected Hamilton.

But I glanced at Principal Truss, who sat next to Officer Bond, and he nodded for me to begin.

I approached the podium and welcomed the students, their families, and friends. Then I cleared my throat and shared my short speech. "Our identities as individuals are linked to our families. Families provide a foundation, a solid footing for what happens next in our lives. As we advance into our teenage years, we take who we've become and begin to modify and further mold our identity based off of the influences and interactions of friends." I paused, and cleared my throat again. "These talented students, for their last writing project, have used the power of words to share how their families have helped to shape who they individually are. This special project has been a wonderful adventure for all of us. Now please, enjoy this evening of reflection, insight, and shared talents."

The applause erupted and I grinned. I announced Blake as the emcee just as Hamilton walked in, accompanied by his sister and mom. I offered him a quick nod, which stirred everyone to twist around and acknowledge our late guests who slipped into the very last row, across from Tracey and his moms.

I stepped away, patting Blake on the shoulder as we exchanged spots. Then I took my seat to the side of the podium and felt a small sense of relief. The event had begun, and Thad Forbes had not come, both of which relieved me.

But while listening to Blake's short introduction, I saw two men talking out in the hall. Just as Blake announced Dillon's name, my breathing paused as Dillon's father and Thad Forbes entered the room.

The two men slid into seats next to Thad's wife. It felt like I'd stopped breathing. When Thad made eye contact with me, I felt flustered and knew my face was red. I glanced over at Dillon, who had made his way to the podium, and I caught his own disorientation as he spotted his father in the audience.

When Dillon shot me a glance, I tried to offer an encouraging smile. But it felt forced and trite. He struggled with his paper, as if stalling to find the strength to start. Meanwhile the crowd shuffled, waiting for the first speaker to speak.

Finally Dillon cleared his throat and began, "Good evening, ladies and gentlemen." As he smoothed his paper out once again, I saw his shaking hands and heard the tremors in his voice. "I'd like to share my essay titled *Father.*" He drew in a loud breath, then he looked up, and his eyes connected with his dad's. Seconds passed, and he kept looking at his dad. The crowd shifted again, some looking behind their shoulders, trying to see what had caught Dillon's attention.

Suddenly, he picked up his paper and said, "I'm not ready to share." He fled the front and collapsed in the chair next to his mom. She swiftly put her arm around him and shot me a glance. With her free arm, she motioned for us to move on with the program. So I shot Blake a look, and gave him the same motion. A little muddled,

Blake returned to the mic. But his words came out full of compassion. "Okay, Dillon. Next up is Anya Truss."

I glanced over the crowd to see Dillon's father looking at his hands. The rest of the audience looked forward, some with eyes of sympathy for the boy who was too scared to share. But Abigail looked at me, and without words, we connected over Dillon's hurt, and his internal struggle.

Fortunately, Anya would balance the moment. And she did. Her words came out strong and confident.

"I wrote a poem to share my feelings and my thoughts. The poem is titled *Life*."

I was given life;
That is important to me,
But nothing as important as the love given by those who raise me.
My genes came from far across the sea.
My stability came from parents who devoted themselves to rearing me.
I may have some differences.
I may not have my mom's nose
Or my dad's eyes,
But I have my mom's compassion;
I have my dad's loyalty.
I have my parents' love.
For that, they have made me a better me,
One who has endless possibilities in who I still will be.

She curtsied at the mic, and the crowd pumped out the applause. The tone of the room had successfully shifted. I glanced at the Trusses. Anya headed straight into her mother's arms, then into Principal Truss's arms. When he glanced at me, his smile beamed and I nodded. Then his wife looked at me. How fortunate they were!

Years ago their hearts had been ready in time to receive this special gift of Anya.

Blake called Tracey up to the stand. He stood, straightened his purple velvet dinner jacket, patted at his styled hair, and then proceeded to the front while his mothers exchanged bemused yet proud looks over their son.

First, Tracey straightened the mic. Then he began, "For my writing, I will share a list of questions. But first I want to thank Mrs. Childs and my friends in this class for giving me the ideas for my piece. They've been to me like rum is to Captain Jack Sparrow." Then he lifted his paper up and began.

Who really does define family?

God?

Blood?

Government?

Those who nurture us?

Those who we have ties with?

Who protect us?

Who are there for us?

Who we run to when something really good happens to us?

Or when something horrible and tragic occurs?

Who will rescue us when we need to be rescued?

"And as my good friend, Todi, said to me," he whispered this as if it were a side note,

Who do you maybe, just maybe, hope to be with for forever?

I don't always understand who I am, all of what makes me ME, but I know that a great deal of who I am is because of who my parents are and how they're raising me.

Again the crowd applauded while Tracey gaited his way back to his seat and dramatically collapsed between his two mothers. Both women drew him into half hugs, and then each clasped one of his hands.

Next Blake called Abigail to present.

She stood and her mom reached to squeeze her hand. Ringlets fell around Abigail's face. She wore a pressed button-down blouse and a pencil skirt, and as she made her way to the front, I marveled at how much she'd matured from that fourteen-year-old girl who had entered my class last August.

Her calm demeanor remained as she approached the podium and set her paper down. However, I noticed she avoided looking at Dillon, who had kept his eyes on the ground since his own public speaking moment. Instead, as she spoke, Abigail looked directly at her older sister Paige and her mom, as if speaking straight to them.

Sometimes we know who we are
And sometimes we get lost.
Sometimes we hold on to things that prevent us from experiencing life.
Sometimes we fail to see all that life has to offer us.
Sometimes we make mistakes that keep us away from who we really are
Or who we really wish to be,
And then family comes and saves us.
Family reminds us of who we really are.
Family provides a refuge for us when our mistakes have thrown us into
a storm.
Family shows us who they see us as even when we can't see.
Family is a lighthouse, a lifesaver, a rescue boat.
My family has saved me.

When she stepped away from the mic, the crowd was quiet. Then it was her sister who began the clapping. She kept clapping while she stood for Abigail to return to her seat, and the rest of the crowd carried on the applause while Abigail's mother wiped tears from her eyes.

Blake called Todi up.

Before she spoke, she glanced at me. My eyes were already full of tears.

I knew how seriously Todi had taken this assignment, how difficult this topic was, and how much she wanted to respectfully complete her tribute. So I held up a box of tissues, which I'd stationed earlier near my seat.

That gave Todi the laugh she needed, and she began.

Family. What does it mean?

A living organism, so delicate and fragile that with the slightest neglect it can sicken, and sometimes even die.

A system so full of little parts, individual needs, and collective needs. Sometimes there are heavy responsibilities, yet also very clear and important belonging.

Without family there is deep hurting.

The basic unit of society. Without a family, one feels a longing, lost, a misplaced human in our society.

Family is a hierarchical need, a necessity.

Without a family, holidays turn into even more lonely days.

No matter the void, or the heartache, or the need, families are essential. They are needed, they are right.

Family is where it is.

So what must I do to start making the most of mine?

Carroll Johnson stood and clapped loudly. Paisley followed; then Anya, Blake, and their families, followed by Tracey and his mothers.

Todi shot me a glance and I nodded at her. "You did it," I mouthed and I felt the tears tumble down.

She ran over and gave me a hug. Then as the crowd reclaimed their seats, Todi ran down and hugged Carroll and Paisley before taking her own seat.

Blake was still clapping when he returned to the mic. "Great job, Todi," he said. Then he smiled at her and she smiled back. Finally he cleared his throat and said, "Now we'll hear from Hamilton Forbes."

His sister looked bored, his mom looked pleased, and his father raised a fist as if Hamilton was heading out onto the field for one of his games.

Hamilton glanced at me first, before he began. I offered a huge grin of encouragement. Numerous times, I'd read all the students' pieces, and although this was most certainly not a competition, the Forbes would be pleased. Hamilton's words would make them proud.

Except when the first words of Hamilton's essay spilled out, I knew something was wrong.

There are secrets. And then there are crimes.

I held my breath, waiting for his essay to slip back into the words I'd already praised him on.

There are victims. There are suspects. And then there are those who inflict the crimes.

I shot Officer Bond a concerned look. He was already looking straight at me, his eyes matching my concern.

I grew up under the shadows of a legend. I was told how my genes dictated who I was destined to be.

Officer Bond stood and held his cell phone in his hand as if it were a bomb.

My own decisions were not to be made, for it was my duty as a Forbes to become what was already determined as great.

Officer Bond moved out the door, avoiding eye contact with Thad, whose face had turned red, his eyes hot with aggression. But his arm remained around his wife, who appeared oblivious to her husband's shifted demeanor.

I had clear footsteps to follow, opportunities that others would beg for, and they were mine.

Who am I to not be thankful for the unlimited chances before me, to associate with the greats, the Hall of Famers, the best of the best?

I squirmed in my seat. Other than Officer Bond, who had left the room, and perhaps Thad Forbes, and certainly myself, everyone else believed Hamilton was reading the approved words which we'd spent months preparing him to present.

My dad said I had no idea what it's like to make it off my talent, my own skills, my own ambition. Instead he has made it so easy for me.

That's according to him.

So what does ruining our family's name do for me?

I saw Thad's neck muscles tighten. He drew his arm away from his wife, and he looked ready to lunge.

How does slandering the values I should have embraced teach me how to be?

I desperately wanted Officer Bond to return.

How does finding a way to bring public shame satisfy your talk of how easy my life is?

I bit down on my lip and looked at Principal Truss.

What is easy about being disgraced by a parent's selfish acts?

Now Principal Truss looked at me. I shook my head at him, trying to signal that this essay was not part of the plan.

After you have destroyed the life of another, as well as the life of all those who claimed to have loved you, what's next? What place do you have in any of our lives?

Officer Bond returned to the room and I felt my shoulders drop. Thad Forbes stood up. Principal Truss turned around. And Hamilton finished with:

You no longer belong to us.

From his hand, Hamilton revealed a dragonfly pendant. Then everything happened at once.

Other than a few stray hands, no one clapped. Immediately, Hamilton came and sat by me and said, "I'll protect you, Mrs. Childs." Blake stood and looked at me, unsure whether he should announce who was next. The crowd looked at Hamilton first, then me, then they turned to the back of the room, which kept their focus.

And I too watched in horror as Officer Bond stood in Thad's way.

"Excuse me," Thad grunted, aiming to walk out the door.

Officer Bond looked small next to Coach Forbes. He shook his head. "Hi, Thad."

"Move, Carl."

"You know why I'm here."

Thad's shoulders heaved up and I held my breath. If he wanted to, he could sack Officer Bond, pushing him straight out the door.

For seconds the two men eyed each other, each waiting for the other to back down. "I have a weapon, Thad. Do you want me to pull it?"

Thad took a step forward, closer to Officer Bond, who kept his voice calm.

"How big do you want to make this scene?" Officer Bond nodded at the entire group which now watched them.

As Thad turned around, the reality of his surroundings sank in.

Just then a uniformed police officer tapped on Officer Bond's shoulder. He stepped aside and two additional officers entered the room.

Thad's arms dropped to his side. "No scene."

Officer Bond's tone was almost apologetic. "We need you to come with us."

In consent, Thad nodded his head.

One of the other officers pulled out some handcuffs, but Officer Bond touched the handcuffs and then shook his head. He truly did not want to escalate this scene.

But it was too late.

"This is an outrage!" Hamilton's mother broke away from the crowd and marched past the two officers to face Officer Bond. "What's going on?"

"It's okay, dear." Thad tried to sound calm but his face still held a deep shade of red.

"We just need to ask him a few questions," one of the officers said.

The other officer placed his hand on Thad's shoulder and motioned him toward the door.

But Thad paused for a moment. He reached for his wife's hand but she shoved him away. "You're Thad Forbes. Whatever this is, you fix it," she said.

He gave her a pained smile. "Protect the kids," he said before letting the officers escort him out.

Mrs. Forbes watched him leave, then she clutched her head in her hands. Principal Truss stood and approached her. He placed his hand on her shoulder, which caused her to turn and meet the eyes of the entire room. For a few seconds, all she did was stare back, as if trying to grasp where she was.

Then, from across the room, she shot Hamilton a look. "Come now," she ordered. Next she turned to look at Hamilton's sister. "Grab your stuff. We're leaving."

Hamilton still sat next to me. "Are you going to be okay?" I asked.

He shrugged. "I don't really care." He tried to sound tough, but I caught the deep sadness in his eyes, and the sense of betrayal which he now held.

"I'm sorry, Hamilton," I said.

"My truck's back from the shop," his words were hollow, "which is where I found this." He handed me the necklace. "It's hers."

I looked at the dragonfly pendant and nodded. My heart hurt for him, and my eyes began to sting with tears. "I know."

"Come," his mother ordered from across the room.

The entire silent audience watched Hamilton obey and the Forbes family leave. Then slowly, one by one, all heads turned back to the front.

I was still thinking of Hamilton when I felt a slight tap on my shoulder. It was Blake. "What do I do?" He held the program of names in his hand.

Almost in a daze, I said, "Do you feel like reading?"

He looked out over the group, who stared at him, and shook his head. "No. Not now."

CHAPTER
Thirty-Five

FROM THERE, THE READING CEASED AND THE GOSSIP began.

Some families quietly slipped out of the room, but others stayed to rehash the scene. Priscilla kept asking, "What does it mean?" while Kyle's siblings scurried to the dessert table.

From a corner, I stared at everyone blankly until I heard, "I wanted to say thank you."

I turned to see Dillon's father standing next to me. I scanned the room, but Dillon and his mom were no longer present.

"I know this didn't go as you'd planned." He gave me a charming, sympathetic smile. "I'm sure whatever this is with Thad, it'll all work itself out. But it was unfortunate, the timing and all."

I nodded.

"And I know it was hard for Dillon having me here. But I just wanted to tell you I appreciate what you've done for him. He said you've helped him a lot."

"He told you that?" My voice revealed my surprise.

A blink of sadness crossed his face. "His mother told me. It's been a complicated year, but it's all for the best."

"It's been a tough year for Dillon."

"I know. That's why I felt I needed to say thank you. Because sometimes when you love a child, and they hate you, you thank God there are other adults who can help your child with what they need. Where his mother and I lacked, you made up the difference. We owe you a lot."

I was speechless, feeling another wave of shock over the night's events. Finally, I said, "Dillon is a talented young man."

"I know he is." In his voice, I could hear the deep love and sadness toward his son.

"I'm glad he still has so many opportunities ahead," I said.

"Me too." Then his phone buzzed. He glanced at it, nodded at me, and then picked up his phone. "Darling, yes, I know, I'm on my way home, right now."

I watched him leave and wondered if he had any regrets.

When I finally left the library, I sat in my car and pulled out Stella's necklace. My fingers touched the blue and white gemstones that made up the dragonfly pendant.

And I cried.

Then I called the station, but it was closed. I tried Officer Bond's phone only to leave a message.

Then I drove home.

I placed the necklace on my kitchen counter, and touched it again.

Finally, I went to bed in search of a reprieve from this sorrow.

The next morning, Officer Bond returned my call. He was headed to the school to meet with Principal Truss and invited me to join them.

Twenty minutes later, I walked down the silent Saturday morning halls of Helam Junior High.

When I reached the office, Principal Truss and Officer Bond were already visiting. I slipped into the room and Officer Bond turned to me and said, "Last night, after speaking with his attorney, Thad confessed."

"Wow," I said quietly.

"Yeah," he nodded. "Lieutenant Fisher had feared this was going to escalate into something like the O.J. Simpson trial, with outsiders scrutinizing how we conducted the investigation. So, this is nothing shy of remarkable."

I stepped forward and handed him the dragonfly necklace.

"Thanks." He glanced at it briefly.

"Do you know how Hamilton's doing?" I asked.

He tucked the necklace in his breast pocket and said, "An officer saw the family this morning, to let them know Thad confessed."

That didn't answer my question, so I looked to Principal Truss. "No. I haven't contacted them yet," he said. "I figured there was nothing to say until now."

"So what happened?" I asked both of them.

"What do you want to know?" Officer Bond asked.

"All of it," I said. "And none of it."

Principal Truss motioned toward vacant chairs and then sat behind his desk. I sat too.

Officer Bond did not. "Well, it was all true about Skyler and Stella," he said. "A nasty relationship and then Thad learned that Skyler hit Stella and he wanted to help."

I thought about Thad Forbes in my classroom, and the fear I'd felt, and the threats he'd made. "How does *helping* end up like this?" I asked.

Officer Bond's face appeared troubled. "An accident, according to Thad. A tragic accident made up of lots of poor choices along the way." Then he shifted, so we couldn't see his face. "Thad says he felt an obligation to protect her. He started walking her to her car, calling to see if she was safe, and taking time out of his schedule for her. At the homecoming game, since she'd stopped going to parties due to Skyler, they went for a drive. And that's when things started between them."

Officer Bond turned back to face us, and we all exchanged sorrowful looks. "What a tragedy," Principal Truss said.

"She fell hard for him," Officer Bond continued, "and for a time he foolishly thought things were good. Until Layne's false accusations happened, and reality hit. He tried to end things with Stella, but she was heartbroken. So he tried to help her, which instead kept ending up as 'one more time.' Then at the end of February, he learned that his unclaimed autograph and memorabilia sales had launched a tax fraud investigation. He came back to Helam that night, just like he told us he had. Although he felt some panic, he also expected to be saved by his accountant and attorney. But he had a greater fear too.

"So later, he took Stella for a drive out into the country to make it clear that things were over between them. Instead, she made an advance, but he refused her. So she used manipulation tools that had been a mainstay in her and Skyler's relationship. She cried, she hit, and she asked him to hold her. When he wouldn't consent, she said she'd kill herself.

"Thad claims he hates liars, so his goal was to point out her false threat. He said 'Prove it. Right now!' She was shocked, and probably hurt, but her adrenaline was rushing. As was Thad's. She said, 'Find me something then.' And he searched Hamilton's truck. It was dark, but he found the bag. Then she said, 'I'd leave a note first.' So he reached into the bag and found the ripped paper. He gave her a pen. She scribbled a quick note and shoved it into her coat pocket. Then she tried to kiss him again.

"He says it was because of the approaching federal investigation that made him react as he did. He yelled. She cried. And then she yelled. Then she asked if this was what he wanted and she slipped the bag around her head using the rope straps as her noose. Then she said, 'But before I'd do this Thad, I'd tell the whole world I loved you. And that you loved me!'

"He says those were the words that triggered him, because he saw this young girl controlled his destiny. He went into a rage. He hadn't planned to kill her. Just scare her. But he went too far.

"After that, he didn't have a plan. He was delirious. He left her in the pasture, figuring he'd come back and make it appear like a suicide. He went home to get supplies, only to find Hamilton. He panicked further, decided to flee, and was heading toward Canada when another coach left the message about Stella and noted that Skyler was the person of interest. So that's when Thad figured he could save himself."

The account made me sick. From the look on Principal Truss's face, he was mortified too.

For a few moments, we both sat in silence while Officer Bond looked at the ground.

I thought I should have some type of peace, or satisfaction, maybe even joy that the mystery was closed. Instead, I just felt dirty and disgusted from listening to the account of Thad's vile actions.

Since I had no words, I stood, nodded at both of them, and headed toward the door, but before I could leave, Principal Truss turned to Officer Bond. "So what did Stella's note mean, *The truth is found here?*"

"I asked Thad that," Officer Bond said. "She'd drawn a heart next to that line. We thought it was a signature, or a doodle, or a decoration. But Thad says the arrow was pointing at him. She was saying she'd be willing to kill herself over her broken heart."

I lingered in the doorway, still with nothing to say.

Because there were no words that would bring Stella back, or stop Thad's destructive acts, or free Hamilton from the weight he and his family now faced.

The act was done, and the repercussions of those acts were now in full force.

"Thank you," I said to both of them. And I left.

From there, I wasn't sure where to go. For a while, I drove aimlessly through town, until I ended up across from the Forbes's home. It was the largest in Helam, and at the moment, three news trucks sat outside waiting for some type of action. And the sickness in my stomach grew.

Hopefully, with this breaking news, there was a pinch of solace for Stella's family.

Yet how far would this news coverage spread?

Most likely the world would stop for a moment due to the horrific violence of the former NFL player, Thad Forbes. For a moment the world would mourn over the life of a young woman, Stella Fabrizio, who had lived in the small but growing town of Helam.

Then the world would move on.

380

We all would move on.

But for some, our lives would never be the same.

I left the Forbes's neighborhood and drove to the library. I slipped all the way to the back, into the vacant room that shared the memories of our triumphant, beautiful, and failed readings.

I thought of Blake, Kyle, and Priscilla, none of whom were able to share their writings. And I thought of Dillon. And of course, I thought of Hamilton.

Then I wandered down the pointless path of *what ifs*, wondering if I'd known how all this would end, would I still have embarked on this special creative writing class.

Eventually, I went and bought a to-go salad from an Italian deli and ate in the park. From there, I went alone to a movie, hoping to briefly slip away from this new reality that the town of Helam now faced.

At the theater, I scanned the movie titles. I refused to watch violence, hoping to give my mind a necessary break. I considered a romance, but feared I'd miss Peter even worse than I already did. So, although I feared stirring up my childless heartache, I selected *Shrek 2* and stepped into a lit theater full of families. There were babies crying, children laughing, and adults chattering. These were the familiar and iconic sounds of this town, and rather than these sounds being acidic to my heart, they instead began the healing of my recent wounds. Circling around me, these families weren't broken with life. Instead these noises were the sounds of hope. This represented each family unit investing time, resources, and their hearts into their children. This was the sound of Helam cheering on life and the bright futures which lay ahead.

CHAPTER
Thirty-Six

THE COMPUTER-ANIMATED MOVIE, ALTHOUGH THEMED all around *happily ever after*, had done its job and entertained me. Light and humorous, the characters left me smiling, the simple storyline offered me cheer, and I left the theater with a reengaged sense of duty toward life.

When I got home, I stepped into the darkness and flipped on the hallway switch. In my entry-way there was a large duffel bag. In slow motion my mind registered the meaning of it. Then I looked up to see Peter in the hallway, staring at me.

Still in shock, I stared back, until the spell broke and I ran to him. I wrapped my arms around him, kissing his clean-shaven cheek, laughing, giggling, giggling some more, giggling like an unreserved teenager who was madly in love.

The giggles kept coming until my mouth found his lips and I pressed into them long and hard.

When I finally pulled back, I was dizzy and sick in love.

"Peter." I giggled again. "Peter." My eyes filled with moisture. "Why are you here?"

"I got home this morning." His body pressed into mine.

"But you told me," my mind was lost in a cloud of shock, "another week?"

His eyes twinkled. "I know."

"You lied to me?"

"I wanted to surprise you."

"But I should've been there. The whole ceremony, the big welcome, I would've had a banner, balloons, and—"

He pressed his forefinger to my lips. "I know you don't like those events."

"But I would have been there," I whispered. "I should have been there!"

He pulled me into a strong kiss and when he withdrew my knees felt weak. "My parents were there," he said. "It was nice."

"But I'm your wife," I said softly.

"And this is what I wanted for us. So, let me be here now. Let me surprise you how I want to, let me be home now."

Every feature about him, his brown cropped hair, his light gray eyes, his deep voice, his broad shoulders, his arms around me—all of this I was crazy in love with, falling for him all over again. "I missed you." My words stumbled out.

"I missed you too," he whispered in my ear.

I thought of telling him everything that had happened since we'd last talked, telling him as fast as the words could take me, spiraling back through the events of the last few days.

Instead, right then, I wanted a break from it all.

My lips went to his neck and my nose drew in his clean scent. Then I whispered, "Bedroom?"

"I was just waiting for you to ask." He scooped me up into his arms and carried me up the stairs toward our room while joyful tears filled my eyes.

Then he set me down in front of the bed, where a beautiful thin box with a large ribbon waited for me.

"You'll want to open that first." He winked at me, and then pulled me close, his lips pressing firmly against mine. When he released me, I had to steady myself against his arms. I had missed this.

He reached for the box, handed it to me, and then stepped away. I opened it to find a satin and lace mauve nightgown. "One of many gifts." He kissed my cheek and steered me toward the master bathroom. "With more to come."

When I stood in the doorway, he stepped back, and for a moment we both stood there, staring at each other, love rich and deep in his eyes. Then I clutched the nightgown to my chest, released a nervous giggle, and shut the bathroom door.

My heart raced with awareness, reminding me of this deep satisfying love which I'd once possessed. Only now, this love had grown deeper.

I paused in front of the mirror. A glow of happiness covered my face.

There were still challenges and adjustments ahead, but Peter was home. Together, we were a unit. Together, we were a family!

I clutched the nightgown in my hand and whispered, "I love you, Peter!"

Sunday evening, Peter made me the most divine meal of roast beef, real mashed potatoes, and savory gravy—comfort food which surpassed comfort, food that tasted like we were enjoying heaven.

I gobbled it up and felt grateful for the rescue from my regular stir-fry meal.

CHAPTER
Thirty-Seven

AFTER THE UNBELIEVABLE AND BEAUTIFUL WEEKEND with Peter, it was hard to return for the final week of school. Graduation was only two days away and spirits were high among the ninth graders. Fortunately, this was a very short week of yearbooks, parties, and excitement—no real work, just play leading up to a fun and joyful summer.

However, as soon as Hamilton walked into his English class, I placed my own eagerness and anticipation on hold.

"I wasn't sure you'd be here," I said.

He shrugged. "I couldn't stay home." His expression was bleak. "Things are crazy there."

I nodded, while the noise of rowdy students caused me to step away and begin class.

Still, I watched Hamilton and at the end of class I met him at the door while all the other students left. I desired to share some comforting words with him.

But I came up empty.

Instead, I said, "I've no idea what you're going through right now, Hamilton."

He shook his head and stared at the floor. "We visited my dad last night."

I pictured the father-son exchange and my heart ached. "How was it?"

"He hates me. But that's a given. He also knows we hate him."

"Hate and love are sometimes more like brothers than strangers," I said.

He glanced at me for a moment, then looked away to brush at his eyes. "I get it. It's like what Dad once said to me, after I messed up on a football pass, 'You've disgraced us but I still love you.'"

"And he does, Hamilton! He does love you. Just like you love him. That's why this all hurts so deeply."

He nodded but looked back at the floor.

"Over these next several years, you're really going to discover how intense and deep that love truly is."

He brushed at his eyes again.

Then he looked at me. "He told us it was an accident, all of it. That he never intended for any of this to happen."

I nodded. "I'm sure that's true."

He heaved out a heavy breath. "He said he wanted the truth out there so we, his family, could move on. He didn't want my sister's and my lives dragged through all this."

"That says something about your father, Hamilton. You know that, don't you?"

He didn't say anything.

So I asked, "Will you still play football?"

He shrugged. "I haven't figured that out yet."

"I'm sure there are lots of big and small details that are still being worked out. And some will just take time."

"Know what he told me?" He looked past me as he spoke. "He told me to write. To write my story, not his story, but *my* story." Then Hamilton looked back at me and shook his head, like the words made no sense to him.

"I hope you do," I said.

He gave me a soft grin. "Thanks."

At the start of sixth period, I approached Blake and asked him a question. Fortunately, he agreed.

So when the bell officially began our final class period, I gave my short and last speech to my ten creative writing students. "I considered doing lots of different things today. But I don't think we will do any of them. Instead, I want to take a short moment to thank you." I had the attention of every one of my students. "It's been a deep honor to have each of you in this class. And I wish you all the very best in your efforts and in your dreams. I hope that in some small way this class, the assignments, and your writings have been worth the investment you gave.

"Now, I've asked Blake to share his graduation speech. I've read it and even though you'll have a chance to hear it then, you'll also be caught up in the midst of your own graduation excitement. And as a class, I want to know you heard his words."

I stepped away from the front and Blake took my place. He stared at the group but didn't say anything. For a moment, it seemed like he wouldn't begin. But then Todi clapped her hands together, and cheered, "Go, Blake!"

He shot her a smile, squared his shoulders back, and glanced down at his speech.

For the next several minutes we listened to a boy speak like a man. He pulled quotes from authors, philosophers, and successful businessmen. He shared thoughts on courage, loyalty, and friendship. And then he shared his recent passion.

"In literature we read of many different types of Lost Boys. For example, in *Lord of the Flies*, the Lost Boys are a group of British boys who get stuck on an island and then try to govern themselves with awful outcomes. In *Peter Pan*, the Lost Boys are a group of orphans with no adult supervision who tend to be ill-behaved and don't want to grow up because they don't want to leave their wild lifestyle. But there is another Lost Boys group, not in literature, but in recent history. This is a tale of remarkable boys who fought against the odds and worked together to succeed. Because of a civil war in Sudan, tens of thousands of boys were orphaned or displaced and had no adult leadership to help them find refuge in Ethiopia, which was a thousand miles away. Some were as young as seven years old, but they banded together and formed their own family units. They called each other *brother* and built a support network. This helped them survive their difficult journey as well as their adjustment in their refugee camps.

"I have met some of these great *boys* and they are my heroes. How they banded together to survive has taught the world courage, dignity, loyalty, and friendship.

"In closing, I wish to challenge us, the class of 2004, both male and female, to not be like the Lost Boys from *Lord of the Flies* and inflict harm on others. Or like *Peter Pan's* Lost Boys and shrink from our responsibilities. Rather, let us become like the example shown to us by the Lost Boys of Sudan. Let us rally around each other and courageously help each other in our individual and collective dreams. Rather than destroy, let us look for ways to be a strength to another.

Let us be like a family unit that chooses to bond together and weather the storms of life together. Let us seek a victory that goes beyond our individual goals. In our climb in life, let us take time to lift others up. Then together we can advance in our great and courageous quest. As we move into our high school, college, and career years, let us do all we can to work together to make the world a greater home for all."

He lowered his paper down and looked at the class.

One by one the students began to clap. Then Todi stood and kept clapping, followed by Anya, then Tracey, Abigail, Priscilla, and Kyle. Darby glanced around the room, but finally succumbed and stood too, followed by Dillon, and then Hamilton.

Once the cheering stopped, Blake returned to his seat and Todi slapped him on the back and said, "You're going to hit it out of the park, Blake!"

An enormous grin spread across his face.

I glanced at the clock. It was time for my ninth graders to head to the quad for their yearbooks. So I dismissed them, and as they piled up at the doorway, I felt a tinge of sadness to see them leave.

Then I noticed Abigail talking with Dillon. Since Friday's reading, his scowl had returned. Yet he now held the door open for Abigail as the two stepped out into the hall.

"Mrs. Childs?"

I turned around to see Todi.

"I wanted to tell you, I didn't get to finish my memoir."

I smiled at her. "I understand."

"But even when I go back to California, I'm going to keep working on it."

"I hope you will."

"And someday, when it's published, I'm dedicating it to you."

"Todi!" Before my eyes even began to tear up, I headed over to my tissue box, but of course, it was empty.

"Wait," Todi called out. I turned around to see her rustling through her bag. "I've been saving these for you. Keep them so you always have them when you need them. Or at least keep them until you run out, and then—well, then I'll send Anya to get you some more."

I laughed as she handed me a little plastic sealed bag of folded tissues. "Thank you, Todi. I will miss you."

"I'll miss you, too."

My voice filled with emotion. "Are you going to be okay?"

She gave me her trademark Todi grin. "It's kind of just who I am. You know, I love my mom, and I wish things were better for her, and for me but, well, your class taught me a lot, Mrs. Childs, about families."

"Did it?"

"Yes."

"If it helped, Todi, I'm so glad."

"My family's not perfect. But Clarissa's my mom, and she does try. She makes mistakes, lots of them, but she still hasn't given up."

"That's a strong statement," I said kindly.

"We've been talking on the phone lots right now, and she says this time she really wants to change and be a better mom for me. Especially since my sis, Cassie, isn't coming back—and I scared my mom a lot when I decided to stay here for the rest of the school year. She says she really got it this time, that if things don't change, I really might not come back to her forever either."

"Todi," my voice was firm, "what we all want is for you to be safe."

She shrugged. "I'll be okay. Two and half years seems long, but it's not. I may even graduate early, and then it'll only be two years. That's all the time she has with me. After that, I've already decided I'm coming back to live here."

I smiled. "I hope you do."

"And if she can't do it while I'm there," Todi looked at the floor and shrugged, "then I'll end up somewhere else."

"If that ends up being the case, maybe you can come back here."

"Maybe." But she frowned. "Carroll and Paisley will be gone for a year and half."

The letter to Peter was still saved on my computer. And in the days ahead, while we re-established *us*, Peter and I would explore what I wrote.

"Maybe there will be other options too," I said, then I grabbed a notepad and scribbled down my email. "Please stay in touch, okay?"

She smiled as she accepted the outstretched paper. "Thanks, Mrs. Childs, I for sure will, 'cause when my memoir's done, you'll have to tell me where to send it."

"Exactly!" I grinned at her.

"Good." Her genuine smile was back. "Are you coming to the quad? I want you to sign my yearbook."

I nodded. "I'll be there soon."

"Okay," she called out as she headed out the door, "see ya in a bit."

From the hall noisy chatter filled the air, but inside my classroom it was silent.

For several minutes I just stood there thinking about the school year, until my classroom door creaked open.

Darby stood in the doorway. "I forgot something." She returned to her seat, looked around, then shook her head.

"What is it?" I asked.

Again, she shook her head. "Nothing." Then she stared at her feet.

"We missed you at Friday's reading," I said.

"Yeah," she scoffed at me. "I hear it was a real showstopper."

We exchanged grins like friends sharing a sad joke.

"That it was," I said.

"Like I told you, no one in my family could make it. And what's the point of reading to myself?" Her eyes shot up to stop me from speaking. "I haven't read it to them yet, my essay, but I will. Sometime I will."

"I figured," I said. "And I'm sorry they weren't able to come."

"Don't be sorry. It's just how it is. They're not even coming to my graduation."

"Really?"

"My dad says he'll try. Mom has work, but she's hoping to run over on a break. And Lena," She shook her head in disgust. "Lena says she has other plans."

I tried to find a positive within her bleak statement. "So that means Lena's at least speaking to you?"

"Hardly! And what sucks is Mom hasn't even noticed. Dad does, but he doesn't care. He just says 'get over it'."

I considered offering Darby sympathy. Instead I said, "I know it's hard, but for what it's worth, I'm proud of you. I think you made the right decision in what you did."

She shrugged, clearly not wanting my praise. "The worst part about it, is seeing what Lena chose over me—that's the part I hate most!"

"Is she still with Skyler?"

"I don't know. She won't tell me anything anymore. But I hope not."

"I agree." Our eyes connected. Then I said, "It's been a tough year."

She nodded, and then extended her yearbook. "Here, want to sign it?"

"Gladly!" I took it, found my regular page, and wrote:

To a future doctor!

May the consequences of good choices steer your life toward greater happiness.

And may one thing learned in this creative writing class benefit you in your journey ahead. I'm very glad you were in the class – you taught me lots.

All the Best,
Mrs. Childs.

When I handed it back she said, "You write a lot!" Then she smiled at me.

"Thank you!" I grinned back at her.

The door opened and Kyle rushed in. "Am I too late?"

I had to hold back a chuckle. Due to the panic on his face, he looked more alert than I'd seen him all year. "For what?" I asked.

"If I turn in my last English paper, that was due last week, will you accept it? I forgot about it. I just ran home, and I ran back. You told me last week that if I didn't get it in, I wouldn't pass the class. But if I turn it in now—?" He paused, clearly out of breath.

"Then you pass the class." *Just barely with a C-,* but I didn't say that, especially since Darby was standing there.

"I pass!" He jumped up and down, until he needed to catch his breath again. "I pass." He looked at me, then at Darby, then back at me. A large smile shone on his face.

"Yes, you did," I said. "Good work."

"Sweet! The only class I have to retake is Math. And that's just 'cause it's *so hard*!"

"Which Math?" Darby asked.

"Pre-Algebra! And my mom thinks she's going to help me pass it through summer school." He groaned. "She's such a *bad* tutor. It's going to be such a sucky summer!"

"I could tutor you," Darby said softly.

"What?" He stared at her.

"I'm pretty good at Algebra."

Kyle kept staring at her.

"I could tutor you," she said again. "I've nothing else I'm doing this summer."

"Do you want money?" He brushed his short bangs from his eyes. "I'm sure my dad will pay you."

"Okay." She smiled at him. "Give me your yearbook. I'll sign it and give you my number."

He froze in place, as if unsure of what to do. His eyes were as wide as his mouth.

"Kyle," I said, "do you have your yearbook?"

Suddenly he awoke from his trance. "Uh, yeah." He quickly fumbled through his bag. "Yeah, I got it right before I ran home." He pulled it out and handed it to her. "Thanks, Darby."

CHAPTER
Thirty-Eight

WEDNESDAY AFTERNOON, I JOINED THE REST OF THE invited teachers and sat on the stand. From my viewpoint, I could look out over the grassy field and see the entire ninth grade body all dressed in their white caps and gowns. From my position, they reminded me of the seeds of a white dandelion, soon to be blown into the wind. Perhaps I, like the other teachers beside me, were the blowers, sending each strand farther into a world of adventures which awaited them.

These students' lives were just beginning, their highs and lows, their thrills and defeats, their independence and their co-dependence.

And as a passionate educator, I was part of their change, this beckoning into adulthood, and now their departure into new terrain.

While I waited for the ceremony to begin, I looked deeper into the whiteness and took a mental tally of how many students I'd taught over these last three years: one hundred and forty-six from this graduating class of 2004.

Then I specifically picked out each one of my creative writing students. First, I found Todi, Anya, and Tracey. They sat together exchanging smiles and giggles as if a bundle of energy was trapped between them.

A row behind them, Abigail sat with several occupied chairs between her and Dillon. Both had quiet, mature looks which surpassed the youthful looks of the students around them.

Farther in the back, Priscilla and Darby, like bookends, sat next to Hamilton. I saw him whisper something to Priscilla and a grin covered her face. Then he turned to Darby and whispered again. A similar grin appeared on her face. And Hamilton was smiling too.

Then all three laughed together, like true friends.

In the last row sat Kyle with his bangs cut and his eyes now exposed. A rich smile stuck to his face; he would be receiving his diploma on this designated day.

On the stands, in the row in front of me, sat Blake. His knees bobbed up and down while his lips ran through his memorized speech.

And then eventually his time came.

When Blake stood his knees looked unstable, but his hands soon clutched the podium and then his voice roared across the grassy lawn.

After he finished, cheers erupted until the crowd rumbled into a standing ovation. Blake's face reddened while he watched the crowd. Of course the greatest sight was his own mother, whose hands were the last to cease clapping, and her body the last to resume a seat.

Then, in time, Principal Truss presented the diplomas and I watched with pride as each student I'd taught received their individual recognition of accomplishment.

I was especially thrilled, when Darby Johnson's name was called, to hear in the far corner of the field the burst of loud cheers. Of course what was even more priceless was to see the smile that beamed across Darby's face. Her family had indeed come.

Then Hamilton Forbes's name was called. And a hush went through the crowd.

Suddenly, a strong applause rippled through the audience until everyone, even Principal Truss, who had asked all to hold their applause to the end, paused himself to applaud. Such a response had been unexpected, especially for Hamilton. But from my position, what I saw was a town that had lost one hero and found another, a hero whose integrity had outshone his own wants and fears.

Eventually the ceremony ended, and then the concentration of white gowns dissipated into the arms of loving families. Through the crowd I watched Todi run, then jump up the stairs and pull Blake into a bear hug. His previously reddened face returned while his former eloquence stumbled into unintelligible words.

Then she was off again, running down the stage, flying past me, only to suddenly halt and run back. Next, she threw her arms around me in the largest hug.

"Thank you, Mrs. Childs. This was the best year! And you're the best teacher ever!"

But before I could respond, Todi was gone.

Instead Abigail was there waiting for me.

"Hi," I said softly.

She held out a wrapped gift. "This is for you. Thank you."

"Wow!" I took the gift and smiled at her.

"I couldn't have made it through this year without you, without the project, without the journals and our group." Her voice trembled slightly.

"It's been quite a year!"

She nodded.

"How are things with you and Dillon?" Before the ceremony, I'd seen them exchange an uncomfortable hug.

"Monday, before we got our yearbooks, was the first time we'd really talked since, you know, we'd broken up."

"How was it?"

"It was okay," she shrugged. "We both agree we love each other. But right now, we're just too young. And so we need time to heal and stuff, alone, away from each other."

I touched her arm briefly. "Are you going to be okay?"

She gave me a genuine smile. "I miss him." She shrugged her shoulders again. "And he says he misses me, but we can't go back. What's done is done. So we'll just do our best with what's next."

I nodded my approval. "You've really grown, Abigail. You've made difficult decisions during some real tough times, and I'm proud of you."

She smiled at me in a way I hadn't seen in months. "Thanks."

"And your mom is too." I could see her mom watching us from below the stand.

Abigail's grin widened. She glanced over at her mom and her mom smiled back. "I think so too," she said.

When she stepped down and returned to her mom, the two enveloped each other in a strong, long-lasting hug, a stark contrast to the short, awkward hug I'd seen earlier between her and Dillon.

As I stepped down into the crowd, Tracey greeted me.

"Guess what?" An enormous smile lit up his face.

It was contagious. "What?"

"For my graduation present, my moms bought all three of us a trip to New York to meet *my* sister."

"Tracey!"

"I know." He clapped his hands together. "Two weeks ago, we got matched up online. We have the same donor, and she agreed to meet. At first, my moms were not cool about it. At all. Especially when I told them I was going to go by myself. But then they got cool and said we'd figure something out, which they did since they just told me about my present, and that we're going this summer. I'm beyond excited!"

"I'm so glad!"

He gave me a quick a hug. "I'll miss you, Mrs. Childs. Thanks for the fun year!"

As I watched him jog back to his moms, I waved to them. Then Tracey pulled both of them into a hug as well.

Off to the right of Tracey, I spotted Darby with flowers in her hands. Lena and her friends had pulled Darby into a group hug and her mom snapped a picture. Then Darby requested a picture of her standing between her parents.

While she posed, she saw me looking at her, and she offered me a smile, a real genuine smile.

Then I turned to see Priscilla practically dancing in front of me.

"Guess what?" She clapped her hands together and smiled at me. "Hamilton's mom had to leave early, so my dad offered to give Hamilton a ride home!"

I grinned at her. "I'm glad to hear it."

"And," her eyes were wide with excitement, "my dad thinks he can work it out so Hamilton can work for him this summer, which means I'll get to see Hamilton even without school! And my dad already told Hamilton if he needs anything that our family really wants to help him and his family, because of all that *stuff* with his dad."

"Oh, Priscilla." I felt tears starting to form in my eyes. "I'm so glad your family can be there to help him."

"Thank you so much, Mrs. Childs." She clutched her hands together and almost squealed.

"I'm not sure I had anything to do with this."

"You told me Hamilton might need me, and now I get to be his friend." She offered me a huge smile. "It's going to be the best summer ever!"

She skipped across the grass, over to her father, who was sitting on a chair, talking with Hamilton.

As she neared, they both turned toward her. Then Hamilton saw me and I waved at him. He waved back.

Truly, he was a hero!

I took a few steps away from the crowd and paused to look over the entire group one final time. This was a school with good kids, special kids, young adults with great purpose. Life gave each one of them trials, and bit by bit each one of them was rising above those challenges. For me, it'd been a grand privilege to work alongside this wonderful Class of 2004.

After one last deep breath, I began to walk off the field and a final rush of emotion came over me.

These students were making choices. And it was through their choices that these students showed the great power within them. For with those choices, they revealed how they would handle the lives they'd been given.

And this gift of choice was the same for me.

I glanced at my watch. Peter would be picking me up shortly to take us on our next adventure. I was ecstatic at this. I needed this.

And I needed this upcoming summer.

For I was in the midst of my own healing, my own making peace with my God, because at an early age, I'd committed my life to Him. When I'd made those commitments I'd seen children in my future. And now years later, children did surround me, but in a different manner, facing challenges I could have never before foreseen. But they still needed me, just like I needed them.

For this is my beautiful life, a life in which I choose to embrace.

Looking for ways to connect with Tara C. Allred?

Share an online review.
Sign up for her newsletter @ www.taracallred.net.
Follow her on Facebook, Twitter, or Google.

Looking for more adventures from *The Other Side of Quiet*?

Check out www.othersideofquiet.net for more character info, insider views, and some sneak peeks at upcoming character projects.

Also visit www.othersideofquiet.net for an online creative writing experience. You can read writing lectures from Mrs. Childs, writing samples from aspiring writers, and writing tips from guest professional authors.

If you'd like to receive feedback on your creative writing project, please visit the site for submission guidelines.

LOOKING FOR WAYS TO STRENGTHEN YOUR FAMILY?

The Power of Family is an organization that provides resources and education to encourage greater love in the home, healthier marriages, and stronger family relationships.

The organization also provides financial assistance to families, couples, and individuals, who are in need of counseling and professional help.

To learn more, visit www.thepoweroffamily.org.

Acknowledgments

I wish to thank the youth that I grew up with, the youth I have since taught, the teachers who cared and taught me, and my sister Amber, a gifted teacher who has richly shaped my life. All of you were the inspiration and motivation behind this story.

In researching aspects of this novel, thank you Ken and Marlene Littlefield, Rachel Woolbright, Melissa Young, Aubrey Gubler, Shaunell Glasglow, Laekin and Yolanda Pascua-Rogers, Alisha Larson, Alisa Brough, Alisa Mercer, Libby Lloyd, and Marni Law for the perspectives you shared.

Also it was a remarkable experience to share this novel with the talented creative writing students from Venture High School. Thank you for your feedback.

Mom, thank you for your help on this project and for teaching me what the word *family* means.

Kelley, you are an extraordinary person! Thank you for all you have done for me and this story.

And Jeff, you have taught me what truly matters. Thank you for your support, sacrifice, and perspective on this project and in all the aspects of my life.

TARA C. ALLRED is an award-winning author, instructional designer, and educator. She has been recognized as a California Scholar of the Arts for Creative Writing and is a recipient of the Howey awards for Best Adult Book and Best Adult Author. She lives in Utah with her husband.

Her other published works include *Sanders' Starfish* and *Unauthored Letters*.

Made in the USA
San Bernardino, CA
16 April 2016